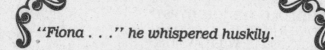

"Fiona . . ." he whispered huskily.

She gave a muffled snort, and he started, discovering belatedly that the green eyes danced with merriment.

"Oh—I am sorry," she gurgled with not the smallest appearance of remorse. "I know I shouldn't laugh, but—really, you do it so well. Much better than Torrey plays the hero."

She was more shrewd that he had fancied. Perchance she was not quite as smitten as he'd supposed. His life might well depend on his making sure she was suitably captivated. Easy enough of an accomplishment. Smiling his tenderest smile, he drew her closer again and, running the tip of one long finger down beside her ear, said softly, "Is it so unbelievable, dear lady, that my reason is simply what I implied?"

THE DEDICATED VILLAIN

Patricia Veryan

Book VI of
"The Golden Chronicles"

FAWCETT CREST • NEW YORK

A Fawcett Crest Book
Published by Ballantine Books
Copyright © 1989 by Patricia Veryan

Library of Congress Catalog Card Number: 88–30810

ISBN 0–449–21800–7

This edition published by arrangement with St. Martin's Press, Inc.

Manufactured in the United States of America

First Ballantine Books Edition: March 1990

Dedicated with respect, gratitude, and humble affection to the memory of Mr. Jeffery Farnol, whose books provided me with lifelong enjoyment, and without whose inspiration and guidance my own works might never have been written.

✍ PROLOGUE ✍

Flanders
August 1743

The raindrops, plinking fitfully onto the sagging roof of the hut, provided the only source of distraction. Roland Fairleigh Mathieson, who for many and various reasons at present went by the name of Otton, lay very still, his right hand tight gripped in the straw of his crude bed, and his eyes closed as he shut out pain and thirst and concentrated instead on the uneven sounds and wove them into the melody of the little song that drifted aimlessly through his mind.

> Come live with me (plink, plink, plink) and be my love, (plink, plink)
> And we will some new (plink, plink, plink) pleasures prove (plink)
> Of golden sands, and crystal brooks, (plink, plink)
> With silken . . .

Golden sands and crystal brooks . . . Would he ever see such sights again? England in the springtime. Clean yellow-green leaves, fresh bracing air from off the sea, cheerful happy people, warm sunlight . . . He shivered convulsively as a dank draught stirred the straw and winced as he jarred his broken collarbone. Lord, but he was so damnably thirsty, and the water jar had been empty since breakfast time—or what he guessed to have been breakfast time. His watch and cardcase and Bond's watch and cardcase had both gone to the peasants who lived on the small farm and scratched a living from the flat Flanders land. François and Madame, who had taken him in, a half-dead enemy with a broken head and a musket ball in him, and with half

1

a dozen French hussars in hot pursuit. A terrible risk had François and Madame taken for the sake of avarice. A risk they must have repented, for they had stuck him out here three, or was it four days ago? They had tended him when they thought of it, roughly and grumblingly, and had fed him scraps of food and left him a daily jug of brackish water. But he'd had not a drop since early this morning, so that he was nigh shrivelled up with thirst and tantalized by the rain that splashed on the roof only a few feet away.

His left arm was itching fiendishly, but if he reached across to scratch it, his other flea bites would start to itch again. He gritted his teeth and fought the need until it became an obsession so that he moved too fast, and pain clawed its savage way through him. The verminous hut faded into a merciful dizziness that blotted out both pain and itching for a little while . . .

"We've taken Worms, thank God, but rumour has it that those damned Frenchies are massing in Flanders . . ." The loud voice echoed through the mists of memory, and he could see Major Cunningham's dark eyes glittering with zeal. "I want two of you young fellows to volunteer for a reconnaissance of the area . . . Splendid! You then, Otton, since you speak the language like a native, and—you, Bond. Good luck, and God speed. And especially—speed! We must know at the earliest possible moment what the bastards are about . . ."

The major's voice faded and, sighing, Otton returned to the harsh reality of this rainy afternoon and a new distraction. A busy rustling amongst the straw. His dark head, swathed in the dirty bandage, turned very slightly. Even with caution it was a painful effort and exhausting. His suspicion however, was verified, for he perceived that the Comte de Flanders was back and once more heading at an ungainly but determined run for the mouldy crust of bread that was the only bulwark against starvation.

Otton relaxed his grip on the straw and reached out gropingly until he detected his tiny pile of ammunition. Taking up one of the miniature pellets of wax, which he had gathered from the tallow drippings, he deposited it on his ribs, took a bead on the large cockroach, and flicked a skeletal finger. His missile whizzed at the enemy, and the comte scampered madly to the side. Otton informed the insect in a faint but pithy voice of his ancestry, and reached for another wax pellet. How he could have managed to drop the crust so that it rolled out of reach, he didn't know, but sometimes he seemed to drift in and out of this unending nightmare so that it was difficult to tell where dreaming ended and reality began.

There was no dreaming his thirst, however. That was all too real. Surely François would come soon? Or Madame? A fine madame she was—poor creature. More like sixty than forty; scrawny and bent and faded long before her time, stinking of dirt and sweat, soured by hardship and poverty. He'd never heard her speak without a whine. Although he'd not expected to be nursed by the woman, she could at least have washed him once in a while or tried to make him more comfortable, rather than abandoning him to this cold and verminous hut with only the fleas and cockroaches for company and not a soul to speak a kind word when the pain was so bad.

He grinned in faint embarrassment to so indulge his sense of ill-usage, but the grin faded when he recollected that the card-cases had both been of gold, and together with the timepieces, should have brought a pretty penny. François and Madame had been more than well paid, and could have been kinder, blast it all! For all their hard-hearted treatment of him, however, one or the other usually came at least twice a day. He'd not seen hide nor hair of either one since last evening when François had come in to grudgingly refill the water jug and put down the stale bread and the dried up hunk of cheese. Nor, now that he considered the matter, had he heard the whine of Madame's shrill voice or the grumbling discontent of François. Had they perhaps made off with their profits and abandoned him? His thick dark brows drew together, the shadowed black eyes narrowed with anxiety. If they *had* gone, he would surely die here. Bond had sworn to come back, but poor Bill Bond might never have reached the safety of the Allied lines . . .

He shivered again, and, spurred by a sudden frenzy of apprehension, worked his right elbow under him and dragged himself upward. A rusty lance seemed to rip through him, and he groaned a curse, but managed not to fall back. Drawing a deep breath, he shouted for probably the tenth time that long weary day, *"Hallo? . . . Monsieur François? . . . Madame . . . ?"* His straining ears could detect not the faintest sound of human life. Panicking, he advised his hosts in somewhat disjointed but fluent French of all the flaws in their characters and of his des-

3

perate need for help. But when he was panting and had slumped down, exhausted, there was still no sound, no sign.

They must have gone, then. They had abandoned him to die of thirst and starvation. But an Englishman must not die in a dreadful little vermin-ridden hut on a flat and waterlogged Flanders plain . . . He was, of course, not really an Englishman because he was half French. Still, he was the grandson of a duke . . . Not officially, since he was born, as they say, on the wrong side of the blanket. But even if he was not welcomed at the house of his noble relative (nor in any other noble house, come to that!) to die here, all alone, was not the thing.

One might have hoped, he thought aggrievedly, that Thomas would have bestirred himself and helped a little. Thomas had been *Maman's* favourite of the saints, and it was to him that she had at the end commended the care of her beloved son. Roland had been grateful for this effort, but he had discovered that while St. Thomas sometimes managed surprisingly well, he could not always be relied upon. This appeared to be just such an occasion, wherefore, he must fend for himself.

He eyed the door speculatively. "You may think, *Monsieur Éclat*," he told it, "that I cannot reach you. But—you shall see!" It was a few feet distant; he could manage that surely, if he really tried. "Up, Roland Fairleigh Mathieson!" he muttered. "Up, you lazy lout!" He eased himself onto his right elbow again, swearing in both French and English when his head vied with his shoulder as to the degree of anguish it could inflict. At least, his right arm was workable, and if he could just drag himself to the door, he would be able to drink the raindrops . . . 'Try! . . . Oh, blast and dammitall! Try . . . again . . .'

It was late afternoon when he opened his eyes. He crawled on, inch by miserable inch, resting his thickly bearded face on his outstretched arm when consciousness reeled; sometimes shouting curses at François and Madame, once hearing himself calling to Bill, and, as the light was fading, feeling his fingers touch the rough wood of the door. He pushed at it feebly, and it gave not a fraction. *Mon Dieu*, but he was thirsty! So damnably thirsty! His mouth and throat felt as though stuffed with burning sand . . . And the blessed rain was pouring down— scant inches away. 'Twas said that men deprived of water went mad before they died . . . God! With all his remaining strength he fought again to reach the doorlatch, but he was too weak, and he gave up at last, sobbing with helplessness. The humour that had sustained him was fading, his courage failing. Before his eyes now was *Maman's* beautiful, concerned face. In his ears, the gentle murmur of her beloved voice . . .

"Roly! Roly—my poor old lad! Roly . . . Is this how that rascally pair served you then? Here, dear fellow—here!"

That was not *Maman*! A hand was holding a flask to his lips. Wonderfully cold and clean water was quenching that hellish thirst, gentle hands were easing his awkward position. He peered upward and through the blinding mists discerned a square, bronzed young face, a pair of blue eyes usually filled with laughter, but just now holding a mixture of pity and wrath.

Emotion played havoc with Roland's weakness, and he croaked in a gratitude that defied expression, "Bill . . . you—you damned maniac . . . ! You came . . . back!"

"Well, of course I did," declared Lieutenant William Bond, his voice rather husky. "Blast you, Roly! Did you think I'd leave you here to—to luxuriate in this curst overpriced hotel . . . ?"

Roland Fairleigh Mathieson, sometimes known as Otton, was quite unable to reply, and the mists that blurred his eyes now, were thankful tears.

❧ *I* ❦

England
Late Autumn, 1746

' 'Tis very obvious,' thought Fiona Bradford, burying her face in Torrey's lace-edged cravat, 'that a girl can know a gentle, well bred-up boy all her life and know him not at all!' She drew back her foot. It was a tiny foot, encased in a very high-heeled sandal, and she dealt her admirer a swift kick with it. Unhappily this resulted in more damage to her toes than to Mr. Torrey's shin. She emitted a wail of frustration and her struggles were further hampered by the need to hop on one foot.

"Let—me—*go*!" she panted, pushing at him furiously.

A large young man was Mr. Freemon Torrey, with a husky physique, thickly waving auburn hair now well powdered, and a fine pair of blue eyes that blazed with ardour. Not a few young ladies sighed over him and found him extreme good to look at, but Mr. Torrey had given his heart long since, and his devotion remained undimmed despite occasional brief dalliances into easier fields and the fact that his lady refused to admit she returned his affections.

"Sweeting," he said, his voice low-pitched with desire, "you know how dearly I love you." He seized her chin with one hand and forced it up as he smiled down into her bewitching, if enraged little face. " 'Tis Francis's fondest wish that you should become my wife, and—" His fervent utterance terminated in a yelp as his beloved demonstrated the depth of her feelings by sinking her teeth into his hand.

"I'm sorry," gasped Fiona, succeeding in wrenching herself free and running back a few paces. She blew at a curl that had become dishevelled and was hanging over one eye. "Oh! Now my hair is all come down! Really, Torrey, you have *no* right, absolutely *none*, to—" She broke off, groped under the wide sash tied about her tiny waist, and a small knife glittered menacingly in her hand. "Oh no you don't!"

Angered, he had started forward, but the knife gave him pause. He stared in astonishment, then said indignantly, "Biting is not bad enough! You must resort to knives as well! A pretty way for a lady to behave, 'pon my word!"

"You know perfectly well that I never have had time to learn how to be a lady. Francis gave me this knife whilst we was in Spain, and since you have been bosom bows all your lives, you can apprehend he taught me how to use it! And furthermore, Freemon Torrey," she gave her bodice a little straightening tug, "it may be his wish that I wed you, but could my dear brother have seen you mauling me just now, he'd likely have tossed you into the river and warned you never to darken our door again!"

Nursing his smarting hand, he frowned, but it was a glorious afternoon and Miss Bradford presented a delectable sight as she stood there on the bank of the Avon, the soft breeze flirting with the great skirts of her primrose taffety gown, the warm autumn sunlight sparkling on the water behind her and drawing golden gleams from her tumbled light brown curls. She could not really be termed a beauty, for she was neither tall nor blessed with a straight, Grecian nose or a rosebud mouth. In point of fact, she stood just over fifty-nine inches in her stockinged feet (wherefore she wore high heels). Her nose was very small and uptilted at the end, and her upper lip was a touch too short although, all things considered, it was a vivid and most enticing little mouth. Her eyes were light green and rather narrow, and she had a determined chin, both of which features Mr. Torrey found regrettable, but the eyes seemed always to hold a lurking smile, and the dimple that had a mischievous way of peeping beside her lower lip, more than compensated for the firm chin.

She was scowling at him, but his own frown had faded into an indulgent smile. Her hair had indeed come down. The thick ringlets were a loose but lovely mass on her creamy shoulders, and he had succeeded in disturbing the laces that foamed about her bodice so that the sweet swelling curves of her ample bosom were more evident than usual. The obliging breeze billowed her skirts again affording him a glimpse of a pair of shapely ankles. Sighing, Mr. Torrey said with patience but a sad lack of diplomacy, "I admire your morals, dearest girl, but you have been of marriageable age these four years and more and . . ."

Fiona's eyes flashed fire. "I am just past one and twenty," she exclaimed indignantly.

"Exactly so. And I have waited long enough. 'Tis high time we were wed and setting up our nursery. You know your papa endorses Francis's wishes. He has given me every encouragement and only today remarked that we would deal very well together."

This was a telling stroke, for Fiona was devoted to her erratic parent and the brother who two months earlier had barely escaped England with his head and now dwelt in France. "Perhaps," she said with pronounced acerbity, "Papa misunderstood your meaning and fancied you to be referring to the cards!"

Torrey grinned. "Vixen! He did no such thing, nor were we playing cards for I came to discuss our holiday—until his steward claimed his attention." He drew a jewelled watch from the pocket of his blue satin waistcoat and glanced at it uneasily. "Three o'clock almost. Gad! I promised him I'd take you only for a short drive. He's likely done with Allard long since and awaiting me. Come, sweeting, and we can make our wedding plans on the way back to the house."

Fiona levelled her knife in business-like fashion. "Whatever plans I may have do not include you, Freemon. Be off with you! And you may tell Papa why I sent you packing—if you dare! Go away! I mean it! Go and chatter about your silly holiday—though why two grown men should wish to jaunter about in a caravan like any gypsies, is beyond me!"

It seemed to her that for the briefest instant a grimness came into Torrey's blue eyes. Then he gave her a resigned smile and started towards the light coach that waited up on the road.

He looked well in his dark blue *habit à la française*, the excellent cut of the coat emphasizing the breadth of his powerful shoulders. Watching his manly figure, regret touched Fiona. He was her brother's dearest friend, and Francis probably did hope she would wed him. It would please her to gratify her beloved brother, but unless Papa insisted upon it, she would not wed Freemon. This was not because she hoped to love her husband. Love matches were rare, and Grandmama held they were vulgar. Still, one would wish to have at the least liking and admiration for the man with whom one would spend the rest of one's

8

days. And nights! She did not *dis*like Freemon, of course. They'd been friends forever. But of late she felt uncomfortable in his presence, and his blazing temper and too easily awoken jealousy bored her. She frowned thoughtfully, and wondered why that should be so. By comparison with some of Francis's more colourful companions, Torrey was a paragon of virtue. He'd had his share of *affaires de coeur* of course, but he had remained faithful to her as his choice for a mate. He did not gamble excessively, he was unfailingly good-humoured—even at the breakfast table! His address was good, his manners nice (usually!), and his fortune far from contemptible. As Mrs. Freemon Torrey she would become mistress of Torrey Park—no mean attainment, even if a title was nowhere in the offing. Yet the very thought of becoming his wife, bearing his children, made her say aloud an emphatic "No!" Again—why? He was not a bad man. Most of her friends regarded him as an excellent catch and shook their heads over her resistance. Could it be that she took him for granted? His sire and her papa had been bosom bows all their lives; Francis and Torrey enjoyed a similar depth of friendship, and she herself was extreme fond of Torrey's younger sister, Moira. Torrey Park was only ten miles away, and both families were in London yearly for the Season. Thus, she had known Freemon all her life. Might that be the difficulty?

She gave an impatient little shrug. If it was, she would soon have a chance to miss him, for he and Papa were bound and determined to sally forth in their caravan to, as Papa put it, "Savour the rural charms of our lovely land." She would miss dear Papa . . . especially with Francis now so far away. '*Safely* away, thanks to Ligun Doone!' she thought, and sent up a small and silent prayer for the gallant gentleman who had spirited so many Jacobite fugitives from under the very shadow of the axe.

"Are you sure you won't come, Fiona?" Torrey was leaning from the window of the coach, shouting to her.

He'd likely not dare maul her again, not with his coachman and footman within call. But the prospect of his close proximity did not appeal. She shook her head and waved him on, then watched the departing coach rather glumly. It was a glorious day, but it was also unseasonably warm and a long walk back to Blackberry Manor. Furthermore, her toes were bruised. At least she had her wide-brimmed hat to protect her from the bright sun. She took it up from the grassy bank where it had fallen when Torrey became so odiously amorous. Tying the yellow ribands under her chin, she started off.

She had gone less than half a mile when a donkey cart came rattling along the lane and pulled up beside her.

Mr. Allard, her father's gruff steward who had dangled her on his knee when she was a babe and who she knew adored her, drew the donkey to a halt and raised his tricorne respectfully. " 'Tis not a coach of state, Miss Fiona, but—an you would care to ride . . . ?''

Already hot and with her toes more uncomfortable than ever, Fiona gave a squeak of gratitude and was duly handed up onto the seat.

Allard drove to a wider part in the tree-shaded lane and turned the cart deftly. "I saw Mr. Torrey come home," he said non-committally. "Thought you was with him, miss."

"I was."

The steward's rather small brown eyes flickered to her grim little face and were lit by a spark of amusement. Young Torrey was fairly panting for the girl, but had picked the wrong one to play off his Romeo airs on. Still, she looked dishevelled as well as vexed, which infuriated him. He said impulsively, "If you ever need a—er, helping hand, Miss Fiona. I mean—seeing as Mr. Francis is away, and your papa . . . er . . .''

"Regards Mr. Torrey as a second son?" she supplied with a rueful sigh.

The steward had never been very communicative. He looked embarrassed now, but nodded, then said, "I hope you will forgive if I speak out of turn, miss."

Her heart warmed, she laid her mittened hand on his arm. "You do not. I am most grateful for your interest, Mr. Allard."

The touch of her hand quite broke down his reserve. He faced her squarely. "Some of us do worry a bit. You—well, you should have a chaperone, or—"

"Or a governess!" She laughed merrily. "Poor souls—they tried so hard to make a lady of me!"

"And did a very nice job of it, if I may be so bold. 'Specially seeing as you was so often drug—I mean travelling about Europe with the master. 'Tis just—well, your papa might not always see what—That is, your being a young lady now, and—" He checked with a gasp of shock as a small but razor-sharp blade flashed under his nose.

"I am armed, you see," said Fiona with a giggle. "And Mr. Francis taught me how to use it, if I have to, which God forbid. So you must not worry for my sake, my friend."

Her friend! The steward's loyal heart soared. What a very dear young lady she was, to be sure. "Showed it to him, did you, miss?" he said, grinning broadly.

Fiona nodded. "Mr. Allard," she said thoughtfully, replacing the knife in its leather sheath. "If you were my papa—just supposing, you know—would you look upon Mr. Torrey as—as a second son . . . ?"

Allard's mouth set into a hard line. "No, miss," he said with emphasis. "I would not!"

Blackberry Manor was a large square, grey brick house of the Tudor style. Mr. Mervyn Bradford had seen fit to Italianize it with much ornamentation on the exterior and great elaborately carved mantelpieces and ceilings inside. Francis Bradford endorsed these "beautifications" as enthusiastically as his sister deplored them, but she had to admit he was probably right, for the "improvements" had caused much local comment and several neighbours had expressed the intention of bringing their own properties "up to style."

Having no wish to encounter Freemon Torrey again, Fiona entered the house by a rear door. She felt dispirited as she made her way along the cool hall, taking off her hat and attempting to tidy her hair. The ornate gilt mirror that hung opposite the large dining parlour showed her a flushed face and a shockingly disarranged bodice. The hat had crushed her hair on top, and the fallen curls were tangled and untidy. "Frightful Fiona," she advised her reflection.

An instant later she heard her father's voice from the bookroom she had just passed. ". . . seeking me, Freemon, but we must not be interrupted again! Come."

He sounded stern and Fiona felt a pang of anxiety. Papa had been quite shattered when Freemon's father, his closest friend, had died very suddenly a little over a year ago. Less than a month later her brother had gone rushing off to fight for Bonnie Prince Charlie. Mervyn Bradford had long despised the House of Hanover, so it was no surprise that his son should have enlisted in the ranks of the Scots rebels. Papa had hidden his worries under his customary carefree manner, but Fiona knew how deep those worries had been. They had both been frantic last April when word had come of the shocking Scots defeat on Culloden Moor, and the subsequent brutal hunting down and slaughter of Jacobite fugitives. Her brother had fortunately had the foresight to volunteer under an assumed name, so they had been protected from the dreadful reprisals taken against families of known Jacobites, but for months they'd been unable to discover whether Francis was alive or dead. With typical rashness, Papa had determined to go in search of his son, and several times it had been all that Fiona could do to dissuade him from so dangerous and forlorn an endeavour. Then, tales had begun to drift down to the Southland about a mysterious individual named Ligun Doone, who had set himself to rescue as many as possible of the hapless fugitives. It was a ray of hope, but long weeks had passed before Torrey had brought word that Francis had indeed been helped by Mr. Doone and was at last safely in France.

It had been a nerve-racking year for Mervyn Bradford. For the first time his blithe and unconventionally adventuresome spirit had begun to wilt. Fiona had been shocked to come upon him one day without his wig, a look of despair on his fine face and new streaks of grey in the close-cropped brown hair. He had laughed at her anxieties, but she had not been deceived and for the first time had realized how deeply caring was the impulsive, rather pompous and often irresponsible gentleman who had fathered her. She loved him dearly and would move heaven and earth to protect him from more sadness. And it would both sadden and infuriate him to learn that the son of his old friend was not above mauling a reluctant girl.

Just now, his voice had sounded stern. She could only hope Torrey had not been so unwise as to confess his improper behaviour. Even so, if Papa saw her in her present state, at the very least his suspicions would be aroused. She must not let him see her. She could not hope to return to the back stairs before the study door opened, nor reach the main stairs in time. Desperate, she darted into the small red saloon. This had been a charming room until Papa had installed a massive fireplace that was much too large for so small a chamber. He had not admitted his mistake, choosing to avoid the embarrassment by never again entering the unfortunate saloon. Convinced she had found a sure haven, Fiona swung the door closed, and waited, listening breathlessly.

"This saloon will do nicely," said Bradford. "She'll never look for us in here."

Fiona could have wept. Brisk footsteps were approaching. She flew to the tall corner windows, but her attempt to open one was foiled; the handle turned, but the seldom used casement might as well have been nailed shut and resisted her strongest efforts. Swinging around, realizing she must offer some logical explanation for both her appearance and her presence in this room, she gave a gasp of relief. The jut of Papa's ridiculous great fireplace left a deep recess in the corner beside it which would afford excellent concealment. She pressed back against the wall and pulled her skirts close, convinced that unless the gentlemen walked across to the windows, she would be out of sight.

The door opened and then closed. Chairs scraped. Bradford said, "Keep your voice low, for God's sake, for this is high treason, and our very lives depend upon secrecy."

Fiona's breath froze in her throat. She almost announced her presence, but she had mothered her wild and lovable brother, and her handsome, volatile father since she'd left the school-room, and it came to her that whatever these two were plotting it might well behoove her to learn of it before Papa ran his head onto the block. She closed her lips angrily and waited.

It was a puzzling conversation at first, but gradually it began to make sense. They were discussing the great treasure that Prince Charles Stuart had gathered to finance his fight to restore his father to the throne of England. Jacobite sympathizers had willingly contributed their gold and precious articles to the cause of the handsome young price. From the hushed words of the two men, Fiona now gathered that Prince Charles had tried to smuggle the treasure to France, where it could be used to buy arms and foreign mercenaries. Vigilant English troops and the unceasing naval blockade of the Scottish coast, had thwarted his plans. In desperation, Stuart had sent his priceless hoard to England instead, reasoning that it should be easier to ship to France from there, since such a move would be unexpected. Then, the so hopefully begun Uprising had failed, and bloody Culloden Moor had sounded the death knell to all Stuart ambitions.

'Good heavens,' thought Fiona, her eyes very wide indeed. 'Do these two simpletons mean to go on a treasure hunt, then?'

"The thing I cannot fathom, sir," said Torrey softly, "is—how we are to find it."

Bradford's deep and beautifully modulated voice responded, "A man is coming from France. I've no knowledge of his identity, save that he was a highly placed officer on the prince's staff. To him have been entrusted the locations of all three hiding places of the treasure."

"And we are to gather it together, eh? But—surely 'twould be best left where it is?"

"Apparently not. 'Twould seem the hiding places had to be selected in haste, and now are considered unsafe. The Committee—you know of them, Freemon?"

"They are the group who initially gathered and guarded the treasure, I think?"

"Correct. They also handled the shipment to England, besides doing whatever they might, with Ligun Doone's help, to protect our fugitives. At all events, they've now found a permanent and secure hiding place where the treasure is to be stored until it can be returned to those who contributed."

"A tremendous undertaking, sir!"

"Aye. But one that will save many lives. Have you any notion, lad, of how many families of the men who fought are now dispossessed of home and lands? Of how many are starving? You and I stand to regain funds of course, but 'tis a matter of life and death to those poor souls."

There was a brief silence through which Fiona stared blindly at the picture of two hunting dogs on the opposite wall, her thoughts rioting. This then was the reason behind the "jolly caravan holiday"! She might have known, for certainly the pattern had repeated itself often enough!

Once, while they had been in Spain, brigands had stopped their coach. Ignoring the odds, Papa had fought them, been badly beaten, but almost at once had gone haring off with a few ill-equipped men in pursuit of the villains. He'd come back, triumphant, but with a pistol ball through his leg and a chill that had developed into the pneumonia. A fine time she'd had, fighting for his life! And all over Mama's pearl necklace which she very seldom wore! There was also the matter of the sermon to which he had taken offense and stood up and argued his case in front of the whole congregation, so that the vicar had never since been able to address him with a smile! And that dreadful scene in Drury Lane when Papa had fancied himself a great actor and, having somehow inveigled his way into the play, had left the stage on opening night to plunge into the pit and do battle with the young gallants who'd booed him! A charming riot *that* had caused! One must not forget the boundary dispute with the irascible Sir Gavin Brack, which might yet be resolved with swords, for all her desperate attempts to avert such a calamity. And other fiascoes—oh, too numerous to count—that she *had* somehow contrived to deal with!

Faith, but she'd only to turn her back for an instant, and the impossible creature was at it again! Rushing blithely into a treasonable scheme with no thought of the possible hideous consequences to himself, and all of them! She closed her eyes. Why, oh *why*, did gentlemen have to be so utterly foolish?

Torrey broke the silence to ask slowly, "How are they to know who gave what? Sworn testimony?"

"I think our prince was more canny than that, m'boy. Ninety-nine out of a hundred would take no more than their due. But, human nature being what it is, there's always the occasional charlatan. So Prince Charles had a list kept of all contributors *and* their contributions."

"Good God!" Torrey's chair went over with a crash. "Where a plague is the damned thing? 'Tis a veritable death warrant for all those named!"

"Be at ease, boy! 'Tis en route to us now, and has been guarded well, I dare swear."

"How was it brought out of Scotland?"

"By a courier. A brave man, and cruelly hounded, poor fellow."

"And he is safe? The list is delivered?"

Bradford laughed and said fatalistically, "If 'tis not, our risks may well be for nought, Freemon. But the courier will win through or destroy his message, you may be sure."

"Sure—hell! If he is taken every man or woman named on that list will be very dead and in no need of the return of valuables! For my part, I'd as lief have my head, thankee!"

"Aye—well, we've no choice in the matter. Now, I've told Fiona we leave on Tuesday next. But I fear she may decide to go with us, so we must instead get away at dawn tomorrow."

"What if she catches us, sir?"

"Then 'twill be too late for her to pack. You know how women are—they'll never move without all their frills and furbelows and creams and fal-lals."

They both laughed, but might not have done so had they seen Fiona, who stood fuming, her hands tight clenched and sparks glinting from her narrowed eyes.

"She has no suspicions, sir?" asked Torrey.

"Gad! Don't even think such a dreadful thing! One whiff merely and you may be *sure* she'd try to spoil our fun!"

Fun! Incensed, Fiona fairly sprang out from behind the fireplace. "You are too late, Papa!"

With a faint scream Mervyn Bradford leapt to his feet, his handsome features blanching, "Oh—my God!" he gasped.

"The devil!" exclaimed Torrey, even whiter.

"Neither," snarled Fiona. "Papa—how *could* you sneak and plot and connive behind my back?"

"I . . . I . . ." stammered Bradford, and then blustered feebly, "What the deuce are you about, child? Listening by stealth to . . . to private conversations that you've no right to—"

"No *right*? My dear brother has been forced into exile! You are all I have left," she raged, heartlessly disposing of several dozen aunts, uncles, and cousins, to say nothing of her formidable but much loved grandmama. "You must not attempt so mad a venture, Papa! The roads and by-ways are fairly clogged with troopers hunting Jacobites. Do you not recall all the posters and uproars and alarms because of the coded messages they sought?"

"I do. And that is quite done with, for the cyphers are all safely delivered, praise God!"

"Praise God, indeed! And a ghastly time of it the couriers had, getting those deadly rhymes through! A poem is a very small thing, sir, easy of concealment. Do you seriously think to stuff your silly caravan full of gold and drive it through the military patrols? You'd not get a mile!"

Torrey, his face troubled, murmured, "She has come at the heart of it, I think, sir. The chance is slight indeed."

Mervyn Bradford drew back his shoulders. He was a tall man, well proportioned, of most striking appearance and commanding personality. His dark eyes flashing now, he looked magnificent as he said with the drama he loved to employ, " 'Tis a chance we must take. Brave men have given their lives to guard and return the treasure to the rightful owners. Gentle ladies who have lost their loved ones and their homes to the Cause are dying and watching their children die of exposure and starvation. The return of the valuables they gave so willingly might at least put a roof over their heads and would likely spell the difference between perishing or a new life! Can you truly ask me to turn my back, Fiona? To . . . let 'the other fellow' attend to it?''

"We have lost our dear Francis to this horrid rebellion, Papa! Is that not enough to give?"

"He is alive—thanks to Ligun Doone, a man who risked death a hundred times to help our people."

"He was one of us, and—"

"No, child," interrupted Bradford softly. "He was not!"

Torrey gave a shocked gasp. Staring at her father, Fiona felt as though the ground had been cut out from under her.

"He was an Englishman," said Bradford. "A soldier in the service of King George. He was badly wounded, but retained sufficient humanity to be appalled by what he saw in Scotland, and felt obliged to do what he might to make amends. Because of his compassion for his enemies, my son yet lives. But for him, Francis's head might even now be rotting atop Temple Bar!"

Fiona shuddered and closed her eyes briefly.

Bradford said, "Can you still question my determination to help, when both your brother and I supported the Jacobite Cause? Why, I'd count myself a craven cur did I refuse aid to those who have asked it of me!"

"I can well guess who asked you! This has an air of Grandmama about it! And—what are you supposed to be while you—you venture this forlorn endeavour? Gypsies?"

"Perhaps. 'Twould serve."

"An all-male band of gypsies?" she persisted.

Bradford regarded her in sudden unease.

"Hah!" she said. "And what will the military think when they see so odd a company? You had as well advertise yourselves as frauds!"

"There will be women," said Bradford. "Jacobite volunteers. And listen to me, my girl," he shook a finger sternly under her diminutive nose, "do not be getting any silly notions!"

17

"Certainly not, Papa," she said. "My notion is far from silly. When you leave—I go with you!"

"No!" thundered Bradford furiously. "Damme! I say—*no!*"

"Absolutely not!" cried Freemon Torrey.

Fiona smiled and lifted her little chin.

❧ 2 ❧

The weather, which had been fine coming up through the Cotswold Hills, turned chilly on Sunday afternoon and by dusk a light drizzle was misting the air. Roland Fairleigh Mathieson, sometimes known as Otton, but at present using his own name, had remained at a discreet distance behind his quarry these last four days. He was a man who knew how to bide his time, but he also knew and respected the rebel he followed, wherefore he urged Rumpelstiltskin to a canter, his keen gaze intent on the carriage wherein Rob MacTavish and his bride travelled at a steady pace through the valley below. Mathieson judged it inconceivable that the Scot knew he was following, for he had been very careful, but with the instinctive caution of the hunted, MacTavish had detoured several times, once so successfully that Mathieson's chestnut horse had been obliged to stretch his long, powerful legs in a sustained gallop in order to regain sight of the carriage.

The drizzle became rain and conspired with the dimming light to decrease visibility, and with fiendish contrariness MacTavish was setting a faster pace. A driven man, no doubt, thought Mathieson, his well-cut but rather thin lips curving to a sardonic smile. Well, he himself was driven—had been driven these three years and more in his search for easy wealth. And if MacTavish thought to lose anyone who might be following, he was doomed to disappointment. "Not this time, friend," Mathieson said softly.

Rumpelstiltskin was well accustomed to receiving his master's confidences, and whickered an acknowledgment. Mathieson tensed, but between the pattering of the rain and the distance,

19

there was scant chance MacTavish's postillions had heard. He leaned forward and patted Rump's wet neck, then turned him onto the downward slope.

The straightest line led through a belt of trees, but despite the increasing gloom Rumpelstiltskin picked his way unerringly among fallen branches, shrubs, and bracken. They emerged onto the turf without mishap. The rain had stopped now, but it was very obviously a temporary lull. A cold wind moaned through the valley, whipping Mathieson's cloak and stirring the chestnut's mane, and above them the skies were heavy with towering black clouds.

Narrowing the long dark eyes that had been the undoing of several lovely ladies, Mathieson sought for the coach and at length discerned it briefly outlined against the stormy sky as it topped a rise and vanished down the far side. He'd shortened the distance between them, by Jupiter! Exultant, he spoke softly to the stallion, urging him onward, casting caution to the wind as the rain began in earnest, the great cold drops becoming a steady downpour that promised to last the night out. They reached the rise in a pitchy darkness and were greeted by a wind-driven sheet of rain that made Mathieson clutch at his tricorne and duck his chin into the collar of his cloak. Far off, a cluster of lights promised a village or a hamlet. Too small for Cheltenham, he thought, but likely the Scot would rack up there, if only out of consideration for his lovely Rosamond.

Mathieson smiled faintly. His long search for the treasure that Bonnie Prince Charlie had so obligingly gathered, was surely drawing to a triumphant conclusion. After many months of disappointments, including having suffered a nasty wound at the hands of a fighting rebel, a lesser man might have abandoned the frustrating and perilous road to easy wealth. Not Roland Fairleigh Mathieson. When the trail in England had run quite cold, he'd repaired to Paris. Many hunted Jacobites had escaped to France. Certainly, he'd reasoned, they would be in touch with other fugitives—perhaps those who knew something of the hidden treasure.

He'd been fortunate in encountering an intrepid young man calling himself Dr. Robert Victor. Very soon Mathieson had learned that the worthy doctor was not a physician at all, but one Robert Victor MacTavish, an escaped Scots fugitive in honour bound to return to England to help his people. That any

Jacobite, having once escaped Britain, would risk the horrors of a traitor's death by returning, had seemed to Mathieson the very height of stupidity. He was obliged to admit, however, that he'd been outwitted by the Scot. MacTavish had fallen in love with and won the heart of a lovely English lass whose clergyman brother, although not a Jacobite, was deeply involved with helping them. At the very point of arrest, MacTavish had got his lady's brother safely out of the country, then flummoxed the military into believing he and his love had also fled to France.

Mathieson could not recall their final encounter with pleasure. He and a troop of dragoons had been close on MacTavish's heels at the end of that mad flight to the south coast. It might in fact, have had a very different end, for Mathieson had come upon the Scot and could have earned a nice reward by delivering him up for execution. Unfortunately, in a moment of weakness, he'd given his word not to betray the fugitives, and so had been unable to let the injured and helpless MacTavish suffer the consequences of his folly. A depressing situation in which to be placed. He sighed, but was rescued from gloom by his customary optimism. Eventually, good had come from his foolishness, for he was very sure now that MacTavish not only knew where the treasure was located, but was heading straight for it. With dogged determination therefore, he had clung day and night to the trail of the Scot. He was known both to the fugitive and his bride, wherefore it was necessary they not set eyes on him, but—

He started. He'd been so lost in reflection that for a minute or two he had failed to notice the change in the stallion's gait. He reined up and was out of the saddle in a lithe swing. Investigation brought a groan of frustration. He shook a fist at the dark heavens.

"Why? Why must you fail me now, Thomas? The poor fool is less than a mile distant—the treasure as good as in my hands!"

But it was evident that St. Thomas was bending his energies elsewhere, and the iron horseshoe was no less lost for Mathieson's rageful indignation. He took up the reins once more and led Rumpelstiltskin on through the worsening storm while apologizing to him for the situation in which they found themselves thanks to a somewhat less than efficient heavenly mediator.

"There!" whispered the pretty little serving maid. "The tall gent by the fire. Did ever you see such a face, Bertha?"

Her co-worker peered through the crowd gathered in the tap of The Red Rooster Inn. The gentleman indicated stood directly in front of the roaring flames, which was understandable as he appeared soaked to the skin. The cloak he had discarded was flung over the settle beside him. His wet black riding coat and white buckskins clung the tighter to a slim but muscular frame; a ruby winked richly from the snowy laces at his throat, another graced the fine-boned, long-fingered hand that held the tankard of ale. 'Quality,' she thought. 'And the most handsome gent what I ever saw.'

The thickly lashed black eyes turned in their direction and a smile came into them. Her heart leaping, Bertha dodged past her outraged friend and ran to enquire with a pert smile as to "milor's wishes."

Mathieson waved his tankard at her. "No 'milor' and—no more ale alas, pretty girl," he said in a rich, cultured voice.

She reached for the tankard, her eyes glued to the fascinating dark features, and in an instant his arm was around her, and she was squealing as he planted a kiss on her rosy cheek. He laughed and let her go and, when he returned, slipped a shilling down the front of her bodice. "You're a ripe armful. What's your name, lass?"

"Bertha." She rubbed her hip and said poutingly, "And you hurt me with your ugly sword."

He leaned nearer. "Then I must kiss it better."

"Ooh!" she exclaimed, blushing, but her blue eyes flirting with his brilliant black ones. "What a wicked genelman!"

"Aye, and not easily put off," he murmured, caressing the earlobe that peeped from beneath her laced cap.

She shook her head at him. "You're liable to be put under sod! To wear such jewels on the road at night! Hasn't ye heard that Galloping Nick waits fer the likes o' you?"

"Galloping Nick will stop no more travellers, does he stop me, I promise you." It sounded boasting, but there was that about him which said he did not boast idly. "I seek a friend, sweet Bertha. A gentleman about my own age, but perhaps half a head shorter than I. Today he wears neither wig nor powder, his hair is light brown, his eyes—light—um . . . grey I think, and he goes with a very slight limp. A good-looking man, rather on the lean side. Likely came in shortly before I did. Have you seen such a one?"

She considered and shook her head. "If he comes, would ye wish I tell him as you are seek—"

"No, no. I bring him good news, but I'd prefer it be a surprise. He—er, stands in need of cheering up, d'ye see? Keep your eyes open, my sweet. Tip me the word before he spots me, and you'll find more than a shilling in your lovely bodice."

With spurious shyness she put a protecting hand over the area his eyes prowled so wickedly, but her saucy reply was lost in an outburst of loud laughter from the group of men gathered at the other side of the wide hearth.

"Treasure my grandmama's garter! Had Bonnie Prince Charlie p'ssessed 'smuch treasure as twenty gold p-pieces, he'd've spent 'tall on his misbegotten Uprising! I tell—hic!—I tell you, friends, Romans'n countrymen, if there be any treasure 'tis no more'n the price on that m-misguided fug'tive's unfort'nate head!"

The serving maid tripped away, and Mathieson's gaze turned with faint amusement to the big man who stood holding forth among the rustics. The accent said London and Quality. The attire said eccentricity, for, although bearing the unmistakable mark of a fine tailor, it was more than a trifle flamboyant, the crimson velvet coat lavishly trimmed with purple embroidery, the frogged buttons also purple, the waistcoat white satin, quilted with purple thread. White satin nether garments hugged powerful thighs, and white stockings with purple diamonds were slightly wrinkled over shapely calves. His costume and the amethyst buckled high-heeled shoes he wore proclaimed that he travelled by coach. His demeanour and the diamond patch beside his humorous mouth said that he harboured a taste for the dramatic. His high colour and slurred enunciation told of a generous partaking of the wine that slopped in his glass.

"With all due respect, sir," argued a squarely built man who looked like a prosperous farmer, "rumour says the Scotch prince gathered a great fortune and when he run out of time to spend it on his Rebellion, he hid it away so secret that now he's been obliged to write messages about what he wants done wi' it. We all do know how the army's been hunting down fugitives these five months since the Battle o' Culloden Moor, and—"

"What would you?" interjected the gentleman, leaning precariously towards him. "Fellas are t-traitors. Fought us. Enemies."

A thin man with a sour mouth and a well-cut dark brown habit observed drily that Jacobite fugitives were executed almost as soon as they were apprehended.

"Unless the army thinks as they knows summat," put in an apple-cheeked countryman clad in a snowy smock and gaiters. "Then they do live longer. Say a week or two. And like as not wish they 'adn't! Which do seem a mite 'arsh, but you cannot go fer to deny as they did fight us, Doctor Lowell, and many a fine young English chap lying dead and cold in Scotland on account o' it."

"The Uprising was put down nigh half a year since," responded the sour Dr. Lowell. "No more call for such savagery. Especially when they hound the poor devils for three hundred miles and more, and then nab 'em just as they go to set foot on a ship bound for France. Is inhuman, I say!"

"Ar, well you shouldn't say it, Doctor. Not out loud," put in the prosperous farmer, his shrewd eyes turning uneasily toward the tall young gallant who had undoubtedly heard his reckless medical friend. "And be that as it may, the fact remains as there's been a'many couriers rushing hither and yon carrying pomes, and—"

"Carrying—what?" interrupted the tall gentleman, fascinated but swaying as he stood there, "Do pray eluci-eluci-'splain y'meanin', m'dear f'low."

Two of the bystanders covered their mouths rather ostentatiously, and the farmer flushed.

"Pomes," he repeated with defiant determination. "You know, sir. Words as goes wi' a lilt, and what rhymes."

"Ah . . ." The large gentleman's eyes kindled. He flung his hand high in an extravagant gesture that sent Mathieson a hurried step to the rear so as to avoid a shower of wine. "Like this—perchance?" In a deep and sonorous voice that stopped all conversation in the crowded tap, he recited,

> "No longer mourn for me when I am—
> hic—dead
> Than you shall hear th-the sully surlen bell
> Gi' warning to th'world that I—er—bled
> In thish vile inn and—er—so farewell . . ."

24

There was a chorus of awed gasps, capped by Mathieson's muffled snort of laughter.

The large gentleman, who had been bowing deeply, glanced up in mid-bow and toppled to his knees.

Mathieson found it advisable to turn away to conceal a broad grin.

The laughter faded.

A hand tapped Mathieson's shoulder.

He turned to find the large gentleman's chin thrusting at him, the rather foolish smile having given way to a livid ferocity, and the eyes narrowed and dangerous.

Recognizing the signs and having no desire to draw attention to himself, Mathieson said with his pleasant smile, "Wish you good eve, friend."

"Cannot have a g-good eve when y'take all the heat from th' fire, sir," growled the large gentleman belligerently.

"Very selfish of me," admitted Mathieson, who had long since ceased to consider the well-being of his fellow man. "I am rather damp, you see, but I'd no thought to—"

"To be a fire hog?"

"I apologize." Mathieson's bow was just a touch too deep but so graceful that the two serving maids sighed dreamily.

A few chuckles were heard, and the large gentleman, rightly suspecting he was being mocked, bridled. "And . . . and you steam, sir," he pointed out, making wild fanning motions.

"The logical result of a meeting of heat and water, alas."

"Then ye mean t' go on with it? I din't come in here t'be steamed over, and—and so I tell ye. To y'r face—which I can't hardly see f'r—f'r all y'r c'nfounded steam, sir!"

Mathieson's dark eyes danced with laughter; he lowered them and stepped aside saying meekly that he would endeavour to refrain from steaming. He was, however, quite unable to keep his mouth from twitching and, bristling, the large gentleman advanced.

"You found m' p'formance—amusin', I gather?"

Despite himself, Mathieson asked mildly, "Was not that your intent, sir?"

"By God, but 'twas not, sir! Th' Bard c'n be mos' 'musin' when he wishes to—to be. Not in that p'tic'lar sonnet h'wever. You care to—to step outside . . . sir, an' let me wipe that demned grin off your face?"

25

A small and very hopeful crowd was gathering. The large gentleman was obviously eager for a mill. His dashing adversary was tall and well built, the sword that hung at his side had seen much service by the look of it, and there was about him the slight swagger and arrogant assurance that spoke of a born fighting man.

Mathieson disappointed them. "By no means, sir," he replied, bowing once more. "I admired your rendering of Shakespeare." The gentleman looked somewhat mollified. "I merely fancied your misquote to have been deliberate."

"M-Misquote?" roared the large gentleman, at once choleric. "Misquote, d'ye say? Why, devil take y'sir! I do *not* misquote th' 'mortal Bard. Not *never*! Take it back, sir, or . . . by—by—" Even as he spoke, his fist flashed out. It was a large fist and might have been most damaging had it landed. The wine, however, had taken its toll. Mathieson swayed easily aside, and the fist flew past his ear. The large gentleman lost his balance and plunged.

"Bye, bye," said Mathieson, grinning as he caught and lowered the aggressive Shakespearean afficionado to the floor.

He then offered polite farewells to the amused onlookers, and taking up his wet cloak, made his way to the stables to check on Rumpelstiltskin.

The rain had stopped, a half-moon was playing hide and seek with the clouds, and the wind had sunk to little more than a breeze. There was ample light for Mathieson to see his way, which meant there was also sufficient light for Rob MacTavish to do the same. On the other hand, Mathieson was tired, for he'd been in the saddle since dawn. It followed, therefore, that Mrs. Robert Victor MacTavish, née Albritton, would also be tired.

"Cheltenham eh, Rump old lad," said Mathieson. The big horse whickered and tossed his head. "No," Mathieson told him firmly. "No farther tonight, or I'm like to pass by the Highland gentleman, and we can't have that!"

Ten minutes later, his chances of passing his prey were deteriorating rapidly. The breeze had stiffened into a brisk wind once more; the wispy clouds were gathering into ominous masses that gradually obliterated the moon, and even as Mathieson called down maledictions on England's unpredictable climate, the rain began again. Cursing, he turned up the collar of his cloak and slowed Rumpelstiltskin, narrowing his eyes to peer through the darkness.

Above the drumming of the rain he could soon detect a deeper sound—rushing water. He was sure they'd left the Severn behind, but likely this was some tributary swollen by the heavy rains. After a while he was able to see the water, a dark flood, roaring along beside him. Rumpelstiltskin snorted uneasily, and Mathieson guided him with care, searching for a bridge. They came upon one at last, a rickety wooden structure. Mathieson dismounted and walked cautiously onto the timbers; the chestnut minced along, his cold nose at his master's neck. The bridge seemed safe enough, but Mathieson strode over it rapidly, Rumpelstiltskin's hooves thudding close behind. They were safely across and starting down the incline to level ground when Mathieson checked, listening intently. Almost at once there came another faint cry, startling the chestnut so that he snorted and danced sideways.

"Help! Please . . . help me!"

A woman, and in distress. Mathieson's shout elicited the information that she was "down here," this followed by a breathless request that he "come quickly!"

He left Rump and clambered down the rainswept bank, the roar of the stream sounding ever louder in his ears. But look where he might, he could find no sign of a lady and he was almost to the water's edge.

"Where the deuce are you?" he roared.

"Here! Are you b-blind?"

The voice came from his feet. Shocked, he discerned a cloaked figure lying face down in the mud and he dropped to one knee beside her. "What—on earth? Did you fall, ma'am? Here—let me help you up."

"I can't . . . get up." A young voice, and breathless. "I daren't let go! Please—can you reach it?"

Bewildered, he bent closer. The girl's arms were stretched straight out before her and he realized belatedly that she was clinging to a dark shape that leapt and swung to the pull of the rushing stream. He leaned down precariously.

"Sir—do be careful! A whole section of the . . . bank gave way just a minute ago. I—I think this piece is almost gone!"

He glanced down and was aghast. She was perfectly right.

27

The earth he knelt on was melting away before his eyes. Amazed by such unselfish courage, he gasped, "Good God! Is it someone in the water? Jupiter! 'Tis a treetrunk! What—"

"She fell in and managed to cling to it. I—heard her crying and . . . and came. Oh, have you got a grip on—?" The words ended in a shriek as the bank disintegrated under Mathieson. At one instant he was stretching out to grab the tossing treetrunk; at the next he was up to his neck in icy water that pounded and pulled and tore at him, snatching his breath away, whirling him off his feet, and smashing him hard against the treetrunk that was already providing a precarious haven for another victim of the storm. He clung to it, unable to see who was his companion in adversity, fighting to keep from being torn away, praying that the girl on the bank could hang on just until he could get a purchase on something. Mercifully, his feet found the bottom. He could stand, and he battled the raging current, groping out desperately for dry land. He felt something stable at last—a root exposed by the torrent. With a choked gasp of relief he clutched at it and dragged himself up, somehow managing to haul the treetrunk after him. Other hands came at once to help and, fighting for breath, he was kneeling on firm ground. Soaked, freezing, and feeling as if he'd been battered by two or three unfriendly giants, he spat and spluttered, "Are you—all right?"

"Yes. Oh, yes! And—here she is, poor little girl! Half drowned. Oh, sir—you were splendid! How brave to jump in like that to . . . save her!" The panting voice sharpened. "What's wrong? Did you hurt yourself?"

"Seem to have—twisted my ankle a trifle," gasped Mathieson, pulling a slimy weed from his ear. His boots were full of water and when he attempted to pull one off, his right hand began to hurt as fiercely as his twisted ankle. He managed somehow to empty out the water and replace his boots. He hadn't lost them, at least, and if he'd managed to save a child's life this night, it just might warrant one bright spot on his page in the heavenly record book. *Maman* would be pleased, for Lord knows there were sufficient blots on that particular page! "Never mind about me," he said nobly. "Is the little girl able to walk? I can't see . . ."

"She'll be all right now. I can manage her. We must take care of—of you, sir. Oh, how c-cold it is, and you're wet through!"

28

She took his arm. "Up the bank and just a little way into the trees. It's not too far."

Since it was quite close by, Mathieson did not suggest that the girl ride Rumpelstiltskin, who came snorting up to follow them. With each stride however, Mathieson discovered new aches and pains and it seemed a miserable age before he glimpsed a light through the trees. 'A very small house,' he thought, but then realized it was not a house at all. 'A caravan, by Jupiter! Are they gypsies, then?'

"Here we are," said the girl, a faceless shape in the darkness as she climbed some steps. "Do come in."

His teeth were chattering, but he hesitated. "M-my horse—"

"Will be quite all right for a few minutes, if you tether him on that side, out of the wind." She opened the door and became a dark silhouette against the warm inside glow, her hood close about her face, her cloak protectively covering the child she carried.

Mathieson limped around to the side protected by the wide-spreading branches of a tree. He unsaddled Rump with a good deal of difficulty and a great many oaths, found a comparatively dry piece of sacking, and gave the chestnut a cursory rubdown with his left hand, promising to come and do it properly in a few minutes, and wondering if he could manage such a feat.

"Do hurry, sir! You must be frozen!"

He responded to that urgent call and made his painful way to the steps once more. The girl had removed her cloak, and stood waiting for him. She ran to take his arm, advising him to lean on her as he negotiated the steps. He contrived to do so. She was very short, but she was young, and he thought glumly that if she was also comely and lived alone in her little caravan, he might soon have made them both warm, save that fate had been so unkind as to disable him. She pushed the door open and, sighing regretfully, he glanced at her, only to recoil instinctively.

From head to toe, she was mud. It streaked down her forehead, covered her face, and sullied her pale green gown. Her hood must have been of little protection, for her hair was soaked and had plastered itself in wet strands around the oval face and hung in a lank straggle about her shoulders. She might as well have been wearing a mask, for all he could really distinguish were her eyes, which were a rather odd shape, somewhat narrow and slightly uptilted at the corners, but of a clear light green. They twinkled at him now, and she said rather illogically, "Oh dear, you *are* a mess! Poor man! And—alas, I've no fire to warm you, for the rain put mine out. I have saved hot water though, thank goodness." She went to the rear of the caravan, calling over her shoulder, "You must take off your clothes at once!"

Mathieson could have wept. A golden opportunity, ruined! That it truly *was* ruined became more evident when he started to unbutton his cloak. His right thumb was swelling and so painful he could scarcely endure to move it. He fumbled with his left hand, stifling the curse that rose to his lips, but the girl must have been watching because at once she was standing directly before him again, peering up with anxious if bizarre solicitude into his face.

"What is it? Why do you just stand there shivering instead of taking off your clothes?"

She was a bold lass, if nothing else. Confound the luck! But the humour of it all struck him, and he held out his hand saying ruefully, " 'Fraid I'll have to disappoint you tonight, my pretty."

"Oh, dear!" She touched his thumb with one feather-light finger. "What a pity. Is it dislocated, do you think? My brother did that once, and it was exceeding painful until Papa re-set it."

"A sprain, more likely, and a confounded nuisance." He added with a suggestive wink, "Tonight, especially."

She nodded. "I should probably bandage it so you do not use it for a while, but first we must have your garments off, they're fairly dripping mud!"

"So are yours," he pointed out. "I can manage. Do you tend to yourself and the little one." He glanced about. "Where is she?"

"Under there." She indicated a blanket lying in a bundle on the upper of two narrow bunks attached to the left wall of the caravan. "She's warmer now, poor mite. I'll fetch some hot water and be back in a minute." And she was gone with a whirl of petticoats and a slam of the door.

Mathieson had never been inside a caravan before and as he shivered and swore his way out of cloak and coat, he was intrigued to find things cramped but very neat and orderly. A straight-backed wooden chair with a brightly embroidered cush-

30

ioned seat stood in the far corner, which would be the front end were they moving. A tall narrow cupboard was bolted to the wall beside it, and on the left wall were the two bunks. Several books and periodicals were piled on a small shelf enclosed by a guard rail, and a large brass-bound trunk did double duty as a table. Strings of onions and a rope basket of vegetables hung from the ceiling. The remaining wall space was home to a small mirror and innumerable pots, pans, cooking implements, and extra candles, all very precisely disposed. And the unmistakable imprint of feminity was evidenced by the immaculate red and white cloth that was spread on the trunk, the little vase of flowers that stood there, the occasional water colours nailed up amid the pots and pans, and the faint aroma of powders and perfumes that pervaded the air.

He had succeeded with all but the last of his shirt buttons when the laces at his left wrist became caught on the ruby pin in his cravat. His right hand was useless and however he struggled, for some reason he could not detach the pin which seemed to have become inextricably entangled with his ruffles. Fuming, he snarled, "Of all the stupid—"

The door opened, admitting a rush of colder air, and the girl hurried in. A towel was draped over her arm, and she held a tray on which were set a steaming bowl, a sponge, and a cake of soap. "Can you undo your . . . er . . . ," she enquired, slightly pink.

He lowered his hand to the buttons of his nether garments and, of necessity his head followed. "Is somewhat difficult," he admitted, bent double and craning his neck to grin up at her.

"What—on earth . . . ?" she gasped.

He waved his left hand, the laces still securely attached to the ruby pin.

Her laugh was a musical ripple. She was undoubtedly just as cold and almost as uncomfortable as he, yet she could laugh. A pearl among women, this gypsy lass.

"Poor fellow," she exclaimed, setting the pan on the trunk. "Here—let me!"

He flung out his right hand to ward her off and cried theatrically, "Release my ruffles only, an you will, ma'am. I am not without me pride!" He grinned boyishly. "Besides, I'm afraid you may first have to help me shed my boots."

Chuckling, she reached up to disentangle ruffles from ruby.

It was most fiendishly enmeshed, and soon her lips were slightly parted with concentration, revealing small white teeth and the tip of her tongue. Mud or no mud, she was all female, and Mathieson, not one to miss an opportunity, leaned to her mouth.

She had finished her small task even as he bent however, and went hurrying off to rummage about under a pile of pillows on the lower bunk.

He sighed.

"Poor soul, you are exhausted," she said with mistaken sympathy.

"Ineffectual, certainly."

"We'll soon have you feeling cozy." She shook out another large blanket and held it up, screen-like. "Do you remove your shirt and then wrap this about you."

"No such thing!" He leaned over the top of the blanket, smiling down into her upturned face. "We have not been so much as introduced and I'll have you know I am one for the proprieties!"

There could scarcely be anything less proper than their present situation and, predictably, that rich trilling laugh rang out again. "Very right," she said, in her low, husky voice. "Therefore, out of respect for your privacy and my reputation, I shall close my eyes—thus. Now you may proceed, Mr. . . . ?"

"Mathieson. Roland Mathieson." He took off his shirt, wrapped the blanket around him toga-fashion, and sat down on the chair. "I might better have introduced myself as Caesar."

"And of a certainty, the little one and I almost buried you!" The green eyes opened and twinkled at him. "Put your foot out and I'll pull off your boots."

Despite all the mud he noted that her gown was of fine India muslin, well cut, and worn over many petticoats; altogether of much better quality than he would have expected of a gypsy girl. His brow wrinkled—come to think of it, she spoke in refined accents, also.

She knelt. "Your foot," she prompted, looking up at him.

He hesitated. "No, please get up, ma'am! You're cold and wet. Perhaps I can manage."

He bent and tugged at his boot, trying to spare his right hand. His ankle protested vigorously, his thumb throbbed, and he bit his lip and wished with profane intensity that Sorenson, his invaluable man of all work, was here.

32

Two small hands gently but firmly detached his grasp. "Just lean back," she said, "and be quiet."

"But—"

"I do this for my father all the time, you know."

She probably did, for whatever her past station in life, certainly she now lived in a caravan. Perhaps she even had admirers who visited her in this leafy glade. He apologized for being such a nuisance and stuck out his leg.

"Nuisance, is it? Have you forgot? I am greatly . . . indebted to you, Mr. . . . . Mathieson," she panted, tugging.

"Ow!" gasped Mathieson.

She staggered back and sat down inelegantly, clutching his boot. "I am sorry. But—it's off at all events," she said cheerfully, clambering to her feet, no more perturbed by her fall than was Mathieson, who'd enjoyed a fine view of ankles and petticoats.

The second boot came off more easily, at least less painfully, and she gave a little crow of triumph. "Excelsior! And I am Miss Fiona Bradford." She dropped a swift curtsey, flourishing the boot in her hand, then set it neatly beside its mate. "Now—while you wash, I am going to go across to my father's caravan and change my dress and get some of this mud off. I'll come back in just a few minutes, I promise, and tend your poor hand."

"Never mind about me. What about the little girl?" He glanced anxiously at the bunk. "She hasn't moved!"

"How very kind you are." Miss Bradford went over to lift a corner of the blanket carefully. "Oh, she's fast asleep. She'll be all right, never fear. Now—keep warm. I'll be as quick as I can."

It seemed a rather haphazard attitude to adopt toward a half-drowned child, but women knew more about these things, of course. He waited until Miss Bradford had closed the door behind her, then began clumsily to wash his face and hands. The water was black when he finished, but he felt much restored. The blanket was warm and ample, and with it wrapped around him he was quite cozy and no longer shivering. His head was nodding when Miss Bradford knocked and then came in carrying a steaming pitcher and with a basket over her arm.

33

"Here I am, at long last!" she cried brightly, then halted, staring.

He had made shift to order his thick black hair, but it was wet from his ablutions and a few strands curled untidily about the features that were so breathtakingly handsome that she felt a twinge of unease.

Mathieson, staring in turn, came clumsily to his feet.

Miss Bradford had changed into a charming but simple gown of light blue. The mud was gone, revealing an oval face that had little claim to classic beauty. Her small nose was slightly uptilted, her upper lip was too short, even if it did curve very sweetly to meet its mate, her candid green eyes were inclined to be narrow, but held such a smiling look, and a dimple lurked beside her firm little chin. Her hair hung in a damp light brown mass about her shoulders. Despite the fact that she was so little, her figure was prettily rounded, but he was dismayed and muttered, "Good Gad! You're scarce out of the schoolroom!"

For an instant she did not move, standing there clutching the pitcher and gazing up at him. Then she gave a rather strained laugh and hurried to put the pitcher on the floor and pick up the bowl of dirty water. "I'll have you know I am of age, sir! Just," she amended hurriedly.

Mathieson breathed a silent sigh of relief and sat down again. She was an odd chit, devoid of sophistication or a proper shyness, which was not to be wondered at in a girl who dwelt in a caravan. Still, she had evidently been taught how to speak properly, and there was something about her that intrigued. He determined, in fact, to visit her once this business with MacTavish was successfully concluded. It would not hurt, he thought, to lay a little groundwork.

Miss Bradford had gone outside to empty the bowl, and now returned to refill it with fresh water from the pitcher. "Now, mighty Caesar," she teased, "I have brought bandages in my basket. We will tend your hurts, if you please."

"But—" he protested, looking to the child.

Miss Bradford did not exactly smile. Rather, her entire face seemed to glow; almost, he thought, as though someone had lit a candle within her. "Of course," she said softly. "You are so kind, and must think me quite heartless." She went to bend

34

over the pile of pillows, folded back the blanket, and took up the other storm victim.

Mathieson uttered a stunned exclamation.

Miss Bradford held a small, scrawny, tabby cat, its fur all standing up in spikes, and its small pink mouth wide open as it yawned at him.

3

"What—the—deuce?" snorted Mathieson, momentarily bewildered.

"Do you see, sir, why I so admire you," said Miss Bradford earnestly. "How many gentlemen would throw themselves into a raging torrent only to save a cat?" She glowed at him. "And not even a purebred!"

"You said," he pointed out with increasing choler, " 'twas a little girl!"

"She is a little girl cat, and—Oh! You never really thought—" For a moment she looked dismayed, then she laughed softly. "Oh, but you are funning, of course. As if I would have left a child untended after so frightful an experience!" She raised her hand as Mathieson attempted an impassioned denunciation. "No, 'tis no use disclaiming. It was the bravest thing I ever saw. Especially since many gentlemen do not particularly care for cats."

"You may number me among them," he said icily.

"Oh, yes. And next you will be saying you did not risk your life for her sake." She held the purring kitten to her throat, bending her head above it, then raised twinkling eyes to meet Mathieson's scowl. "Come now, stop your teasing and make her acquaintance, sir."

It was on the tip of his tongue to tell this deceitful chit exactly what he thought of having been so diabolically used. Especially since his ankle hurt vilely, and his sword hand was out of commission just when he might have to face MacTavish's steel—did he ever come up with the blasted Scot! But then he noticed that the revolting little cat was held against a particularly delectable

36

bosom, and it came to him that he was not **playing** his cards well.

He summoned his whimsical smile. "As you say, ma'am," he murmured, and swinging the end of his blanket over his shoulder with a jaunty flourish, he advanced.

The cat blinked at him.

Mathieson's eyes however were upon a different target, and he reached out eagerly.

The cat spat and clawed the approaching hand. Mathieson jerked back.

"Oh, dear!" said Miss Bradford, her lips twitching suspiciously. "What a naughty girl! A fine way to show your gratitude, Picayune!"

Mathieson had another name for that treacherous little feline, but he gritted his teeth and suggested gently that Miss Bradford might know of another way to repay him.

"Of course I do, dear sir," said she with a melting look, and dropped the small cat upon the cushions. "Come here."

He brightened and limped closer.

Miss Bradford giggled, "Oh, you *are* a sight to see! Pray sit down."

Fuming, he glared at her.

She threw a hand across her mouth but over it her eyes danced with merriment. That sparkling look was hard to resist and his vexation faded. With a reluctant grin, he said, "Lost my dignity, have I? I'm not surprised. Wretched girl!"

"I know! I am! I am! But—is it not hard to change what we are? I do try, I assure you, but Papa despairs of me, alas! Come—sit here like a good boy, and I will do as best I can."

He might have made another attempt at flirtation, but he was tired and his sensibilities were ruffled, so he sat down, feeling decidedly hardly done by.

Miss Bradford poured hot water into the bowl and sprinkled yellow powder into it.

"What's that stuff?" enquired Mathieson, without enthusiasm.

"Mustard. You were very wet, dear sir. I cannot have you catching a cold on top of all else."

She stood before him, holding the bowl and trying not very successfully to look grave. He likely did present a ludicrous picture, wrapped in his blanket and without his boots. Small wonder he had failed to entice her, and the more fool he, for having attempted it! He resigned himself and prepared to inhale the wretched vapours, only to be attacked by a gargantuan sneeze.

"There!" she said. "You see?"

He mopped an end of the blanket at his eyes, then gave a gasp as Miss Bradford knelt and seized his leg. Perhaps he was not so ludicrous after all! "What are you about, naughty chit?" he enquired hopefully.

"You cannot put your foot in with your stockings on, foolish creature!"

Put his foot in . . . ? Of all the revolting suggestions! "I have not the remotest intention—" he began, starting up.

His intentions were foiled. Miss Bradford had already been so immodest as to roll down one of his stockings and she gave a tug at his undamaged ankle in the same instant that he attempted to stand. Caught off balance, he fell back into the chair and sneezed violently once more. Momentarily, he was helpless and quite unable to foil the two small hands which firmly grasped his foot and popped it into near-boiling water.

With a howl, Mathieson whipped it out again.

"Too hot?" She clicked her tongue and poured some cold water into the bowl while her patient eyed her smoulderingly. She tested the water with her elbow, pulling up the frill of her chemise sleeve and bending over the bowl in a no-nonsense fashion. From this angle Mathieson had an excellent view of her bosom which was so delicious that he was absorbed and raised no objection when she requested that he replace his feet in the bowl.

Still kneeling, Miss Bradford observed this procedure critically.

She really did mean well, and certainly had not intended either that he fall in the flood or that the little cat take such a violent dislike to him. Besides, it was the first time he had been fussed over since his mother's gentle spirit had winged its way heavenward. Repenting his ill humour, Mathieson lowered his voice, leaned towards her, and murmured at his most seductive, "You are very kind, Miss— May I call you . . . Fiona?" He stroked her long hair which was almost dry and a pretty shade of light brown enlivened by russet highlights where the light from the candles shone on it. His hand rested on her shoulder then drifted lower.

Miss Bradford glanced up, that glowing look in her bright eyes. "Of course you may," she said, taking his hand and patting it kindly.

He pressed a kiss on her palm, then allowed his lips to slide softly up the inside of her wrist—a sure shiver-getter—while telling her in a hushed and intimate voice that he was indeed a very lucky man tonight.

"Oh, yes," she agreed. "But your toenails want cutting."

It was quite the most unkind remark that had ever been made to him in a boudoir. He snatched his hand back and said a curt, "Thank you." He also curled his toes under.

Oblivious of her offense, Miss Bradford instructed, "Now just sit here quietly, and I will fetch you a hot posset."

Beyond a vague knowledge that hot possets had to do with illness, he was ignorant, and he asked stiffly what the drink would contain.

"Why, hot milk and wine, of course. And spices."

"Thank you. But—no."

She bent over him, patting his shoulder as one might soothe a recalcitrant child. "Poor soul, are you tired. This will help you sleep. Do you pull off your breeches first and I will—"

"Devil you will, miss!"

The deep voice fairly thundered through the caravan.

Mathieson looked up, his nerves twanging a warning.

A large gentleman stood upon the threshold. He held a heavy riding crop. His face was a thundercloud, and it was a familiar face, for this irate individual was the Shakespeare lover from the tap. Evidently, he loved more than Shakespeare. Perhaps he had set up this little lass in her nest, and was irked by an apparent invasion of his territory. Amused, Mathieson drawled, "*Tu peux être tranquille*, Falstaff. I can—"

"Quite so, Papa," cried Miss Bradford, cheerily untroubled. "For there is nothing to worry about. And you are come home!"

Papa? Mathieson all but reeled. Zounds! Whatever else, the man was undoubtedly a gentleman. If this unorthodox chit was his daughter, then one normally quick-witted soldier of fortune had properly compromised himself with the type of female he knew well enough must be avoided like the plague! A lady of Quality—of marriageable age! 'My dear God!' he thought, frantically. 'I've fallen into parson's mousetrap! I'm ruined!'

"Aye, I'm home!" grated the new arrival, his eyes narrowed with rage as he watched Mathieson stand. "And only just in time, 'twould appear! I give you fair warning, sir—you'll answer to Mervyn Bellamy Bradford for this!"

"And to me, by God!"

Another man had come in. A man as large as Bradford, but some twenty years younger. He had auburn hair, a pair of blue eyes that fairly hurled wrath, and a square chin which was heroically outthrust.

"Oh, now really, Papa," cried Miss Bradford, stepping in front of her infuriated parent. "Mr. Mathieson is a brave gentleman who came to—"

"To have his head blown off," snarled the young man, wrenching a long-barrelled pistol from his belt.

This farce, thought Mathieson, had gone on long enough. Entering it, he stood very straight, clutched his blanket about him and lied on two counts, "I am an honourable man, sir. You may be sure I had no designs on your daughter."

"Ha!" snorted the large young man. "It don't much look like it!"

"Do be quiet, Freemon," said Miss Bradford angrily. "Papa, Mr. Mathieson has behaved as a perfect gentleman."

"*Sans* apparel," growled Bradford, pacing forward, lifting his whip.

"*Will* you listen, Papa?" Miss Bradford held out her hands in appeal. "This gentleman—"

"Took you for some gypsy wench, I'll be bound," snorted Torrey murderously. "Alone and unprotected. So he decided to bed you and—"

"No!" cried Miss Bradford in desperation. "Papa! Only listen to—"

Low and grim, Bradford commanded, "Step aside, Fiona."

Mathieson moved the girl to one side. "I have not harmed your daughter in any way. But if you mean to strike me, sir, 'tis only fair to tell you I've not the least intention of permitting you to do so."

"We'll see that," jeered Torrey, coming up beside Bradford.

"We'll also see a lot more of Mr. Mathieson, is he obliged to drop his blanket so as to defend himself," pointed out Miss Bradford. "In which case I shall be properly compromised!"

Mathieson grinned at this logical summation and promptly sneezed.

"Here," said Bradford, peering at him narrow-eyed. "I know you! You're the young puppy made a mock of me in the tap. And now you've ruined m'daughter!" His arm flew up.

The girl flung herself at her sire, reaching up to grasp his wrist and crying urgently, "He helped me save Picayune, sir, and threw himself into the river to do so! I could do no less than bring him here—surely you see that? Surely, you do not doubt me, my dear one?"

"What stuff," said Torrey with derision. "As if a man would risk drowning for the sake of a miserable alley cat!"

Bradford was looking into his daughter's face uncertainly, but at this he rounded on the younger man. "Do you dare to name Fiona a liar, Freemon Torrey?" he thundered.

"I assure you, the lady speaks truth," said Mathieson. "I am all too aware that I do not appear heroic, which is perfectly logical since I am very far from being so." His lips quirked. "I might better admit that 'my cue is villanious melancholy.' Especially in this unfortunate costume."

An appreciative twinkle came into Bradford's eyes.

Fiona released her father's wrist and turned to beam at the accused.

Torrey glared and pointed out acidly that no true gentleman would disrobe in front of an unwed lady of Quality, no matter what the circumstances.

Bradford looked at Mathieson thoughtfully.

"Mr. Torrey," said Mathieson, in the soft drawl that would have warned many who knew him, "I think you and I should discuss this matter at some future date."

"Not too distant, I trust," snapped Torrey. "Mr. Bradford, 'tis evident to me—"

"Enough!" Bradford threw the whip down and said impatiently, "I'll believe my daughter, Freemon, and I'll thank you to keep a still tongue in your head about this!" He advanced on Mathieson, scanning his features intently. "What have you to say in the matter, sir?"

41

"I put it to you, Mr. Bradford," said Mathieson ruefully, "do I *look* like a man engaged in an *affaire de coeur*?"

Bradford blinked from the bare feet to the blanket, to the tousled black locks, and gave a throaty laugh. "Begad but y'don't. Blest if ever I saw a *less* romantical fellow!"

"Exactly so, Papa," agreed Miss Bradford, demurely.

Mathieson was unable to decide whether he had won, or lost.

"That blasted cat," grunted Bradford, sitting on the edge of the bunk in his caravan and watching Mathieson who was sprawled sleepily in the lower bunk opposite, from which Torrey had been pre-empted. "Well, I'm obliged t'you, not to refine on it. My girl is quite capable of having clung to the treetrunk until both were swept away!"

Mathieson was finding it difficult to keep his eyes open. "I'll own I was somewhat surprised," he murmured, "that a lady of Quality should be out here, all alone, on such a night."

"Aye, I'll admit that was nobody's fault but my own." Bradford's fine face reddened, but his gaze did not falter. "Fiona is very dear to my heart, whatever you may think. I left Freemon here to guard her!"

Freemon Torrey, who Mathieson now knew to be a lifelong friend of the Bradfords, was sitting cross-legged on the floor, and at once declared with gruff resentment, "She ran me off, sir. As I told you. We quarrelled over—nothing really. You know how—how unreasonable Fiona can be at times . . . I was enraged, and—left her, God forgive me! I own 'twas bad, but you know I mean to marry her and would never do anything to harm her. Truly, I thought Mrs. Dunnigan and Japhet would arrive at any moment, not—" his eyes flashed to Mathieson. He growled, "You may be sure 'twill never happen again!"

"One would hope not," said Mathieson with pious insincerity.

"Damn you!" Torrey's fists clenched. "Were you not disabled, sir—"

"Well, he is," Bradford interpolated irritably. "And furthermore, Torrey, it might well have been another type of man who found my child alone and unprotected! I thank the good Lord a gentleman of Mathieson's moral calibre came upon her! No thanks to you! Be damned if I'm not a mind to leave you in this wilderness!"

42

"You cannot," sulked Torrey. "You need me to guide you to the—"

"Estate," put in Bradford hurriedly. He turned to Mathieson. "We journey to the estate of Lord . . . Tyson, who is—"

"My uncle," declared Torrey, just as hurriedly.

Mathieson looked curiously from one to the other, then sat up in sudden alarm. "Jupiter! My horse should have been rubbed down half an hour since!"

"Not by you, young fella," said Bradford. "Not with that hand. Torrey will tend the animal."

Mathieson frowned. "Thank you, but—no, sir. I shall—"

"You'll stay where you are. Oh, never fear, m'boy. Torrey's a block at times, but he's a good man with horses."

His smile forced, Torrey muttered something about making amends, and went out.

Mathieson settled down again. "Sir—will he . . ."

"Never fear. He may feel like pummelling you, but he won't take it out on your hack, I'll say that for him. You set a store by that big stallion of yours, eh?"

"Yes. He is one in a million."

"I see." For a moment Bradford watched the candlelight flicker on the lean planes of the remarkable face in the opposite bunk. Then, he leaned forward, hands clasped between his knees. "I feel the same about my daughter." He flushed again as he saw Mathieson's brows lift slightly. "Oh, I know you must think otherwise. And—God help me, 'tis true I've been a sorry failure as a father!"

"Is none of my affair, Mr. Bradford. I'd not presume to—"

"I know, I know. But you saved the lass. You're entitled to an explanation."

Mathieson was more tired than curious, but he listened resignedly.

"My wife, sir," said Bradford, staring at his hands, "was the very loveliest little creature that ever walked upon this green earth. You've seen Fiona . . . how beautiful she is . . ." He shrugged. "Need I say more?"

'Considerably,' thought Mathieson cynically, but he smiled and strove to look sympathetic. "You are a widower, sir?"

"Yes. Since '39, alas— And I am doomed, for I shall never find the like of my lovely Cassandra." A sparkle came into the fine brown eyes. He added with a grin, "Besides, with so many lovelies, 'tis far more gratifying not to be confined to one . . . eh, m'boy?''

Mathieson laughed and became less drowsy. ''Couldn't agree more, Mr. Bradford.''

''Aha! I fancied you were a young rascal and had a thing or two in common with me!'' He was still smiling, but now the smile did not reach his eyes. ''Good thing Torrey and I arrived—when we did, eh?''

''You're wondering if you really were in time, are you sir?'' Mathieson said gravely, ''I'll be honest. Where *l'amour* is concerned, I rate myself something of a—skilled artisan. Had I not been covered in mud, been hampered by a twisted thumb and a wrenched ankle, I might well have regarded a pretty girl, alone in a caravan, as a choice delicacy—'' He saw Bradford's eyes narrow and the strong fists clench, and went on levelly, ''However—even in that event, sir, I have ever yet found it either necessary, desirable, or in any way the business of a gentleman, to force a reluctant girl. I'll own to being a rascal. I resent being judged a libertine.''

For a long moment the eyes of the two men held steady and stern. Then Bradford nodded. ''I'll accept that, and apologize for my doubts. I've never known my girl to lie to me, but—a young fellow with your looks and address . . . Still, I should've—Aye, you may grin, but only wait till *you* become a father! Gad, what a responsibility!''

''A responsibility I've no least desire to take on, thank you, sir! But I can sympathize. To be left alone with children to be reared must be something of a task.''

''Ah. There you have come at the very hub of the wheel! I engaged governesses, of course, and I'll own my boy . . .'' the light died from Bradford's face, ''was no trouble. But—Fiona . . .'' He shrugged. ''I've tried. I *meant* her to be properly instructed and chaperoned. But—I have suffered setbacks, Mr. Mathieson. Many cruel buffets of Fate, climaxed by a great financial—disaster's the only word.''

'The tables, or the ponies?' wondered Mathieson, cynically.

Bradford sighed. ''Lost everything. So 'tis we are reduced to these revolting vehicles. A nomadic life. And now I go to appeal for help from my childhood bosom bow.''

''Mr. Torrey's uncle?''

''What? Oh—yes! That's true. The boy's sadly smitten, as

44

you saw. And there's no doubting we are indebted to him already." He drove a fist into his palm, his head bowing. "If you *knew* how it grieves me that my sweet child should be reduced to the humiliation of living in a caravan!"

"She don't seem crushed to me, sir."

The dark head lifted. Bradford said proudly, " 'Twould take more than the loss of our estates to crush my Fiona! She may grieve what we've lost, but she'd die sooner than let me see it! That's what makes it so—so *damnably* hard, d'you see? She has such complete trust—such courage. Why, bless her brave heart, she's never uttered one word of reproach, never blamed me. The dear little soul is as full of confidence in me as if I were—ten times the man I am! And I'll tell you, Mathieson, a girl like that can *make* a man ten times himself!" He sighed wistfully. "But—never fear. I'd be granting you the greatest possible gift, but I'll not demand you make an honest woman of her!"

'Hmmnn,' thought Roland Fairleigh Mathieson, chilled.

He was unarmed, alone, and desperate. He ran frantically, although his right foot dragged a heavy ball and chain. Behind him pounded Bradford and Torrey armed with great gleaming war axes. And in every pew of the great cathedral, ladies he had loved, men he had fought, and countless outraged mamas, howled encouragement—to his pursuers.

"St. Thomas!" he pleaded sobbingly. "Help!" But from high in the shadowed buttresses came a faint response, "Gone fishing . . ."

He could see the altar now, the archbishop standing before it. A man of no great stature, with hands clasped, mouth droopingly contemptuous, and a great dog lying beside him, its head resting on one of his high-heeled shoes. "Muffin," he groaned. "Help me!"

The Duke of Marbury shook his stately head. "We do not help those who are beneath contempt!"

Fiona Bradford walked slowly from the choir stalls and stood beside the ducal archbishop. She wore a glorious gown of white lace and satin, but her face was all mud.

And he was doomed, for Bradford and Torrey had gripped him by the arms now and were dragging him forward.

"No!" he screamed.

"Wrong answer!" snarled Torrey, and raised his weapon until the razor-sharp blade of that great axe bit into the captive's throat.

The duke looked put out. "You must say—'I do,' " he chided.

"I won't," Mathieson cried defiantly. "Kill me, but I—"

Another lady drifted into view. A dainty lady of peerless beauty and great sad dark eyes. She floated above the altar, her shining wings outstretched, a glowing aura about her loveliness. "Oh, Roly," she murmured. *"Mon fils . . . mon fils . . . que faire?"*

And sweating, horrified, he knew what must be done. He could not bring tears to his beloved *maman*. He was trapped. He would marry the muddy girl and have dozens of muddy children . . . Good God!

"Very well," he muttered through dry lips. "I . . . do."

"Well I do not!" cried Miss Fiona.

A great gasp arose from the crowded pews. The archbishop threw up his hands; Torrey and Bradford uttered shocked cries.

He himself stood trembling, not daring to hope.

Pointing one finger, incensed, Miss Fiona shrilled, "His toe-nails want cutting!"

He looked down. He was barefoot.

"I'll cut 'em!" roared Torrey, and swung up his axe.

With a shout of terror, Mathieson woke up.

He was in the caravan, his heart thundering. "Thank the Lord!" he gasped, enormously relieved. Deep rumblings emanated from the opposite bunk, but the one above his own appeared to be empty. Mr. Torrey had found other accommodations for the night.

Panting, drenched with sweat, Mathieson lay back again, and as his breathing eased and the vivid nightmare faded, he listened drowsily to the steady beating of the rain and wondered where Rob MacTavish was spending the night and how soon he would be able to come up with him. If he lost his chance at that Jacobite gold when he had at last come so close to the end of the rainbow . . . Still, if he hadn't been riding this way last evening it was very likely that foolish chit would have hung onto the tree until the bank gave way beneath her. He frowned at the upper bunk. She should never have been left alone by her charming but irresponsible father. And as for Torrey! His frown became a scowl. Was that where the surly block had gone? But—no, it was unlikely. Evidently Torrey's intentions were honourable; he actually wanted to marry the chit. A fine chance he stood! She might want for manners and have no notion of correct behaviour, but she was kind and warm-hearted and deserved better than the likes of Freemon Torrey . . .

By ten o'clock Mathieson was well on his way, riding at a steady canter, bathed in a warm and beneficient sunlight. He had risen before dawn and, thanks to the vibrations of Mr. Bradford's snores, had been enabled to don the clothes which he'd found on the solitary chair, and limp outside, undetected. It had stopped raining, and the brilliance of the morning had also revealed that Miss Fiona had done remarkably well with his garments. His shirt and cravat were clean, if not ironed, and most of the mud had been brushed from his breeches and cloak. If it should rain again, which it very likely would, he'd look no worse than any other bedraggled traveller. He suffered a momentary qualm to think of the chit staying up half the night to achieve such results for him, but perhaps she considered this fair payment for the rescue of her repulsive cat. At all events, it was as well to put as much ground between them as possible, just in case her flamboyant papa should change his mind and turn the nightmare dream into a horrid reality!

Rumpelstiltskin was in high spirits, eager to run. Mathieson gave him his head, guiding him on a course that ran parallel to the highway, but remaining, as far as was possible, out of sight of any traveller. Swaying easily in the saddle, his keen eyes alert for a sign of his valuable quarry, Mathieson's thoughts drifted to the task before him.

He suffered no qualms of conscience regarding his intention to divert as much as possible of the Scottish treasure into his own pockets. That those who had contributed their gold and valuables now stood in dire need was no concern of his. 'The fools brought it on themselves,' he thought contemptuously. Nor was he much interested in the bitter plight of those Jacobites who had escaped the slaughter on Culloden Field only to be hunted like animals the length and breadth of England. He had no intention of persecuting them himself—unless they carried information of use to him—nor had he the least desire to inform against them or hand them over to torment and slaughter. But as to helping them—rubbish! They were grown men who had known the risks when they took up arms against the Crown. One

47

made one's decisions in life and, if those decisions went awry, one contrived somehow, without whining, or repining, or involving others in one's difficulties.

He'd had his own difficulties, heaven knows! He'd come within snatching distance of the treasure when its existence had first become known. But as is so often the case, just when everything was going along nicely, a fly had to plop into the treacle. In this case the "fly" was personified by a set of curst interfering persons he designated The Busybodies. Many of these idiots had been violently opposed to the Cause of Charles Stuart; some of the men had actually fought against him. Yet all were so appalled by the ruthless persecution of escaped Jacobites and the privations of their hapless families, that they had banded together to help in any way possible. They had impeded his own efforts several times and were now intent upon a plan to restore the treasure to the original donors—a dastardly scheme he was determined to sabotage.

Half an hour later, he still had caught no glimpse of the MacTavish coach. The odds against picking up a trail lost for over twelve hours might well have discouraged another man, but not the least of Mathieson's attributes was his unquenchable optimism. A decision was indicated, however, and he pulled Rumpelstiltskin to a halt, and considered his next move carefully.

He was convinced that for the treasure to have reached England in the first place, it could only have been sent down the west coast aboard ship. Prince Charles was known to have spent considerable time in the Isles of the Western Sea, which fact seemed to lend credence to this theory. Mathieson's personal opinion was that for Charles Stuart to have sent his treasure to England was as brilliant as it was daring; certainly it must have been the last move his enemies would have expected. Further, if the valuable cargo had indeed been hidden in haste, as he had reason to believe, it followed that the hiding places must be near the coast. Therefore, although MacTavish had yesterday turned eastward to Cheltenham, it seemed unlikely that he would continue to the east, but more probably would at this point either swing north toward Kidderminster and Wolverhampton, or strike west through the Malvern Hills into Herefordshire. But which?

Mathieson put the matter up to his four-legged friend.

"Rump," said he whimsically, "an you toss your head once we will immediately turn west into the hills. Two tosses, and we continue to follow the river, at least as far as Tewkesbury, hoping for a sight of the elusive bounder."

As was his fashion when addressed by his master, Rumpelstiltskin snorted amiably and tossed his head.

"Once, is it?" Mathieson patted his glossy neck, then reined around to the west. "As you will, then."

∂ 4 ∂

Mathieson came upon the hedge tavern by following the smoke that drifted up from behind a fine stand of oak trees. Riding slowly down the hill, watching the vista gradually unfold to reveal a wandering stream, a goosegirl herding her flock across an emerald meadow, and the old tavern standing in thatched and whitewashed serenity amid its oaks, he was not surprised to see an artist at work. An elderly man, seated at his easel, absorbed in his task.

Mathieson was as absorbed in the goosegirl. Even from this distance it was apparent that she had a comely figure. He grinned, and whistled the command that urged the well-trained stallion into an immediate stretching gallop. They reached the meadow with a flurry of air and a thunder of hooves, and Mathieson dismounted to bow to the pretty creature. The geese scattered. The girl was frightened, wherefore it was only common kindness to soothe her. Besides, she was even prettier than he had hoped, with that special prettiness that comes from youth and fresh-scrubbed cheeks innocent of paints and powders. He questioned her cautiously about the MacTavish coach. She answered with shyness and regret that she had seen no such vehicle. However, she proved more than willing to make up for this lapse by returning his kisses, nor did she raise any objection to a roving hand, even if that hand was bound up in a rather grubby bandage . . . Still, he dared not linger too long—the Scot was not far ahead, he was sure of it. Reluctantly rearranging her bodice, therefore, he lifted his head to smile at her, met a yearning look that suddenly became scared, and from the corner of his eye glimpsed a large dark shape hurtling at him.

50

He had forgotten the artist. His left hand blurred to the jewelled hilt of his Arabian jambiya dagger, his right grabbed instinctively but abortively for his deadly colichemarde. He heard the goosegirl scream, had time only for a half-formed thought that the old fool might believe he was abusing the girl, then something heavy slammed into his back, and he measured his length on the turf.

A warm, wet object was flapping about his neck; heavy blows thudded at him, driving the breath from his lungs; whines and smothered grunts, familiar but impossible, were in his ears. Disbelieving, he flung up an arm to protect himself, and rolled over. The goosegirl had departed. A great head, neither Alsatian nor mastiff but something of each, hung over him, powerful jaws grinning, and big brown eyes adoring him.

"Beast!" he gasped, incredulous, and was at once deafened by a bark that must have been heard three miles away. What appeared to be a yard of pink tongue sloshed across his mouth. Spluttering, he loosed his hold on the dagger, and sat up, drawing his sleeve across his face, fending off the dog's rapturous excitement, caressing him even as he damned his ears, his own eyes darting to the side, then fixing there. Incredulity became stupefaction.

The artist stood watching. He was of no great stature, his shabby clothing seeming to indicate a minimum of success in his chosen profession. His grey hair was thick and neatly tied back. He had a wide mouth, a thin hooked nose, bushy eyebrows, and there was a smear of green paint down his long chin. Not, one would say, a figure to strike awe into the heart of such a fighting machine as was Captain Mathieson. Yet that ruthless young man's jaw dropped, his black eyes were glazed, and, forgetting his manners he gasped, "M-Muffin . . . ?"

The bushy eyebrows lifted. A gleam of amusement lit the pale blue eyes. "You recognize me," murmured his Grace the Duke of Marbury. "But how charming. And quite remarkable, under the circumstances. You were very fast with your dagger, Mathieson. I commend you, though I trust you will feel inclined to spare Beast and return it to its sheath. Thank you. No—pray do not stand. I purely detest being obliged to look up to you."

Mathieson flushed, but one did not remain in an ungainly sprawl while one's grandparent stood. He compromised by kneeling. His bewildered gaze roved the duke's person, then sought about for attendants.

"I am disturbed that you were rather tardy with that ready sword of yours," said Marbury. "A man in your—er, profession—Ah, but you have hurt your hand, I see. That explains matters. Are you looking for my servants? I am quite alone."

"B-But—sir . . ." Mathieson absently removed Beast's tail from around his jaw. "Surely—That is—I mean—Why on earth would you—"

"Yes. I quite see that an explanation is required." The duke sighed and seated himself upon a convenient rocky outcrop of the hillside. " 'Tis nothing more devious than that I find it necessary at times to run away from my responsibilities. I cannot mingle with my fellow man in my customary garb. Not, at least, without drawing the type of company and attention I seek to escape. Hence," he indicated his worn and humble clothing, "my disguise."

"If ever I heard of such a thing!" exclaimed Mathieson, much shocked. "You should not risk yourself in such a way, your Grace!"

"I was a man before I was a duke, my boy. 'Tis naughty, of course, but you can have no notion of what you avoid by being— ah—exempted from the line of succession." He saw his deplorable grandson's fine mouth close with a snap and the familiar chill come into the dark eyes. A wry smile touched his own lips. "Are you, might one enquire," he went on, "in the way of effecting an escape yourself? Or do you pursue, rather, your usual . . . line of endeavour?"

"Such is my intent," drawled Mathieson, pushing Beast away so that he could regain his feet. His ankle, which had been less bothersome today, had not benefited from the dog's enthusiasm and was throbbing again. He strove to keep most of his weight on his left foot, brushed his coat, scowled at his twice muddied breeches, and returned a cool and veiled gaze to his illustrious grandparent. "Wherefore, your Grace, with your permission, I shall be about my business."

The duke pointed out gently, "But I have not granted my permission, you see. Be so good as to assuage my curiosity by favouring me with a minute or two of your so valuable time." His grandson's handsome head being stiffly but respectfully inclined, he folded his fine-boned hands and went on: "Thank

52

you, dear boy. I am intrigued, for example, to learn whether at this particular point in time, you are a Fairleigh, a Mathieson, or hide behind that repulsive pseudonym—Otton.''

"I use my own name, sir.''

"Ah. An improvement.'' Marbury watched Beast return to sink down at his feet. "Provided,'' he appended, "you are not involved in that which will *further* tarnish it.''

As usual, thought Mathieson gritting his teeth, although he towered above the old gentleman, he felt about six inches tall in his presence. He shrugged, assumed a bored smile and murmured, "Too late for this leopard to change his spots, sir. Did you require anything more of me?''

The duke sighed. "Only that which you are incapable of giving, alas. Honour . . . loyalty . . . integrity . . .'' Another ripple disturbed the proud set of his grandson's jaw. 'The boy is easily stung today,' he thought. "You are both bored and impatient, I know,'' he said. "How are you hurt? Not another duel, surely?''

"A fall, your Grace.''

"Taken, I presume, in a brawl.'' The faintest of frowns disturbed the ducal brow. "The price you pay in this endless pursuit of easy riches!''

"The fall was in no way connected with my—quest, your Grace.'' Rumpelstiltskin had started to graze, and Mathieson whistled. The big horse at once cantered to his side and whuffled affectionately at his shoulder. "No food for you, rascal,'' said Mathieson, stroking the velvety muzzle. "We've to let you cool off before you eat your luncheon. Can't have you getting a bellyache.'' The stallion did not seem to argue with this, but Beast roused himself and came to push between man and horse, wagging his tail and grinning ingratiatingly. "Jealous,'' scolded Mathieson, amused.

The duke nodded. "In more ways than one. How many commands have you taught that stallion of yours?''

"Lord—I never counted, sir. Dozens.''

"Not all spoken, I think?''

"Oh, no. Many by a particular whistle, some by voice or hand signal.''

"The devil you say! Either the brute is of great intelligence or you must have expended a great many weary hours training him.''

53

"He is superbly intelligent, your Grace, and there is nothing wearisome about the time I spend with him, believe me."

"I do. It was a foolish remark on my part, for 'tis very obvious that animal is the only living thing for whom you have a particle of affection."

"Say rather one of two living things, sir." Having said which, Mathieson caught his breath and wondered in a near panic why he should have been so stupidly rash.

The duke stared in astonishment at the hurriedly averted but very red cheek. Surely this young scoundrel was not admitting to a fondness for—himself? He probed carefully, "An you have found your lady, my boy, I think it improper that you rush about kissing every wench who—"

In a gruff, unwontedly halting voice, Mathieson said, "I—did not mean that—I have not found my . . . lady, your Grace." A twinkle brightened his eyes. "In the singular, that is. Which is as well, for I likely could not support her if I did so."

'Good God!' thought the duke, undeceived by the frivolity. And more moved than he would have admitted, he drawled, "I was under the impression I had indicated a willingness to provide you with adequate funds for your own and—er, other support."

"You did, sir, and I thank you. But—it is not necessary."

His grandfather's expression at once assumed its customary cool serenity, but Mathieson knew that he had offended. Feeling a clumsy oaf, he asked hurriedly, "Am I permitted to see your work? I had not known you've a penchant for art."

"But then, we know so little of each other—you and I, dear boy."

Was there a touch of wistfulness to the voice now? Nonsense! More of the duke's biting sarcasm, most likely. Which being the case, he drawled, "I think you know all there is to know of me, your Grace."

A moment's pause, then Marbury stood and started towards his easel, Mathieson, horse, and dog following.

The painting was near completion and depicted not the charming rural scene, but the head and shoulders of a young woman. Her dark hair hung in glistening ringlets about a pair of snowy, dimpled shoulders. She was half-turning to smile from the canvas, and her beauty was breathtaking, the features daintily formed, the green eyes great pools of bewitching mischief.

54

Entranced, Mathieson gazed in silence. The duke, covertly watching him, gave a shy little cough. " 'Tis not necessary that you feel obliged to utter polite falsehoods, Roland.''

"She is—exquisite . . . I've the feeling I have met her somewhere. Who is she?''

"A lady who was dear to my heart once. Long ago.'' Wistfulness was in the voice now, beyond doubting. "I have always to be in the hills before I attempt to put her on canvas, for the last time I saw her was in the mountains . . .''

Mathieson said an awed and sincere, "Jove, but you have a rare talent, sir. You must have cared for her very deeply. But she was not my *grand-mère*, I think?''

The duke's head flung up. "She most assuredly was not! But—care for her? Aye, I cared for her! As you will someday care for a lady. God grant that when you do, Fate is kinder than she has been to me!''

The mouth was twisted with cynicism, the flush now was of rage, and in the eyes so fierce a glare that Mathieson was aghast and in an effort to alleviate his *faux pas* said with a grin, "Fate has been sufficiently kind, thank you, duke. I have cared for only one lady in my life, and she was wise enough to choose another. I doubt I shall ever find her like again and, faith, but I'm not at all sure I want to.''

"If you can speak of it so lightly, you did not really love at all. But the day will dawn, I warn you, when your heart will be given. You are more a Mathieson than a de Fleury, thank heaven, and we're an odd breed. Our women are passionate creatures and tend to have many loves. Our men love once and if they lose their lady, may have their—diversions, but never love again.''

The slight to his mama's family had brought a quick frown to Mathieson's brows and his chin lifted haughtily. "Then I will cling to the hope that I never find my love, for surely she would be a lady of Quality, and as surely would have nothing to do with a man of my reputation. I'm much better off with old Rump and a carefree life.''

"Is it so carefree? Or have you gone hungry for your pride?''

"Hunger-'tis said, is good for the soul.''

The nonchalant shrug, the bland air of indifference infuriated the duke. "Why—in the name of heaven?''

Mathieson hesitated, then replied, "Not so long ago, sir, you

warned me to expect nothing from you. You named me, as I recall, a heartless, soulless, mercenary rake and opportunist."

From under his brows Marbury scanned the six feet of arrogant defiance that was all he had left in the way of immediate family. "I was explicit, I see. Still, I referred, I believe, to your hope of a legacy. Not to your present needs."

"Because my obvious poverty would be an embarrassment, sir?" Mathieson's lip curled. "I can appreciate that. But—I manage. One way and another."

"True. 'Tis the 'another' that disturbs."

"I have no wish to disturb you, duke. But nor will I avail myself of your—charity . . ." The older man's eyes flashed fire and his jaw set, but Mathieson stood his ground. "Loathsome as may be my moral standards, I neither break my given word, nor ignore my obligations. If I should please you, sir, by leaving England, it will not be to escape any condition you might impose on me in return for an allowance. I am everything you think me, and more. But I have not yet sunk so low as to accept the bounty of a man who brought bitter sorrow to a lady I loved very deeply."

Marbury stiffened and stood as straight as did his tall grandson, and because he had, like any good general, taken the higher ground, Mathieson was still obliged to look up to him. "I am impressed, dear lad," said the duke with the faintest suggestion of a sneer. "No, really, I am impressed. You would appear to not only have a few scruples, but to harbour a conception at least of the meaning of loyalty." His voice became steely. "Am I correct in thinking that you also have the insufferable presumption to condemn me on your mother's account?"

Gad but the man had a tongue like an asp! Through his teeth, Mathieson snarled, "You presumed to judge *her*. And she was a saint!"

"Had Juliette de Fleury been a saint she'd not have attempted the ruin of an inexperienced boy! Her mistake was that her victim's father had already been so ruined, and recognized her for what she was!"

"That is not so! Quite the reverse in—"

"Do—not—*dare*," interpolated the duke very softly, "take that tone to me!"

All his life Mathieson had feared and respected this man. All his life he had secretly yearned to be accepted by him. But now

56

he was too angry to care, and he flashed back just as softly, "I dare, your Grace, to defend my mother. Against any man living, I will defend her! I collect you really believe what you say, but in this instance, you are wrong. The *truth*, sir, is that my father seduced and ruined *her*!"

"In which case, you are indeed your father's son! How many girls have *you* seduced and ruined, my pure defender of the innocent? Ten? A dozen? More perhaps?"

Mutually enraged, the two men glared at each other.

"Many more, sir," drawled Mathieson, his voice quivering with passion. "Faith, but my by-blows fairly treble the population! You can tell 'em," he held out his left hand, "by the fingers."

Now it chanced that down through the centuries certain men of the House of Mathieson were born with a small defect, this being that the middle and third fingers of the left hand were identical in length, instead of only the middle finger being longer than the others. It was such a small flaw that few people had even noticed it, but the duke himself had inherited this peculiarity.

His Grace's breath hissed through his teeth. He stood very still, staring down at his grandson's hand. Then he moved a step closer. Through a long moment of almost unbearable tension Mathieson was sure he was going to be slapped for such impertinence, and he thought, 'Hit me, you arrogant, opinionated old devil! See if I give one damn!' But in that moment, looking into the cold, proud features of this noble kinsman, he suffered a sharp and contrary pang of remorse.

"You compound insolence, sir," said Marbury in that same hushed yet awful voice.

Mathieson's head bowed. "Yes. Your pardon, duke."

"How regrettable it is, that even when we do occasionally meet, 'tis only to quarrel. You may leave now." Marbury turned away and seated himself at the easel once more, and Beast sank down beside him and arranged his head comfortably upon the worn boot.

Mathieson said his farewells in a polite, colourless voice and strode off, refusing to allow himself to limp.

The duke's eyes followed the lithe erect figure, noting the slight cavalry swagger to the walk. "What a great pity, Beast," he murmured sadly, "that Dudley was so very young when that mercenary little Frenchwoman lured him to Paris and broke his heart so that he would not even acknowledge their son. By the time I found Roland, the wretched trollop had thoroughly poisoned the boy's mind 'gainst his family. And how splendid he might have been, instead of so utterly immoral, so lacking a single particle of decency.''

Beast offering nothing more comforting than a snore, Marbury sighed and turned wistfully to the beauteous face on the canvas. "I'm an old fool," he confessed. "But—just sometimes, you know, I cannot help but think of . . . what might have been.''

He took up his brush but did not use it, continuing to gaze at the canvas, remembering. A deep voice echoed in his thoughts; 'one of two living things, your Grace . . .' A slow smile crept into his eyes. Perhaps, after all, there *was* a faint vestige of affection in that merciless young devil . . .

"Hmmnn . . .'' murmured the duke, and gently removed his foot from under Beast's heavy head.

After a hearty luncheon Mathieson went somewhat apprehensively into the yard, but there was no sign of his noble grandsire. The old boy had taken himself off. Without a word. Natural enough, and just as well, of course. But he kicked a stone across the cobbles with brooding concentration until Rumpelstiltskin's friendly whicker lifted his spirits. The stallion had been rubbed down, fed and watered, and was well rested, and in a very few minutes Mathieson was riding out of the yard and into the hills.

Late afternoon found him following a high ridge, still keeping to cover wherever possible, and irritable because he had as yet seen no sign of his quarry. Of course, with the weather as bad as it had been last evening, it *was* possible that he had outdistanced MacTavish. That worry, which came more and more frequently, made him glance back the way he had come, but there was no sign of anyone save for a farm labourer, made small with distance, plodding along behind a plough.

Turning again, Mathieson tensed, every nerve suddenly alert. Down the slope to his right a solitary horse was grazing. A saddled but riderless bay mare, the reins trailing. He guided Rumpelstiltskin into a copse of beeches, whispered a command that he stay, and dismounted. His ankle all but forgotten, he moved swiftly and silently to reconnoitre. There was no sign of

58

a rider. Perhaps MacTavish had left his bride in some safe haven and gone on alone. The Scot had, Mathieson knew, taken a tidy blow on the head last week. Perhaps, in riding, he had exhausted himself and toppled from the saddle. But even if that remotely possible sequence of events had taken place, where was he? Also, MacTavish had an eye for a horse, and this animal was a rawboned mare of poor conformation and advanced years. Of course, MacTavish might have been obliged to hire whatever was available. At all events, decided Mathieson, circling the mare, it behooved him to proceed with caution. Opposite him now was a shallow depression, much overgrown by shrubs and stunted trees. Perhaps MacTavish had spotted him and was lying in wait, musket aimed.

"Thomas," whispered Mathieson, "are you at work this afternoon?" One could but hope that saints did not slough off their obligations on Sunday afternoons and go fishing (as had been the case in his nightmare), just when they were most needed.

There was a wide stretch of open grassland between himself and the depression, but, taking advantage of the flurryings of the branches during a sustained wind gust, he ran across the turf and down into the depression. He discovered too late that it was much deeper than it had appeared. The "shrubs" he had seen were in fact the tops of small trees, and the "stunted" trees now appeared as healthy specimens twenty- or thirty-feet tall. He shot down a near vertical slope, but his frantic attempt to hold his balance failed as his game ankle gave out under him, and he tripped and rolled helplessly, crashing into various obstructions until brought up short by a violent collision with some immovable object. The breath knocked out of him, he lay there, hoping dizzily that MacTavish was not advancing on him with sword drawn, and thankful that he did not appear to have broken any bones during his precipitous descent.

Despite the absence of any major discomfort, he was groaning painfully, which was an affront to his pride. His attempt to choke off the sounds, failed. This was puzzling, and he lay there, frowning up into the tossing branches of the tree, wondering if he was more seriously hurt than he realized.

Gradually, his befuddled head cleared and with a return of rational thought it was borne in upon him that the sounds he heard did not emanate from his own throat. He propped himself on one elbow and, peering about, discerned one of the objects with which he had collided. It lay some way up the bank—the huddled figure of a man. The Scot? Mathieson gathered himself together, stumbled to his feet, and reeled to the prone victim.

"Rob? I'd no intent to . . ." But as he drew nearer his words faltered to a stop. The man was pitiably emaciated; unkempt, unshaven, a living skeleton clad in ragged coat and breeches, his long dark hair tangled about a cadaverous face lit by two blue eyes that blinked from darkly shadowed hollows. From the white lips of this pathetic creature a name was whispered incredulously. "R-Roly . . . ?"

"Good God!" Mathieson dropped to one knee. "Are you . . . not—" Again, his sentence went unfinished as he stared into that ravaged face. It *could* not be! The eyes were the same, but—dear heaven! "Bill . . . ?" he breathed, horrified.

A quivering smile dawned. A claw-like hand trembled out to touch his arm. Mathieson was so stunned he could not speak for an instant, but his own strong fingers closed over that feeble clasp. "My . . . poor fellow!" he faltered. "What on earth . . . ? Were you set upon, or—"

He gestured, impatient with himself. William Bond, whom he last had seen wearing the dashing uniform of a lieutenant of light cavalry, was in terrible straits. Old Bill, to whom he owed more than he could ever repay, without whom he would surely have died three years ago in that ghastly Flanders hut! Bill must have medical attention! And soon! He clambered up. "Hang on, old sportsman. I've some brandy in my saddlebags. I'll—"

Bond gave a feeble wave of the hand. "No . . . time . . . Roly, I'm . . . done . . . but—"

"No, no!" argued Mathieson, appalled, but kneeling again. "We'll have you to a doctor, and you'll be well in no time! Can you get up if I help?" He slid an arm under his friend and was further dismayed by the ease with which he was able to lift those fragile shoulders. A well-built fellow had been Bond. A sportsman to his fingertips, full of energy and laughter and mischief. What on earth could have happened to him? He was of good family, and, even if he'd lost his entire inheritance, it was hard to conceive that in only three years he could have come to such a tragic pass.

Bond's coat fell open then, and Mathieson caught a glimpse of a darkly stained bandage. He ceased his efforts at once. "You're hurt! Whatever—" And he caught his breath to the awareness that there might be a tragically logical explanation for the tattered clothing; the dirty bandages. "*Mon Dieu!* Bill—never say—" He groaned. "You infernal lamebrain! You're involved with those blasted rebels!"

Another faint grin tugged at the pallid lips. "I . . . am Catholic, Roly. Half Scots. Was out with . . . with Charlie . . ."

Stunned, Mathieson stared down at him. Bill? Dear old Bill— an accursed stupid Jacobite? And, Lord, but he looked as if his life was measured in seconds! A lump rose in his throat. "To hell with that," he said gruffly. "I'm going after the brandy!"

The thin hand tightened on his arm. "No," Bond panted. "Desperate. Need—your help. Don't leave . . . me . . ."

Mathieson bit his lip and sat down, cradling Bond in his arms, trying to shield him from the wind. "Anything you ask, my pippin," he said in a voice that very few people had ever heard. "I'll not leave you. Only tell me what you would have me do. Then we must find you a doctor."

"No—use," sighed Bond wearily. "Thank God you . . . came . . . Sorry to involve—"

"Idiot. D'you think I'll ever forget how you came back for me across enemy lines? D'you think I've forgotten how you hauled me all that way—got me to that clean farm and decent care?"

"Clean! Place was . . . little better than—than your hovel. 'Sides, you'd've . . . done . . . same. This means—frightful risk and—"

"Risk my eye! But for you I'd not have had these three years! Name it, Bill. Do you want me to get you home? Must I take news to your mama?"

The untidy head stirred weakly against his arm. The voice was fainter now. "Letter hidden . . . must tell friends . . . where 'tis . . ."

A letter? Mathieson's thoughts raced. When instructions for a more secure storage of the treasure had been sent down from Scotland, it had been by way of four coded poems, each containing part of the message. The cyphers had been carried by four different couriers, and a desperate race they had run, with the soldiers, the populace, and a crew of bounty hunters hard

61

after them. But the cyphers had all been delivered safely, he knew that much. Only one thing remained—the list of those who had contributed the gold and valuables to the Jacobite Cause. All the couriers had been relentlessly hunted, with large rewards offered for their capture, but the man carrying the list rated the highest reward and bore the heaviest responsibility. With the uneasy suspicion that poor Bill was the fifth courier, he looked down.

Bond was watching him. "Please, Roly. Life or death to . . . so many . . ."

Mathieson said quietly, "The list, is it?"

The pleading eyes widened. "You—know? You—you're one of us . . . then?"

One of them? It was comical, really it was! How shocked this brave man would be had he the faintest idea of how far from being "one of them" was his good comrade! But Bill did not know, and this was no time for the truth. "No," he replied smoothly, "I'm no Jacobite. But some of your people are my good friends. Go on, Bill. Where is the confounded—"

Bond's face convulsed suddenly, and he was gasping in anguish. Mathieson gripped a claw-like hand and held it firmly until the frightful paroxysm eased, and Bond lay limp and trembling in his arms. Whether he had fainted or was simply too weak to open his eyes, was hard to tell, but Mathieson had seen that greyish shade of skin often enough that he knew the end was near, so he made no attempt to investigate the wound or to fetch the brandy, but settled his friend as comfortably as was possible, spread his cloak over him, and sat quietly, not moving save to touch the drawn cheek from time to time, to be sure life remained.

The wind blew, the rain started to come down, and the moments slid past, and still he sat there, keeping Bond as warm as he could, and waiting.

It seemed a very long time and his legs were getting numb before the blue eyes opened and blinked up at him. In a stronger voice, Bond said, "Oh, hello, Roly. You're still here. You know about the list, do you?"

Mathieson had seen such a revival before. He bit his lip but it was all he could do to answer calmly. "I expect 'tis the famous list we hear so much about. All the names of those who contributed in response to Charles Stuart's call for funds. And a proper death warrant for the lot of 'em if that piece of paper falls into military hands. A fine pickle you've got yourself into, my William.''

With incredible courage, Bond attempted a grin. "The first copy we sent out was—was lost, y'know. Vital we had another, because it proves . . . who donated what. They're starving, Roly. Lost their homes, most of 'em. Destitute. May mean—difference 'twixt life'n . . . life'n . . .'' He sighed wearily. "Troopers after me—all the way down. Got to Chester . . . think 'twas Thursday. Had to hide in barn. Was—was hit—y'see. A bit—knocked up.''

"Poor old fellow. But someone helped you, no? Who bandaged your wound?''

"Vicar. Very . . . kind, but—couldn't stay, Roly. Too—dangerous for him.''

"I see. So you found a barn to hide in. Is that where you hid the list?''

"No. Smithy. Mouldy old harness on wall behind . . . behind forge. Stuck it inside . . . You find it, Roly. Take it to—to . . . Boudreaux—or Geoff Dela—Dela—'' The words trailed off and Bond's eyelids drooped.

"Bill,'' said Mathieson softly, "can you tell me the name of the inn?''

Again, Bond rallied. "Seven . . . Birds is it . . . ?'' He groaned fretfully, "Oh, Gad! Cannot seem to 'member . . .''

"I don't suppose it could be The Seven Geese, just south of Chester?''

"That's it.'' Bond sighed with relief. "Y'know place?''

"I know it.'' Mathieson bent lower, scanning the grey features compassionately. "Are you in much pain, dear old boy?''

"No. Feel better, in fact. No pain 'tall now. Only—confounded tired, y'know. Just . . . so tired . . . Have you . . . still got Rump?''

"Yes. Splendid brute.''

"I'm glad . . . And—what've you been doing with yourself . . . all this time? Reconciled with—with y'r grandsire? Only man I know, who's grandson of—duke . . .''

"Wrong side of the blanket, don't forget.''

"P'raps so, but—dashed if you ain't the best sportsman I . . . ever . . .''

The words faded away. He shivered, then said quaveringly, "Dashed cold, ain't it? Are you—here, Roly?"

Mathieson thought with a pang. 'He's looking straight at me!' "I'm here, Bill. I won't leave you, my tulip."

Bond shivered again, staring at him fixedly. "Can't see you. 'Spect that—that means . . . I'm not 'fraid any . . . more. If—you should see my mother . . . give her my love and—and tell her I did my—my best . . ." He began to shake violently, his words panted out, barely audible. "Thanks, Roly . . . for—for staying . . . Jove, but—how—very cold—'tis . . ."

Five minutes later, Lieutenant William Bond, aged twenty-eight years, left the cold behind him forever.

And sitting in the chill little hollow, Roland Fairleigh Mathieson—rake, duellist, soldier of fortune, dedicated villain—bowed his head over his friend, and wept.

An hour passed before Mathieson began to toil up the slope. He had wrapped Bond in his own cloak and buried him in a narrow trench at the bottom of the cut, over which, with the aid of a sturdy branch, he had been able to collapse part of the walls of damp earth. He'd piled as many rocks as he could find atop the lonely grave, and strewn bracken and branches over all so that it was quite concealed. A temporary arrangement, which he would relay to Bill's family so they might later make more fitting burial plans. His prayers had been clumsy, for in matters spiritual he seldom went beyond his arguments with St. Thomas. He had, however, asked his mother to keep a kindly eye on the valiant Bond, and had sent his patron saint an excellent character reference and the request for a hospitable reception for the newcomer.

Now, clambering up through a deepening dusk, he grumbled bitterly over the predicament in which he found himself. Not that poor Bill was to blame, God rest him; although he might have had more sense than to get mixed up with so forlorn a cause.

A frigid blast made him shiver and he clutched at an elm to keep from sliding back down the slope, then struggled on.

What bitter irony, that he—of all men—should now be responsible for that accursed list! He had not the slightest wish to restore the treasure to its original owners! The list would work against—not for him. He would be wise—in fact, to find and destroy the blasted thing! Indeed, he thought aggrievedly, if he delivered it, he was no better than a traitor to his king and country! But—if he did not deliver it, he broke his given word and betrayed the man who had saved his life. He frowned at the lowering heavens and hoped Thomas was pleased with himself. One thing—he could do nothing about the list at the moment, for he must come up with MacTavish as soon as possible. The list was perfectly safe where it was, and the time to distribute the treasure was distant, after all. Perhaps, when he'd made sure of his own share, he would retrieve the list and send it to Lord Boudreaux, or to Geoffrey Delavale, as Bill had requested. Meanwhile, the Bible said somewhere, "Sufficient unto the day is the evil thereof." He brightened. So all was settled, respectably, and with no fuss or feathers!

It was almost two hours since he had left Rump. Luckily he never had to tether the big horse, and the animal had doubtless grazed and wandered about, but he should have been rubbed down, and if the rascal had decided to roll, it would play hob with the saddle and equipment. There'd been no choice in the matter, of course. To be with poor Bill had taken precedence over all else. Such a good man to die so young, so needlessly . . . He forced away the crushing sense of loss. Life was full of partings and a chancy thing at best.

He was up the bank at last, and began to run unevenly across the turf. It was still drizzling and the cold evening wind cut knife-like through his clothing. When he reached the copse he whistled the high warbling note that would bring the stallion to him. He heard a sudden scrambling. Rump whinnied but did not appear. 'Gad,' thought Mathieson suddenly anxious, 'never say he's stepped into a rabbit hole!' He sprinted in the direction of the sounds, which became more agitated. He heard a man's muffled imprecation, then a frantic neighing and plunging about.

Rage blazed through Mathieson and weariness fell away. Some sneaking swine was trying to make off with his horse! The sword whipped into his hand. "Hey!" he roared furiously, then began to whistle the shrill notes that would make Rump a handful even for skilled horse thieves. The command went unfinished. A twig cracked behind him. Even as he whirled around he was struck a stunning blow that sent trees, ground, and lowering heavens spinning into a crazy confusion. From a great distance he heard a shout, and then he was falling sickeningly down an endless darkness . . .

The hack's gait was jolting and every hoofbeat seemed to land on Mathieson's throbbing head. Slumped forward in the saddle, he kept his eyes closed against the glare of the morning sunlight and tried to pretend he felt perfectly well while forcing his sluggish brain to take stock of the situation.

It could scarcely have been worse. He had lost one of his few friends. He had lost Rump. MacTavish's trail was cold as last week's boiled mutton. And he was not succeeding in ignoring his head, which felt thoroughly caved in, though it wasn't, thank heaven.

On the brighter side, it had stopped raining. Furthermore, when he'd awoken this morning, he'd been astounded to find that the thieves had not only thrown some sacking over him to protect him from the cold and wet, but had left his saddlebags, complete with all his belongings, lying beside him. Equally astounding, his purse had not been touched, and Bill's hack had been unsaddled and hobbled nearby. Such consideration was beyond belief. His brow wrinkled painfully and he lifted one hand to explore the large lump on the back of his head. Inflicted by a cudgel, no doubt. Likely wielded by a thieving gypsy. But at least the skin was unbroken. And why in the world would gypsies not have taken poor Bill's hack, to say nothing of his own weapons and saddlebags? Perhaps they'd been satisfied, realizing what a rare prize they had in Rumpelstiltskin, whose only faults were that he had a slight—just slight—Roman nose, and his ears were a trifle too long. To compensate for which, he possessed rare endurance, a silken gait, high intelligence, and an affectionate disposition. Devil take the miserable hounds who'd laid their filthy hands on the beautiful animal!

Mathieson groaned faintly and drew a hand across his eyes. Fear was a rare emotion, but he felt it now, and the pain of loss was keener than the hammer blows to his head. What a beastly run of luck that so much could have gone wrong. It just went to show that a fellow could be quietly about his own business, bothering nobody, and without warning Fate could pull everything down about his ears and bring his well-laid plans to a grinding halt.

"Halt!"

The hack gave a snort and a half-hearted shy. Swaying with instinctive grace to the sudden movement, Mathieson clutched his head. His thoughts were becoming almost as loud as spoken words, by Jupiter! Perhaps he was delirious . . .

"Well do not just sit there moaning, sir! I require assistance!"

The voice was shrill, feminine, and imperious. Mathieson scrinched one eye open and peered reluctantly into the morning's glare.

An incredible personage was perched on a fallen treetrunk. An infinitesimal lady, tiny in everything but the jut to her determined chin and the spark in a pair of green eyes that were rather astonishingly lovely for a lady of advanced years. She wore a rust-coloured cloak thrown back to reveal a gown of orange muslin draped over large hoops. Her wig was awesomely high, and her cheeks were as bright as those of a young country miss.

As if reading his thoughts, she declared belligerently, "Yes, I raddle 'em. And you'd be the first to notice such conceit, unless I mistake your character, for no man with your looks could fail to know all there is to know about women!"

"Nor miss the chance to be of aid to a fascinating lady," said Mathieson, managing a smile, and swinging from the saddle.

The personage snorted. A lady-like snort but still a snort. "Very pretty, I'll allow," said she with disdain. "Why do you go about groaning and with your eyes closed? Are you drunk, sir? And why—" She flew up from her treetrunk suddenly and was at his side, one arm about him. "Zounds, but the boy's in a proper state! Lean on me. Come now—this way . . ."

Mathieson, who had been struck by a sudden wave of dizziness, blinked down at the tiny creature who held him in such a firm clutch, and gingerly placed one hand on her shoulder. In

68

addition to her lack of stature, she was evidently afflicted, for she walked with a pronounced hobble, so that he was obliged to support her rather than accept her aid. They came in a most clumsy fashion to the treetrunk, whereupon the lady commanded that he sit down, then seated herself close beside him, peering up at his face, for all the world he thought, like some bright little robin.

"Gin?" she asked, not beating about the bush.

"I wish it was, ma'am. Thieves. Stole my horse and fetched me a clout that put me out of time for a while. But I'm perfectly fine now, so—"

"Perfectly fine and white as paper. Put down your head, you great long creature and show me where you were struck."

Meekly, he obeyed and contrived not to swear when her fingers explored the lump.

"Hmmnn. Well, 'tis not cut, at all events. Is your vision blurred?"

"Merely dazzled, ma'am," he answered, straightening cautiously.

Her eyes softened. "I judged you rightly, I see. You may present yourself, if you feel able. No, I require neither that you stand nor bow, which would be stupid, for you'd likely fall down and I should be obliged to lift you all by myself. Ah! I saw that grin! I suppose you fancy me a helpless old hag, too shrunken and racked by gout to be able to lift anyone!"

"I beg to present Roland Mathieson to your Grace's attention," he said, suppressing the grin with difficulty. "And my vision would be blurred indeed did I fancy you to be any of those things. How may I be of service? Never say you also have been robbed?"

"Well, I won't. Nor am I a duchess, though I might have been I do assure you had he not had a great stomach and been sixty when I was eighteen. I've mislaid my coachman. One of the carriage wheels split, or some such thing, and, faith but I could not blame it, for we'd been jolting over that dreadful road with its potholes and mud since dawn. Or nine, or thereabouts! My poor bones could endure no more, and the sun was so bright, and the countryside is always so—countryish and delightful. Provided one stays no longer than three days. I sent Cuthbert off and told him I would wait. Only he did not come so I began to walk about and became lost and then the heel of my foolish slipper broke off. You will say I should have stayed where I was, but—I was lonely, something you know nothing of, Roland. Nor did I, at your age, but I do now." Her eyes were wistful suddenly, and she sighed as she continued, "For in spite of wealth, servants, houses, and so-called friends . . . age is—lonely, alas."

"What fustian," he said, greatly daring.

The infinitesimal personage stiffened; the small mouth became a tight line, the chin jutted ominously.

"No lady with eyes like yours could ever be lonely," he went on, "else all the middle-aged gentlemen are betwattled! Am I to be favoured with the name of my companion in adversity?"

For an instant it appeared that he was not, for she continued to glare at him. But laughter danced in his velvety black eyes, he was young and good to look upon and showed besides promise of an ability to amuse. Further, although he was still pale, he gave no sign of discomfort. The infinitesimal personage admired courage, and thus the twinkle was back when she said, "I am Lady Clorinda Ericson." She extended a tiny hand but cried, "No! Do not bend, or you will hurt your head. Here."

To his amusement, she pressed her fingers to his lips, and when he had dutifully planted a kiss upon them, she drew back regarding him with approval.

"Faith, but you flirt deliciously, Roland. Are you wed?"

Startled by such a home question on short acquaintance, he said, "No, my lady."

"I suppose you think me a prying old woman, which I am. But as we grow older, gossip becomes so delicious. Now that I think on it, I always found it a delightful pastime, and so exquisitely wicked. Speaking of which, you must be Marbury's bastard." She gave a cackle of mirth. "Lud—only look at the boy fire up! An I have shocked you 'tis because you young people today are so incredibly and unnaturally prim!"

Mathieson had been called many things, but "prim" was so divorced from any of those things that he forgot his vexation and gave a shout of laughter, whereof he winced, and had to bite back an oath.

"Say it," invited Lady Clorinda. "Too much the gentleman, are you? Then I'll say it for you!" And she did, so explicitly that Mathieson could barely refrain from uttering another devastating laugh and at length had to plead that she refrain from so cruelly amusing him. "Tell me, rather," he begged, "why you are lonely. Have you no family, ma'am?"

"Family! If ever anything should be poxed in perpetuity, 'tis 'Family'! One bears children—well, you won't, of course, but your poor wife will!" She twinkled at him. "And I say 'poor wife' for many reasons, Roland Mathieson! Where was I? Do not interrupt! Oh, yes. I bore children. Three. All by my first husband, unfortunately. One died. My daughter ran off with a charming rascal and has the poor taste to be happy with the creature! My son is eight and forty, and as rash, irresponsible and bothersome as the veriest child! My grandson—humph! And my granddaughters both are buxom, opinionated wenches with more sauce than sense, who should have been wed long since save that one lost her love and will not accept the man who seeks to take his place, and the other wasted her sympathy on her brother, who is a reckless scamp, and now wastes her youth on her father—the idiot! I mean her father is the idiot—not my granddaughter. Oh, I am a wretch and have made you laugh again! My apologies. Why do you vex Marbury so?"

Mathieson's laughter died abruptly and his eyes became cool and veiled. "I have the greatest respect for my grandfather, ma'am."

"Have you? I heard he is grown to be an impossible creature! You do not resemble poor Muffin, but you are very like him, for all that the relationship is so—*à huis clos*, as it were."

"Yet 'twould seem you know of me, my lady, so his secret is not so well kept, after all."

Her bright gaze flickered over his countenance, noting the faint look of polite boredom, the perfection of nose, mouth, and chin, the high, well-cut cheekbones, the dusky inscrutability of the long-lashed eyes, and the proud tilt to the dark head. She kept silent for a moment, thinking many things. Then, she murmured, "You really hate the poor man."

A flash lit the cold eyes, and he started to his feet. "You will forgive madam, an I leave—"

"Hoity-toity!" Her frail little hands tugged heartily at the skirts of his coat. "I will do nothing of the sort! I am a lonely, abandoned old lady. Would you go away and leave me to the mercy of passing thieves and murderers? Sit down! Sit down! I have a good hold on you, unkind one, and do assure you I shall

71

not relinquish it. You will have to drag me—screaming—all the way!''

Mathieson could visualize such a scene, and fought an appreciative chuckle. Still, it was true that they were not very far from where Rump had been stolen, and this sharp-tongued old lady wore some remarkably fine diamonds on her slightly gout-twisted fingers. Therefore, he tightened his lips, but sat down again.

''That's a good boy,'' said Lady Clorinda, retaining her hold on his coat.

''Madam,'' he corrected, ''I am neither a boy, nor do I hate my grandfather.''

''Of course you don't,'' she soothed solemnly. '' 'Deed but you love him so deeply that when he is mentioned all the animation dies out of your face, and you become so much like a marble statue that I wonder nobody has bought you and put you on display in London!''

Mathieson's lips twitched. ''Might one ask why you should concern yourself, my lady?''

''Because Clifford Augustus Fairleigh Mathieson, Duke of Marbury, Earl of Nettering and Mathie, et cetera, et cetera, was the hero of my girlish dreams when I was very, very young and he was a dashing—oh, such a dashing—ensign.'' My lady blushed like a girl and lowered her roguish eyes. ''Well, enough of that! Suffice it to say that I knew your grandfather when he was simply young Lord Fairleigh, who allowed himself, when he was barely eighteen, to be tricked into marrying that horrid cat Mary Frobisher because she said he had got her with child! Which was nonsense, if ever I heard any, for Muffin was shy—in those days. However, never mind that. The thing is, she gave birth to Dudley—your father.'' A frown pulled at her brows making her suddenly formidable. ''And your father I knew well.''

Breathless, Mathieson almost stammered, ''And—did you perchance . . . know my mama?''

''Oh, yes.'' She asked shrewdly, ''Is that what you hold against your grandfather, lad?''

He was silent, for it was a painful topic, and one he discussed only with Rump. But, perhaps because his head pounded so mercilessly, or because for all her teasing there was a kindliness in those bright eyes, he answered at length, his voice low-pitched, almost as if he spoke to himself alone. "She was the loveliest, sweetest natured, most unselfish, and truly good lady I shall ever know. My father—" He broke off, his jaw tightening, then went on, "But Mama was always kind; always understanding and ready to listen . . . even when she was so very ill, at the end . . ."

My lady watched him and wisely held her tongue.

After a minute, he muttered broodingly, "And the duke rejected her—dared to condemn her and hold her vulgar and—" he spat out the word "grasping! My God! If he did but know . . ." His hand clenched tightly and he was very still, gazing into the bitter past.

"Even so," she prompted carefully, "your papa must have been very proud and pleased with her, that she had given him such a fine son, if—"

Mathieson's harsh laugh shocked her, and she drew back eyeing him askance.

"Oh, my dear lady," he said, the cynical sneer very apparent, "your gossip serves you indifferent well, I think. I would have supposed—"

Lady Clorinda did not like to be interrupted, and therefore interrupted in turn, "Never underestimate a gossipy old woman, my lad! I know much of you. For instance, that you distinguished yourself on the battlefield, but are no longer received anywhere. That you are a reckless gamester, a soldier of fortune, a regular Don Juan with the ladies—and a very generous one, 'tis said! That you hover constantly on the brink of being clapped up for debt, yet live extravagantly. That is the sum of it, no? And not so very dreadful, surely."

"Because, ma'am, 'tis but the tip of the iceberg. I am a social outcast—by my own choosing. I live by my wits and by my sword and have few, if any, scruples. Indeed, my depravity has been finely honed and polished. I do assure you I am a thoroughly dedicated villain and enjoy my trade."

"Why?" She looked into his cynical smile curiously. "Vengeance?"

It seemed to my lady that for an instant he did not breathe, but then he chuckled, and said with a careless shrug, "Indolence, ma'am. Pure and simple." He turned to look at her fully, one dark brow mockingly upraised. "My regrets do I disappoint, but you would have the truth."

73

"What a pity," she sighed, relinquishing her hold on his coat so as to pat his cheek very gently, "that I did not get it. Ah! Here is my lazy Cuthbert at last!"

Mathieson, who had regarded her with stark horror and jerked his head away when she touched his cheek, recovered his aplomb only to lose it again when he glanced to the coach which came lumbering along the muddy lane.

It was an enormous vehicle painted a rich dark red and lavishly adorned with gold shells and swirls and flourishes so that it bore more resemblance to a coach of state than to a private conveyance. This illusion was enhanced by the four white horses, and the red and gold livery of the two footmen who stood up behind. 'Zounds!' he thought. Raising his fascinated stare from the equipage, he met a pair of amiable grey eyes in a broad, ruddy visage. This large individual, who was more conventionally attired in a black coat with big gold buttons, must be the mislaid Cuthbert.

"Lovely, isn't it?" murmured Lady Clorinda.

"There are—er, no words."

"Evil creature," she exclaimed with a giggle. "I like ostentation. Sometimes. And I can afford to indulge my whims. Come along now."

She held out her hand imperiously. Mathieson offered his arm and led her toward the carriage which had come to a halt. A very young footman sprang down and ran to open the door.

My lady glanced critically at William Bond's hack. "Tie that poor creature on behind, Japhet. Truly Roland, I wonder that Muffin cannot at least mount you better than that!"

"Is not my horse, ma'am." He handed her onto the first step. "I've the finest chestnut stallion in the world—an opinion shared, evidently, for he was stolen, whereby I collected this lump on my head."

"Yes, of course. I had forgot you was robbed. How dreadful! Have you any hope of finding your animal?"

"Oh, I shall find him, ma'am," he said grimly. "I'll catch the miserable varmints, I promise you."

"What—on that?" My lady pointed to the old horse. "Never! We must find you a better mount, sir." She peered at him uneasily. "Though you do not look at all well, and must not ride any more today. I forbid it! You shall drive with me, and tomorrow—"

Touched, because kindness was something he received even more seldom than he gave it, Mathieson smiled at her. "You are very good, and I thank you, ma'am. But I cannot delay. Rumpelstiltskin is *absolument irremplaçable*. I must get after him at once."

She frowned and said grudingly, "I suppose I must respect you for that. Do you mean to return to Tewkesbury to hire a mount?"

"From the look of the tracks the thieves headed north, and I daren't waste time going back to Tewkesbury. I'll hire another hack at the first livery stable I come to."

The coachman coughed portentously.

My lady glanced up at him. "You've a stable in mind, Cuthbert?"

"One or two, ma'am. But I was wondering . . . Did I hear you say—a chestnut stallion was stole, sir? He wouldn't have two white stockings and a blaze on his nose, I don't s'pose?"

"He most certainly would!" Mathieson stepped back and looked eagerly into that square face framed by the blue of the sunlit sky. "Have you seen such an animal today?"

"Aye, sir! A big fellow, sixteen hands if an inch. I recollect thinkin't that 'cept fer his ugly Roman nose and them mule ears, he'd—"

"That's my horse, by God," cried Mathieson, too elated to take offense at the aspersions cast on his beloved Rumpelstiltskin. "Where, man? When? Did you see who had him?"

The coachman rubbed the handle of his whip against his chin. "Lessee now . . . Musta bin about—sevenish, I'd say. A pair of country-lookin' coves was ridin' him, and—"

"Both of 'em? Damn their eyes! You sure they weren't gypsies?"

Cuthbert shrugged. "Mighta bin, at that. They was dark enough—dark as you, sir, now I think on it."

Mathieson gave him a searching look, but the broad face was guileless. "And where were these two rogues heading? North?"

"Lor' bless yer, no sir. South. I says ter meself, 'Them two ain't got no business with that beauty, Cuthbert, me boy! Like as not they stole him. They're makin' fer a cozy hideaway in the Forest o' Dean, they is!' "

"Blast!" muttered Mathieson under his breath. If the thieves were gypsies and reached the fastness of the forest, they would disappear as if into thin air. Moreover, if he turned south now he might as well abandon all hope of catching up with Mac-Tavish. He brushed the thought aside. The all-important task was to find Rump. Glancing up, he found my lady, coachman, and footmen watching him interestedly. "My apologies for wool-gathering," he said. " 'Twould seem I must decline your offer, ma'am, for my route lies in the opposite direction, alas."

"Ah." My lady nodded but her smile was wistful. "I should have enjoyed your company, but I wish you well in your search, Roland."

Two minutes later, having rewarded the observant coachman and been so bold as to plant a kiss on my lady's cheek—much to her delight—he waved as the great chariot rumbled away with a tiny handkerchief fluttering from the window.

The mare was stubborn and resisted all attempts to urge her to a respectable speed. For one of the few times in his life, Mathieson wished he owned a pair of rowelled spurs rather than the short-necked pair he wore and that he seldom employed for even the lightest touch to Rump's sides. Fumingly abandoning his efforts to hurry the animal, he rode on, and half an hour later was searching for the livery stable a farmhand had told him was "just down the lane, left at the signpost, and stay on 'crost the fields, due east a mile or so, like."

His thoughts turned, as they so often did, to poor Bill Bond and some of the wild times they'd shared. There had been one particular leave in Dover . . . He sighed, and concentrated instead on his meeting with the tempestuous Lady Ericson. Now there was an interesting little creature. Likely she'd a lively past; certainly she had been a beauty in her day. He was convinced that she must have been pointed out to him at some time; in Paris, perhaps, for something about her was so familiar. She had— Ah! Here was the hamlet, and he could hear the ring of a smith's hammer.

He rode along the single street. A small girl in a faded blue dress stood watching him, a bright red ball clutched in her chubby little hands. An old man in a snowy smock sat outside the tavern smoking a long clay pipe which he lifted in a companionable greeting. A dog woke up as the mare trotted past, and rolled onto its back to remain thus, all four legs in the air. The only other person in sight was an extremely fat gentleman who stood in the open door of the smithy, apparently chatting with the smith while he waited for his horse to be shod. 'Poor beast,' thought Mathieson. 'With a load like that to carry, 'tis likely glad of a rest.'

That the fat man's mount was not the only one in need of a rest, he discovered to his horror. His horse sat down.

Scrambling from the saddle with neither grace nor elegance, Mathieson stumbled, swore heartily, and added to his humiliation by sitting in the road beside the hack. The sudden violent movements exacerbated his headache which was not at all helped by an outburst of delighted laughter. Furious, he peered upward. The fat man, may he rot, was convulsed, and clung for support to the grey-haired smith, who howled in a lower key, but just as raucously.

"You cannot know how glad I am," snarled Mathieson, "to provide you with amusement, gentlemen!"

The smith straightened, mopping at his eyes with a grubby handkerchief. "No offense intended, sir," he said in a great boom of a voice. " 'Twere just as I hasn't never seen no horse sit down like that 'un."

"Blister me!" moaned the fat man. "No more have I. A—a *rara avis* you've got there, sir! You might—might put her on exhibit and collect enough money to—to buy yourself a horse!" And he and the smith were off again. Uproarious.

Glaring at them, Mathieson turned when a shrill squeaking added to the assault on his battered head. Drawn by this unexpected entertainment, the small girl was nearby, jumping up and down. Her golden ringlets bounced and her dress swirled. In her innocent delight she clapped her hands and dropped the ball, which rolled down the hill toward Mathieson. He took it up, then tossed it to her, smiling, and she caught it and beamed at him, her joyous little face to some extent alleviating the gloom of this miserable morning.

He regained his feet, but his head throbbed so that he raised a hand to his temple involuntarily.

The smith's eyes sharpened. "Feeling a mite out of curl 'smorning, is ye, sir?"

Mathieson brushed dirt from his already disreputable breeches. "My horse is, certainly," he said wryly.

"Gad, but you're a sportsman, sir," chortled the fat man. "Admire a fella who can laugh at adversity. But you *are* a touch green about the gills. I shall buy you a tankard of ale, sir, deuce take me if I don't! Nothing like good English ale to put the spirit back into a man!''

"Thank you," said Mathieson. "I only wish it might put my own horse back under me! I was robbed last night gentlemen. My stallion was taken and this poor old slug left in his place."

The smith shook his head and clicked his tongue and said it was "sinful goings on."

The fat man was more vocal. "By Gad, you don't say so!" he cried with great indignation. "Handled you roughly too, did they? Thieving gypsies, likely. Devil take it all, what is England coming to? I ask you! Not a moment ago I was telling Enoch here I damned near hauled in an ugly little lot late last night, and would've by Gad, had we a constable in the village! Rogues, or I'm a Dutchman, sir! Three of the dirty bounders. Unshaven, sir. A disgrace! I doubt there was a groat betwixt the lot of 'em, yet they'd a—Zeus!'' His round little eyes grew rounder. "What like was your horse, sir?"

Mathieson described the chestnut. The smith and the fat man stared at one another.

"Cor," said the smith, awed. "White blaze and all! Sounds like the stamper, Mr. Reed."

"The stamper?" snapped Mathieson, tensing. "My horse has the habit of stamping is he at stand. 'Tis why I named him Rumpelstiltskin. Have you seen him, then? Do you say these men had my horse, sir?"

Mr. Reed nodded with owlish solemnity. "Or I'm a Dutchman, sir!''

Mathieson seized his arm. "By God, but I'll buy *you* that ale, Reed! And you too, smith! Now—tell me where I can get a decent horse, but first—late last night, you said? Could you describe me these rogues and tell me where they were bound? Into the Forest, eh?''

"Dean, sir? No, sir! Devil a bit of it! Tall, skinny fella—gypsy, likely. Big rascal wearing a knitted green cap. Bigger rascal—forty-ish. And all riding *north*, sir. Most definitely north, sir. *North!* Or I'm a Dutchman, sir!''

Mathieson bought ale for Enoch the smith, and Mr. Reed. He also bought a black cloak and a fine grey horse and, although these transactions left him rather dangerously short of funds, he was pleased to find that the cloak was warm, and the grey was a good goer.

His further discussion with Mr. Reed had convinced him the man was in the right of it, and that Rump had indeed been taken northward. Lady Ericson's coachman must either have been mistaken as to the thieves' route, or they had changed direction after he saw them, perhaps in an effort to confuse any pursuer. Knowing that they would put as much ground as possible between them and himself, Mathieson headed steadily northward. Despite their good progress, however, his mood deteriorated as the hours slipped away with no sight of his quarry, the dread that he might not find Rump compounded by his frustration because MacTavish had eluded him.

A light meal at a friendly farmhouse restored his nerves, and, his headache a little less vicious, he mounted up once more. He had scant hope of obtaining word of his horse from hamlets or inns, being convinced the thieves would steer clear of such places, but he asked nonetheless, of carters, pedlars, shepherds, blacksmiths, a man with a load of feathers, a tinker with an irascible donkey, sundry farmhands, and a dimpled dairymaid. He was answered variously with indifference, courtesy, garrulity, and (by the tinker) a curse. The farmhands scratched their heads and tried in vain to recollect such an animal as he described. The dairymaid blushed and fluttered her lashes, but could provide him with nothing more useful than a kiss, which he took without leave and returned when she dimplingly demanded it.

By late afternoon his hopes were fading into a fuming helplessness. The wind was warm but blustery, sending the clouds to racing the shadows they cast onto hill and dale. He had crossed into Shropshire, and, still avoiding main roads, was high in the hills with lush green valleys to either hand, and far below the sparkle of a river that he rather thought would be the Teme. Beautiful, unspoiled country. Ahead, the thatched roofs of a tiny hamlet peeped above the trees, and a few thin strands of smoke rose only a short way before they were whipped into invisibility by the hurrying wind. Mathieson spurred the grey to a gallop, then reined up frantically as a startled shout rang out, and a young boy with flaming red hair darted from the undergrowth almost under the grey's hooves. He was clearly scared half out of his wits, but he stopped when Mathieson demanded it, and faced him, trembling.

Mathieson leaned forward in the saddle and surveyed him thoughtfully. The boy kept his hands behind him, but when he first had burst out from the long grasses he had been clutching a knife and a piece of wood. Hiding from his tasks, no doubt, while he whittled a wooden pistol, or a doll for his sister. Mathieson could sympathize with such truancy, and he smiled and said kindly, "My apologies did I frighten you."

"Ain't f-frightened," the boy gasped, his lips pale and the freckles standing out like small beacons all over his white face.

"Glad to hear it." Mathieson was weary of his questioning, and it was doubtless a waste of time, but, "You've a fine pair of eyes," he said. "Do they see well?"

The boy looked puzzled and a little less ready to swoon. "Yes, sir."

"You've been—er, resting on this hill for some time—have you?"

Cautiously, the bright head nodded.

"If I was ready to pay—sixpence, say—for information, d'you think you could remember everyone you've seen?"

"Ain't seen any rebs, if that's what you means, milor'," said the boy, taking on a bold and swaggering air. "Else I'd have ambushed the dirty traitors and tied 'em up and drug 'em to the village constable."

"I'm glad to hear you're a patriot. However, I'm not after Jacobites, but my horse. He was stolen by thieves last night, and I've been riding like fury trying to come up with the villains. Three men, and a chestnut stallion with—" Mathieson stopped, his heart giving a great leap, for the young face was suddenly alight with excitement.

"I saw 'em, your honour! A fine big horse with long ears, a white blaze on his face, and two white stockings—be that the one?"

"Your bright eyes just earned you sixpence!" Mathieson took out his purse. "Now, tell me—which way were they going?"

"Shrewsbury, I 'spect sir. Likely they'll try to sell your horse on market day."

Mathieson spun him a coin. The boy caught it and gave a joyous squeal, but pointed out honestly, "You said sixpence, your honour. This is—"

Mathieson was already riding away, and his voice echoed after him. "Keep it! A bonus!"

The sun was setting before Mathieson caught his first glimpse of the thieves. Three of the filthy swine, just as Reed had said. And dear old Rump, moving with his peerless, silken stride, God love his hooves and hocks! By Beelzebub, but the big clod bestriding him would pay dearly for his villainy! Still, it would behoove him to take them by surprise, rather than to attack now, for two could keep him busy while the third rode off with Rump.

He kept them in sight, therefore, staying always in the shade or behind shrubs, as they journeyed on through the peaceful countryside. They were heading for Shrewsbury all right. He smiled unpleasantly and eased his sword in the scabbard. He'd see to it they never reached that bustling town!

The sunset was glorious and when it began to fade he edged nearer, determined that they not escape him, even if he had to take them on, all three. The wind had dropped to a fitful breeze on which was borne the tang of wood smoke. He rode past a farm where cows stood hock deep in the rich meadow grasses, chewing complacently. A tantalizing smell of cooking wafted from the open windows of the whitewashed house. Faint with distance a bell chimed the hour. Eight. Small wonder he was hungry. He dismissed such a minor annoyance and spurred the grey eagerly as the three thieves skirted the edge of an area of marshland. Cover was harder to come by here, with fewer trees and shrubs, but he noticed that the thieves never looked behind them, apparently convinced they had been too clever to be followed. They passed into the woods where the thick branches screened out most of the crimson light, and without warning were lost to sight.

Mathieson drew the grey to a halt, slipped from the saddle and held the animal's nostrils, listening intently. Nearby, a woman was singing, and surprisingly, it was a quaint little French lovesong, sung with an impeccable accent. The scents of woodsmoke and cooking blended with another smell. He frowned, puzzled. Fresh paint . . . ? He tethered the grey, drew his sword, and crept forward, crouching a little, moving rapidly over the thick carpet of bracken, the garrulous birds covering the few sounds his boots made upon twigs or fallen leaves.

He could hear male talk now, interspersed with low laughter, and was again surprised because the voices were cultured and did not employ the strange Romany language of gypsies. There were more than three men by the sound of it, and womens' voices as well. His brows knit in vexation. He would have been better off to have confronted Rump's captors when first he'd seen them. They were evidently members of a large gang of horse thieves. It might not be quite so simple a matter to reclaim Rump as he had imagined.

He could hear the crackle of flames. The trees thinned and he viewed a large shadowy clearing around the edges of which stood six large caravans. Cooking pots hung suspended from iron trivets over the two fires which blazed in the open central space. A plump young woman with abundant dark ringlets bent over one of the pots, stirring the contents and peering at them anxiously. She wore a cream-coloured gown; a white towel was tied about her waist, and with her free hand she held her voluminous skirts clear of the flames. Nearby, a slender young fellow clad in simple riding habit and knee boots sat cross-legged on a blanket, poring over what appeared to be a map; he was not wearing a wig, and his light brown hair was very short and curled close against his head. A tall, dowdy looking middle-aged woman was perched on the steps of one of the caravans, peeling potatoes. At first Mathieson thought she was alone, but a peeled potato suddenly shot past her to splash into her bowl, and he saw then that she was assisted by another female inside the caravan, of whom only the lower flounce of a pale green gown, and two small slippered feet were visible. Directly opposite, beyond the caravans, was an improvised rope paddock in which a dozen or so horses and donkeys were grazing and where a very small woman wearing a frilly red cap stood with the three thieves, admiring Rumpelstiltskin.

'Is a regular robber's roost, all right!' thought Mathieson.

From behind him there came sudden rapid hoofbeats. A man shouted, " 'Ware! A spy! 'Ware!"

Without an instant's hesitation Mathieson leapt into action, sprinting straight across the clearing for Rumpelstiltskin, his dagger whipping into his left hand, the colichemarde glittering in his right. The man on the blanket sprang up, grabbing for weapons. A woman screamed. Running at top speed, Mathieson whistled loud and clear. Rumpelstiltskin whinnied shrilly and reared, trying to get to his master, but two of the men clung to his head, pulling him down. The hooves thundered very close and Mathieson knew that he could not reach Rump in time. He felt a rush of air, ducked, and the horseman shot past, the clubbed musket he aimed whizzing so close to Mathieson's head that his tricorne was sent flying. The individual who had been sitting on the blanket sprang forward, sword in hand. The largest of the thieves ran to the attack swinging up a hefty cudgel. The tall and powerfully built rogue who'd worn the stocking cap was closest and darted in with rapier levelled. Mathieson engaged the rapier and with a strong glizade sent it spinning from his attacker's hand. The curly-haired fellow's sword would get him, if the cudgel didn't, he thought grimly, but he parried the one, and with a swipe of his dagger, deflected the other. Then he was out of time and luck. The cudgel smashed the sword from his hand. The rapier wielded by the man in the stocking cap was again thrusting at his throat. He flung himself to the side, felt a swift burn of pain as the rapier sliced across the side of his neck, and swore furiously as merciless hands grabbed and held his arms, a vicious grip wrenched at his hair, jerking his head back, and the rapier was aimed again. Mathieson had a brief and confused impression that at some time he had met this dimly seen lout.

A piercing scream cut through curses, shouts, and confusion. A feminine voice shrilled frantically, "Stop! He is a friend! Don't hurt him!"

The man from the blanket beat the rapier away with his own sword and said in a lisping drawl, "Not thporting, old boy. He ith quite outnumbered, you know."

The man with the rapier growled a curse, but his weapon was restrained.

The strong hands did not by an iota yield their grip, but neither did Mathieson continue to struggle and every head turned as a girl ran down the caravan steps flinging out her hands in supplication.

Astounded, Mathieson saw a small face convulsed with anxiety, lips still parted from her cry—the upper one a trifle short but curving very sweetly to meet its mate. She was tiny and slender but nicely shaped, with a delightfully ample bosom.

"The devil!" he gasped. "Miss Bradford!"

⚘ 6 ⚘

Fiona Bradford fairly flew across the clearing, the wind whipping her pale green skirts, the men making way for her. "Let him go!" she cried frantically. "Oh, you have cut him!" She flung herself between Mathieson and the large man with the rapier. "Torrey! How *could* you? Let him go!"

Torrey! Mathieson started, but he saw now that it was so. Even in the dim light, he might have recognized this man save that one sees what one expects to see and it had never occurred to him that the unshaven thief wearing the stocking cap might be the same gentleman he'd met in the company of the Bradfords.

"He's a spy, Fiona," growled Torrey angrily.

"For what possible reason would I spy on you?" snapped Mathieson, wrenching free of his captors and extricating the handkerchief from his pocket.

"I cannot imagine," murmured the wigless young man who lisped. "You are acquainted with the gentleman, ma'am?" The words were calm and unhurried, the accent was undeniably cultured and, despite the lack of his wig, from close-cropped head to shining knee boots, there was about him the air of poised assurance that speaks of breeding.

"He is Mr. Mathieson, the gentleman who came to help me in the storm." Fiona gazed anxiously up at the intruder's scowling features. "And I am greatly indebted to him, which—"

"Which is why we rescued his horse," put in another voice.

Holding the handkerchief to the shallow cut across the base of his throat, Mathieson stared in deepening astonishment at the diminutive female who made her way through the throng.

Lady Clorinda Ericson bore little resemblance to the richly clad aristocrat he had met that morning. Her fashionable orange gown had been replaced by one of simple grey cloth. The expensive wig was gone, dark hair rather suspiciously untouched by grey was braided and wound into a neat bun behind her head, her only concession to fashion being that bright red cap, richly frilled and threaded by a pink riband, but having not a particle of lace. Yet she was still every inch the great lady, and her green eyes seemed more bright and roguish than ever as she went on, "How very clever of you to find us, Mathieson."

His mind was whirling with conjecture, but wrath was still uppermost and he responded curtly, "My lady, how it comes about that you are here I cannot begin to guess. But you are in error. My horse was stolen rather than rescued! I followed the thieves here, and was nigh murdered for—"

"And you demand an explanation," she interrupted, adding to his bafflement by smiling up at him and patting his arm without the least appearance of embarrassment. "Quite right. You shall have one, but—"

"We need explain nothing," interjected Freemon Torrey harshly. "With respect, ma'am, the less this fellow hears, the better! He is a threat to us all, as you know, and—"

Her face flushed with anger, Fiona interrupted in turn, "We know nothing of the sort! Mr. Mathieson is a brave gentleman who very gallantly rescued me and Picayune. And in return he has been most unkindly dealt with."

At this point the largest thief hove up through the dimness and as the light from the fires fell upon him Mathieson saw that it was milady's coachman—Cuthbert. "Very likely, miss," he said in his growl of a voice. "Still, what Torrey says has merit. We took Mathieson's horse so as to—"

"You own it, do you? Now damn your lying hide!" Enraged, Mathieson sprang at him but was at once seized again, and jerked back.

"Mr. Mathieson," said my lady, her sharp voice cutting through the commotion, "pray do not swear. I cannot like swearing, and it says in the Bible—"

"Thou shalt not steal," he interpolated. "Furthermore, madam, to involve this innocent girl with a band of horse thieves is—"

"We ain't horse thieves, curse your insolence," roared Torrey, glaring at him.

"You blasted well admitted you stole my horse." Mathieson strained against the hands that held him. "And if you're not thieves, I'd like to know what—"

A sturdy, broad-shouldered young man with a pair of muscular but bowed legs sprinted across the clearing.

"What is it, Alec?" asked my lady sharply.

"Rrrredcoats!" he panted.

The burr to the "r" was pronounced. 'He's a Scot, by Beelzebub!' thought Mathieson, and was stunned by an idea as fantastic as it was unexpected.

Mervyn Bradford had run up after the Scot and now said in a low and breathless voice, "We're rehearsing, don't forget! I'll—" He caught sight of Mathieson and exclaimed, horrified, "You! What the devil—"

There were certain army officers who had good reason to most earnestly desire a discussion with Roland Mathieson. Chief amongst these was Lieutenant Brooks Lambert (formerly Captain Lambert), who held a gentleman he knew as Roland Otton directly to blame for his demotion. There were other bones of contention between the two men, and the lieutenant was known to be of a vindictive nature, wherefore Mathieson intervened tersely, "What rank is the officer?"

The young man named Alec looked bewildered, but answered, "Captain."

Mathieson, poised for sudden flight, relaxed.

There was no time for more. Into the clearing rode a troop of dragoons, a craggy-faced captain at their head, with sabre in hand and triumph in his eyes.

"No, no!" cried Bradford imperiously, his back to the soldiers, his warning gaze on Torrey. " 'Tis all wrong! Like this . . ." He struck a pose, flung up one hand and recited with booming resonance, " 'I would give all my fame for a pot of ale, and safety.' "

Very pale, Freemon Torrey stared at him blankly. There was an instant of taut silence. Mathieson's quick wits grasped the situation. Stepping forward, he quoted with equal drama but from the wrong play: " 'It goes much against my stomach. Hast any philosophy in thee, shep—' "

"Be still, sir!" interjected a harsh voice. The captain had

dismounted, and now stamped towards them; a chunky man of about five and forty, with formidable chin outthrust, and pale rather watery grey eyes narrowed and suspicious. "What are you people about, hiding here in the forest?"

Bradford responded grandly, "We make camp for the night, sir, we do not hide. And we are about nothing more menacing than to perform our entertainments. You behold a troupe of humble players. We wander hither and yon across the bosom of this noble England, doing what we may to bring a fleeting joy, an escape into tears or laughter, a veneer of the arts, to lonely village, true-hearted yeoman, and simple peasant."

"Indeed?" Clearly unimpressed by this rodomontade, the officer gestured to his men and the troopers spread out around the clearing. "Pray bring a 'fleeting joy' to some humble soldiers," he went on with a sardonic curl of the lip. "My name is Lake. I'd like to hear yours, if you please."

Bradford swept him a flourishing bow and introduced himself, then added, "This lady is my mother, Mrs. Clorinda."

'Mon Dieu!' thought Mathieson. 'Then he must be "the idiot"!'

Looking worried suddenly, Bradford demanded in a normal voice, "What crime have we committed? Is there some law that says we may not make camp here? I was told 'tis open land. Have we to—"

"One hopes you have committed no crimes, Mr. Bradford," the captain interrupted brusquely. "In which case you have no cause for alarm. It will be necessary, however, that your caravans and possessions be searched, and that each member of your—er, company, provide some proof of his or her identity."

The troopers dismounted, some requiring documents from the "troupe," others stamping off to search caravans.

"My gracious," exclaimed Lady Clorinda, shrinking closer to Bradford. "What ever are you looking for, sir? We're honest folks. We haven't done wrong."

Captain Lake shrugged and took the sheaf of papers Bradford offered. "England is littered with Jacobites fleeing their just deserts. One in particular carries a list of traitorous conspirators. A reward of two hundred guineas is offered for his capture." He raised his voice. "D'you hear that, you people? Two hundred guineas!"

"What doth he look like?" lisped the thin young man, interested.

The captain returned Bradford's papers. "Would that I knew. Like you, perhaps, whatever your name is. Your identification."

"My name ith Heywood, thir. I have only thith letter."

"You are an actor, also, Mr. er, Thaddeus Heywood?" asked the captain, glancing in a bored fashion at the letter.

Torrey sniggered and said a wicked, "Why, yeth, of courth."

Heywood flushed, and although no champion of the rights of others, Mathieson experienced a deepening of his desire to deck Mr. Torrey.

"I am a dramatitht, Captain. I write, or rewrite whatever play we plan to give, according to the number of people we have, or lack." Heywood met the officer's cold stare with an engaging smile. "Now, really, thir. Do I look like a dethperate fugitive?"

Lake did not deign to reply, stretching out an imperative hand for Mathieson's identification. "Sergeant," he shouted, while running his eyes down the letters given him, "set the other men to searching the caravans and that atrocity of a coach, and—" He checked, then looked up keenly, "You did not use your own name whilst in the army, Mathieson? Might one ask why?"

"My grandfather appeared to think that up to that point I had not covered it with glory, sir, and so I took another to spare him."

This was not entirely true, but Lake had his share of tyrannical relations and nodded sympathetically. "What caused you to revert to Mathieson again? According to this, you served with distinction and attained the rank of captain. Did those achievements soften up the old fellow?"

Mathieson smiled and said with becoming, if insincere, modesty, "Far be it from me to boast, sir . . ."

Lake chuckled and returned his eyes to the letters. "And you were under the command of Colonel Archibald Cunningham? Is he the stern disciplinarian they paint him?"

"If he is, then I'd say he has calmed down considerably. We thought of him more along the lines of a man-eating tiger!" And grinning in response to the captain's laugh, he added, "Yes, sir. He was my commanding officer in the Low Countries. Though he was a major at that time."

"Well, 'tis to your credit that—What's all this?" He flicked

Mathieson's cravat aside, renewed suspicion flaring in his eyes. "Why is your neck bleeding?"

Mathieson returned his handkerchief to the cut, but before he could comment, Miss Bradford was smiling up at the dragoon and saying earnestly, "They become quite carried away with the drama, sir. I think they should use wooden swords, do you not agree? Real swords are so very dangerous."

The captain's gaze travelled from the glossy ringlets to the little shoe that peeped from beneath her gown. His expression changed subtly. Returning her smile in a way that Mathieson found excessively revolting, he said, "You are very right, Miss Bradford. Do you appear in these plays?"

"Sometimes," she answered, dimpling at him.

"Then I shall endeavour to see a performance." He stepped closer and possessed himself of her hand. "Which way do you travel, ma'am?"

She hesitated, and attempted to pull away, but he held her hand tighter. "We continue northward, Captain Lake."

"Alas. And my way leads to the south. However," he moved even closer, " 'tis not out of all reason that I might be able to—"

"Come and watch us?" intervened Mathieson heartily. "Indeed we hope you may, sir. 'Tis always a pleasure to have a real gentleman lend dignity to our proceedings."

The captain regarded him with a marked diminution of approval, but released the girl's hand. "It would be interesting to know sir, why a man of your background would travel with these people."

"Necessity, alas," said Mathieson with a sigh. " 'Tis not a life any of us would choose, but hunger is a stern taskmaster and Mr. Bradford was so kind as to accept me into his company."

"Not a matter of kindness, dear boy." Bradford's eyes were rather wide, but he carried it off nicely, patting Mathieson on the back and beaming at him. "Roland frequently plays our hero, sir. Much to the delectation of the fair ladies in the audience."

"I see." More scornful than impressed, Lake asked, "And are you prepared, Captain, to pledge me your word as an officer and servant of the Crown that there is no involvement with rebels here?"

A cold finger seemed to touch Mathieson. He was very sure

now that Lady Ericson, the Bradfords, and this whole motley crew were either Jacobites or Jacobite sympathizers. If he swore that they were innocent and they were later arrested, it would surely put his head on the block. On the other hand, it looked as though he might, by a roundabout road, have come closer to MacTavish. The point now was whether the prize was worth the risk . . .

"Jacobites?" he said, all innocent incredulity. "Jove, but we want no truck with that scurvy crew. Our sole concern is with entertaining the populace."

"We are loyal subjects of the king, sir," struck in Bradford, indignant. "Of what do you suspect us, pray?"

"An I suspected you in the slightest degree, Mr. Bradford, I'd have the whole lot of you clapped up until we came at the truth—one way or another! That Captain Mathieson vouches for you is good enough for me. At the moment. Nonetheless, should you be stopped again, you will be well advised to make sure that no rebs are skulking in your company." The officer stamped over to mount the tired horse a trooper held for him. "Unless, of course," he finished grimly, "you value the traitor more than your own heads." He reined around. "I shall hold you accountable, Mathieson. Take care you—"

"Captain! Captain!" His voice squeaking with excitement, and his accent pure Welsh, a trooper raced from one of the caravans. "Look ye at what I do ha' found, sir!" He waved his hands. From each clenched fist hung ropes of glowing pearls, chains of gold, pendants that glittered with diamonds, and precious stones.

'Oh, God!' groaned Mathieson mentally. 'Now I've lost it before I found it, and I'm going to be shot for not having revealed it!'

There was an instant of stunned silence. The dragoon captain, his eyes starting from his head, flung himself from the saddle. "Damme, but we've got the dirty traitorous dogs,' he exclaimed, sabre flashing into his hand.

"Avast ye lubber!" Leering villainously, Mervyn Bradford lurched forward. "Steal me pirate gold, will ye?"

Mathieson's narrowed eyes darted to the girl. Her father had evidently lost whatever wits he might have had, but somehow, she must be got out of this damnable bog. To his surprise, Fiona gave a little trill of mirth.

Lady Ericson said, "Oh, pray do not, Captain Lake. Our trinkets cost a pretty penny, and we lose enough to pickpockets who fancy them to be real gems."

The captain, who had faced Bradford, his sabre ready, scowled and hesitated.

'Very neat,' thought Mathieson.

Grinning broadly, Bradford said, "Sir, 'tis nought but a chest full of fairings. We use them in our pirate farce."

The officer put up his sabre, took a pearl necklace from the trooper's hand, bit it, and peered at it narrowly.

Mathieson watched Fiona Bradford. If she was afraid, she hid it admirably. As for her sire, he appeared about to explode with mirth. Faith, but one could not admire the gentleman. My lady also looked slyly amused. Freemon Torrey had recovered his poise, but he was still pale and as if aware of it, stepped back from the firelight.

For once in his life praying that he had not come upon Prince Charlie's treasure, Mathieson watched Lake.

"Peel!" snarled the captain, and flung the pearls from him.

The man was in a proper rage. He'd find some outlet for it, was he not provided a graceful escape route. Mathieson provided one. "I'll have to admit I made the same mistake as the trooper, sir. For a minute or two I really thought I'd found the Stuart treasure. I fancy for a knowledgeable man those trumperies are easy enough to detect."

"Glass, and poor imitations at that," said the captain scornfully, tossing down a "ruby" necklace and a "diamond" pendant. "Restore this 'treasure' to the pirate's chest, trooper. And try to be less guillible in future."

His face rather red, he stalked to his horse looking neither to right nor left, flung into the saddle and with a wave of one gauntletted hand led his covertly grinning men from the clearing. Torrey sniggered audibly as the man who had discovered the "treasure" ran from the caravan and followed the troop.

Lady Ericson hissed, "Quiet!"

The hoofbeats faded into silence. For a few seconds nobody moved, then Miss Bradford said anxiously, "Come, Captain Mathieson, and we will tend that cut. I wish—"

Cuthbert flung out a detaining hand.

Freemon Torrey whipped out his rapier and held it levelled at Mathieson's throat. "I think not, Fiona!" he said loudly.

"If you thought at all, you would keep your voice low!" Lady Clorinda's fierce eyes swept the small crowd. "Alec—make sure the soldiers have gone, and set Japhet to keep watch for us."

The young Scot nodded and hurried off, calling to a red-headed youth of about seventeen who had stayed by the horses throughout all this.

My lady regarded Torrey's dramatic stance with faint disgust. Flushed but defiant, he continued to hold his sword steady, and Mathieson made no attempt to step clear. My lady gave a slight shrug. "We will all speak softly, if you please. Captain Mathieson, some explanations, sir."

"But—Grandmama," Fiona protested, "he helped us!"

Solemn-faced, the others closed in around them. A quiet but determined circle that left Mathieson in no doubt but that his life hung in the balance.

"Firstly," said my lady, chin out and eyes flashing, "why were you so anxious to know the rank of that nasty captain?"

"I am known to several dragoon officers, ma'am. One or two would give much to lay hands on me."

"For what reason?"

He sent a swift glance around the ring of grim faces. "A few weeks ago," he said slowly, "I assisted a fugitive to take ship for France."

Murmurs of approval greeted this deadly admission, but the old lady's expression did not change. She was silent for a moment while the others waited, watching her with the respect that is accorded an acknowledged and proven leader. "I do not disbelieve you," she said at length. "But even if what you say is truth, it does not explain why you would pretend to be of our company."

"Because he is a spy," cried Torrey. "You heard that dragoon say he's a captain. Sent here by the army to—"

As though belatedly recovering his wits, Mathieson interrupted hotly, "I came only to reclaim the horse you people stole from me. Did you suppose I'd make no attempt to get him back?"

"He could have told the soldiers about that," Fiona pointed out. "But he very kindly did not!"

"Why not?" demanded the dark-haired saturnine individual. "Such noble forbearance isnae natural in a body, y'ken!"

"We ken that you talk too much, Gregor," said my lady

sharply. "And if Captain Mathieson wasn't aware of your birth-place before that revealing little speech, he assuredly knows it now."

"All the more reason to finish the dirty creeping—" began Torrey, advancing his rapier so that Mathieson was obliged to swing his head back to avoid being spitted.

The lisping Mr. Heywood's sword flashed out and for the second time beat Torrey's weapon aside. "The man did uth a favour! Let him talk."

"He very likely will," snarled Torrey. "To his army friends! I tell you, he knows too much!"

"And you are too quick with your steel!" cried Lady Clor-inda jabbing a finger at him. "Oblige me, sir, by putting it up. Now, sir!"

Torrey hesitated, looking angrily in search of support.

"Man, are ye daft?" growled Cuthbert. "Ye'll not challenge the Committee?"

'The Committee?' Mathieson's ears perked up. He'd heard of the small, select group who had been instrumental in spiriting many desperate fugitives to safety, and who were said to guard the treasure. Was this dainty little old lady one of their number? Surely that was unlikely. Yet if she was indeed, he had pro-gressed much farther than he'd dared hope. 'Roly, my lad,' he told himself, ' 'twill be a very great bore to journey with these busybodies, but you must endeavour to do so.'

With a muttered curse, Torrey slid his sword into its scabbard and stood glowering at Mathieson with brooding dislike.

"Thank you," said my lady ironically. "Captain Mathieson, we must have your answers at once, but I grow tired. Come with me, if you please." She rested her hand on Cuthbert's arm and he led her towards the caravan from which Fiona had come, the Bradfords walking with them, Fiona talking to her grandmother in a low, impassioned voice.

Torrey shoved Mathieson roughly and unnecessarily, since he had already started to follow. Mathieson darted a grim glance over his shoulder at the powerful young man, but said nothing, and they all fell into a small procession in my lady's wake.

The caravan was large and light green, and at some time in the past an artistic but too liberal hand had embellished the sides with twining vines and flowers, now faded. Fiona ran lightly inside, to return with a cushion which she placed on the top step, and Lady Clorinda settled herself down, ordered her skirts and petticoats, and perched there like some tiny feudal empress, with the small group gathered before her.

Mathieson's eyes flickered from face to face. Freemon Torrey stared back with scowling hostility; Bradford looked troubled in an heroic way; and the expressions of the lisping Mr. Heywood and the dark, gaunt Scot, Gregor, reflected a sober withholding of judgment. Cuthbert betrayed no emotion whatsoever, and the younger Scot—Alec—had not yet returned. In addition to my lady and her granddaughter there were two other females, the plump dark girl with the long ringlets who had been stirring the cooking pot when first he arrived, and the woman who had been peeling the potatoes; tall, middle-aged, with a careworn face and sad blue eyes. Both of them looked upon him with interest, and he was confident there would be help from that quarter, should it come to a vote in which they were permitted to participate. The girl, he noted, had a singularly sweet expression, a ruddy, full-lipped mouth and big dark eyes, and her figure was lush and enticingly—

"You are no fool, Mathieson." Lady Clorinda's high-pitched voice cut through his reflections. "You have reached a conclusion?"

He looked at her levelly. "My lady, I'd be a fool had I not. You are either Jacobites or Jacobite sympathizers. This acting business is, I think, a screen for whatever it is you really are about."

There was no consternation at this, although the dark girl looked scared and Torrey muttered explosively under his breath.

Lady Clorinda leaned forward. "If you knew that much, you have properly put your head in jeopardy by lying to the soldiers."

"I am aware, ma'am."

"A fearful risk to take," said Bradford, gravely distinguished.

Lady Clorinda murmured, "And a sensible man does not take fearful risks without he has a compelling reason."

This morning, Mathieson had seen a dreaming look of tenderness soften the old lady's shrewd bright eyes. Unless he was much mistaken, she had been a great beauty in her day, probably with her share of *affaires de coeur*. In his experience, time did not dim the romance in a lady's heart any more than the twinkle in a gentleman's eye. And he knew just how to manipulate romantical ladies. This particular lady was deeply fond of her granddaughter . . . He allowed his eyes to drift to Miss Fiona. How anxiously the chit watched him. Smitten. Yes, there was no doubt she was smitten, which might be useful. He gazed at her for a moment, with just the right touch of wistfulness, saw the uncertain smile curve her lips, and, aware that my lady had missed not an instant of the little byplay, acknowledged, "*Very* compelling."

There came a sudden rush of colour to the girl's cheeks and the thick lashes drooped shyly. 'Oh, nicely done,' he thought. 'Or was that pure innocence?'

Freemon Torrey had also missed nothing of the interchange, and although he did not comment, his hand dropped to caress his sword hilt, and his eyes said very much indeed.

"Favour us with this so compelling reason, sir," growled Cuthbert.

"Actually, there are several," Mathieson explained, not altogether fallaciously. "I myself take small interest in politics, but I number some of your, ah—colleagues among my close friends."

"For instance?" demanded my lady.

"For instance—a fellow named Carruthers, and a fugitive who called himself Lascelles."

Bradford smothered an oath and Cuthbert started visibly. Lady Clorinda's eyes widened, but she said nothing.

"Also," continued Mathieson, "I am favoured with the friendship of a regular blockhead, by name Anthony Farrar, whose affianced bride wangled a promise from me that fairly forbids I should inform against such as—yourselves." He shrugged and gave them his wry, winning smile. "Wherefore I am, you see, unable to betray you even did I wish to do so. And, to say truth, I have no slightest desire to betray anyone to the—er, peculiarities of military justice. Perhaps I was unwise in telling the dragoons I am a member of your troupe, although it seemed to answer at the moment, but I'll be glad to travel with you for a while, in case Captain Lake should feel driven," he smiled at Fiona, "to find you again."

"No!" objected Torrey. "Lady Ericson says he is dangerous, and a soldier of fortune, which is why we snabbled his horse and sent him off on a wild goose chase."

95

Mathieson caught his breath and his head jerked around to Lady Clorinda. She frowned irritably, but did not interrupt.

"What if he is also a damned bounty hunter?" Torrey went on. "We've seen how quick-witted the fellow is! Heed the lies and fustian he tells and we all might pay with our heads!"

Several voices were raised in endorsement of this remark. The stern faces become sterner. The lives of these men and women were at risk every hour of every day. The slightest threat must be harshly dealt with were they to survive. It was a philosophy Mathieson could understand, but that very understanding told him his chances had diminished.

Cuthbert growled, "Ma'am, I'm not one for unnecessary killing, but—we must protect our own lives—and our mission."

"Aye," struck in Torrey eagerly. "Do you not see, my lady, that this fellow is the slippery type? With that pretty face and his beguiling ways, he needs no flute to charm a serpent. He thinks that by travelling with us, he'll learn something of real value, and once he does—may the Lord help us!"

Mathieson drawled, "That would depend on what you term 'real value.' "

"The location of the Jacobite treasure, for instance," jeered Torrey. "Or—the real identity of the gentleman who calls himself Ligun Doone. *That* would be a good saleable item, eh? How much would you get for selling *his* head?"

Mathieson's fists clenched hard, and a glint came into his eyes. Ligun Doone had not been heard from of late, but not long after the Battle of Culloden that intrepid gentleman had run the English victors a merry dance. Dozens of fugitives had been spirited away from under their noses; wounded rebels had been helped and hidden until they were well enough to be carried off to safety in France. Vital cyphers concerning the disposition of the Jacobite treasure had been sent out and safely delivered. And all accomplished without the loss of any more English lives, for Doone was known to believe there had been too much of death in this bitter struggle. Despite threats and intimidation, Doone's fame had spread, his courage and brilliance heartening the crushed populace as much as it infuriated the occupation forces. Enraged and outwitted, the notorious Duke of Cumberland had offered a huge reward for information that would lead to Doone's capture, but until the day he had vanished from the scene, not one single farthing of that reward had been claimed. Still the reward posters flaunted their message, and now, always hopeful of making an example of the man who had thumbed his nose at oppression and cruelty, the military had raised the ante: Ligun Doone's brave head was currently worth an unprecedented Six Hundred Guineas; a fortune, in any man's language.

"Do you say," murmured Mathieson, "that *you* are aware of Doone's real identity?"

Torrey grinned and said tauntingly, "Eager, ain't you? But your advice is wasted, Mathieson, for I do *not* know. In point of fact, Doone's identity is known to only one of us here! What d'you think of that, master greed?"

"I think you are a liar, sir."

With a cry of rage Torrey lunged for him.

Mathieson timed it to a nicety, ducked under the flailing fist, and his left came up short and sharp. Torrey shot backward faster than he had advanced and sat down hard.

Gregor whipped out his dagger and sprang forward.

As swiftly, Heywood stepped in front of Mathieson and snapped in an unexpectedly commanding voice, "Let be! Torrey earned that."

Mathieson lifted both hands slightly in the timeless gesture of surrender. "Your pardon, Lady Clorinda, but a man can take just so much. And I spoke nought but truth. There are now *two* here who are aware of the valiant Mr. Doone's real name!"

There were no comments. Indeed, his words seemed to have turned everyone to stone. It was my lady who broke the silence. "I'll admit I would liefer believe you are sincere, than be obliged to agree with Torrey. But I'll not have my people betrayed to the bloody block and axe, nor racked and tortured. If you can prove what you say—you'd best do so. If not—heaven help you, for I'll not protect you further!"

Mathieson moved closer and bent to a whisper so that she alone could hear.

She gave a smothered cry and threw a hand to her throat, staring at him wide-eyed.

"Is it? Oh, is he right?" asked Fiona anxiously.

My lady pulled herself together. "He is perfectly right."

"Is he, by God!" gasped Cuthbert.

Clambering to his feet, one hand pressed to his reddening jaw, Torrey growled, "He likely discovered it by chance! What difference does it make?"

"It makes a muckle difference, mon—as ye'd see had ye a single brrrrain in yer head," said Gregor.

"Indeed it does!" Lady Clorinda's eyes were fixed on Mathieson's face. "Only a handful of us know Doone's true identity. Lord help you if ever the military discover you know it, for they'd flay you alive, and a man can only hold out against the torture for a time."

He said quietly, "Or die, ma'am."

Torrey clapped his hands and jeered, "We have indeed found ourselves an actor! If ever I heard such dramatics! He admits that he's not in sympathy with the Jacobite Cause. Yet he would have us believe he is willing to die rather than betray a man for whom he likely feels no admiration—no allegiance! Fustian!"

Mathieson eyed Torrey thoughtfully but addressed his reply to Lady Ericson. "I owe no allegiance whatsoever to Doone. But I admire him. And—a gentleman does not break his given word."

It was said without bravado, and several murmurs of approval were heard.

"Very well, Roland," said my lady with the hint of a smile. "Since you know who Doone is, and have not claimed the reward, I have no alternative but to judge you a friend. Will you tell us now to what extent you are involved with Doone? Or how you came by your knowledge?"

He had to sternly suppress an urge to laugh. What if he told her the truth? 'Why, ma'am, I was hired by greedy men to arrange his murder, but unfortunately, my ambush failed . . . !' That would wipe away the friendly grins he now saw. By God, but it would! The laugh within him died. Ligun Doone—alias Lord Geoffrey Delavale—had accepted the word of honour of Roland Mathieson to keep his deadly secret. Knowing what manner of man he dealt with, Doone had yet been so unwise as to entrust his life to that dishonored and discredited individual.

"Three months back," Mathieson said slowly, "Doone and I were involved in a little, er—fracas. I discovered his dual identity by chance, and he knew me well enough to rely on my silence." He met Lady Clorinda's eyes levelly. "I wish, ma'am, you could see your way clear to do the same and allow me to journey with you."

"Why, Mathieson?" demanded Cuthbert, but with a note of respect now in his voice. "Ours is dangerous work."

Mathieson grinned. "I like a lazy outdoor life. Especially . . ." he glanced again at Fiona, "with such pleasant companions. Besides, I always had a fancy to tread the boards."

A laugh went up. My lady declared her own willingness to allow Captain Mathieson to join the group and asked for any nays. There were none, even the bitter-eyed Torrey remaining silent.

Mr. Heywood pointed out, "I think we owe the gentleman our gratitude."

Suddenly, they were all eager to shake his hand and wish him well. It was a novel experience. Pleasant, just for a change, even if it was nonsense. But, in an odd way, disquieting.

The green caravan was larger than the one Fiona had occupied, and the end section was curtained off, presumably to hold clothing. The bunks were arranged as in Bradford's vehicle, two on one wall, and a single one on the other. There was also a narrow highboy, and a solitary wooden chair.

Fiona lit two candles set in wall sconces, and Mathieson was divested of his coat and cravat and required to occupy the chair. My lady had intended to tape a dressing over the shallow cut high on his shoulder, while questioning her patient about his association with Ligun Doone. She had no sooner bathed the wound, however, than she was summoned by Cuthbert, and with a speculative look at Mathieson, went out promising to send Moira to help.

"I think it was unforgivable of them to doubt you so," said Fiona, gently spreading a salve over the injury. "Tilt your head just a little, please."

"You are very kind, ma'am," he murmured, complying. "It was, after all, only natural for them to be extreme careful. I cannot fault them for mistrusting me. Indeed, they would have been foolish not to have done so."

"Then I must be very foolish," she said, "for I have no doubts of you whatsoever."

Rather touched, he watched her as she taped a bandage over the cut. She was concentrating on her task and seemed neither flustered by his scrutiny, nor shy because she ministered to a gentleman in his shirtsleeves. Truly the least affected chit he had ever met. Her hands were incredibly gentle and she had a very graceful way with them, as he'd noticed before. He was reminded with sudden horrible clarity of his treatment at the hands of Madame in that ghastly Flanders hut, and he shuddered involuntarily.

At once Fiona bent to peer anxiously into his face. "Oh, I am so sorry. Did I hurt you?"

He smiled. "Not at all." Straightening, he stayed her busy hands by the simple expedient of holding them. "Miss Fiona . . . I—hope I did not embarrass you just now."

"When?" She frowned, puzzled. "Oh—do you mean when you implied that I was the reason you wished to stay with us?"

He blinked, rather taken aback by such candour. She was looking at him with cheerful ingenuousness. Amused, he thought, 'The poor child simply does not know how to go on! Has Bradford taught her nothing of correct female behaviour?' He lifted her small warm hand to his lips and murmured as he kissed it. "Yes."

"Oh. Well don't worry, that's quite all right. If you will let me go, I can—"

He stood, pulling her to him, and gazed down into her face. "But you see," he breathed, "I don't want to let you go . . ."

"Why? Are you dizzy? In that case you should sit down, and—"

He tilted her chin. She blinked up wonderingly into the velvety dark eyes that were so ineffably tender. A wistful smile curved his sensitive mouth. He really was, she thought, almost unbearably handsome.

For his part, Mathieson was thinking that, however gauche, this chit was quite a pleasant little armful. And her skin was remarkably fine—almost translucent. The way with her mouth was oddly fetching too, and her lips were full and vivid . . . "Fiona . . ." he whispered huskily.

She gave a muffled snort, and he started, discovering belatedly that the green eyes danced with merriment, and the dimple beside her mouth was very much in evidence.

"Oh—I *am* sorry," she gurgled with not the smallest appearance of remorse. "I know I shouldn't laugh, but—really, you do it so well. Much better than when Torrey plays the hero."

Considerably shaken, he said with a marked diminution of his usual smooth expertise, "So you think I am playing a part."

"Well, of course, but there is no need, you know, whatever your real reason for wanting to travel with us."

His eyes narrowed. Was it possible that, of them all, this strange slip of a girl had seen through his deception? "My—*real* reason . . . ?" he echoed softly.

"Oh, pray do not be cross," she said, twinkling up at him. "It doesn't matter, you see. Perhaps 'tis something you cannot tell us at this moment."

"I see." He drew a deep breath. "Then you do think I have lied to you."

"Say rather, you are not telling the—the whole truth." He frowned, and the look that she could not like hardened the dark eyes and tightened his lips to a thin, rather frightening line. "But it doesn't matter," she reiterated hurriedly. "Whatever your reason, I know you would never harm us, for you are the very soul of honour. Why, I feel safer, only because you travel with us."

He did not share her feelings. She was more shrewd than he had fancied, and could well be a danger to him. Perchance she was not quite as smitten as he'd supposed. His life might well depend upon his making sure that she was suitably captivated. Easy enough of accomplishment. Smiling his tenderest smile, he drew her closer again and, running the tip of one long finger down beside her ear, said softly, "Is it *so* unbelievable, dear lady, that my reason is simply what I implied?"

"Very unbelievable," she answered, with a matter-of-fact nod. "I have had my share of beaux, Captain Mathieson, but I am not so henwitted as to believe myself the type of dasher who could attach the heart of such a one as you."

'Good God!' he thought, but fought on, murmuring fondly, "What a thing to say! And besides," he leaned closer to her lips, "you are quite . . . mistaken . . . ."

He was only a breath away from claiming those lips when she snorted again in a vain effort to muffle her mirth.

Releasing her hurriedly, he stepped back. How in the deuce could a fellow make love to a girl who giggled when he tried to kiss her? "You little imp!" he said, half laughing, half exasperated.

"Yes. I am really dreadful," she trilled, then bowed her head and folded her hands meekly.

Baffled, Mathieson watched her.

She looked up, her eyes very solemn now and her mouth prim, but with the dimple hovering ominously. "I will behave," she promised. "Do please go on. 'Tis only that it's—it's so funny to be wooed by a real rake."

Funny! "The devil! What next will you say? And who told you I am—"

"Grandmama. I am like her, you know, for I do not like swearing."

"My apologies. I should have said—'Oh, bother!' "

"Yes. It is not proper to say 'The devil!' in front of a lady."

Her eyes danced at him, and he was won to a helpless laugh.

"Grandmama bade me have a care," advised Fiona. "For she thinks you have wicked eyes, though I find them more—"

"Never mind!" He snatched up his coat and shrugged into it. "Ma'am, I assure you, my intentions are—"

The plump dark girl tripped up the steps and paused in the doorway, looking from one to the other with a questioning smile.

"Come in," called Fiona gaily. "Captain Mathieson, this lady is Miss Moira Torrey. Freemon's sister, you know. Thank you for coming, Moira, you are just in time to hear Captain Mathieson tell me of his inten—"

"Nothing of the sort, you wretch!" interrupted Mathieson, yearning to spank her.

"Oh," said Fiona, her eyes wide and innocent. "What a pity. Moira would have so enjoyed it. Are you finished, then?"

He said through his teeth. "Quite finished!" And bowing, retreated in considerable disorder, horribly conscious of the muffled squeals of laughter that followed him.

Descending the caravan steps, he overcame his ire by wondering when he would be able to have a look at the contents of the "treasure chest."

ℳ 7 ℳ

The last week, thought Fiona, had been both fascinating and worrying, mostly because of the dashing young man who now lounged against the treetrunk beside her, while she painted busily.

The weather had been idyllic for the time of year; golden, glowing days, radiant dawns and sunsets, brisk evenings and chilly nights. They had journeyed ever northward, and there had been much to do, with three performances of the play, scenic pieces to be repaired, and the endless work with harnesses and horses, wheels and axles, cooking and mending and washing and setting up and taking down their camp. But there had been time also for walking or riding together, talk and camaraderie and laughter.

She'd found it highly diverting to watch Mathieson. The poised sophisticate, obviously not accustomed to exert himself to be sociable, had struggled to subdue the boredom that would come into his eyes when Gregor prosed on and on about the politics of the Uprising, or to curtail the cynical curl of his lip when Torrey was aggressive in his loyalty to the Stuart Cause. Mathieson listened politely to Gregor, but he baited Torrey so subtly that his victim was unaware of it and would rave on in defense of his theories until the helpless laughter of the others would alert him to his own gullibility. At once his hot temper would boil over, whereupon Mathieson would confound him by apologizing so humbly as to leave his victim the choice of either laughing with the rest, or appearing a poor sportsman. Torrey made a show of taking this in good part, but Fiona had noticed a few of the glances he slanted at Mathieson when he thought himself unobserved, and she knew that he both mistrusted and disliked the newcomer.

At the opposite extreme was Mrs. Dunningan's son Japhet. His father, to whom the boy had been devoted, had been severely wounded fighting with the rebel forces at the Battle of Prestonpans, and had died a month later. Refused permission to accompany his mother on this dangerous venture, Japhet had followed anyway, and had proved so persistent in declaring his right to help, that his determination had been rewarded and he'd been allowed to become a member of the little band, assisting Cuthbert with the horses and performing many other tasks about the camp. It was inevitable that Mathieson, with his good looks and devil-may-care self-assurance, a known duellist and a former cavalry officer with several battles behind him, should win the awed admiration of the freckle-faced redhead. By the second day Fiona had begun to fear that the boy, dogging his idol's footsteps whenever possible, watching him with the eyes of hero worship, might constitute an annoyance. Mathieson however, tempered his sardonic tongue with Japhet and was amazingly patient with him. Mrs. Dunnigan, Lady Clorinda's devoted and long-time abigail, was grateful for the young gallant's tolerance and when her awkward and gangly son went into ecstasies because Captain Mathieson had volunteered to teach him some of the finer points of swordplay, the woman could not say enough of good about him.

The others warmed towards him also, for he had great charm—when he chose to use it. Thaddeus Heywood seemed especially drawn to him and his was such a warm and friendly nature, his ways so unaffected, that the two young men were very soon on a first-name basis and able to insult each other without fear of offense. Grandmama was guardedly pleased with Mathieson, Alec Pauley liked him unreservedly, as did Moira; Papa thought him a splendid fellow and a potentially good actor. Cuthbert and Gregor said nothing, but Fiona sensed they tended to side more with Torrey and distrusted Mathieson.

Her own relationship with this adventurer was another matter. There was no use denying that she found him much too attractive for her peace of mind, but she was not a fool and kept her guards up. Roland Mathieson was a threat, not because she feared him, but because she feared herself. He sought her company whenever possible, but she told herself it was only to bedevil Torrey who was already seething with jealousy. If they passed some especially lovely spot, or some pretty foal or animal or object of interest, Mathieson was eager to draw her attention to it, his magnificent black eyes would smile into hers, his voice become so gentle and persuasive that her beseiged heart would quail. She admired him beyond measure, for he was the epitome of gallantry. But she was very sure that this was for him a fleeting episode that he would forget the instant it was over. He was being kind; he scolded her as her dear brother might scold. His eyes said, "Let us share this peaceful time—let us be friends." But his eyes sometimes held a flirtatious gleam that awoke far different feelings, and she gathered her defenses, refusing to allow herself to dream impossible dreams, for she knew he thought of her as a pleasant but rather wayward child—not as a desirable woman.

They were not to move camp today, for there was a fair nearby where posters could be put up announcing their next performance. There were other things to be attended to also; things connected with their real purpose, about which she asked no questions. It was a glorious morning, and so soon as breakfast was done and the dishes were cleared away Japhet had gone eagerly to the fair, Torrey and Gregor had ridden out somewhere, and Fiona, declining her father's offer to accompany him, Mrs. Dunnigan, and Heywood to the fair also, had set herself to repaint some of the scenery damaged when rain had found its way through the caravan roof.

" 'Tis nigh eleven o'clock," observed Mathieson, who had been grumbling about all the hard work to which he was subjected. "I was up at dawn. And whilst *you* were still dreaming, *I* had already started the fires and put water on to boil, though such tasks are far beneath my dignity."

Unmoved, Fiona concentrated upon applying her paintbrush to the palm tree on the large section of the desert island.

Mathieson contemplated her drowsily. For a travelling troupe—especially, so small a troupe—to devote two caravans to scenery, costumes, curtains, properties, et cetera, he thought illogical. At least, the *ostensible* purpose was illogical. Few troupes of strolling players carried set pieces, usually conveying their scene purely by costume and the play itself, or occasionally by utilizing painted sheets or screens that could be unrolled and hung where appropriate. The pieces of scenery hauled about by the Avon Travelling Players were wooden and mounted on wheels to facilitate handling. Each piece was double-sided, with a two-inch space between the sides. He had commented that this caused the pieces to be more cumbersome and that they might better have simply painted both sides of a single piece of plywood, but Bradford explained that when they'd attempted this the scenic pieces tended to bend when hauled about and would not stand properly. "The audiences," he said solemnly, "were not impressed by a bent pirate ship, and the mood suffered." There were seven of these set pieces in all; three depicting part of the desert island on one side and the deck of the pirate ship on the other; another three portraying the exterior of the farmhouse, backed by the withdrawing room of the villainous Sir Roger's glooming mansion; and the seventh, a representation of the forward half of a royal frigate, which was attached to a rope and drawn across the stage behind the "palm trees" in the final scene, much to the excitement of their various audiences. When first he had laid eyes on these large pieces it had occurred to Mathieson that the hollow areas between the sides might actually constitute a hiding place for valuables. His eager and surreptitious investigations had proved only that the "treasure" was indeed brass and glass, and that the hollow centres of the set pieces contained nothing more exciting than air and a few cobwebs.

Fiona having offered no comment upon his grievances, he now informed her with a sigh that she was a hard-hearted woman. "Have you no sympathy for my backbreaking labours?"

She chuckled in that soft little ripple of sound he found remarkably attractive, and pointed out that they all worked hard. Mrs. Dunnigan did a great deal, but had her hands full caring for the ladies and helping with the cooking, and Japhet worked endless hours helping Cuthbert or anyone else who needed his services. "Besides," she added with a marked lack of sympathy, "to the newest member of any group falls the most onerous tasks."

"I believe you, Miss Kindliness," he said mournfully. "Your papa has also required that I practice my part in the play."

"Oh dear. Do you find *that* an onerous task, Sir Lazylump?"

"Not—entirely. There are one or two scenes that are—er, bearable." She gave a squeak of indignation. His mouth

106

twitched; he added blandly, "In fact, those are the parts I think need more rehearsal. I'm sure you will be more than willing to oblige your father by going over them with me."

She glanced at him under her lashes, well aware of both the gleam in his eyes and the fact that her cheeks were becoming heated. "Which scenes?"

"Well now, let me see . . . Ah, yes. There's the one at the beginning—"

"Scene One," she corrected.

"So you guessed, clever child!"

Of course she'd guessed! She would have wagered her garter that he would pounce on *that* particular scene! But—"No, I didn't," she denied, blushing. "I was merely providing you with the proper terms."

"Realizing that my own—terms—are quite improper?" 'And there,' he thought, 'goes that intriguing little dash of dimples again, and how very daintily she blushes!'

"But of course," she agreed provocatively. "Now what is the difficulty about Scene One?"

"It's that part where brave Captain Jack Firebrand declares himself to Beautiful Dairymaid Barbara and sweeps her into a passionate embrace."

'Naughty rascal!' thought Fiona. "But Jack is not Captain Firebrand at that time," she demurred, "and does not become so until after he is betrayed and sold into slavery."

"Later becoming the dashing scourge of the Spanish Main! Yo and ho!"

She looked up at him rather ruefully. "You think it a very bad play, do you? I suppose it *is* rather simple."

He could not like to see that downcast expression on her face, and he said quickly, "It has been my experience, Tiny Mite, that some very bad plays have been written by famous men who forgot how to be simple and tried merely to be clever, thereby boring everyone in their audience save for those who are impressed by the incomprehensible. Heywood's play is not intended to be profound. It is instead jolly good fun, and I think country folk and probably a lot of city folk will enjoy it enormously and leave the hall with a smile rather than a sigh. Not so ill an effect in these difficult times." Considerably surprised by this flow of volubility, he added, "None of which has anything to do with you and I rehearsing the scenes in which I need—ah, assistance.''

''Is very true that you lack expertise,'' she agreed, her eyes downcast.

He looked very hard at her, then said grittily, ''*Merci mademoiselle.* Now, as I recollect, we are in the withdrawing room and I seize you—''

''Well, do not,'' she interjected hastily, waving her paintbrush at him as he prepared to stand up. ''Let us try a—er, less tiresome scene.''

''Tiresome!''

''I mean one not so—active.''

''Oh. Well, the other part that I do not seem to have learned properly is the scene in Act Two in which I have escaped and must sail away and leave you.''

''Hmmnn. You mean where you bid Miss Barbara farewell and vow your undying love?''

''While pressing her to my heart, and—''

Her brush faltered. Over it, she looked at him in mild surprise. ''I do not recall that you do that.''

''You see? You too need practice. Now put down those silly paints and we can—''

The dimples flickered enchantingly. ''No, really. I must finish this.''

Mathieson groaned and lay back again. '' 'Woman's at best a contradiction still!' Though I demean myself to supplicate in an ungainly sprawl at your pretty feet, you will not aid me!''

She chuckled, but, watching all the lean unconscious grace of him, wondered if it was possible for him to be ungainly.

''Hasten, fair but heartless artist,'' he sighed. ''I await your pleasure.''

''You will wait a shorter time an you allow me to concentrate.''

''I shall be dumb.'' He closed his eyes. ''Wake me when your masterpiece is a *fait accompli*.''

''Wretch!'' She began to paint again. In a short while the palm tree was complete. She surveyed it with her head held on one side. ''How does that look, Ro—Captain Mathieson?''

He snored loudly, but when she advanced on him, paintbrush poised, he opened one eye, then sat up quickly. ''Evil child! What were your intentions, I wonder?''

"To paint the end of your nose bright green, Master Tease!"

"One masterpiece a day, Tiny Mite. Now—I am ready to view your progress . . . Turn it this way a little." He leaned back on his hands, crossed his long legs, and inspected the "palm tree." "Jolly good," he said admiringly. "But—where's its head?"

She fixed him with a stern stare. "Where is—what's head?"

"Grammar! Grammar! And besides," he pursed his lips, "I didn't think they dwelt on desert islands. Are you sure they do?"

"I am sure you are an odious man," Fiona informed him, not mincing words. "An you think my work so funny, try if you can do better!"

"I did not say 'twas funny. I merely asked if peacocks dwell on—"

"It is—*not*—a peacock! 'Tis a palm tree, as you know perfectly well, horrid creature!"

"Oh." He looked searchingly at the palm tree. "Well—now that you tell me, of course, I—"

With a squeal of indignation, she snatched up her painty rag and threw it at him. "Wretch! Evil—*actor!*"

"Oho!" he laughed, catching the rag. "The ultimate insult!"

"You are jealous! You know you could not make so fine a—"

"Stunted little weed—"

"Is *not* stunted! I stood on tiptoe to paint it, and—"

"Small wonder it looks stunted! Now if you but had a few more inches to you; say twenty or so—"

He dodged the paintbrush in the nick of time and as Fiona began to stalk away, he called, still chuckling, "Come now, Tiny Mite. Do not be a poor sportsman. You never mean to abandon me here? Suppose your great love comes upon me? I shall be most foully done to death and none to give me aid!"

She turned at this, disclosing a frown but eyes full of merriment. "I can hear your teeth chattering. But you may rest easy. Freemon will likely not return until dinner time. Now farewell, I've to help Grandmama."

"But you promised to read over those scenes with me."

"I did no such thing! Besides, 'tis more important that this be done. Do you try *your* skills at palm trees. The scenery must be dry by tomorrow in time for your debut as our Stupendously Dashing Hero."

Feigning indignation, he started up.

Fiona laughed and danced away.

Grinning, Mathieson settled back to watch the breeze billow her skirts and ruffle the soft brown ringlets tied behind her head with a broad riband of peach velvet. She was a cheerful little soul, he thought musingly, as full of mischief as she could stare, which was as well, for a lesser girl must have been crushed by fear of the danger which hung over them all. Not that she was so naive as to be unaware of their peril. Far from it. During this past week he'd learned much of Miss Fiona Bradford, as he had learned much of all the troupe members, and he knew that behind her cheerful light-heartedness there dwelt courage and resourcefulness and a deep devotion to her family.

It had not been as gruesome a period as he'd feared. For one thing, he was glad to be away from Town for a change. For another, he found the play amusing and enjoyed both watching the others at their rehearsals and the performances he had seen. As for his companions, well, they were a foolish lot, beyond doubting, but he was finding them less insufferable than he'd anticipated.

For instance, aside from his ridiculous and unending political speeches, Gregor was an expert musician and it had been quite interesting one evening when he'd discoursed knowledgeably and at length upon the origins of the bagpipes and the old Scots and Gaelic melodies. When referring to his family history, Gregor's saturnine features would become touched by sorrow and although he said little on that particular subject, one gained an impression of a tragic past that might well account for his gloomy attitude.

Pauley was as sunny-natured as Gregor was morose; open and uncomplicated, the product of a well-to-do family of shipbuilders. The large house where he had been born had been burned down during the Uprising, but instead of bewailing the fate that had destroyed his home, he was only grateful that his family was safe and well, and had cheerful expectancies of rebuilding their fortune once the treasure was distributed. Unfortunate, thought Mathieson, that he was in for a disappointment on that score, but his ebullient spirit would doubtless sustain him.

The boy, Japhet, was a confounded pest and deserved to be sent off with a flea in his ear. But he was very young. And perhaps because of his own bitter youth, Mathieson had not yet been able to bring himself to give the boy the setdown he warranted. Besides, his mother was my lady's trusted abigail, and was grateful to him for bearing with the lad. It might well be a matter of boredom invested against the possibility of some future profitable return.

He had been unable to learn much from Cuthbert. The big man was taciturn and unwilling to be friendly. He was devoted to Lady Clorinda, and that devotion appeared to extend to the Bradfords, but he said little, and to his credit seldom participated in the long-winded political discussions that would develop around the campfire in the evenings.

Mathieson was more than ever of the opinion that Freemon Torrey was not the mate for Miss Fiona. Torrey was all unrestrained impulse, fire and fury, and although it was clear he worshipped the chit, she'd be little better off as his wife than she was as the daughter of Mr. Mervyn Bradford. Worse, in fact! Bradford was as irresponsible as any stripling, true, but full of fun besides, and despite his theatrical manner there was a warmth and an underlying kindness to the man.

A much finer candidate for Fiona's hand, in Mathieson's opinion, was Thaddeus Heywood. He had in fact already dropped several hints in Heywood's ear, pointing out Miss Fiona's many attributes, and in turn had suggested to the girl that Heywood was a splendid fellow. There was a mystery somewhere in Heywood's background, but Mathieson thought he knew what it was. He had noted a slowness to respond when Heywood was called by his surname, and, suspicious, he'd experimented with the casual use of "my lord" as a form of address. Heywood had responded with immediacy and no trace either of surprise or of consciousness of the title. Very likely he was a peer using an assumed name. Further, unlike Freemon Torrey and Gregor, Heywood had little to say of the pros and cons of the Rebellion, wherefore it was doubtful that he was a Jacobite at all. Far more probably, he was one of those kind-hearted but ill-advised individuals who felt obliged to help the hounded fugitives and their unfortunate families. A failing, admittedly, but by and large he was a nice fellow, just the kind to make his chosen lady a devoted husband, and not go wandering off into little dalliances on the side. By God, but he'd better not do so! Mathieson

111

scowled. She was a sweet little chit and if she had a fondness for his lordship, he'd damned well better be good to her, or—

He sprang to his feet. *Nom de Dieu*, but this was an irritating subject! Be curst if he would have any more of it! He stamped over to the set piece and gingerly removed a fly which had committed suicide on Miss Fiona's "palm tree."

"Torrey doesn't like it." My lady turned the pages of the play and set the chair to rocking slowly. "But your papa feels we must make the change just in case Captain Lake should come up with us again, and I agree. Besides, I've a notion young Mathieson will excel in the role of Firebrand—he's a swashbuckler if ever there was one, eh?"

"Hmmnn," said Fiona, standing in the open doorway of the caravan and watching the distant Mathieson busily at work on the piece of scenery.

"Torrey says he will seek to take advantage of you on stage," my lady went on. "You must tell me at once an he does so. I've no intent for you to be made uncomfortable. As it is, for Torrey to have to watch Mathieson making love to you will likely cause more bad blood between them."

"What?" said Fiona, turning with a shocked little gasp.

My lady shook her head reproachfully. "I doubt you heard a single word." She set the play on the table and came to stand beside her granddaughter. "What is it that so fascinates—Oh." She frowned. "I see. Never form a *tendre* for that one, child. He's a pretty rogue, but a rogue for all that, and has broke more hearts than—"

"Well, he'll not break mine! Besides, Captain Mathieson thinks of me as his little sister, and is determined to bring me up properly."

My lady's jaw dropped. "To . . . what?"

"He considers Papa to have been remiss in my education," said Fiona demurely.

"Well! Of all the impertinence! How dare he presume to judge your father? Not but what he ain't perfectly right, for Bradford never has seen to your proper guidance, being quite content to allow you to mother *him*, rather than be a responsible father to *you*! But for Mathieson, of *all* men to censure—La, but I must have been all about in my head when I let him join us!"

Fiona asked pensively, "Why did you allow it, Grandmama?"

"Oh . . . curiosity, perhaps." My lady returned to her chair and said with rather a wistful sigh, "I wanted to see if he is as black as he's painted. Besides, 'twill do no harm to have another sword in case things go badly, and I'd sooner have him under my eye than . . ." She paused, then went on militantly, "But not if he is trying to fix his interest with you, miss! That I'll not stand for!"

"What do you think of Thaddeus Heywood as a husband for me, ma'am?"

Lady Ericson sat very still for a moment. Then, her tone casual but her eyes very intent she asked, "Have you a kindness for him, child?"

"I have indeed. Thaddeus is the dearest of creatures. But, I believe the poor soul has already lost his heart, Grandmama."

"Hmmnn. Did he tell you so?"

"Not in so many words. But we have talked often, and I sense an inner sorrow. Perhaps he has been rejected."

"Hah! And a prodigious silly chit to reject so prime a prize. The boy is charming, not unattractive, gentle, honourable, will never be able to spend a fourth of his fortune, and is a baron besides!" My lady's chin jutted. Eyes flashing, she muttered, "Little fool!"

Fiona's wonder at such vehemence was drowned in her deeper astonishment. "Thaddeus—*Heywood*? A peer?"

"Yes, and lud what a gabbling gossip I am! You will please to forget I've told you. Now—enlighten me pray, as to how our fine instructor means to improve you? I'll own he's had sufficient experience with the fair sex to know what he's about."

"Evidently, ma'am," said Fiona. "For I rather suspect Captain Mathieson has reached the same conclusion as you have done, and means me to marry Thaddeus."

My lady gave a slow smile. "Generous of him. But—as well perhaps, since 'twill prevent him from flirting with you himself, eh my love?"

"A gentleman does not flirt with his—little sister."

Something about her granddaughter's twinkling eyes gave my lady pause. She said suspiciously, "Now what are you about, Mistress Mischief? I have marked how you tease him, and I warn you, Roland Mathieson is a very dangerous man! Both in

113

matters of the sword and *l'amour*. By all means let him waste his efforts by playing matchmaker, if he's of a mind to do so, but tread carefully around him, child. I'd never forgive myself were you to be hurt.''

Fiona swooped down to hug her diminutive grandmama and plant a kiss on the rouged cheek. ''Never fear, dearest. I am not so gauche but what I've learned that one always allows the gentlemen their little games.'' She started down the steps and at the foot glanced back and said over her shoulder, ''Is so much fun to watch them blunder about, poor dears, and then point out the error of their ways!''

''Why not?'' demanded Mathieson, sitting on the grass beside the table and frowning up at Miss Bradford.

''Because,'' she said, stirring busily at the large bowl, ''I must make these.''

The afternoon sun woke golden gleams in her hair, especially on one little curl that danced above her temple. Watching this curl, he complained, ''You always find something that *must* be done. I want to show you what I have accomplished with your peacocks. Is a lovely afternoon; your light o'love is away, and—''

''Freemon Torrey is not my light of love, sir!'' She waved her spoon at him. ''But an you do not stop aggravating him, there will be blows struck, and—''

''There have already been blows struck. Faith, but were I not such a trusting soul, I'd begin to suspect the gentleman don't like me.''

She looked at him sharply, saw the laughter in the dark eyes, and was won to a smile, but said, ''I am serious, Roly.''

''Captain Mathieson,'' he corrected primly. ''Which is the very thing I want to talk about.''

''My manners, do you mean?'' She glanced around the meadow. ''Surely we do not have to stand on ceremony now that we are alone.''

Had any of Mathieson's *chères amies* uttered so encouraging a remark under such circumstances, he would immediately have turned it to good account. But not one of his lady loves would have said it in just that particular fashion. There was no flutter of eyelashes, no coquetry, no come-hither look. Fiona beamed at him, all innocence.

In return, he frowned at her. "An you say things like that to Freemon Torrey, 'tis small wonder he fancies himself in love with you."

"Goodness me!" She rubbed her nose, thus leaving the tip white with flour. "I only said—"

"To tell a gentleman he need not stand on ceremony with you when you are alone together," he pointed out severely, "is a very improper remark, *ma belle*. And you've put flour all over your nose."

She lifted her apron to wipe the offending item, but her gown was caught up also and revealed a delicately formed little ankle. "Is that better?" she asked meekly.

"Much!" replied Mathieson, grinning. With an effort he tore his attention from the revelation. Flour now adorned her left ear. "No. Lord! Don't do that! Tidy your dress, do!"

Her second attempt to repair the damage had all but shown him her knees. Bewildered, she glanced down at the area that usually claimed the attention of the gentlemen.

"Not there," he said, exasperated. "Your skirts! Gad, but our hot-blooded Torrey would be beside himself!"

"Oh." She restored her gown, smiled at him sunnily and said, "Then how fortunate I am that you are so cold-blooded."

He came to his feet with supple ease and advanced purposefully.

"I thought you meant—here." Fiona gave herself a little pat, leaving flour all over her creamy bosom.

To all intents and purposes, they really were alone. Cuthbert and Lady Ericson were in her caravan, poring over some papers which Mathieson would have given much to see, and Alec, badly smitten with the shy Moira, was helping her shell peas and had eyes for no other.

Despite this however, Mathieson glanced about carefully, then shoved his handkerchief at her. "Dust yourself, child."

She wiped without much effect at her nose and when he shook his head and pursed up his lips, she sighed and gave him back his handkerchief. "Am I making it worse? Well, you do it for me, please."

He obliged with frowning concentration. It was a ridiculous nose. So tiny. Very much like Lady Clorinda's. Of course, Lady Clorinda had been a great beauty, whereas this exasperating chit . . . He paused, gazing down at the small face so trustingly

115

uplifted. And he realized with something of a shock that Fiona *was* beautiful. Not in a classic Grecian way, perhaps. But in her own inimitable fashion she would put any classic beauty to shame. 'Her beauty,' he thought, 'comes from within. She is such a happy, caring little mite . . .' Her lips were close and vivid, and slightly parted. Even as he leaned to them they curved to a smile.

"Did you get it all?"

He started, and recollecting his task, looked her over and saw the flour on the sweetly rounded breasts. Seldom had fate offered a finer opportunity. He reached willingly to oblige, only to be thwarted by an irritating reminder of her innocence. "Here," he thrust the handkerchief at her. "You must do the—er, rest."

She dusted busily, then blew downward.

Mathieson was obliged to look away. "What," he croaked, convinced he was suffering from softening of the brain, "are you making?"

"Crumpets. 'Tis as well to cook them a little ahead of time and let them sit for a while."

Reminded of last night's dinner, he grunted unkindly, "Not so long that they become petrified, one trusts."

"You mean, like my dumplings." She sighed. "I am not the world's best cook, alas."

"You have no business cooking. You have no business being here at all! If I had my way—"

She folded her hands in front of her. "Yes, Captain Mathieson?"

He chuckled. "I'm glad to see you properly subdued."

Her smile was rather wan and once more the sight of that small troubled face awoke in him a most unfamiliar and urgent desire to brighten it. "Never look so stricken Tiny Mite. Am I being utterly ruthless?"

"No, of course you're not." She gave a forlorn gesture. "You only try to help. I know how—how clumsy I am at times, and you—"

"You are not in the least clumsy! You have a sweet and sunny nature, and if you—Well, what I mean is—I'd not have you exchange your innocence only to—" He scowled, and hesitated.

"To become a poised and properly behaved young lady? But—that is what I should be, surely? 'Tis what Papa would wish, I know. That I not behave in so—so gauche a way, I mean. And poor Grandmama quite throws up her hands over me. Is not grace and propriety what *you* would want in a lady, Roly?''

He thought of many of the ladies he knew, and his smile was twisted and mirthless. For no reason he could identify, he was irritated and impatient with her, and said with a bored shrug, "What I want has nothing to say in the matter. You must not look to me, child.''

She tilted her chin and remarked judicially. '' 'Tis difficult, I'll own.''

He grinned at that. "To look to me?''

"To look *at* you. Since we are in a critical mood, Ro—Captain Mathieson, I will admit that I could wish you were not *quite* so handsome. 'Tis rather unsettling, and although I know you are the last man to be conceited, it—'' She checked as he gave a shout of laughter. "Oh, my! There I go again! Roly, you *must* help me, or I shall surely wind up an old maid!''

"Never,'' he gasped, but his mirth faded into a scowl. "Oh, Gad! We *were* alone.''

"Picayune!'' Fiona bent to pick up the vociferous little cat. "What is it, my precious?''

"Don't believe a word that wretched animal tells you.''

"She could have only good words for you, sir. Did you not save her life? Come now, Picky—say your thanks.'' She held the cat out, and urged, "Do pray stroke her. You'll see how loving she can be.''

"I have not the faintest desire—'' he began, but the smile in the green eyes overbore his better judgment, and he reached forth a tentative hand. "Ow!''

"Oh, dear!'' Fiona set the cat down hurriedly. "Did she bite hard?''

"Hard enough! Dratted little pest. I wish I'd hit her this morning!''

"With the brick?''

"Brick? The de-deuce!'' The dimple was peeping slyly at him. Fascinated by it, he muttered, "With my colichemarde, rather. I've a fancy for a fur cap.''

She laughed merrily. "Oh, what a rasper! 'Twas an apple core, merely. And thrown wide, at that.''

"How do you know, Miss Sauce? And you should not use cant terms.''

"Because I saw you, pseudo-rascal. And later, Thaddeus was laughing about it with my papa." She crossed to the fire and began to ladle spoonfuls of the mix onto the smoking griddle slung above it. "He said Picayune was in your boot when you put it on, and she became a proper pincushion, which—ah, upset you."

"The foul little brute tore my foot to shreds, if you care to know of it. But," he added sardonically, "pray do not grieve so."

She giggled irrepressibly. "Thaddeus said you howled like a banshee."

He stood and wandered over to hold the bowl for her. "Did he indeed? You may be sure I'll repay him!"

"But of course. Probably by handing him over for summary execution."

The carefree words were sobering and his jaw set. How glibly they chatted. As though there were no shadows over this golden afternoon. No shadow of block and axe. No shadow of the hoard of gold he meant to wrest from them for his own uses. This trusting child would find out about him then . . . by God, but she would! And what matter if she did? It was as well. She was *too* trusting by half, and the sooner she learned how cruel life could be, the better. Everyone had to grow up and face reality sooner or later.

"Oh, I am a horrid girl!" Fiona was gazing at him in dismay. "I was only funning! Truly, I did not mean it!" In her anxiety to make amends she rested her hand upon his arm. "I know you like Thaddeus."

"Yes, as a matter of fact I do. As I've said, he would make you a good husband." His smile bland, he enquired, "Should you like that?"

"Do you really think there might be a hope for me in—" she blinked up at him, "—in that direction?"

"*Hope* for you? Why the devil should there *not* be hope for you? Only say the word and I'll—"

"Force him to the altar at sword's point?"

"Scarcely. Could you—er, like Heywood in—in that particular way?"

She tilted her head in the grave fashion she sometimes affected. "I think he is the dearest gentleman, though I'd not perhaps considered him as a husband. How very good of you to

118

point out to me that he would make a nice one. Perhaps you would be so kind as to discover from him if—"

Good Gad, did she expect him to arrange the match for her? His temper flared. He snapped, "Lord, I scarce know the man!"

"But—you just said—"

"I was making a suggestion, merely. If you fancy the fellow, desire your father to—ah, look into matters a trifle."

"What matters?" She asked anxiously, "You never think there is something—unsavoury about Thaddeus?"

"*Mon Dieu!* Have I said it? I merely—Madam, *I'm* not your papa!"

She trilled a laugh. "Don't be silly! Of course you're not. But how can I ask Papa to speak to the gentleman if I don't even know that he is interested in me?"

"He is." Mathieson scowled at a passing ladybird. "I've chatted with him about you, and—"

Fiona squeaked with excitement. "Oooh! How good you are! How *very* kind and good! But still—if there is that about his character which disturbs you . . . I have no objection to his lisp, you know. After all, a girl who dwells in a caravan cannot have the expectations of a diamond of the first water." She raised limpid eyes to his. "But of course, you know all about that."

She looked so guileless, so innocent. But—was she? Or was she laughing at him? He decided that this was unlikely. Women might smile at Roland Fairleigh Mathieson, but they did not laugh at him. "Faith, but you cannot expect me to say that you are not a diamond of the first water," he said silkily.

"No, for you are much too well bred to say something so unkind. But you know all about such creatures, and—and high flyers and opera dancers too, I daresay."

Disconcerted by this candid response, he clapped a hand to his brow and groaned, "You should not even speak of such matters, much less accuse a gentleman of knowing all about 'em, you impossible child."

"Why not? You do. Grandmama said you do."

He stiffened and said icily, "Did she indeed! 'Tis surprising that Lady Ericson would address such a remark to a brat who has not been much about the world."

"Why are you getting all starched up? Besides, I *have* been about the world! I've been to France and Portugal and Spain and been chased by brigands and I shot one though I don't think I hurt him very much because he came that night and serenaded me under my window. Most dreadfully off-key,'' she added, her brow wrinkling critically.

Mathieson's ire was banished. His eyes alight with amusement, he suggested, "Perhaps he was taking his revenge."

"Perhaps he was. Poor man. Papa emptied the water pitcher over him." Her musical little laugh blended with his deep one. "Enough of my singing brigands," she persisted. "Tell me of the dark secret in Mr. Heywood's past that renders him ineligible."

"Wretched Mite," he said, still chuckling. "I know nothing of the gentleman save that I rather doubt Heywood is his true name. And I'm sorry to have to advise that your crumpets are all breaking into holes!"

"Just as they should, sir. But I must hurry. Would you please spread that linen towel on the table and bring the slice? Quickly!" She turned back to dole out more spoonfuls and asked, "What did you mean about Mr. Heywood's name?"

"Only that he sometimes forgets to answer to it." He sought about on the table. "Not that 'tis any of my affair. Likely he seeks to protect himself, which is understandable, heaven knows. I cannot find your confounded article! Slice of what?"

"Good gracious, how could you not know? A slice is a flat, thin-bladed kitchen tool."

"Alas for my ignorance," sneered Mathieson.

"Don't pout."

He checked, glancing up at her with brows elevated.

The bored look on the handsome face was a challenge. She twinkled at him. "Tit for tat. You correct my naughty ways, so you must allow me the same privilege."

He grinned at that and murmured seductively, "I will allow you any privilege you desire, lovely Mite."

"Aha, the rake is come back. What fun!"

Shaking his head at her, he took up the slice. "This, *Madame la chef*?"

"Yes, that's it! Now hurry and turn over the crumpet on the end, if you please."

He drew back. "What? Me? Roland O—Mathieson, dedicated villain, man of fashion, and et cetera."

"O'Mathieson?" she echoed, curious.

"A slip of the tongue, merely."

"You're quite sure?" Her quivering little grin quizzed him. "You *do* know your own name?"

"Very well, ma'am. Depending upon which one I chance to affect at the time."

For an instant her eyes searched his face. It was tranquil now and unreadable. She scoffed, "Prankster! Come now, dedicated villain, man of fashion, and kitchen maid's helper. Turn over the end crumpet if you please! *Vite, monsieur! Vite!*"

Wielding the slice, he approached the crumpet gingerly, almost dropped it but succeeded in turning it and was at once inordinately proud. "Excelsior! Is there no end to my talents?"

Fiona put down the bowl and clapped her hands, amused by the boyish enthusiasm of this man who usually seemed the epitome of poise and sophistication. "Well done! Oh, well done!"

He offered a flourishing bow.

"I shall give your grandfather an accounting of your progress," said my lady, who had come up unobserved to watch this domestic little scene. "I see Fiona has you in training, Roland. But she must do without you. I need some ink. You shall have to ride into the village for me."

"Madam! Would you deprive me of this invaluable course in crumpeting?" And, demonstrating his newly acquired technique for her, he went on gaily, "Seriously, my lady, may I not finish here, and then ride with Miss Fiona into the village?"

Lady Clorinda looked for a long moment into his smiling countenance and unreadable eyes. "By all means," she said.

Mathieson was jubilant and Fiona gave a little jump of delight. But, walking away, my lady was frowning.

"You don't think they will spoil, sitting there on that towel?" asked Mathieson, his thoughts still with the neatly spread crumpets that waited at the campsite. "I did not slave over a hot fire all day only to have my culinary masterpieces ruined!"

Fiona guided her little bay mare closer to the tall chestnut. "In all my experience with crumpets, I have never known a failure."

"How many times have you made them?"

"We were discussing Thaddeus, I believe," she evaded mischievously. "You may be right about his using an assumed name. I wonder if that is why he is so sad."

He shook his head at her. "Pish! You imagine it, romantic child."

"And you only say that to keep me from worrying."

"Now why in the name of creation should you worry about him? You'd not considered him as a matrimonial prospect until I suggested it."

"I worry about the people I like, even if I do not mean to marry them. And don't pretend to be hard and cold, sirrah, for you cannot deceive me. He is your friend, and you worry about him too, because, being the type of man you are, you could not do otherwise."

He thought, 'Could I not?' And said with the sneer she so disliked, "I cannot afford friends, ma'am. And if 'tis because of *your* friends that you are involved in this particular mess, you'd be better off without 'em."

Briefly, she was silent. Then, she said slowly, " 'Tis because of Francis."

"Your brother? Ah! He was a reb, then?"

She did not answer, but regarded him with unwonted gravity.

"Gad," he exclaimed. "What a clod! Forgive. *Vraiment*, I never said it!"

She smiled faintly. "Are you French, Roly?"

"My mother was. Do I speak the language often? Deplorable habit."

"I find it not at all deplorable; and you seldom speak it, but when you do, your accent is *sans reproche*. She was beautiful, no?"

The hard look in the dark eyes eased. He said in a low voice quite different from his customary drawl, "She was exquisite."

"And you loved her very much. Then that would explain it."

"What would it explain?"

"Why, that you are always so very gallant to ladies."

Mathieson thought of Penelope Montgomery. He looked away quickly, and because guilt was an unfamiliar emotion, squirmed uneasily in the saddle, and spurred with unaccustomed force.

Rumpelstilskin gave a surprised snort, reared, and was off like a thunderbolt, charging up and over the brow of the hill even as Fiona, also surprised, brought the mare to a gallop.

Vaguely, Mathieson had been aware of a distant turmoil. He

was aghast, however, to find himself plunging full tilt into an angry crowd, sending people scattering right and left. "What— the devil!" he cried, belatedly trying to quiet the nervously rearing stallion.

"Don't ye go for to interfere now, drat 'ee!" shouted a fierce little old man in smock and gaiters, brandishing a walking cane threateningly.

"Nay, we doan't need no furriners stickin' of their noses into our business," cried a burly villager.

Mathieson saw then the ducking stool at the side of the pond, and the wretched woman who sagged, half-drowned, against the iron band that held her in that cruel instrument of torment.

"Get ye gone!" shrilled a fat woman, shaking her apron at him.

Several men seized the see-saw-like beam to which the sturdy wooden chair was attached and began to tilt it so that "stool" and victim sank into the pond.

The old woman screamed piteously for mercy but none was given and her head came ever closer to the murky water.

"Now, see here," began Mathieson, indignantly, as the crowd re-formed about him.

Another thunder of hooves and they scattered once more as Fiona rode towards them. "How splendid of you," she said, turning a look of glowing admiration upon Mathieson. "I wondered what you heard to send you away at such a rate."

She was at it again! "I did not—" he began.

"Stop," she cried furiously, riding into the throng. "Pull her up at once!"

The villagers were in an angry mood and showed no inclination to stop, continuing to force their sobbing victim down until the dark waters closed over her head, while they shouted defiance at the girl.

'This,' thought Mathieson, 'could be ugly.' He guided Rumpelstiltskin forward. With loud cursing and desperate scramblings the crowd retreated before the big horse.

"Miss Bradford!" shouted Mathieson. "We must get—"

"She do be a witch!" A burly villager who wore a wig that made Mathieson shudder tugged at the pole and the stool surfaced, water streaming from it, the woman choking frenziedly. "Ye doesn't hold wi' witches, does ye, me fine gent?"

"Fiona," said Mathieson, eyeing the old creature uneasily. "We would do well to—"

"Yes, and we will," she declared, her voice ringing with zeal. "How dare you so abuse the poor soul?" She slid from the saddle, and ran to release the bar which confined the hapless victim. "Come, ma'am, and—"

Momentarily awed by such high-handedness, the crowd had fallen silent. Now, the fat woman shrilled, "Oo be she to come a'telling of us what us mayn't do? That old hag overlooked me prize sow, and the whole litter was stillborn! Ducking's too good fer the likes o' Jane Shadwell! Don't ye listen to these fancy folk wi' their long noses! Jane be possessed, I tell ye, and must be ducked till the evil spirits leave her!"

Roaring endorsement for these proper sentiments, the crowd surged forward.

There is a well-known maxim that a man would do better to stand alone against the might of a Roman legion than to face a crowd of enraged British rustics. Well aware of this, Mathieson dismounted in a leap, and took Fiona's arm. "Dear Mite, really we cannot—"

"I agree," she said grimly, and jabbed her little gold-handled knife at the burly man who grabbed for the failing woman she supported. The burly one yowled and swung up a clenched fist. "Ye stabbed me! Ye danged little bitch!"

Mathieson froze and his lips tightened into a thin line. One hand whipped Fiona aside; with the other he struck hard and true. The deplorable wig sailed from the head of the burly man, and drifted into the pond after him.

As Mathieson had foreseen, this action failed to please the mob. Shouts of rage were augmented by the sudden appearance of cudgels. Stones began to fly.

"Ye Gods and little fishes!" He dragged Fiona behind him, and whistled shrilly. A rock struck home above his eye and sent him reeling back, but already a ringing neigh was transcending the howls of the villagers. The crowd split before a chestnut fury that reared and bucked and spun, hooves flailing, big teeth bared and snapping busily. Shouts became shrieks. Men and women ran for their lives.

"Here . . . Rump!" wheezed Mathieson. Snorting, the stallion danced to his side. Mathieson seized Fiona and threw her into the saddle. "Go!"

She grabbed the reins but sent Rumpelstiltskin spinning again. "No! Not without her!"

The old woman had sunk to her hands and knees and was coughing and spluttering helplessly. With a groan of revulsion, Mathieson lifted her. Despite the fact that she was tall, she was skin and bone and weighed very little, and it required no great effort to hoist her up behind Fiona. The crowd, thwarted and ugly, was re-forming. He slapped Rump on the flank, and the big horse was away, ignoring Fiona's desperate efforts to halt him.

Mathieson made a dash for the bay mare, but the villagers, normally gentle and peace-loving, were inflamed now by the mindless violence of the mob and surged in to cut off that way of escape. "Blast!" he muttered, and crouched, the dagger whipping into his left hand, the sword into his right. Momentarily, the glitter of cold steel gave pause to the villagers but only momentarily, for they were many and he but one. The burly man dragged himself from the pond and brought a good-sized stone with him. He heaved it with power and accuracy and as their target staggered, the others were encouraged and the hail of rocks began in earnest. Mathieson threw up one arm to protect his head and gave a gasp as a well-aimed missile smashed home against his wrist. The dagger fell from his numbed hand and his arm dropped helplessly. The angry crowd sent up a roar of delight as another rock drove him to his knees.

Their enraged, hate-filled faces began to blur before his eyes. He thought dimly, 'Dammitall, this is what I get for abandoning my principles . . .'

The shot was deafening. Swaying dizzily forward to the support of his right hand, Mathieson heard the clear, girlish voice as from a distance.

"You are behaving like skulking cowards, instead of honourable Englishmen! The first one brave enough to throw a rock at that most gallant gentleman will be shot. In the tummy, I think, though I cannot be sure, for my aim is not very good and I might accidentally shoot the person standing next to him. Captain Mathieson—be so good as to mount up, for I want my dinner."

It required a considerable effort, but somehow he reclaimed his dagger and was on his feet, still clutching his sword and weaving towards the bay mare whose reins Fiona held with the same little hand that was locked on the stallion's mane. He wondered in a vague fashion how she had managed to control Rump . . . How she could have fired one of the damn great pistols he always kept loaded in the holsters of his saddle. Then he had dragged himself up, and they were away.

8

Mrs. Shadwell guided them to a belt of woodland edged by a hurrying stream; a quiet lonely spot where they felt safe in halting for repairs. Mathieson meekly obeyed instructions to sit on the bank, and Fiona knelt beside him and washed the blood from his face. " 'Twas the bravest thing I ever saw," she declared, gently dabbing his handkerchief at the cut on his temple and regarding him glowingly.

He felt properly battered, his head hurt miserably again, and he deserved it all for having behaved like a prize fool. He knew a strong impulse to disillusion the Tiny Mite, and would have done so, save that he could not seem to muster the effort just at the moment.

"Aye, 'twere brave all right," agreed Mrs. Shadwell in a soft country accent.

She looked halfway human, he thought, now that she had wrung out her skirts and tidied her greying hair. A tall woman with an odd dignity and dark piercing eyes that seemed to skewer right through a fellow. Come to think on it, be damned if she didn't look just like a witch! He drew back uneasily as she pounced at him, but fear was replaced by embarrassment when she seized his hand and pressed it to her lips.

"No, no!" he said, striving, horrified, to reclaim his hand. "You must not!"

"Ye saved Oi, zur," she said intensely.

"You thank the wrong person, madam. Had this lady not been with me I promise you I'd have ridden away and left you to your fate, so do not be—"

A slow smile softened her stern features. "That ye would not,

127

sir, though the ending might've been different. And Oi do indeed thank your pretty lady. Oi done nothing wrong, mistress! Oi bean't no witch, Oi do swear it!''

"Of course you're not.'' Fiona smiled kindly at her. "If you had been, you could have saved yourself.''

"Mebbe so. But 'cepting fer ye good folks, Oi'd be drownded dead this minute and fer nothing worse than knowing how to heal wi' herbs and roots, and having no roof over me poor old head.''

'Hmmnn,' thought Mathieson cynically, and reached for his purse.

Mrs. Shadwell muttered, "Oi could teach they fools a thing or two . . .'' Her head flung upward and she said with a proud gesture, "No, sir! Oi be enough in yer debt! Put up yer gold. Oi doesn't know how to thank ye, but—mebbe Oi can tell ye summat o' what lies ahead.'' She turned Mathieson's reluctant hand and scanned the palm frowningly.

"Oh my,'' whispered Fiona, awed. "Can you tell fortunes, then?''

"Not fortunes, mistress. The past. The future—sometimes . . . Ah!'' she glanced up at Mathieson and said sympathetically, "Ye has known much o' grief, young sir. And have a hard road afore ye. But there be joy—ah, great joy, for a little while. Then—'' She stopped speaking, staring down at his hand with breath held in check, then drew back from him, her eyes very wide. A moment longer she remained thus, then jumped up. "Oi must go, 'fore they comes arter me. They brung dogs last time. Oi hates dogs, Oi do!''

"Wait!'' cried Fiona. "You did not finish! What—''

"Nay. Oi cannot! But—'' Staring at Mathieson, she cried, "Ye've a good heart, lady. Doan't ye give it to one as will—break it!'' She turned then, and limped quickly toward the trees.

Fiona knelt up. "But—where will you go? Will you be safe? Perhaps you should come with us!''

'Good God!' thought Mathieson.

Mrs. Shadwell stopped at the edge of the woods and turned to face them again. "The Folk be hereabouts. Oi'll be safe wi' me own, never worrit.'' She raised her arm as if in benediction. "God bless ye both—poor childers.'' And she was gone, vanished into the quiet shadows of the trees.

"What a strange woman,'' murmured Fiona. "I wonder

whatever she meant.'' She turned to Mathieson and surprised a grim look. ''Have you really 'known much of grief,' Roly?''

''Only,'' he said drily, ''since I met you, Little Mite!''

''I most certainly would never have done so mad a thing!'' declared Mathieson indignantly, as they rode slowly towards the encampment. ''Rump bolted, is all, and I would have beaten a strategic retreat had you not come up with me. Gad! When I think of how you embroiled me with that horrid crowd of yokels, I wonder I did not turn snow white! What with your cats and your old witches, my girl, I—''

Fiona gave a low trill of laughter. ''Oh, Roly! Why will you never admit how splendid you are? I vow, to listen to you, one might fancy you the greatest villain of the century!''

''I try,'' he said modestly. ''You, on the other hand, are a true heroine, albeit a vexatious one. How a'God's name you were able to manage Rump and your mare and that da-dashed great pistol of mine, is quite beyond me.''

'' 'Twas near quite beyond me,'' she admitted with a droll shrug. ''Which is why I dropped one.''

''*What?*'' He groaned. ''Not my beautiful *Les la Roche*?''

''Oh, I am so sorry! But—when it went off, it jumped right out of my hand!'' Brightening, she added, ''Still, you were able to retrieve your pretty dagger, and at least I did not drop the other pistol! Besides, I expect we could go back and—''

''Saints forfend! And I should be flogged for an ingrate! Child, do you not know what you risked? You were mad to come back even for my glorious carcass.''

''How could I do otherwise when you charged so gallantly to rescue that poor woman. Only think of what—''

''Don't,'' suggested Mathieson. ''The entire episode is best forgot. Gad, but I'm starved! I believe I can smell our dinner.''

''Yes. There is the camp, thank goodness. And only look! Picayune is coming to meet—What on earth is that in her mouth . . . ?''

The small cat approached with great strides over tufts of grass, a white, shapeless object firmly grasped between her jaws. She stopped abruptly, tossed her prize into the air, then sprang to seize and shake it, whiskers bristling.

''Devil take that revolting animal,'' cried Mathieson, outraged. ''She's been into my crumpets! I told you they'd not be safe! Well for you to laugh, madam! If you was to ask me, that *cat* is what those blasted rustics should have flung into the pond!''

Mathieson was the hero of the hour at dinner that evening, which irked him until he noted how much it infuriated Freemon Torrey. His spirits picked up as they sat gathered around the fires, but he was disgusted to find the crumpets as light as any bricks, and from boastfully claiming to have played the major role in their manufacture, he immediately denied any involvement whatsoever. There was much amusement at this, but Torrey observed contemptuously that anything Miss Fiona cooked could only be perfection.

There was singing when the meal was done. The evening air held the briskness of autumn, but the fires warmed the heart as well as the feet, and listening pleasurably to the clear voices of the ladies threading among the deeper tones of the men, Mathieson experienced a contentment he'd not known since his army days. His bruises and his battered head ached, however, and after a while he slipped quietly away. In the red caravan he shared with Heywood and Alec he took off his coat and boots but lay on his bunk without undressing and promptly dozed off.

Waking in the night, he was cold and pulled the covers over him. By the time that was accomplished he was not only wide awake, but could not seem to find a comfortable position. He was unused to sleeplessness, but the several matters that preyed on his mind would not give him any peace. He spent an hour tossing and turning, by which time he was so irritated with this pointless behaviour that he abandoned all attempts at sleep. Climbing down from the upper bunk to which he'd fallen heir, he forgot the protruding nail on the support post and swore heartily as he gave his finger a deep scratch. He was just sufficiently irritable to contemplate waking Thad or Alec and badgering them into conversation, but there was no sign of either. Grumbling, he pulled on his boots—having first shaken them out to guard against feline occupation—and went into the silvery darkness.

A full moon hovered above the trees and a soft night wind stirred the meadow grasses. Rump was easy to find in the rope paddock. Mathieson whistled softly and the big stallion woke up and came trotting over to nuzzle him affectionately. He took the rope loop from the fencepost and the stallion thumped through. Mathieson stroked the warm sleek neck and they walked together, the horse patiently watchful, the man with hands thrust into his pockets and head down.

"Do you suppose we have lost Rob MacTavish, Rump?" he murmured thoughtfully. The stallion snorted, and tossed his head. Mathieson said, "You may be right, but I rather think not. Unless I mistake it, we are even now en route to rendezvous with the gentleman." He smiled cynically. "That will be a jolly reunion, eh? Perchance the reb will lead us to a real pot of gold." He thought with a touch of weariness, 'And an end to my battles.'

From the moment that at the age of nine he had disgraced and bitterly humiliated his father at the hunt, his life seemed to have been a continuing series of battles, among which the brief Parisian interludes with *Maman* shone like bright oases. *'Cher Maman . . .'* And, Gad—how maudlin he grew! Impatient with himself, he said, "Stuff! I've had my loves, you know that, Rump. And friends, too!" The stallion whickered an apparent agreement, but Mathieson was startled by his own words. Friends? What need had he of friends? Much he wanted them!

He kicked at a root, then stared moodily across the moonlit meadow. The piquant face of the Tiny Mite crept into his mind's eye, and he smiled faintly. Rumpelstiltskin nudged him and he strolled on again, muttering, "Zounds, now what maggot has got into my stupid head?"

He seldom thought of women other than to consider how well this one pleased him, or how much that one cost him. Save for Penelope. Penelope, whom he had loved. And knocked down . . . He bit his lip and clenched his hands, bewildered by this unfamiliar depression of the spirits. Was it remorse that plagued him? Why in hell should he feel remorse? He was a dedicated villain. Always had been! Always would be! He would accept no other path, for he had learned very early in life that to the villains of this world went all the rewards, and to the heroes, the hard knocks. Certainly, he had struck Miss Penelope Montgomery. She'd not only had the poor taste to reject him, but had come at him with a poker during that damnable sword fight with Quentin Chandler. It had been her, or Chandler's sword through him! And when Chandler had beaten him (fair and square, blast him!) he *had* taken the reb's sword in his chest,

131

which could well have finished him. To strike a woman under those circumstances was justifiable. 'No, *ma mère*?' But he shrank a little, knowing how his beloved mother would have viewed that deed. It had never troubled him before. Or— seldom. Why must it so haunt him now? Besides, it was becoming ever more apparent that he had not really loved Penelope . . .

Rumpelstiltskin snorted gustily down his neck. He caressed the soft nose, then sat down against a tree watching unseeingly as the big horse began to crop at the grass. And again, he saw Fiona's face, her eyes fixed on his with that look of awed wonder because she'd fancied him to have ridden to the rescue of the witch. 'Silly chit,' he thought resentfully. 'Had she a brain in her head she'd have seen I wanted no part of that fiasco! Devil fly away with her misplaced admiration!' He could console himself with the knowledge that sooner or later, her expression would change; inevitably, her eyes would hold disgust . . . contempt . . . That realization brought no consolation at all, but rather a pang so sharp that he swore and his head bowed lower.

'Our men love once and with a deep and unalterable passion . . .'

Muffin had said that. Well, he had neither the time nor the inclination to indulge a ''deep and unalterable passion''! Besides, the Tiny Mite was not the lady to capture the heart of a man who had been born a century too late; who should have been a real pirate, prowling the Spanish Main; who ever had scorned the virtuous and the virtuous path.

'Oh, Roly! Will you never admit how splendid you are?'

His laughter was short and harsh and held a note that brought the stallion thudding back across the meadow to whuffle anxiously at his ear. Mathieson patted his equine friend, thinking sardonically, 'I am splendid, all right!' He could look back over long years of ''splendour''! Years of womanizing, fighting, gambling, cheating. ''A liar and a blackguard'' someone had once named him, and he'd been proud of it. The one thing he never had sought was the reputation of an honourable gentleman. He had sought only to fulfill the expectations so often hurled at him by his nobly born sire. And to enjoy a damned good time in so doing! He'd *had* a damned good time, hadn't he? Even if there had been bad moments. Rather many bad moments, come to look back . . . But there had been the ladies,

God bless 'em! A small voice whispered, 'Not one of whom would have faced a mindless mob to save your worthless neck . . .'

'The first one brave enough to throw a rock at that most gallant gentleman . . .' *Mon Dieu*, but she had been superb! Resolute, loyal . . . and small and lovely. And pure, dammitall! Pure. He didn't want purity! He wanted a hussy. A woman of the world, who knew how to love. Like Sybil—immoral tart that she was!

And he groaned a curse, because only to think of Mrs. Sybil Montgomery and Fiona in the same breath was a sacrilege . . .

A hand was on his shoulder. A kindly voice enquired, "Are you all right, old fellow? Your head, ith it?"

Heywood, still booted and spurred, was looking at him with obvious concern. Mathieson felt a swift rush of gratitude that his nonsensical aberrations of the mind had been interrupted. It was his head, of course, just as Thaddeus said. Some form of shock, no doubt, and of a certainty he'd had enough of 'em of late: The shock of watching poor old Bill die in his arms, the ridiculous episode with Picayune in the river, the loss of Rump, the rock that had bounced off his skull today. All combining to cause this brief venture into lunacy. He took a deep breath and his drawl was cool as ever when he answered, "Bit of a nuisance, only. And why do you prance about by moonlight, m'lud? Guilty conscience, perchance?"

Still watching him, searchingly, Heywood smiled. "You look like hell, you know."

"Thank you, kind sir. As well I should prepare myself."

"To hear Fiona tell it, hell will be far from your eventual abode. Gad! Your head really doth trouble you. I offer my arm to our bedchamber, mighty champion of witcheth."

Mathieson did not want to go inside. Not just yet. And if he looked bad, Thaddeus did not look so well, either. Not that it mattered how the idiot looked. Still, "Would you object to sitting here and talking for a while?" he asked.

Heywood selected a root, and sat down. Almost, he seemed relieved.

Sharing a companionable silence they watched the moon rise higher to etch the wings of an owl that swooped low over the meadow then soared up with some hapless small creature gripped in its talons.

Heywood murmured, "They look tho noble, and are in fact very cruel."

"Present company excepted?"

"Your fine animal, thertainly." Heywood smiled, but his smile was sad.

Watching him, Mathieson said, "You may ignore this, an you wish, but—dare I ask if there is . . . a lady you admire?" And he waited with an oddly keen anxiety for the answer.

After a moment, Heywood replied quietly, "Am I very obviouth about it?"

Mathieson scowled at his wistful face. "Yes," he said, and as Heywood looked up, mildly surprised by such brutal candour, he added, "For how long have you known her?"

"Five monthth, two weekth, and three dayth—no, four, thinthe 'tith already after midnight."

"Gad! If you are *that* badly smitten, why the devil do you do nothing about it?"

Heywood shrugged. "I am a fool, but not tho much of a fool that I cannot know there ith no hope for me." His voice dropped. He murmured softly, "I found a lady who ith too beautiful. Very poor planning. But—when I thaw—*her* . . . I wath jolly well flattened. I knew there wath very little chanthe, but I offered . . . and wath rejected, of courth. Very gently. I tried to look at other ladieth but—for me, I'm afraid, there *ith* no other lady. Who elth could have that lovely cloud of golden hair . . . or tho perfect a figure? What other eyeth could thmile in that perfectly adorable way . . . ? And that pretty lilt to her voithe when—" He turned dreaming eyes on his companion, started violently and became red as fire.

'What a sickening display!' thought Mathieson, scornfully. 'And the idiot doesn't even know that her hair isn't golden, but a rich light brown with little gold glints in it.' " 'Faint heart,' " he snarled, " 'ne'er won fair lady'!"

Horribly embarrassed, Heywood stammered, "I th-think my heart ith not faint, but I know I cannot win her. Not very remarkable—all thingth conthidered." He gave a derisive shrug. "Only natural that a lady would prefer her man be capable of thpeaking her name properly."

"Do you mean you have no chance because you lisp? *C'est une absurdité!* And I think you wrong her. Besides, the women love a title."

134

"Many do, but— Now damn your eyeth! Who told you I am—"

"A nobleman? You did, you dolt. I called you 'milord' several times and you were so accustomed to it you didn't even notice. Did you join this troupe for the sake of your lady?"

Heywood nodded. "I can at leatht help her, and her people."

"I thought that must be it. I did not fancy you were a Jacobite."

"Gad, no! But—I've a couple of very good friendth who are. Devil of a coil, to get 'em out of trouble, ain't it?"

"If you're fool enough to try," sneered Mathieson.

"Do you hear that, Rump?" said Heywood lightly. "Your friend who will fight a crowd of angry men for the life of a witch, would not bethtir himthelf to help a friend!"

"I have no friends," grunted Mathieson, standing and whistling the horse to him again.

"I wonder whatever led me to believe you were here for that very reathon. You claimed it wath—a compelling one, an I recall."

Mathieson turned to face him squarely. "I was mistaken.'Tis not at all compelling. The lady wants none of me. Do you understand?"

"No. If that were truth, why would you keep with uth? You're no more a rebel than am I, and you dithtinctly claimed you'd not bother to help—"

"Because," snarled Mathieson, suddenly and irrationally furious, "I mean to steal all the treasure and sail off into the sunset with it! Put *that* into your next play, you great block, and perchance 'twill be a success!"

Heywood gave a shout of laughter so that Rumpelstiltskin danced away, eyeing him uneasily. "My public would never pay to thee a tragedy," he chuckled. "I think you play the proper part in 'My Lady Dairymaid.' "

His only response a disgusted profanity, Mathieson started back toward the paddock.

Grinning, Heywood kept pace with him. A few seconds later, he said, "Thpeaking of which . . ."

His tone had changed. Mathieson looked at him across Rumpelstiltskin's back and asked jeeringly, "Well? Do you mean to use some sense and make me into the villain after all?"

"Our prethent villain would be well pleathed an I did tho."

"Aha! So your glum expression has to do with the blithe Mr. Torrey!"

Heywood seized Rumpelstiltskin's mane and drew him to a halt. "You would do well not to treat it lightly, Roland. He ith the type to brood over a grudge. You made him look a fool before the lady he hopeth to wed; you have taken hith part in the play; and Lady Clorinda ith fond of you, but don't like *him* above half—which he ith well aware of. You are a threat to him and he can be a dangerouth man. Have a care."

"Pish! I could cut him into gobbets in five minutes! Less."

"Aye—in a fair fight." Not one to glibly slander another, Heywood paused, then added guiltily, "I am a cad to impugn hith reputation."

Mathieson stood very still. Not looking at his companion, he asked, "Do you believe that Torrey dislikes me so much he would strike from ambush, or pay an assassin?"

"You find that unlikely. Natural enough that you would, for any honourable gentleman would draw back from that kind of cowardly, underhanded—"

"You fail to give the devil his due, Thaddeus. If Torrey chooses the cowardly and dishonourable way, he'll find me no stranger to such tactics, I do assure you. Still, I thank you for the warning. Good night." With the big horse pacing gracefully beside him, he stalked away, his eyes angry and his mouth bitter.

Puzzled, Thaddeus Heywood looked after him. Then he shook his head, murmured, "Cawker!" and, smiling, strolled towards the caravan.

"All these years I have dreamed of finding you again," declared Captain Firebrand, lifting Miss Barbara's hand to his lips.

She swayed to him, and said tenderly, "Much has happened since we parted, Jack. I am changed from the—"

"Louder, Fiona," called Bradford, from the edge of the sunlit clearing they had chosen for this rehearsal.

"I am changed from the simple milkmaid you once knew," she declared in a carrying voice.

Firebrand said ardently, "You are the loveliest and purest milkmaid in all Sussex, and—"

"Shropshire!" shouted Torrey, adding an audible, "Stupid oaf."

Mathieson frowned and referred to the sheets in his hand. "But, it distinctly says—"

"We change it depending upon which county we are in," explained Fiona, helpfully.

"Oh." He smiled down at her. "Then tomorrow you will be the loveliest and purest milkmaid in all Cheshire."

"Brilliant," snorted Torrey.

Mathieson bowed. "Thank you. I am glad to see that you are not *completely* lacking in perception Mr. Torrey."

Torrey swore under his breath and took a step forward.

"Devil!" whispered Fiona and added hurriedly, "Yet, only a milkmaid, sir, and not worthy to be the bride of a gentleman of your station." Mathieson's laughing gaze still held on Torrey, and she prompted a low-voiced, "Sir Roger . . ."

"Sir Roger finds you worthy," he recited dutifully.

She hung her head. "Ah, but—but Sir Roger does not seek my hand in marriage."

"Which goes to prove how slimily stinking a swine he is," intoned the dauntless Captain Firebrand.

"Devil take you, it don't say that!" Torrey, who was now to portray the villainous Sir Roger, flourished his pages aloft and stamped onto the impromptu stage.

"Then it should," said Mathieson, adding politely. "Now do please go away, Sir Roger. You spoil our nice scene."

"Yes, but Freemon is perfectly right," Fiona pointed out, her eyes sparkling. "You are supposed to say—'Which proves him a wicked man.' "

"That, too," said Mathieson agreeably. "But I really think my words are more forceful, Thaddeus."

Heywood, sitting on a tree root, grinned broadly. "Very true, dear boy."

"Forceful enough to offend every lady in the audience." Mervyn Bradford's resonant voice overrode the smothered chuckles of the watching group. "Come now Mathieson, you must stay with the part as writ. Torrey, we'll have your fight scene after this." He turned to Mathieson and murmured softly, "And no slips of the fist, else I'll let Torrey play Firebrand, you rascal!" In a normal tone, he added, "Now try to finish from memory. You take the leading role tonight, and you must be letter-perfect."

137

Torrey gave a contemptuous snort and marched into the trees again. "Damned popinjay," he growled to Alec Pauley.

Pauley, whose bowed legs provided Torrey with much amusement, had no love for the man. "A fine actor, for all that," he said, his hazel eyes amused. "Especially in that final love scene with Miss Bradford. Do ye no agree, Miss Moira?"

The dark girl said shyly, "He does make it seem so real. In my scene with him, where I cut the ropes and free him and he kisses me on the cheek . . ." She sighed. "Oh, he does it passing well."

"Does he so?" muttered Pauley, a frown chasing the smile from his eyes.

Torrey gave an exclamation of impatience. "Much you know of it, Miss Innocence! But I'll tell you this—clever Captain Mathieson may succeed in fooling all you silly females, but he don't fool me! And he'd best not take advantage of his role to molest either you or Fiona!"

"Molest!" gasped his sister, dismayed. "But I promise you, Freemon—"

"Quiet!" shouted Bradford irritably. "May I *beg*, dear my daughter, that you continue? 'No matter what . . .' "

Torrey glowered his resentment but was silent. Alec looked at him with a curl of the lip, then caught Moira's anxious eye and forgot his dislike of her brother.

"No matter what may chance," said the much tried milkmaid, "no matter how long we must be apart—I shall never forget you, Captain Jack." And she whispered provocatively, "Nor your crumpets!"

Firebrand stepped closer and took her hand in his. "Why do you speak as in farewell? I shall be gone two days—no more. My dearest girl . . ." he slipped an arm about her slender waist. She lifted her hand to his shoulder and gazed up at him. And there was no teasing in her green eyes now—only a deep tenderness. The faint aroma of her perfume was in Mathieson's nostrils; such a clean, sweet fragrance. The simple dairymaid's cap framed her little face . . . her mouth surely was formed for kissing. "I do so—love you," he said huskily.

"Then why not share your emotions with your audience?" howled Bradford, incensed. "With luck, they'll hear you in the front row!" He glared at his silent mother and snarled, "One would think they shared a secret!"

138

"And I—you," responded the pretty milkmaid with yearning softness. "Until death, and beyond . . . my dearest, dear . . ."

"Oh dear, oh dear!" whispered Lady Clorinda.

"Lord! Lord! *Lord!*" raged Bradford. "You're not just talking to *him*! Here—let me show—No! You DO NOT kiss her, damn your eyes!"

Mathieson blinked at him innocently and, very aware of Miss Fiona's rosy blush, said, "Good gracious, did I mistake it? It says—'they embrace,' so I thought—"

"Devil you did!" Infuriated, Torrey again rushed forward, fists clenched, but was seized and held back by Heywood and Cuthbert.

"*What* a fuss," drawled Mathieson. "We are only acting, are we not, Miss Bradford? Your pardon an I offended."

Her pulses racing madly, Fiona stammered, "Why—no—I mean, yes, of course. That is—well, it *does* say that, Papa."

"It don't say he is to *kiss* you!"

"Dammitall, I'll not have you pawing my betrothed!" raged Torrey, struggling to free himself.

"I am *not* your betrothed!" said Fiona indignantly.

"You will please to keep quiet, miss," interposed Lady Ericson, her voice cold. "Captain Mathieson, I allowed you to journey with us because you said you wished to be of help."

"That's *exactly* what you said," bellowed Bradford. "We all heard you!"

My lady gave him an irritated glance. " 'Tis not helpful to cause bad feelings between our people, and I warn you, young man, I'll not tolerate it."

"No more shall I!" said Bradford grandly. "Give you some personal instruction so you will understand the directions, and—"

With acid disdain my lady interpolated, "Nonsense, Bradford! Mathieson knew perfectly well what was implied by Mr. Heywood's directions. He chose to take advantage of the situation."

"But, Grandmama—" began Fiona. My lady's eyes turned to her, and she quailed into silence.

Mathieson said quietly, "You are perfectly right, ma'am. The temptation was—extreme, but I had no right. I apologize."

"As you should. No, Fiona! Take yourself to your caravan.

Do you speak again you'll stay there for the rest of the day—rehearsal or no!''

Scarlet, the girl fled. My lady returned her attention to Mathieson. ''I will accept your apology. This time. An it happens again we must judge the—ah, 'temptation' too strong for you, and will have no alternative but—''

''Of course it will prove too strong,'' said Torrey, blazing with fury. ''He can scarce keep his hands from her. Send him off, before—''

''Before . . . what . . . ?'' asked Mathieson, in a soft deadly voice.

''Enough!'' shrilled my lady. ''When I require your advice Freemon Torrey, I will ask you for't.''

''I have a right to defend the lady I mean to wed!'' argued Freemon, loud and defiant.

There was a moment of complete stillness while every eye was fastened on the three tall men and the small but invincible figure of my lady.

Flushed, and her bright eyes the brighter with anger, Lady Clorinda looked at Mathieson but he, more skilled than Torrey in the ways of women, kept his own eyes lowered and remained silent.

''Your rights, Freemon Torrey,'' said my lady coldly, ''exist only if your claim is valid, and—''

Torrey turned to face Bradford. ''Tell her, sir! I am to marry your daughter. You gave me your word!''

Mathieson frowned, and directed a narrow look at Bradford.

With monarchial dignity the tall man declared, ''You have evidently forgot that my word was qualified, Freemon. I promised that if my daughter was *willing* to take you to husband, I'd give you my blessings. No more. No less.''

''And since my granddaughter has made it perfectly clear she does not consider herself betrothed to you,'' said Lady Ericson, ''your rights in the matter extend no farther than those of a friend and a—''

''It has been understood for years—'' stormed Torrey.

''*Silence*, sir!'' The old lady stood very straight, head high-held, fine eyes flashing, chin outthrust, and the power of her such that everyone in the clearing was breathlessly still. ''Twice,'' she said awfully, ''you have dared interrupt me! I suffer few men to do so. A third time, sir, and you will leave us, just as surely as will Mathieson does he displease again! Do you take my meaning?"

For a moment Torrey glowered at her rebelliously. Then he said, "I do, madam," and offered a stiff bow.

"Thank you," said my lady crisply. "We will not speak of this again, I trust. Bradford, shall you wish another rehearsal? We must be on our way by two o'clock."

Her son consulted his ornate pocket watch. " 'Tis precisely ten minutes past twelve. We should, I think, apply ourselves to luncheon first, and then we'll have time to try the duel scene again, before we pack up."

Alec Pauley turned to Moira. "The duel!" he muttered. "We'll be lucky do those two gamecocks not fight a real duel before we've the chance tae stage one!"

"How dreadful." Contrarily, Moira's dark eyes glowed with excitement. "But, surely my brother knows he would stand small chance with Captain Mathieson."

"I fancy he is aware o' that fact," said Pauley drily. "I wonder . . ." he frowned and did not finish the remark.

"Whether we should speak to Mr. Bradford? Is that what you were going to say?"

Pauley shook his head. "No lassie. I—I just wondered . . . what chance Captain Mathieson stands with little Miss Fiona . . ."

'Or the other way around,' thought Moira.

Alone in her caravan, Fiona was wondering much the same thing. Mathieson's eyes had been ardent during their love scene. *Had* that been mere acting? Despite all the consternation, he had only kissed her on the brow, yet her heart had thundered a response that had shocked her by its intensity. It was the very height of folly to indulge such feelings. From the beginning she had known it would be dangerous to give her heart to such a man. And yet . . .

Agitated, she sprang up from the chair and began to pace about. Oh, why must life be so difficult? Why could she not be comfortably in love with Freemon Torrey, who was genuinely fond of her, and was not, after all, a bad man? Nor was she the only one in a pickle; there was Thaddeus Heywood, who Grandmama said was a titled gentleman, and who certainly was grieving and likely rejected by some silly girl. And only look at poor Moira—so shy-eyed and blushful whenever Alec Pauley looked her way. And he, poor lad, so enamoured of her it was a wonder

141

Torrey did not see it. Heaven help them when he did notice, for there'd be trouble a'plenty! Freemon Torrey had larger plans for his sister than a practically penniless young rebel. It was all so unfair and—She whirled about as the door opened to admit Lady Ericson.

"Well, there's no cause to look at me as though I were a two-tailed dragon rather than a feeble little old lady," scolded the grande dame, sinking onto the chair and fanning herself with her diminutive handkerchief. "Oh, how very warm it is for October. And Lud, but I miss the refinements of life—my kingdom for a proper fan!"

Fiona knew her too well to be taken in by this carefree attitude, and handing her a week-old copy of *The London Gazette* which her father had purchased in Cirencester, she waited in silence for the storm to break.

My lady fanned herself with the *Gazette*, and hummed. "The play goes along well, I think," she remarked airily. "Young Mathieson makes a dashing Firebrand, do you not agree? But of course you agree. That is very plain."

"Is it, Grandmama?"

"Oh, very." My lady sneered, "La, but you must learn not to be so transparent, Fiona. Had I behaved as warmly to the gentlemen who courted me as you do to Mathieson—"

"Who is *not* courting me."

"Pah! I'd like to know what else you would call it. Those wicked black eyes of his fairly devour you, innocent that you are! Foolish child, I warned you before. 'Ware the likes of Rascal Mathieson. He was not fashioned for your kind."

"For whom was he fashioned, ma'am?" asked Fiona meekly, but with a spark dawning in her green eyes.

"For opera dancers. His type always is—until they run out of funds. Whereupon they find themselves some indulgent and wealthy widow, usually years older than themselves and often slightly touched in the upper works. They marry the widow, whether or not she smells of the shop, keep her pacified with an occasional kind word or a night's *amour*, and spend most of her fortune and their time between the muslin company and the tables." My lady leaned forward, suddenly grim, and shook the newspaper under her granddaughter's sagging jaw. "Aye, you think me a properly vulgar old woman! Well, perchance I am, but I've seen forty years more of life than you have. And I know

142

a rogue when I see one. Oh, never tilt your chin up at me, miss! You may not think Mathieson a rogue, but—''

"I think him the bravest, most honourable gentleman I ever met," declared Fiona, cheeks flushed and small hands clenched.

"And the most handsome, eh? La, the pity of it! D'ye know the dance he'd lead you?—even were he honourable, which he ain't! The women wouldn't let him be faithful for a minute! You'd not know from one night to the next whose bed he was sharing, and—''

"Grandmama!"

"Tush and a fiddlestick! 'Tis time you faced facts, child. I've small use for Freemon Torrey, but by heaven I'd sooner see you wed him than lie down your heart for Roland Mathieson to stamp on! And don't pretend you're not halfway in love with him already, for you show it each time you look at the young devil. By heaven, but I've a mind to send him packing, even as Torrey asks!"

"And what will happen do we encounter Captain Lake again? Can you really judge the risk—to all of us—warranted, ma'am?"

My lady set her small chin and frowned into her granddaughter's defiant face. "I must consider the risk to you, also," she answered slowly.

Remorseful, Fiona sank to her knees beside the chair. "Dearest Grandmama, I do not mean to cause you worry, truly I do not. Captain Mathieson likely flirts with all the ladies and means this as no more."

My lady smiled faintly, and reached out to stroke the silken curls. "So the child is not all innocence, after all."

"No, but how could I be? Francis used to chatter with me of his—his *chères amies*, and—''

"That lecherous boy! To what extent?"

"Oh, nothing naughty—or at least, not very naughty." Fiona rested her head on my lady's knee and murmured sadly, "I miss him so."

"We all do, child. Be thankful he is safe away. But, for his sake as well as your own, I could never countenance a match with Roland Mathieson."

Fiona sighed. "Now, dearest one, has he approached you in the matter?"

"No. Nor will he, for he is shrewd enough to know I have

143

taken his measure. My fear is . . . Oh, pretty one, I'd not see you hurt!''

There were tears in Lady Clorinda's eyes, and, deeply moved, Fiona leaned to hug her tiny but so formidable grandmother and kiss the rouged cheek.

It was sweet, but not quite the answer my lady had hoped for.

9

The village hall was crowded with virtually the entire populations of both Nether- and North-Brackendale. Outside, the wind was rising to set doors and windows rattling, but the drab little hall was brightened by a row of rush lights that flickered merrily along the edge of the small stage, and by the "sand dunes" and "palm trees" on which the Avon Travelling Players had expended so many hours. It was seldom these country folk were able to enjoy an entertainment, especially one with such ambitious scenery, and they sat entranced as the drama unfolded.

Mathieson had come successfully through the first two acts of Heywood's play, and if he had at times remembered the dialogue imperfectly, he had improvised to such good effect that none of the spectators had detected the substitutions. They had now reached the third act.

Clad in a white open-throated shirt and black breeches, with a crimson sash around his waist, Captain Firebrand flourished his cutlass at the great treasure chest that spilled its bounty onto the island sands. "There, wanton!" he cried disdainfully. "Fill your greedy hands, since gold is your only idol! You sold me into slavery! You sold yourself to that—that unspeakable cur—" he gestured towards the palm trees "—who even now comes to claim you!"

Miss Barbara, delectable in a gown of pale pink muslin trimmed with ecru lace, sobbed, and ran to the edge of the stage. "Ah, how can he be so cruel?" she asked the enthralled audience. "Yet—he does not know . . . and how may I tell him I—sold myself . . . in exchange for his dear life . . . ?"

"I'll tell him, lass!" shouted a sturdy farmer, springing to

145

his feet. "Like any other fine gent, he cannot see past the end of his nose!" (Loud shouts of endorsement.) "Hey! Firebrand!—" Here, he was pulled down by his embarrassed spouse and subsided into surly growls that faded into awe as the bows and 'midship of His Majesty's Frigate, *The Vengeance*, rumbled and lurched into view behind the shuddering palm trees at the right rear of the stage. The audience cheered lustily, and the muscular Alec, concealed behind the left-hand curtains hauled on the guide rope until the frigate jerked to a swaying anchorage.

Resplendent in a great periwig, purple velvet coat, beribboned breeches, and a flowing black cloak flung back from the left shoulder, Sir Roger sprang over the "side" of the vessel and bellowed, "Avast, you scum!" He suffered a small embarrassment when his cloak caught on a splinter in the frigate almost toppling it, so that he was obliged to prop it up and free himself, to the raucous amusement of some of the more rowdy elements in the audience. His temper was not improved by the sight of Mathieson's covert grin, but at last he was able to wrench out his sword and advance on the dashing pirate. "An ye want the girl," he shouted in his fine, resonant voice, "fight for her!"

"I'll not fight for your leavings," declared Firebrand, sheathing his cutlass, and folding his arms proudly.

Barbara flew to sink to her knees before him.

"Ye silly gert gowk," howled a big wheelwright in the front row. "She's give up all fer ye'self!"

Mathieson had never dreamed that playacting could be so entertaining. He sent a delighted grin flashing at the captivated playgoer that brought yearning sighs from many female throats and caused the vicar's wife, a fragile and romantically inclined lady, to grope dazedly for her vinaigrette bottle.

Behind the curtains, costumed as Firebrand's rascally uncle, Bradford whispered, "It's going along famously, Mama. Mathieson's got 'em in the hollow of his hand. Jove, but the boy's a natural-born actor!"

"Hmmnn," said my lady drily. "You may be right at that."

On stage now was the clash of swords as Firebrand and Sir Roger fought for the girl they both loved. The duel had been rehearsed several times and on each occasion Mathieson had seen hatred peeping from Torrey's blue eyes. As always, the close brush with danger was exhilarating and he moved about

146

nimbly, amused because it was so easy to lure his opponent into ever wilder attacks not included in the scenario.

Fiona watched with real anxiety, and when Captain Firebrand at last neatly disarmed Sir Roger, her sigh of relief blended with more cheers from the audience, while off to the side Thaddeus Heywood shook his head and muttered something about a day of reckoning.

Sir Roger, panting and thwarted, drew back, and the brave captain, only slightly out of breath, recommended that the distressed girl go away with the man to whom she had sold herself.

Barbara again appealed to the audience. "You know I am a good girl! I was betrayed!" She pointed dramatically at Sir Roger.

Loud boos and hisses sounded. Two men sprang onto the stage and made a run at Torrey, fists clenched and intentions clear. Cuthbert and Gregor sprinted to head them off and remind them it was "Just acting, sirs. Just acting." Smouldering, they allowed themselves to be shepherded back to their seats and Barbara proceeded to confess the noble self-sacrifice that had led to her fall from grace, and to identify the villain responsible.

Brave Captain Firebrand advanced on Sir Roger. "You shall pay for that villainy, sir!" he cried and swung up his fist.

At this point, the sound of a healthy blow was supposed to be heard, whereupon Torrey would stagger backward and fall. Heywood, perched on a stool behind the curtains and out of sight of the audience, made no attempt, however, to pound on the head of cabbage. Mathieson glanced to the side, and Torrey instinctively doing the same, the closely aimed blow actually grazed the villain's cheek. "Whoops," said Mathieson under his breath. The crowd howled its approbation, and Torrey had no need to feign wrath as he staggered and went down.

Triumphant, Captain Firebrand held out his arms.

"I am forgiven!" Betrayed Barbara flew to the embrace of her pirate as tears flowed and handkerchiefs fluttered. The lovers, arms about each other, did not see Sir Roger recover sufficiently to slink over to the treasure chest and begin to stuff his pockets with gems. Howls of outrage and warning rang out.

"Jack!" cried Barbara, becoming aware of Sir Roger's dastardly behaviour. "That scoundrel steals your treasure!"

Captain Firebrand laughed and drew his lady close again. "Not so, beloved! *He* has found some pretty baubles." He looked down at her adoringly. " 'Tis I who have found the only *real* treasure!"

Gregor's flute and milady's paper and comb played a triumphal air, and amid more cheers and a veritable thunder of applause, Bradford and Gregor came in from each side, drawing the curtains closed.

"Oh, oh! It went so *well*!" cried Fiona, clinging to Mathieson's hand and dancing with excitement.

"You did that deliberately!" snarled Torrey, advancing in a very different frame of mind.

"No, really," protested Mathieson. "I looked across to see why Thad did not whack his cabbage, is all, and you moved in the same direction. Like a gudgeon," he added sweetly.

"I'll gudgeon you," growled Torrey, snatching for his sword hilt.

My lady said tautly, "Oh, stop your silly quarrelling, do! Very well, Gregor."

The curtains were pulled back and the cast of "My Lady Dairymaid" joined hands, walked forward, smiling, and took their bows to sustained cheers and applause.

The curtains closed once more.

"Heywood should make his bow as playwright, no sir?" enquired Alec.

"Aye, was he here," agreed Bradford, glancing about. "Where a'pox has the boy got to?"

Fiona frowned a little. "Cuthbert is not here, either."

"Well, they'd best hasten," said my lady with a twinkle, "else they will miss our surprise party."

"A party?" Moira Torrey clapped her hands. "Oh, wonderful!"

"What for?" asked Fiona eagerly.

"My brilliant debut," drawled Mathieson. "Naturally enough." He laughed at the storm of derision that greeted his boast, but his nerves were taut. Thaddeus Heywood was not the man to shirk his responsibilities, no more was Cuthbert. My lady, who might have been expected to be annoyed by such conduct, seemed not at all put out. Perhaps she had sent Cuthbert off to fetch supplies for her surprise party, but that did not explain Heywood's disappearance. His blood began to tingle, and he eased his jambiya dagger in its scabbard.

* * *

148

Beyond noting that she stood between two men, one of whom was Cuthbert, Thaddeus Heywood's attention was so fixed upon the cloaked figure of the girl that had the village suddenly disappeared he'd likely have been unaware of it. Just before the duel scene he had heard horses outside and with the eternal vigilance of the pursued, had investigated. His position behind the curtains at the far right of the small stage allowed him convenient access to both an outside window and the back door, and his cautious glance through the one had sent him plunging through the other.

She stood with her back towards him, and the hood had fallen onto her shoulders so that he could see the shimmer the moonlight awoke on her unpowdered fair curls. She was speaking in the soft, lilting voice that had haunted his dreams, and he halted a few paces away and stood motionless, gazing and gazing.

The man beside Cuthbert had seen Heywood's approach, and he tensed, crouching a little, then smiled and relaxed again.

The girl spun around with a swish of petticoats. She was perhaps half a head taller than Fiona Bradford, and although she looked startled she was very pretty indeed.

The man she knew as Lord Thaddeus Briley whispered yearningly, "Beth . . . oh, Beth . . ."

Her great dark eyes widened with shock. She gasped, "Th-Thaddeus!" and reached out to him.

Heywood took her hands and pressed a kiss on each. And they stood there, unmoving, looking at one another in a poignant silence.

Cuthbert said drily, "I take it introductions are not required."

"Pardon?" The girl started and blushed scarlet. "Och, no! I am acquainted with his lordship.

Thaddeus flinched very slightly.

Cuthbert exclaimed, "His—*what*?"

"I am known here ath Mr. Heywood," explained Thaddeus, his voice still rather hoarse and uncertain. Belatedly, he glanced at the second man and gave a groan of exasperation. "Oh, God! I thought you were thafely out of England, you idiot!"

His outstretched hand was seized in a strong grip. "As you see," said Robert MacTavish, the smile lingering in his grey eyes, "I'm no illusion. How are you, Thad? You risk your foolish head for us yet again, do you?"

"Foolish indeed!" exclaimed Miss Elizabeth Clandon, her

pale face full of anxiety. "Ye've nae right tae run such awful risks, Thaddeus!"

His lordship replied quietly, "I think I have every right, ma'am."

Her eyes fell and she murmured something flustered and unintelligible.

Heywood forced his attention back to MacTavish. "Rob, you know you are quite mad to be here. Did you bring your lovely bride?"

"Rosamond waits at my home in Wales and as . . . for—" MacTavish was interrupted by a sustained spell of coughing.

"Jupiter, Rob," Heywood exclaimed, taking his friend's arm supportively, "You're ill, man!"

"No, no," denied MacTavish, gasping for breath. "I've had a stupid . . . cold merely. And now this cough's a—a confounded nuisance, but—"

Miss Clandon, no less concerned, interpolated, "He pushes himself night and day, Thaddeus. Time and again we've warned him, but he'll nae listen."

"And that's the truth," grunted Cuthbert. "You're vastly important to us all, MacTavish, and for all our sakes should have a care for your health. Would that your lady wife was here, for she—"

"Would nag and bully me off to my bed, I dinna doot." MacTavish tried to laugh only to again lapse into the harsh, racking cough.

Heywood gripped his hand. "Now thee here, Rob! Good God! You're afire with fever! I thought you looked poorly but—"

Irritated, MacTavish jerked his hand clear. "Och, away wi' ye! Dinna fash so!" And reverting to impeccable English, he clapped his friend on the shoulder and said apologetically, "You're a good fellow, Thad, but I've neither the time nor the patience to be maudled over. 'Tis a cold—nothing more. Now— the plans are laid and all preparations have been made for the transfer of—" He was again interrupted, this time by a storm of applause from inside the hall. "One gathers your play has ended."

Heywood gave a dismayed groan. "Oh, egad! Lady Clorinda will have my head for not being there to hit the cabbage!"

"Hit . . . the *cabbage* . . . ?" echoed Miss Clandon, astonished.

He laughed. "I have found my true calling, ma'am. I am a cabbage hitter thecond to none! Rob—will you come inthide? I imagine you're eager to talk with everyone."

"I am. But I think 'twould behoove me to wait till your audience departs. And my news will better be told to all of you at once. Now, tell me how come you to be with the troupe? Do you know who is this dragoon Cuthbert tells me dogs your footsteps?"

Longing to be alone with the lady he worshipped and whom he'd feared he would never see again, Heywood's innate courtesy prevailed. "I learned that Frank Bradford had been out with Charlie and had to run for hith life after Culloden. The Bradfordth are old friendth of my family tho I went to thee if I could help in any way, and they allowed me to join them in thith little—endeavour. Ath to the—"

The doors to the hall swung open and the audience began to surge out chattering happily about the play and the performers.

The three men and the girl edged deeper into the shadows.

Mervyn Bradford lifted his tankard high. "A toast!" he shouted.

"A toast!" echoed the jubilant players, gathered merrily in the stage area of the hall.

A triumphant note in his voice Bradford said, "To the end of the first part of our journey!"

There was an instant's incredulous silence, then his words were echoed with joyful vigour and the toast was drunk in ale and wine and cider.

'So that,' thought Mathieson, watching Fiona over the rim of his tankard, 'was the reason for the surprise party. We have reached our destination; the treasure must be very near at hand!' Cuthbert had probably ridden out to notify some key Jacobite figure (MacTavish, very likely) that they were here at last. Which meant also that the threat to Roland Fairleigh Mathieson grew more deadly with every second that passed. The time had come for the villain of the piece to fold his tent and steal softly away to where he might watch the plotters without risk to himself. He set his tankard down and began to drift towards the back door, only to hesitate, frowning. That clod Torrey was pestering Fiona again, and she looked troubled. Damn the fellow!

"I have been patient for years," Freemon Torrey was murmuring. "My dearest girl, you know how much I care for you, but if you won't have me, do not I beg, throw yourself away upon Mathieson. No—never be angry. I say it only because I deplore his kind of man, and it worries me to see you falling into his trap."

Fiona tapped her foot and said coolly, "If Captain Mathieson has set a trap, Freemon, it must be a very poor one, because I continue to escape it."

"Do you?" Seizing her hand he declared, "I've marked how he hangs about you. You are so sweet, so innocent—you don't realize what he has in mind for you."

Irritated, she pulled her hand away. "Then since you seem to read his mind so well, perhaps you should tell me of my intended fate."

"Now you're angry." He sighed heavily. "How do I offend, that you must be so unkind? I long only to care for and protect you. To keep you safe from harm for as long as I live."

Fiona's eyes softened. He really did look crushed, and they had been friends for so many years. Perhaps she *was* being unkind. Surely, the greatest of compliments was to be loved; to be desired as a wife, and offered the lifelong devotion of an honourable gentleman. She said repentantly, "Am I unkind, Freemon? I'm very sorry if that is the case. You've always been a good friend to us, and I am indeed honoured that you want to make me your wife."

"More than anything in the world," he said ardently.

His blue eyes were fixed on her face and held a look she longed to see in another pair of eyes. The awareness of that longing scourged her so that she began to feel a monster. "I wish I could give you the answer you want," she said falteringly, staring at the small cake she held. "But—the thing is—"

"Oh, you need not tell me," he interrupted, at once firing up. "I know I have been very cleverly replaced in your affections by that posturing mountebank! I warn you, Fiona—he will bring you only sorrow!"

His opinion was shared by others, she knew. Grandmama, Papa, even the poor woman they had saved from the ducking stool, Mrs. Shadwell, had warned her against Roland. Shaken, she responded with what dignity she could muster. "You are quite mistaken. Captain Mathieson has never even hinted that he has a *tendre* for me."

152

"I do not doubt that! 'Tis not his way! He is too clever, and you so innocently gullible as to be deceived by his Frenchified charm! Well, never say I did not warn you! Keep on as you are going, my girl, and between your flirting and his cunning lechery he will bring shame and disgrace your way!"

"How *dare* you say such things! I have not—"

Her attempt to move away was foiled. Mr. Torrey had drunk deep of the wine and caution was drowned. He seized her wrist and said in a voice harsh with anger, "I think I know a rogue when I see one, and he is a rogue and a charlatan if ever—"

"Did someone call me?"

The quietly cynical drawl brought a sigh of relief from Fiona, but heightened the blaze in Torrey's somewhat bloodshot eyes. "I called you just what you are," he declared thickly.

"Indeed?" Mathieson regarded him with a bored smile. "I bow to your perception, but do you think it wise? Lady Clorinda warned us only today that we—"

"I've another warning for you! Stay away from my betrothed, or you—"

"But of course I will keep away from the poor girl," smiled Mathieson. "Only point her out, and—"

"Damn you!" Maddened, Torrey whipped out his sword and lunged fiercely.

Fiona screamed. Alarmed shouts rang out. Quick as a cat Mathieson flung himself sideways. Even so, the sword whispered across his arm.

"For shame!" thundered Bradford. "There are ladies present!"

Blind to everything but his jealous hatred, Torrey pressed his attack, shouting, "I've held my temper with you long enough, you slippery scoundrel!"

Mathieson's colichemarde had slid into his hand once more and he parried the following thrust in the nick of time. "You call *me* a scoundrel?" he sneered. "You treacherous cur! I've not yet sunk so low as to stab a man without warning."

"Desist!" roared Bradford, striding forward and flinging up one arm majestically.

My lady said shrilly, "Let be! Better they should fight it out than always be sniping at each other."

The swords flashed and rang together. The onlookers drew back to make room and watched eagerly.

Deploring what Torrey had done, Fiona could not wish him dead, but nor did she wish Roland to fall. She gripped her hands together, her heart pounding wildly. An arm slipped about her shoulders and she glanced up to meet her father's eyes. "Disgraceful behaviour," he muttered. She leaned against him, anxious and frightened, yet thrilled by the desperate conflict.

Torrey fought in the Italian manner, staying mostly with the *tierce* position. Mathieson, an advocate of the French school, preferred *sexte*, relying as always on speed over force. Their demeanour was as different as their style; Torrey flushed and intent, all power and fury, Mathieson's supple grace bordering on the careless, his taunting smile deepening occasionally into a chuckle that made Torrey grit his teeth with rage.

A shout went up as Mathieson stumbled over a fallen tankard. Torrey ignored the Code of the Duello, and allowing no quarter, thrust hard. Mathieson parried desperately as he fell to one knee, then sprang lightly to his feet again, but it was a near thing. Fiona had thought him doomed and closed her eyes for an instant.

"Lord help us!" whispered Moira. "I pray my brother is not killed!"

Fiona forced her eyes open. Roland was still alive and fighting well.

"No one will be killed," said my lady. "First blood, gentlemen! Bradford! See to't."

Mr. Bradford drew his sword obediently and moved forward prepared to strike up the blades of the antagonists should there be a hit.

Somewhat relieved, Fiona looked to Moira. Her friend's face was chalk white, but her head was turned away from the duellists. Following her gaze, Fiona discovered a new menace. Troopers were positioned all along the back of the hall, and Captain Lake stood nearby, arms folded, watching the fight appreciatively. He made Fiona a slight bow and held one finger to his lips in a request for silence.

Turning from him, her eyes flew to her grandmother, but the old lady's attention was fixed upon the swordsmen as another shout of excitement went up. Alarmed, Fiona was in time to witness a furious flurry of flashing blades and ringing steel. Torrey shouted and sprang forward, but Mathieson turned the thrust and chuckled audibly. Inflamed, Torrey launched a powerful thrust over the arm. Mathieson parried with the dangerous *prime parade*. Instead of retreating then, he moved forward, bearing on Torrey's blade. With a shout, Torrey tried to disengage preparatory to a thrust in *carte*. Smiling grimly, Mathieson counter-disengaged, using the *forte* of his sword to force Torrey's blade upward.

Alec Pauley gasped.

Seizing his arm, Fiona asked tensely, "What? Alec, what is it?"

"I do believe he means tae attempt the disarm! Chancy! Verrra chancy!"

In that same instant, Mathieson moved so fast his actions seemed to blur. His left foot advanced; with his left hand he seized the shell of Torrey's sword in an iron grip. Torrey flung his weight forward and kicked hard, but Mathieson had already thrown the right side of his body back. To Fiona's astonishment, his sword whipped behind him and came around from his left side, his wrist supported on his hip, the point of his blade presented steadily to Torrey's stomach. With his sword still inexorably in Mathieson's grip, and that wicked colichemarde menacing his middle, Torrey panted a groaning curse, relinquished his blade and retired from distance.

A spontaneous roar of applause rang out. Breathless, Mathieson spun about and for the first time, saw the redcoats. An instant, he paused; then, with a flourish of both swords, bowed low.

Heywood, who had come in with a beautiful young lady on his arm, walked up to clap Mathieson on the back. "You dog! By God, but you can fight!"

"Not—as well as some," acknowledged Mathieson. "But better . . . than others."

" 'Twas a braggadocio boy's trick," muttered Torrey sullenly.

" 'Twas rash and reckless and superb," grinned Mervyn Bradford. "Which is a deal more than could be said for *your*—" Belatedly, he saw the redcoats and stood motionless.

"Good evening, Captain," drawled Mathieson.

Lady Clorinda came through her quieting people. "So you found the time to attend our performance, Captain Lake. I trust you were not disappointed?"

The dragoon nodded condescendingly. " 'Twas a grand fight,

ma'am. My congratulations, Captain Mathieson. I must take care never to cross swords with you! But as to your performance, alas, I missed it. Unless— Surely, you do not tell me this fight was part of it, Mr. Bradford?"

Bradford grinned but stood in numb silence.

Mathieson thought fleetingly, 'He has frozen solid!' Tossing Torrey his sword, he said, "I think you are not a fool, Lake. This was a personal matter I'd not expected to settle tonight, with ladies present."

Captain Lake glanced at Torrey's red face and lifted a scornful eyebrow. "Forced on you, was it?" He clicked his tongue reprovingly. "Not the thing, sir."

Torrey rammed his weapon into the scabbard, and, aware he'd behaved atrociously, muttered, "I admit that, Captain. But—" he looked angrily at Fiona "—there's a lot you don't know."

Wondering why the dragoons were here, wondering how her cousin Elizabeth had reached them, Fiona struggled to appear calm.

Captain Lake turned to smile at her. "Ah—so that's the way the wind blows. I quite understand." He moved to bow over her hand. "How do you go on, ma'am?"

"Very well, I thank you." Despite her efforts, her voice trembled a little. "Our audience appeared well pleased, at all events."

"And you are tired. I promise not to delay you for very long, though I am most distressed that I missed seeing the play, Miss Fiona."

"You shall have to come again," urged Mervyn Bradford, recovering his wits sufficiently to offer an insincere smile.

"I wish I may. Where do you go from here?"

"Into Cheshire, Captain. We are to give a performance in the vicinity of Chester."

"Alas, then I shall miss it, for I am transferred to Salisbury in the south. I shall tell my replacement to look in on you, lucky fellow."

"A promotion, sir?" enquired Mathieson, with not a vestige of interest in the matter.

"An advancement, certainly. For me. But a demotion for the man who takes over my command. Poor chap let some traitors slip through his fingers. Beastly luck, but—well, I'd best say no more, save that I fail to remember this lady . . ." He turned to

156

the girl beside Thaddeus Heywood. "Your name if you please, ma'am."

"This is my niece, Miss Elizabeth Clandon," said Bradford. "Have you your papers, my dear? This gentleman will wish to see them, I expect."

Miss Clandon produced some forged papers from the prettily embroidered reticule that was of the same stuff as her green cloak. Taking his admiring eyes from her lovely face the Captain scanned the papers briefly.

"So you are from Plymouth, Miss Clandon. You journey a long way to visit your kinfolk."

"My papa is by way of being in business, sir, and had to be in London, but I have been a little unwell, so he preferred I breathe pure country air for a time."

"Sensible gentleman. What—er, type of business occupies your father?"

"He inherited quite a large lending library, Captain. We serve teas and coffees also and have a quality line of dress stuff and fancy goods."

"I see." He found this petite young woman vastly pretty with her big brown eyes and golden hair, and enquired smilingly, "And just where is this—ah, establishment? I might like to pay it a visit."

"We shall look forward to it, sir. Our library is situated just a short distance from the Citadel."

"Ah. I had hoped 'twas in Town. Plymouth is rather a long way for me to go, I'm afraid. But I shall be in London very soon. When do you return, ma'am?"

Miss Clandon hesitated. She recognized the signs and had no wish to be pursued by this grim-looking officer, nor dare she offend him.

Mathieson, who had not failed to notice the intensity with which Thaddeus Heywood followed this conversation, interposed blandly, "Perhaps you should rather ask her affianced, sir. Miss Clandon is by way of being betrothed to Mr. Heywood."

Surprise and delight were mixed in Heywood's tawny eyes. Miss Clandon blushed becomingly and looked shy and conscious.

The captain stiffened. "Indeed? My congratulations, sir." He returned the girl's papers, swung around and said with a sudden dark frown, "It all sounds a touch havey-cavey to me. What do you make of it, Mathieson?"

Over Lake's shoulder, Mathieson could see Fiona Bradford's pale solemn little face. Her green eyes met his own with unwavering confidence. Lake was suspicious, obviously, which was extreme dangerous. But again, fate offered him a chance to save himself. A few words only and he would be protected from the possible wrath of military justice. They, of course, would all be hauled off to the Tower . . . The Tiny Mite, my lady, young Japhet. To say nothing of Thaddeus Heywood for whom, against all logic and reason, he had formed a grudging affection. It was irritatingly nonvillainous, but he had no wish to save his neck at the cost of destroying these people. Besides, he hadn't toiled all these months only to now lose every chance at the treasure. He answered, "I do believe 'tis all above board, sir. I knew Mr. Heywood's affianced was to join us."

The captain grunted. "Very well." He looked sternly around the silent group. "Keep your eyes open, Mathieson. There are rebels about. Dammit, I can smell 'em!" He saluted in the general direction of Fiona Bradford and stamped from the hall, his men following.

By common consent there was silence until the hoofbeats faded into the distance. Then, my lady turned to Mathieson. "You've a quick wit, lad. Again, we have to thank you."

"I—motht of all—am eternally indebted to you," said Heywood, his eyes upon Miss Clandon with such obvious worship that there could be no doubting this was his love.

Amused, Bradford said, "My dear, allow me to present the gentleman who announced your betrothal—Captain Roland Mathieson."

Bowing, Mathieson said laughingly, "I trust you will not feel bound as a result of my impudence, ma'am."

"Irretrievably," murmured Heywood, his eyes wistful. "She cannot ethcape now that it hath been formally announthed."

Miss Clandon offered her hand and said with a twinkling little smile, "Now see the pickle you have got me in, Captain Mathieson."

Heywood had long since abandoned all hope of winning the lady, but her reply held an encouragement that he scarcely dare acknowledge. He turned so white that his freckles stood out darkly and he stared at her, dazed and tongue-tied.

Taking pity on him, Fiona said, "Again, you have risked your life for us, Captain Mathieson. Though why you should do so after the treatment we mete out to you," her eyes rested scornfully on Torrey, "escapes me."

"It escapes me also," said Mathieson thoughtfully. "I had quite meant to denounce you all and thus save my own neck!"

There was much laughter at this. Then, hugging her newly arrived granddaughter, Lady Clorinda asked in eager impatience, "Where is MacTavish? He did come with you, no?"

Mathieson stood perfectly still, breath held in check.

Cuthbert, who had come into the hall in time to hear the end of this, said quietly, "Rob's away again, my lady. Should never've come. The young jabbernoll's properly sick. When we spotted the dragoons he knew he'd be unable to bluff 'em, as poorly as he was feeling, so he's gone back."

Mathieson drew a quivering breath of relief and his taut muscles relaxed.

Bradford asked anxiously, "What ails him?"

"He says 'tis a cold, Uncle Mervyn," said Miss Clandon, shaking her head dubiously.

"More like an inflammation of the lungs, was you to ask me," grunted Cuthbert.

Clearly worried, my lady said, "Lord protect the lad. We cannot have him ill! How ever should we go on without him? Did he send any word for me?"

Cuthbert nodded and lowered his voice. "We have messages, ma'am."

It was decided the messages must wait until they were packed up and had returned to their camp, and a rather subdued troupe set to work.

Mathieson, assisting in taking down the curtains, became aware of a sudden silence, and swung around, ready as always, for violent action.

Freemon Torrey stood behind him, pale but defiant, fists clenched and shoulders pulled back. "A word with you, sir," he said haughtily.

Mathieson turned to face him. The silence deepened, the others pausing in their labours to watch this exchange. "Well?"

"I—" Torrey bit his lip. "No, sir. Is not 'well.' What I did—" His auburn hair glowed in the candlelight, the costume accentuated his muscular figure, and he looked magnificent, but his head drooped. Staring at his boots, his face suddenly scarlet, he went on, " 'Twas—despicable. Dishonourable. Disgusting. I—was—"

"Very jealous."

Torrey's head came up angrily.

"But—quite without cause," soothed Mathieson. "The lady is *très beau*, a delight, a pearl beyond price." And quite aware that Fiona watched and listened, he finished, "But I, you know, am a wanderer—an impoverished, unemployed soldier. With no fortune, no estate, no prospects. Sorry competition for such as you . . . eh?"

Torrey eyed him with suspicion. "But—you admire her. Don't deny it!"

"*Hein!* I said I am without fortune—I did not imply I am dead, sir!"

Hearing smothered chuckles, Torrey bristled again. "Now see here!"

"*Oui.* Forgive. I interrupted your so humble apology. Pray continue."

Infuriatingly, Torrey could not think what to say, and stammered, "Yes. Er—well, I do not expect you to—to forgive the offense. It was unpardonable."

"Quite. And deplorable. My poor fellow—*whoever* taught you to fence?"

Heywood, standing nearby, was overcome and shouted with laughter, the others joining in.

"Dammitall," raged Torrey, but Mathieson's eyes were gleaming with mischief, and, won to a shamefaced grin, he went on, "I'd no suspicion I fought the world's best swordsman, curse you!"

"Second best," said Roland Fairleigh Mathieson modestly.

∂ 10 ∂

Picayune, who had enjoyed left-over sausage for breakfast, half woke as the caravan jolted over a pothole. She yawned, stretched, and proceeded to drag herself into a more comfortable position on Elizabeth Clandon's lap.

"Never in my life," admitted the girl, stroking the little cat absently. "I suppose that is why I so mistrust your Captain Mathieson. No man should look like that. 'Tis most unfair. Only think how 'twould be to love such a one!" She shuddered. "Heaven forfend!" Fiona remaining silent, Elizabeth glanced at her curiously, then steadied Picayune as the caravan rocked again. "Were you offended by what he said to Torrey last evening?"

"I've no objection to being named *très beau*—even if it is not true. Or—a pearl beyond price . . ." Fiona gave a soft little chuckle. "The sly wretch."

"A 'sly wretch' is it? Yet you think he is a good man, dear coz?"

"I know he is. Grandmama likes him. And Papa."

"And Torrey." Elizabeth's eyes twinkled. "Oh yes, I could see the liking between *them*!"

Fiona said with a shrug, "Torrey is jealous."

"With reason?" And noting the hesitation, the heightened colour in her cousin's cheeks, Elizabeth, who was fond of Freemon Torrey, thought, 'My heavens!' and asked anxiously, "Never say you have formed a *tendre* for Captain Mathieson? He is an adventurer if ever I saw one. Surely Grandmama does not approve your—"

Fiona's chin tilted upward. "He saved my life, Beth. And I

161

told you about the poor creature he rescued from the ducking stool.''

"Aye, but you say he claimed he merely tumbled into the river, and—"

"Oh, that is just his way. He is so modest he never will take praise for what he does. We are to believe Rumpelstilskin only *chanced* to run away with him. 'Twas *accidental*, one gathers, that he threw the poor woman and me onto his horse and stayed behind to face that horrid mob alone. Stuff!''

'Lud! What vehemence!' thought Elizabeth. "But why would he say such things an they are not so? Surely every gentleman wishes to appear brave and dauntless rather than proclaim himself a rascally creature.''

"Yet how many gentlemen who appear to be brave and dauntless are all talk, and when called upon to do something that might hold an element of risk or of inconvenience to themselves, contrive to be elsewhere, or claim some pressing obligation which will not allow them to help? Roland Mathieson is exactly the reverse. He *says* he is a villain, yet *acts* bravely and without an instant's hesitation where many a lesser man would do nothing—or run away! You saw him fight last night, Beth. He was splendid, was he not?''

Deeply dismayed by the depth of enthusiasm, by the revealing glow in her cousin's sweet face, Elizabeth said carefully, "He is a magnificent swordsman, I allow. But—rather frightening. No, did you not mark the way his eyes shone? How he laughed while he faced Torrey's steel? He enjoys to fight! The last time I visited you, dearest, I heard my uncle say that Torrey was very good with the foils—yet Captain Mathieson made him appear a rank amateur.''

"Must I like him less because he is a first-rate swordsman? We may stand in dire need of such skills. And soon!''

"Yet, if my grandmama really trusted him, he would have been admitted to the meeting last night after we came home. He wasnae, Fiona.''

"Was *not*,'' said Fiona, with a smile that took the sting out of the correction. "Besides, Lord Thaddeus was not admitted to the meeting either. Yet you both like and trust *him*. No?''

It was Miss Clandon's turn to blush. "I have very good reason to trust Thaddeus Briley—''

"I said 'like,' also. "And 'tis *Heywood*, coz. Be careful!''

162

"Och awie! I *must* try to remember! And of course I—I like him. He is a close friend of Ligun Doone, and although a full-blooded Sassenach—"

"Not a half-breed, like Papa and Francis and—"

With an irked exclamation Elizabeth leaned across to tug at one of her cousin's glossy ringlets. "Ye ken well what I mean, you wretch! Thaddeus almost lost his life while helping our fugitives escape Inverness. He's as brave as he can stare. The very finest kind of gentleman."

"Yes." Fiona took her hand and said firmly, "And you are in love with him! Oh, never deny it, Beth, 'tis writ all over you. Why did you not accept the poor creature, for heaven's sake? Was it because of dear Jamie? He's been gone over a year, now."

Elizabeth shook her golden head sadly. " 'Twas not for that reason, though I do mourn Jamie and always shall, God rest his brave soul. When first I met Thaddeus I thought him a silly, dandified creature. But I soon found out differently and I began to like him—more than like him, but . . . We are worlds apart, Fiona." Agitated, her accent became pure Scots again. "I'd nae wish then tae become a baroness, y'ken. Nor tae leave my dear Scotland."

"But Thaddeus seems so kind and considerate a gentleman. Surely he would understand your feelings and allow you to spend part of the year at least with your family?"

"Aye. He did offer that. But . . ." Elizabeth drew a hand across her eyes wearily. "Och, but I could only think of how awful it would be to become the wife of an English noble-man . . . All the pomp . . . The haughty English ladies looking down their noses at the wee Scots lassie who caught the gentleman they'd hoped to snare. Tae—tae be presented tae—royalty!" She shuddered again.

"Is *that* all? La, Beth, but what a simpleton you are! Only look at yourself. How many ladies can claim a tenth of your loveliness? Why, within a month you would be the Toast of London! And if Lord Thaddeus has a country estate, as I fancy he has, he would doubtless rather spend most of the year there than subject you to unhappiness—if to be in Town would be distasteful to you!" She shook her head at her blushing cousin and added, "When I think of all the Toasts who would give their ears for such as Lord Thaddeus Briley to glance in their direction—and here you refuse the poor soul, and send him off, eating his faithful heart out for you! I *knew* something of the sort ailed him, for when he thought himself unobserved his eyes were so sad. Beth, Beth—are you not ashamed to have teased him so?"

Remorseful but eager, Elizabeth asked, "Was he really grieved, then? How dreadful! I'd not have caused him a moment's sorrow—not for the world! I thought he soon would forget me, even if *I*—" She broke off in confusion, then continued hurriedly, "I never dreamed he would run himself into danger again—and only for my sake." Her lips curved to a fond smile and she murmured tenderly, "Such a bonnie wee lad. . . ."

Watching her, Fiona smiled also and thought that by the grace of God, Thaddeus Heywood would take a bride back to London with him.

"Utter folly!" muttered Heywood, jerking the collar of his cloak higher about his ears, and chirruping to the team he guided along the narrow lane. "Beth ought never to have come! Damme, but thometimeth I wonder what Lady Clorinda ith thinking of!"

Reining Rumpelstilskin around a large puddle, Mathieson asked, "Why *did* Miss Clandon come? I'd think Cuthbert able to be trusted with any message from MacTavish."

"No doubt of that. The thing ith—" Heywood paused, glancing at his companion from the corner of his eye.

"Have a care, milord," warned Mathieson with a grin. "You know I mean to abscond with the caravans and all the treasure!"

"Clod." Heywood paused again, then added rather diffidently, "I think I know men, Roly, and I'll admit I'm glad to have a fellow of your calibre to help uth. I fanthy you're aware we mean to load the treathure very thoon. Mith Clandon hath been arranging the matter of how it ith to be carried on from here."

Mathieson was touched by the shy compliment, but that reaction was drowned in the ramification of Heywood's following sentence. His mind fairly buzzing with conjecture, he managed to ask coolly, "And she came down from Scotland to do so?"

"Clever, ain't you? How'd you know where the lady come from?"

"Because I am astute as well as talented. And just occasionally Miss Clandon has the very faintest trace of an accent. When are we to collect the treasure?"

"I don't know ekthackly, but I imagine 'twill be within a day or two, and that it will take a little time."

It would take a great deal of time, thought Mathieson, if the treasure was as large as rumour said. Yet it could not be of vast size, else how could they transport it in six caravans, most of which were already crowded? There was milady's ridiculous coach of course, wherein Cuthbert slept at night, but even that outsized and outlandish vehicle could not carry a great deal—certainly not without being detected. Besides, the flamboyant coach, certain to draw all eyes, went on ahead when they approached the town or village in which they were to present the play. On these occasions large banners heralding their arrival were hung from each side of the coach, and Cuthbert and whoever went with him posted notices announcing the time and place of the performance. No—of all their vehicles, the coach was the most public—it could not logically be used to transport the treasure.

He had lost the thread of Heywood's remarks and was brought back to the present by the mention of Fiona's name.

". . . for her to be traipthing about the countrythide like any gypthy girl! A lady of Quality! Appalling! Enough to ruin her forever!"

"Oh, I cannot allow that, old lad. The girl is well chaperoned—her papa and grandmother are both here to guard her."

"Aye, and to allow her to *perform*! In a *play*! Come now, imagine what the *ton* would have to thay!"

"Gad! I dare not! I bow to your superior wisdom. She would be ruined fairly. Lucky we are so far from London."

"And luckier ith the lady not identified before we're done with thith mad venture! And no need for it in my opinion. We could have had an all male troupe."

Mathieson jeered, "I wish I may see it! At a time when there's a widespread hunt for a hoard of treasure, here comes a group of men jauntering about in caravans, claiming to be a theatrical troupe! No, my lady is not such a fool! Everyone knows 'tis the pretty girls bring in the custom for such ventures. She knew the military would have pounced on such an unlikely lot."

"I may be a fool," argued Heywood grimly, "but how will you like it an we are hauled off to the Tower? Have you pictured Mith Fiona in ironth? Or put to the quethtion? Curl your mocking lip over *that* pretty prothpect, friend!"

"Now—damn your eyes!" exclaimed Mathieson, whitening at this reinforcing of his own fears. "You blasted well know we'd all die sooner than allow such a thing to happen!"

"I know we'd all be willing, but a man don't alwayth have the opportunity to act ath he intended. We've already four ladieth to protect. And now—to have Beth Clandon at tho dreadful a rithk!" His comely face darkened. "God! It don't bear thinking about!"

Considerably shaken, Mathieson muttered, "It doesn't. But I imagine each of them was fully aware of the danger and chose to share it rather than allowing some other woman to take such a chance. One can only admire them for their courage and devotion." And again, he was reminded of Fiona looking so small, so intrepid, on Rump's back, and holding that mindless mob at bay with his pistol . . .

"You're abtholutely thertain you have no objection to Torrey courting Mith Bradford?" Heywood, his eyes crinkling at the corner with sly laughter, watched him.

"When did I ever make such a remark? Poor fellow," Mathieson shook his head sympathetically. "I collect you were so besotted over your lady at that moment, you did not hear what I said."

Heywood reddened, but persisted determinedly, "I heard you tell Freemon he need not be jealouth on your account, but—"

"As to that of course, he must make his own determination."

Heywood stared at him. "But—you dithtinctly—"

"I told him he had nothing to be jealous about, which is perfectly true since the lady in question is not interested in him—in that particular way."

"Why—you deviouth charlatan! You gave him to believe—"

"Not so," protested Mathieson, injured. "I was the soul of honour and honesty and gave him a clear accounting of myself. I even asked if he supposed me to be poor competition. Now," his eyes sparkled irrepressibly, "if the silly fribble really believes *that* to be so . . ."

Driving the lead caravan, his mother bundled in her fur-lined pelisse on the seat beside him, Mervyn Bradford glanced back curiously. " 'Tis going to rain, as if there was not already water everywhere one looks! But only listen to Heywood laugh. He's a happy man this morning. It's all midsummer with him! I think one of your granddaughters is destined to be a baroness, ma'am.''

"And the other is falling in love with a rascal," she muttered.

"No, no, Mama," he said, highly amused. "Faith, but you romantical ladies have but to see a fellow compliment a girl and—*voila*! 'tis a lifelong attachment! Be at ease. That suave young devil is not the man for my daughter, and well he knows it.''

"He's not the man for any woman with half a brain in her head. I'd have thought Fiona the last girl in the world to interest him. But—do you know Bradford, I begin to believe he is—intrigued, to say the least of it. He can scarce keep his eyes from the child and a time or two I've thought to catch a look . . . The last sort of look one would expect from such a rake.''

"And why not, I'd like to know," said her son huffily. "Fiona is a beautiful girl with a warm and loving nature and a happy disposition that would charm—''

"Tush and a fiddlestick! She is a hoyden, sir! You have seen to it that she has been taught little of feminine wiles and maidenly propriety! She says what she thinks—when for a lady to think at *all* is fatal! She *walks*—or dances!—instead of mincing! She laughs aloud when she should shyly smile or titter behind her fan! I doubt she even dreams of how improper is this desperate business—nor would she care if she did, by heaven!''

"Yet you appear to think those very qualities have intrigued a suave and polished individual such as Roland Mathieson," her son riposted triumphantly.

"Such a conquest gives you pride, does it?" she sneered. "Though you did but say he was not the man for her!''

"Not for marriage—certainly not! I'll not deny I like the rascal. But nor will I have my daughter claimed by a fellow with no fortune and precious little respectability, come to that!''

My lady gave a derisive snort. "Marbury saw to it he'd a name, at least, if that is what you mean. 'Tis not his bastardy which concerns me, but his character. Or lack of it!''

Despite his basic selfishness, Bradford was deeply fond of his daughter and at this he drew himself up and said majestically, "I'd fancied him a gentleman, whatever his background, but an you know of things to his discredit where the ladies are concerned, then I must insist that we get rid of the fellow at once.''

"Don't be more of a fool than you can help, Mervyn! You

knew perfectly well why I ordered his horse be stolen, and why Cuthbert broke his head to keep him away from us.''

Bradford flushed and said sulkily, ''You said he was a dangerous man, but when you changed your mind, I thought—''

''I changed my mind for—for several reasons. Mostly, because I'd had no suspicion he was in sympathy with our people, nor that he'd helped several get out of England. I judged him by his reputation.'' She sighed wearily. ''Lord knows why. One should never do so.''

His jaw dropped. ''But—you just said—''

''Oh, why must you argue so? Do you not see how few we are? We cannot turn away a swordsman of Mathieson's skill. Not while he is of use to us, that is.''

''So you would sacrifice my daughter—''

''Nonsense! I'll own I cannot like to see her partiality for him, but—if worse comes to worst I can make an end of it. Meanwhile, we play a dangerous game which, God grant, is almost done.'' She frowned and lapsed into a silence her son did not dare break. At length she said musingly, ''The Mathiesons are a strange breed. If Roland *should* give Fiona his heart it could work to our advantage—for a little while. Certainly, his ties to us grow stronger with each day that passes, which is as well—especially now that poor Robbie MacTavish is ill.''

''Humph. I said all along we should have more men. Lord knows there were enough willing.''

''Aye, and all with tongues to wag and knowledge to be forced from them should they be taken. No, the Committee judged it best to keep our numbers as small as humanly possible. The temptation of what we will carry is too great. Besides, a fine show we would make riding with a full escort of gallants! Might as well send out a proclamation of who we are! Can you not hurry the beasts along, Bradford? The sooner we reach this Sandipool village Robbie has chose for us, the better I shall like it! Small wonder the poor lad has fallen ill. Did ever you see so much damp? Pools and meres and rivers wherever one looks! Lud, what a swamp of a county!''

'' 'Tis held to be very beautiful, Mama.''

''On a hot summer's day, perchance, but—Here comes the rain! More water! Enjoy the beauty, Bradford! I shall go inside! Turn up your cape, for heaven's sake!''

* * *

Despite its inauspicious beginnings, by eleven o'clock the rain had stopped, and the day brightened. A little breeze came up to blow the clouds away and soon warm sunshine was lifting everyone's spirits and awakening countless sparkles and glitters from new-washed leaves and grasses. Cuthbert, who had ridden out at dawn to find the campsite MacTavish had chosen for that night, returned to lead them to it, and now they drove along muddy lanes but with lovely Cheshire appearing to her best advantage.

A squeak brought a twitch to Mathieson's lips and he guided Rumpelstiltskin to where he might follow the lead caravan. Fiona had opened the window in the back door and waved merrily as he came up. "Oh, Roly," she cried, her eyes as bright, he thought, as the sunshine, "is it not beautiful?"

"Captain Mathieson," he corrected, but with a smile. "Very beautiful."

"Yes, and—hello Rumpel— Oh, *do* look! *What* a pretty village! I declare it would make anyone reach for paints and canvas."

"If one could paint, which you cannot—or so you said."

"Very true. You see *I* do not tell wicked falsehoods—" she slanted a bewitching twinkle at him "—as do some unprincipled persons. And you need not think to have changed the subject, for I— Only see that cottage! Oh, I never saw such beautiful half-timbering!"

"Nor I such a scatter-wit. Where is your shawl? The wind is chill and— No! Never mind about the village pond. 'Tis exquisite—and the ducks are all very well bred and superior, I grant you. Yes, even that fat goose waddles with *savoir-faire*. Not another word until you have your shawl. And then you may tell me of the alleged 'wicked falsehoods.' "

Fiona snatched up a shawl as carelessly as though it had not been very carefully chosen to complement her pale lemon muslin gown. Throwing it quickly about her shoulders, she said, "No—did you think I meant *you*, Captain Mathieson? Now what falsehoods might you have told, sir? Unless—'twas that you do *not* find me *très beau*?"

"I find you a creature of vast conceit," he drawled. "Torrey and I were discussing your grandmama, if you must know it, and—Good God!" (as a squeak interrupted him) "*Now* what bucolic wonder must I admire?"

169

"That! *That!* No—turn your Mathiesonish head this way, do! There—now—what is it?"

"Mathiesonish . . ." he echoed dubiously. "Hmmnn . . . Do for heaven's sake stop squeaking like any dormouse! 'Tis a covered bridge, child. Surely you've seen one before?"

"No! Never! There are none near our home and I've never seen one in London!"

He sighed. "One must presume you close your eyes each time you cross London Bridge."

"Do not be supercilious, Roly! London Bridge is like a regular street, with shops and goodness knows what else besides! One can ride along it and scarce realize it spans the river. This is like—like a stretched out barn. How very quaint! And I do believe we are to go across! Oooh . . . !"

Amused by her enthusiasm, he chuckled. The horses plodded patiently, their hoofbeats becoming suddenly hollow and echoing. The wheels rumbled a sharper song, and the light faded as they passed under the roof of the old bridge.

Mathieson leaned closer and said in sepulchral tones, "The daemon of this bridge has teeth a foot long and he devours squeaky little girls for his breakfast! Prepare to be boiled and spread on toast!"

"Poor daemon—how dreadful when he goes to the dentist. Oh, how *deliciously* daemonish it smells in here! Is that by reason of his toast, do you think?"

"Revolting child! You should shrink and quail and shake in your pretty slippers! Faith, but you are a great disappointment to me."

"What stuff! As if anyone would be afraid of a silly old bridge!"

Mathieson chuckled, his thoughts far away.

Watching the gleam in his eyes Fiona asked curiously, "Where have you gone? Come back, please. Of whom are you thinking now?"

"My apologies. I was thinking of a very fine fellow. A dashing captain of dragoon guards. Er, that is to say he *was* a captain. Now he seems to have—ah, tumbled a little way down the ladder of rank. Nonetheless, he is most impressive. Very good-looking. All splash and dash. And purely terrified of covered bridges."

She giggled. "But has fought bravely in countless terrible engagements, I take it?"

"Oh, yes. He's a terror on the battlefield. But—show him a covered bridge, and he'll run a mile!"

"Roly, you dreadful creature! What fibs you tell. But I do love your stories. Pray enlighten me as to why this so dashing fellow suffers from such an affliction. If you can manufacture a satisfactory cause, that is."

" 'Tis already manufactured, you little wretch. It seems this dashing young captain rode his dashing mare onto a covered bridge one evening at dusk. A flock of bats chose the same instant to leave the bridge with the result that our military friend, who has a horror of bats, suddenly found himself surrounded by dozens of the creatures at very close quarters. His mare who is all nerves and show, took fright, shied, and threw him and I'm told he came nose to nose with the king bat. They say our valiant captain beat his mare to the end of the bridge . . ."

Laughing, Fiona said, "The king bat, indeed!"

"Well, perhaps just a crown prince." He grinned. "Gad, how I should love to have seen it."

She eyed him uncertainly. "Are you serious? It really did happen?"

"Oh yes. It is perfectly true. Only see how I tend to your education. Today we have learned of bats and covered bridges. Now—as to the dentists who tend daemons—did you know that they also have to be of the daemonish persuasion . . . ? I once knew a daemon went to a regular human dentist, and . . ."

The golden moments slipped away while they enjoyed a whimsical discussion on daemons and dentists, punctuated by much merriment, and ending with the mutually agreed upon conclusion there was little to choose between them.

Half an hour later they came to their campsite and Mathieson slipped away to attend to a matter which he had postponed longer than was expedient. When he had finished, he led Rumpelstiltskin to the paddock Alec had fashioned. The young Scot was still there, chatting quietly with Moira Torrey, and, to cover his embarrassment at being caught alone with her, promptly demanded to know where Mathieson had been.

"Attending to my friend's toilette," replied Mathieson lightly. "You would seem to have put your time to better use, dear boy."

Miss Torrey turned quite pink, but she was more perceptive than her shy admirer and, looking past him, exclaimed, "Oh, whatever have you done to your fine animal? His pretty white stockings are gone!''

Alec's eyes sharpened. ''And the blaze on his face. For why, mon?''

''Because I am reminded that there are certain dragoons who know Rumpelstiltskin almost as well as they know me.''

''And if they recognized him . . . ?'' asked Moira in a scared whisper. ''Would that be very bad?''

''It would not be—shall we say—very good.'' Mathieson looked into her wide dark eyes and grinned deprecatingly. ''For me, ma'am. I might, in fact, be called upon to pay an overdue debt. And I've no doubt it would be collected—with interest.''

''At all events,'' said Captain Lake, strolling across the muddy courtyard of The Four Fiddlers Inn, ''there are worse places to be quartered.''

The tall young lieutenant beside him was of fair colouring, well built and very handsome, a splendid example of British manhood. His blue eyes were hard, however, and the fine mouth had a bitter droop. He glanced about the old inn yard without favour, and with a toss of his powdered head grunted sourly, ''And better.''

''Small doubt of that.'' The captain shouted for his orderly, halted, and while pulling on his gauntlets turned to face the younger man. ''Take my advice, Lambert. There's a reb in the vicinity—I can feel it in my bones. Keep your wits about you and your men more in the saddles than out of 'em, and you might be a captain again sooner than you think.'' His horse being led out, he glanced critically at his accoutrements and prepared to mount up. ''Well, I'll be off. Good luck t'you.''

As they shook hands Lambert looked glum. ''God—if you but knew how I envy you! To be going back to the south country! What is there up here but yokels and desolation?''

''Another chance, man!'' said Lake bracingly. ''Cheer up! You're a roving commission. If you sniff a Jacobite—hunt him to earth and exterminate the swine! Or better yet, haul him in alive. I'll wager it wouldn't take much to restore you to favour again. As for envying me, why, you've had a set-back, but it could be worse. You didn't lose your commission, and many a man would envy *you*! A young buck with your looks—well born, good education; and you've a grand battle record, I marked that."

Lambert said nothing, but the blue eyes were brooding, and, curious, Lake said, "I've no wish to pry, but—if you don't mind my asking, just what the devil did go wrong?"

"Everything," muttered Lambert. "And just when life seemed perfect. Beware the whims of fate, friend! Six months ago I'd the world at my feet, or so I fancied. My aunt's fortune was to be mine; I was preparing to marry the lady I'd been courting for some years; my record was spotless. Then . . ." His mouth twisted. "My greedy uncle plotted against me; the woman I courted betrayed me; the friend who promised his help, instead conspired with my uncle to so entrap and ruin me that I lost my lady, my rank, *and* the fortune!"

"A fine friend!" exclaimed Lake, shocked by this litany of treachery.

"A devil, rather," muttered Lambert. "But we'll meet again, I promise you . . ." A glint came into his eyes, and his smile was not pleasant.

"And when you do," said Lake uneasily, "you'll call out the dirty swine, eh?"

Lambert did not at once answer. Then he looked up. His smile was warm, his expression so open and cheerful that Lake thought he must have imagined that rather horrible and secretive look.

"Something like that, sir," said Lambert. "But never heed me. I brought it all on myself, belike, and must take the consequences."

"Good man." Lake swung into the saddle, then reined around. "Oh, and don't forget—if you're up Chester way, look in on that acting troupe I mentioned. They put on a damn good show, and there are a couple of dashed pretty fillies . . ." He winked. "Impoverished now, but were once of good family, I'd think. Might be just the sort of—ah, diversion you need."

"Thank you, sir. Good-bye."

Lake waved his riding crop and started across the yard, his orderly and his escort falling in behind.

Lambert stared after him until horse and man had left the yard. His smile vanished then, and he spat contemptuously at the cobblestones. He could find all the "pretty fillies" he

173

wanted, and with his looks he wasn't obliged to sink to the level of actress whores for his "diversion"!

By the time luncheon was finished the afternoon sun had become quite warm. Mathieson, who had been discovered to have a flair with the scissors, was required to trim Bradford's hair, the big man complaining it was getting so long as to be too hot under his wig. When this task was completed, Mathieson offered his services to Heywood, but that devoted swain had seen his love carry some mending to the steps of the caravan she now shared with Fiona and Moira Torrey, and he lost no time in hurrying to keep her company. Mathieson contemplated wandering past the red coach to try what he could overhear of what Cuthbert, Torrey, and Gregor were plotting with my lady. The risk of being detected at this stage of the game seemed unwarranted, however. Now that Rob MacTavish was apparently too ill to join them, he could bide his time—at least for the next day or two.

Alec was repairing some saddle leathers, but his hazel eyes kept turning hopefully towards the table where Mrs. Dunnigan and Miss Torrey prepared vegetables for the evening meal. Alec, thought Mathieson, starting off in search of firewood, was sorely smitten. He wondered how it would end.

His own time here was almost at an end, that was certain. He had learned to respect life's often bizarre coincidences and even with the threat of MacTavish's arrival postponed, he knew it was not beyond the bounds of possibility that at any moment— particularly during a performance—some acquaintance might see him and denounce him for what he was. The phrase galled. "For what he was . . ." What was he? Had he yet reached the depth of depravity his father had foretold? Was he truly an evil man?

He was in the gold-splashed shade of the woods now, and halted as a small and familiar shape came towards him, sounding a friendly trill. So the little cat had not forgotten that he had (however inadvertently) saved her life. He glanced around furtively. No one in sight. Rumpelstiltskin had a weakness that was shared by both the cat and dog of one of Mathieson's few friends. It was possible that Picayune suffered the same addiction. He groped in his coat pocket and brought out the carefully wrapped piece of cheese he'd saved for the stallion.

"Here, cat," he whispered, dropping to one knee and offering the bribe.

Picayune sat down and considered him.

"Here, you bad-tempered, silly-looking, flea-bag," said Mathieson dulcetly. But when the cat merely yawned, he raised his voice to a squeak and uttered the approved, "Kitty, kitty."

This address appeared to be more the thing. Picayune got up, wafted her tail high, wandered close, sniffed, and accepted. Afraid of frightening her, Mathieson remained still, watching her devour the cheese and tidy up with feline fastidiousness. Finding no more crumbs, she looked at him expectantly. "I have no more, Madam Glut," he informed her. She replied with a friendly "mew." Very slowly, he reached out to stroke her. She turned her head against his hand in a friendly way, then suddenly gave him a fast swipe with one well-equipped paw and shot into the woods.

"Chat révoltant!" he flung after her, rubbing his scratched hand. He stood, and brushed mud from his knees. It was a very small scratch, but quite typical of the spiteful creature. He should have known better.

Grumpily, he returned his thoughts to more pleasing subjects—such as the unappetizing Freemon Torrey, or that complete toad, Lambert. But with the weird perversity of his mental processes of late, he was seized by guilt. Lord knows, of all men he had no right to judge *any* other! His own past was so disgraceful that he was unfit to— He pulled himself up short. What the *devil* ailed him? It was every man for himself in this harsh world, and if he was deceiving a parcel of witless idiots, well and good. Idiots deserved all they were dealt. And he worked hard for the eventual reward. He was bored as hell, but he dutifully played their silly games, acted in their foolish play, pretended to accept their so gullibly offered friendship . . . "I'll admit I'm glad to have a fellow of your calibre to help uth . . ."

He swore, and muttered defiantly, "Dammitall, Roland! Do not be wishing to have been born a good man, for 'tis too late. You cannot keep searching the soul you don't have! You're within sight of your goal—your *gold*. Snatch it with both hands, lucky man, and stop moping about!" He found that he was nudging his toe aimlessly at a tuft of grass, and swung a savage kick at it, which achieved nothing save to startle a moth and get mud all over his glossy boot. In a black rage he stamped deeper into the trees, took up a fallen branch and began to cut viciously at the shrubs he passed.

A splash, followed by a squeal, brought him up short. At no great distance a breathless female voice gasped, "You horrid, *horrid* beast! Now see what you've done!" And, interspersed with a succession of thuds, "Vile . . . besotted . . . *damnable* . . ."

Mathieson was running, his previous anger as nothing to the blazing wrath that now possessed him. By God, but if any man had *dared* . . .

He burst through the trees and was on the bank of a stream, where he halted abruptly.

On her hands and knees, red in the face and considerably wet and dishevelled, Fiona looked up at him in patent dismay, blew a curl from her heated forehead, and gasped, "Oh, Lud! I collect you heard me swearing. Well 'tis too late now, and I'm not sorry, so if you must preach at me about propriety—do so, but you shall have to manage in between my oaths and curses!"

Following which erratic speech, she began to pound a cudgel at the sodden lump of white cloth which huddled without visibly aggressive tendencies on a small boulder.

"What—the *deuce* are you doing?" panted Mathieson. "I thought—some loutish ploughboy was assaulting you!"

Awed, she stopped, and, her cudgel still upraised, looked at him, the cloud clearing from her brow and her stormy eyes beaming once more. "No! *Did* you? And is that why you raced through the trees like some avenging knight-errant? Oh, how *lovely*!"

He fought back a laugh. "Lovely, indeed! Not when I came up in time to hear such frightful language! Terms that never should pass a lady's lips."

"I know." Her eyes fell and a dark blush stained her cheeks. "I am very bad." She peeped up at him, put aside her cudgel and said contritely, "I'm doing the laundry, you see, while Moira and Mrs. Dunnigan prepare our dinner. Only I don't think I'm very good at it, because 'tis much dirtier now than when I began. Indeed, I wouldn't blame you at all if you decided I am a sadly faulted pearl and not of 'great price' at all."

"Well, I might," he warned. But his lips twitched, and there was teasing in the black eyes.

Relieved, she clapped her hands whereupon the garment she had attacked promptly slithered onto the muddy bank once more.

With a shriek, she snatched it up, thus splashing suds on her cheek. "The nasty thing has done it again!" And inspecting the new stains, she cried tragically, "Oh—*Roly*!"

"Foolish child, 'tis not the end of the world. Here—let me help." He seized one end of the garment, which appeared to be a nightdress, and held it up gingerly. "Gad, it *is* a trifle grubby, isn't it! Why were you hitting it?"

"That's what they do in India, and those places. My Uncle Henry brought back a book of his sketches, and there's one that distinctly shows ladies smashing away at washing on the banks of the Ganges, so I thought I'd have a try."

He eyed her dubiously. "I don't see how you can beat away at the things without getting mud on 'em."

"Nor do I." She sighed, then went on brightly. "Unless— perhaps you have to get *in*! Oh, why did I not think of that!" She began to take off her pattens.

Wrenching his appreciative gaze from her beautifully shaped ankles, he commanded, "Disabuse your mind of that notion, Tiny Mite! Uncle Henry's sketches or no, you are *not* going to immerse yourself in the stream! And furthermore—stand up, Miss!—you have soapsuds all over your face!"

She stood obediently and held up her face to be de-soaped. Mathieson wrung out a corner of the nightdress and bent to her. The breeze stirred her hair, and the errant curl flirted down her forehead again. Half laughing, she reached up to push it back.

"No—do not," he murmured, arresting her hand.

She smiled up at him, and the sunlight cast the shadow of her lashes across her cheekbone and emphasized the pert shape of her little nose.

It seemed to Mathieson that she was wrapped in light—a shimmering creature, more fragile than the finest crystal, her daintiness breathtaking, every line of her lovely self so wondrously perfect. He stood utterly motionless, afraid that if he dared move or speak, or touch her, this enchanted moment would shatter and never again would he know such unspeakable delight.

Looking up at his rapt face, the merriment in her own faded into a new look; a tender awareness that had nothing in it of the child, as he had chosen to call her. He marvelled at the realization that this bewitching creature was a woman. A loving, kind, gentle woman, made the more dear, the more enchanting, because of her lack of affectation, her swiftly changing moods, and the loyalty that bound her to those she loved. Here, surely, was a chance for—

Shock ripped through him. He drew back, and suddenly he was terrified. The garment he held slipped from his unsteady hands and he laughed harshly, avoiding Fiona's eyes as he took it up and wrung it out.

"Alas, but now I've done it, and you'll be properly vexed. You've no right to be slaving like this, little one. And you shall not!" He strode over to the ridiculously ambitious pile of laundry she had brought, and gathered it up while talking rather feverishly. "I'll have no more of this manual labour by a lady of Quality. We're to camp here tonight and I gather we will return here after the performance tomorrow, no? There'll be ample time for some deserving and industrious washerwoman in Sandipool, or however the place is called, to benefit from all this extra custom. Come, Mademoiselle Tiny Mite. I shall endeavor to escort you safely home through the menace of the dandelions and then take these to be properly and professionally cleansed." And still without meeting her grave eyes, he led the way through the trees and into the meadow.

Five minutes later, Fiona watched him ride out, a large bundle tied to his saddle. With a slow and tender smile she murmured, "Coward!"

∂ II ∂

It was warm and fragrant in the hayloft and Mathieson laughed softly as the girl who lay in his arms uttered a faint whimper and pressed closer against him. Beams of mellow afternoon sunlight slanted through cracks and knotholes in the old wooden walls and illumined her flushed face; a comely face, and a beautiful and tantalizingly well-rounded young body. He'd not dreamed when he'd bowed his head to enter the washerwoman's small cottage that upon looking up again he would encounter the admiring gaze of so pretty a wench. Having completed the transaction for the laundry, he had enquired as to the whereabouts of a tavern. With coy immediacy, Jenny had offered to show him the way. Her mother's cottage was a little distance beyond Sandipool, and long before they'd reached the toll road whereon the tavern was located, Jenny was comfortably settled on the saddle in front of Mathieson and he had claimed his first kiss. It had at once become clear that although it was the first embrace they had shared, it was far from being the first she'd known. Her mouth was practiced and eager; her eyes invited; his caresses had won answering caresses, and his suggestion that they find a quiet place to "chat" had resulted in her guiding him to the lonely old barn.

Jenny was a hot-blooded young creature, and Mathieson, no less so, was delighted by her lack of any pretended shyness. Her low-swooping blouse had but three buttons which were soon unfastened. His expert attentions to the loveliness thus bared had brought her eager fingers to divest him of his shirt, since his coat had already been thrown aside. Now, he bent to her

179

again, his teasing half-closed eyes roving her with the glow of desire that had prompted her little eager cry.

A rustling in the nearby straw. A cat trilled a greeting.

Mathieson tensed and his head jerked up. A small tabby wandered toward them, tail jauntily high-held.

"Come on, come on . . . me lovely lover . . ." urged Jenny huskily.

He stared at the cat. Impatient, the girl seized his hand and held it to her breast. With an effort, Mathieson tore his attention from the tabby and bent, smilingly to Jenny. The cat uttered another enquiring trill and came closer. Mathieson swore under his breath.

Jenny saw a frown replace the passion in those incredible black eyes. Irritated, she cried, "Get away! Dirty old mog! Get away and leave us be!" She had kicked off her shoes and now snatched one and flung it at the tabby, who fled with a yowl and a flash of grey stripes.

But it was done. It was no use. He didn't want this chit, however buxom—however willing. He desired her—but even his desire had not been so fully kindled that he was unable to draw back. He felt soiled and vulgar and wretchedly stupid, and he sat up, still frowning, and began to shrug into his shirt.

"Here!" cried Jenny, indignant. "What you a-doing of, me-lor'? Bean't I good enough, then?"

His eyes softening, he touched her cheek. "You are adorable. Only— Here, *mon petit chou* . . ." He pressed a gold sovereign into her willing hand. "Buy something pretty to grace your pretty self."

She sniffed, and flirted her shoulder at him as she restored her blouse, but ceased her angry mutterings when he swooped from behind her and kissed the back of her neck. Swinging around, she threw herself into his arms, and he kissed her once more, but differently. Trembling, she lay against him, then she sighed and sat up and began to button her blouse. "You love some fine lady, does ye? Aye—I see it in your eyes. I know that look, though most gentlemen don't care. Ah, well . . . she be one of the lucky ones."

Mathieson's eyes became bleak, and his mouth twisted, but Jenny was busied with slipping on her shoes and did not see. With a flutter of petticoats she ran to the ladder and clambered rapidly down it.

"You can find your own way to the tavern," she called, "seein's ye don't want me!"

Watching her ruefully, Mathieson bowed low. When he straightened she was standing in the open doorway, looking back at him, a shapely but faceless silhouette against the brightness of the golden afternoon. "I do hopes as she be worthy of ye," she called, then ran from sight.

Mathieson discussed this with Rumpelstiltskin, man to man as it were, while he guided the stallion at a canter towards the tavern Jenny had suggested.

"Do you know, Rump, I really begin to think my moral values are being undermined by all these damnable heroes I've been consorting with of late! Either that, or my mind is failing! Jenny probably thought so, too." He frowned. "More likely she thought I was unable to— *Sapristi!*" He drew rein and as Rump danced in a frustrated circle, his indignant gaze flew back across the tranquil meadow. "Of all the stupid dolts! I *must* be demented to so risk my reputation!"

Ten minutes later, seated on a wooden settle under a tall ash tree, Mathieson was still musing over his downfall. 'I do hopes as how she be worthy . . .' He waved away a bee who was interested in the contents of his tankard, then followed its flight until he lost it among the leaves. His gaze travelled higher. The sky was deeply blue, the clouds tinged with mellow gold. 'You did this, Thomas,' he thought. '*You* sent that confounded tabby to remind me of—of a lot of silly foolishness. And for what purpose? You know how worthy is Mademoiselle Fiona. And you most certainly know what *I* am! So what point is there in showing me what I cannot have . . . ?' He took up his tankard and muttered, "You won this time. I hope you're satisfied!"

"Well, I ain't," growled a harsh and vaguely familiar voice.

Mathieson started and blinked dazzled eyes at the roughly dressed man who stood beside him, coarse features scowling, and resentment in every line of his big frame.

"Sacré nom de nom!" drawled Mathieson, astonished. "I thought you were dead!"

"No thanks ter you I ain't," grumbled Ben Hessell. But, knowing this individual, he did not presume to sit on the opposite settle until Mathieson waved an inviting hand and called up another tankard.

"A fine mess you got me inter, Captin Otton," Hessell went

181

on then, keeping a cautious eye on that deadly right hand. "Jest a quiet little kidnapping, says you. Jest fer a lark, says you. We're jest a'goin' ter borrer the lady fer a coupla hours—no more, says you. So what happens? We—"

Mathieson interpolated coolly, "You knew the risks when you took my pay."

"We didn't know as how poor Feeney was goin' ter get scragged stone cold. Nor as how that horrid friend o'yourn would put a pistol ball through me!"

"Friend? Brooks Lambert is no friend of mine! If he ever—" And Mathieson stopped, for the less Hessell knew of his dealings with Lieutenant Lambert, the better.

In a prudently low-voiced continuance of his grievances, Hessell said, "Me and poor ol' Feeney didn't even know what it was all abaht. We was holding the gal fer ransom, we thought." He grinned jeeringly, "Fat lot o' ransom yer got, eh mate?"

Mathieson had gained nothing at all from that little ploy, which had been devised not for ransom money, but to force the hand of a good friend, Meredith Carruthers, who'd been shielding one of the Jacobite couriers. The attempt to acquire the cypher carried by the Jacobite, and to learn from it where Prince Charles Stuart's treasure was stored, had failed, even as Hessell said, and for a while it had seemed that in the process Mathieson had lost one of his few friends. Later, however, Carruthers had appealed to him for help and (for a price) he had obliged. His assistance had been invaluable to Carruthers, but had also brought demotion to the scheming and ruthless Brooks Lambert. Mathieson had no regrets insofar as Lambert was concerned, but the kidnapping was a black mark against him. The lady had been mauled by his confederates and the reminder made him squirm. His eyes glinted angrily, but he said nothing until the approaching waiter had provided Hessell with a brimming tankard.

"I am not your *mate*," he murmured as soon as the man had gone away again. "Wherefore I would advise you to keep a civil tongue in your head."

Hessell leered ingratiatingly and snatched up the tankard. "I didn't mean nothin', sir!" He drank deep and dragged his sleeve across his loose-lipped mouth. "But you gotta admit as it was crool hard. Perishin' hard on a man with a poor wife and lotsa innercent babes ter—"

182

Mathieson sneered, "You rend my heart. One wonders what your poor wife might have thought had she seen you pawing Miss Ramsay!" The malevolent glare Hessell slanted at him brought a scornful shrug. "So you still hold the grudge, do you? Typical! You've no cause. I didn't force you to it. We all took the risk. We lost. 'Tis done and nothing to be gained from brooding over it. Set it down to experience man, and perchance you may learn from it. Meanwhile, tell me what mischief you are about up here."

"Cor, you gotta nasty tongue, sir," whined Hessell, injured. "I ain't up ter nothin'—'cept starving. What I couldn't do with a good bitta roast beef, or a slice'a ham, mebbe . . ."

Mathieson grinned his appreciation of the tragic gaze that came his way. "Faith, but you're a slithery rascal. Very well, I owe you that much."

The waiter was summoned again; a plate of steaming beef and potatoes was brought forth, and between all too generous mouthfuls Hessell related the sad tale of his slow recovery from the bullet wound Lambert had inflicted. "He only shot me dahn fer fear I'd tell as he was in on it, too," he muttered indistinctly. "A wicked lot *he* is and no mistake."

"As are we all. Which does not explain how you come to be up here."

"Ar." Overlooking that unkind aspersion, Hessell conscientiously mopped his plate with a piece of bread. "Well, me old woman's brother lives in Liverpool, so I'm makin' me way up there, so fast as ever I can, sir, ter find honest work on the docks."

"If that's the truth, which I doubt, it'll be the first honest work you ever did."

Hessell gave him an aggrieved look, salvaged the gravy laden piece of bread which was sliding down his greasy waistcoat, and threw it into his mouth more or less accurately.

Mathieson shuddered, and stood hurriedly. "I must be off. I've to be in Town by Sunday. Good luck in your search for—er, honest work, Hessell."

The big man sprang to his feet, wiping his hands on his hat and bowing humbly. "And good luck t'you, too, Captin Otton. Proper kind o' you to give me what to eat. *Generous* is what it was. You allus was a generous gent. I—I don't reckon as you

183

could spare a groat, p'raps? A half-crown, mebbe? Fer old times' sakes, sir . . . ?''

Mathieson eyed his fawning obsequiousness with amused disgust, but handed over a sovereign, and with grateful thanks ringing in his ears, made his way to the stables and the more pleasing company of Rumpelstiltskin.

Hessell curled his lip and swore at the sovereign, then wandered after Otton's tall figure and watched him ride out. So the wicked captain still had that fine hack, did he? Funny, but he'd have sworn the stallion had a coupla white stockings. Now *there* would be something worth the stealing! And the cold-hearted perisher owed it to him, after all! A paltry sovereign! "Muckworm," he growled. "Much *you* care if poor Feeney's dead and buried!'' Not but what Feeney had been a perishin' fool. Still . . . He wandered moodily across the yard, tucked the sovereign in his waistcoat pocket, drew out the other item that had resided there, and halted, looking down at it.

The button was silver, embossed with the crest of some proud old family, though which one, he had no idea. Stolen, likely, because Otton had give it to him during that horrid business with Mr. Carruthers. "If you ever have word fer me,'' the perisher had said, "show this here ter me man—Sorenson—and he'll come and get me quick-like.'' Well, he'd not had no words fer Captin No-Good Otton fer a coupla months and more. Hessell turned the button, wondering how much it would bring in a pawnshop. He only half considered that possibility, for it seemed to him that there was something sniffy going on. You could'a knocked him dahn with a feather when he'd seen that murdering Captin Lambert yestiday. Ex-captin, that is. He chuckled. Jolly good that they'd taken him dahn a peg or two. Serve the bastard right.

A thought struck him forcefully, and he scowled, grappling with it. From what Otton had said, him and Lambert wasn't friends no more. But that there Otton had closed his choppers mighty quick over something. They was up to no good, that was sure, and likely in it together, same as last time. There *might* be a shilling or two come outta this yet. Meanwhile, it wouldn't hurt ter keep a eye on the almighty Lambert. Them Quality coves thought they was better'n everybody. Well, they'd find out they didn't fool Benjamin F. Hessell! He returned the button to his pocket with care. You couldn't never tell when a thing like this might come in handy . . .

Rumpelstiltskin wanted to gallop, and Mathieson let him have his head, the peaceful countryside blurring past as the stallion shot through drowsy meadows, thundered along lanes guarded by fragrant hedgerows, and slowed at last as they came to the hill where was the camp.

Mathieson patted Rumpelstiltskin's damp neck. "Brought me home fast, you rascal. Were you afraid I'd go back after the buxom Jenny?" He consulted the beautifully enamelled watch he had bought to reward himself after the business with the Alderman's lady and her misplaced pomander. "Woe is me, Rump! Half past four o'clock, and I quite forgot to gather the firewood! I'll be in deep dis—" His light words faded.

The faint sounds he had heard all the way up the hill were clearer now. The laughter became loud and the shouts raucous and unfamiliar. Listening intently, he drew Rumpelstiltskin to a halt. Someone had arrived. Someone important, to judge from all the hilarity. MacTavish?

A girl screamed then. He thought, *'Fiona!'* And the stallion who seldom felt a spur, reared to a hard jab and was away like a bolt of lightning.

Crouched low in the saddle as they burst into the clearing, Mathieson received a series of impressions that flashed with incredible speed across his mind. Cuthbert, sprawling beside the fire and trying feebly to get up, despite the efforts of a burly youth in a purple coat with one pocket torn off, who repeatedly kicked him down again; Heywood, sagging in the grip of two men whose garments proclaimed them "gentlemen," while another of their kind aimed a fist at his already bloodied face; Elizabeth Clandon, crouching at bay, her back to a tree, both her little hands clutching a long sword while another Buck howled with glee and dodged her desperate but clumsy lunges; Mervyn Bradford, dead or unconscious, lying huddled atop the steps of his caravan; and a wild fight raging between Pauley, Gregor, and two more intruders. All this was noted and filed away. His frantically searching eyes found and held to one figure. Her hair streaming about her shoulders, a sleeve of her gown ripped away, Fiona sent her little knife darting at the great lout whose laughter ceased as he grabbed her flying wrist. "Let be," he commanded merrily, holding her captive while with his free hand he began to tear the rest of her gown off. "Don't want t'hit ya, m'pretty, but you and me—"

In that shocked split second, Mathieson saw her little face, white and distorted with fear and rage. A roaring came into his ears. The scene before him blurred oddly around the edges. He must have cried out, for the big lout turned enquiringly as he launched himself from the saddle. A jarring impact, shouts, blows that were as nothing, the joy of feeling his fists thud home once, twice, three times against that dissipated, flabby young face. They were up and then down again. Fiona's voice shrieked, "Look out!" He rolled aside, seized the boot that had barely grazed his ribs and heaved—seemingly not very hard, yet his attacker howled and soared from view. Wild, crazed laughter that he suspected might be his own. He was on his feet once more, a face before him, slowly turning purple. Another shock drove him to his knees; boots were all about him. Heywood's breathless yell, "Hang on . . . dear old boy!" In the brief respite he managed to whistle for Rump. Came a thunder of hooves. The boots scattered. A shock that hurt this time, vaguely, distantly. A man screamed. He was up again. Two of the Bucks, less elegant now and much more grim, ran at him, both holding cudgels that looked like chair legs. Alec was beside him with a roared, "Yoicks!" and briefly, they fought side by side. Mathieson downed his man, but his gaze sought for and found the inexpressible swine who had touched her, who had dared tear her gown. The lout was reeling away. With a snarl, he raced in pursuit. The lout turned a bloodied, scared face, and drew a pistol. Mathieson launched himself, as he'd learned in France, kicking out savagely, and the lout screamed and hurtled back, dropping his pistol. He had him by the throat once more. The filthy, stinking animal would not touch her again, by God! He'd never molest any other helpless . . .

"Stop! Mathieson! *Stop!* Good Lord! Get him off, he'll kill the block!"

Hands were tearing at him.

"Roly—let be, you maniac!"

Enraged, he hung on, cursing them.

"Roly! Roly—please don't kill the beast! Please . . ."

Fiona. He relaxed his grip, and the lout lay very still beneath him. He reeled to his feet, and she was there, reaching out to

him. His arm went about her. He panted frantically, "You're all
. . . right? They didn't hurt you?"

There was dirt on her face, and a scratch on her chin, but her
eyes were like stars. "I'm all right," she said in a scratchy voice.

He felt dazed and weak with relief, and with a muffled sob
crushed her against him.

"I knew you'd come," she whispered, "I *knew* you'd come!"

He drew back, smiling down at her. And despite the tangled
hair, the dirty little face, the scratched chin, her green eyes
blazed with happiness and pride. Pride in him. There was no
one else now; the clearing ceased to be. They were alone in a
shimmering magical silence. Once more that sense of fragile
perfection touched him. Once more he stood on the brink of
something rare and beautiful and so dear as to touch his very
soul. This was all he needed. This was of greater value than any
gold ever minted, any jewels ever set. This was the most splendid prize life offered. And it was his for the asking. Only this
time, he knew how much he wanted it. He knew that she loved
him; and that he would never let her go . . .

"It appears," said Lady Ericson, standing by the steps of the
caravan and bathing the cut on the back of her son's bowed head,
"that two of them were in the audience last night and were much
taken with our betrayed dairymaid. Try to sit still, Bradford.
They went on to a bachelor party, drank for most of the night,
and by this morning were properly in their cups and halfway to
being convinced we carry the Jacobite treasure."

Cuthbert sprawled on the bench beside the table they had
righted, his right arm stretched out on the top. Watching Fiona
and Gregor apply makeshift splints to the big man's broken wrist,
Mathieson muttered, "*Très magnifique!* So they brought their
friends along to help them find it, I collect."

"And caught us properly napping, mon," said Gregor painfully.

His eyes grim, Mathieson scanned the disaster that had been
their camp. The cooking pots lay on the ground, the contents
scattered. Two of the set pieces had been pointlessly kicked
apart. The "pirate's treasure" littered the ground. The lid of the
chest had been ripped off. Costumes had been flung from the
property caravan and trampled in the mud. Of more importance
was the human toll. Bradford had a badly cut head and Lady

Ericson suspected a concussion; Cuthbert's wrist was broken, and both men would require the attention of an apothecary. Heywood's nose had been thought to be broken, and although he now claimed it felt "perfectly fine," he had taken a brutal beating and was obviously barely able to function. What would surely be an horrendous bruise was already starting to discolour the right side of Gregor's face from cheekbone to chin. Pauley, who had now gone to check on the horses, had suffered the least damage, in the form of a badly bruised arm that had been dealt a heavy blow with a cudgel.

Mathieson was so inflamed with suppressed rage that his own various cuts and bruises were annoyances relegated to the background of his awareness. His voice harsh, he said, "We were napping in more ways than one!"

Lady Clorinda straightened her back wearily, and glanced at him. She looked pale and haggard, and the buoyant sparkle was gone from her eyes.

In a kinder tone he asked, "Were you hurt at all, ma'am?"

"They pushed me into the caravan when Bradford tried to stop them from taking the 'treasure chest.' " She was obviously shaken, but she was a brave woman, and there was only the faintest tremor to her voice. "When they hit him, he fell 'gainst the door, so I couldn't get out."

"Papa was wonderful," said Fiona, with a glowing look at her father.

"Not very," groaned Bradford, lifting his battered head with one hand and blinking blearily about. "They made short work . . . of me, I regret to say."

"You did well, Mervyn." My lady patted his shoulder in a rare display of affection. "When I heard you fall, I thought— for a minute I thought—" Her voice shook now, and she was unable to continue.

"Why . . . Mama," said Bradford, looking up at her won-deringly.

Perched on the remains of a broken chair, Heywood held a gruesome handkerchief to his nose with one hand, while Miss Clandon bandaged the broken knuckles of the other. He com-mented rather shakily, "We're a fine bunch . . . of protectorth. Had you not come, Mathieson . . ."

" 'Come' is it?" Cuthbert's voice was strained, but he made a gallant attempt to smile. "He did not *come*, man! He exploded

188

among us like a thunderbolt hurled from the right fist of Zeus! Mathieson—I've seen some fighting men, but when I'm able . . . I'd like to shake your hand.''

"I claim that prrrivilege now," said Pauley, grinning as he hastened to join them. "Our horses are all present and correct, at least." He shook Mathieson's hand warmly, then said, "Och, sorry mon. Bruised, is it? I canna wonder! Never in all my days hae I seen such a firrre-eater! Mon, ye were in six places at once! And had we nae drrragged ye frae that clod—''

"You'd have throttled the life out of him," finished Heywood.

Still frowning, Mathieson said, "I think you did the world no favour by stopping me. Though—God knows we should have seen that something like this would come and been prepared for it.''

He spoke as a committed member of the little group and Fiona paused in her bandaging and looked at him, her heart in her eyes. Meeting that revealing glance, Mathieson's own heart sang. How dauntless she was, his little love; most ladies having suffered such a terrifying experience would have fallen into hysterics, or fainted away. Miss Fiona Bradford pushed her own shock and ill-usage aside, and, shaken but inextinguishable, helped others.

"My fault," sighed Lady Clorinda, applying sticking plaster to Bradford's drooping head. "You are perfectly right, Mathieson. We should have guards posted at all times, but we have been lucky, so I grew careless—lulled by the peace of this place, and the fact that it was bright daylight. Inexcusable.''

Wrenching his eyes from Fiona, Mathieson said, "There are seven full-grown and halfway intelligent men in this group, ma'am. Not one of us had the sense to remember that the world abounds with crude clods who would be enticed by the beauty of our ladies, and lusting after what they thought to be . . . the real—treasure." He knew that his voice had faltered on the last few words, and that Fiona watched him curiously, and he wondered with a dimming of his new-found joy if she even suspected that he, too, had lusted after their treasure . . . That he was here under false pretenses.

"We can thank God that nothing worrrse came tae us," said Gregor.

Her voice quivering on a sob and her lovely eyes tearful, Elizabeth said, "Amen tae that!"

189

Heywood stood, his face very stern, and put his arms around her, and she clung to him weeping softly.

Mathieson felt sick and had to turn away. While Fiona had been menaced, while she had fought those brutes with such intrepid courage, he had been romping in the hay with a village strumpet! He thought, '*Mon Dieu!* What if I *had* stayed with Jenny?' and was obliged to walk rather blindly towards the paddock.

Her bandaging done, Fiona left Cuthbert and hurried after Mathieson. Somewhere deep inside she was still trembling with the shock and horror of this terrible afternoon, but stronger than shock or horror was gratitude, and stronger than gratitude another emotion she dared not recognize but that clamoured to be acknowledged. She had thought herself destined for the ultimate in brutality—and had prayed he would come. And he had come. Truly, this peerless young man was her knight in shining armour. Perhaps his sojourn with them would be a brief one, no more than a bright flame in the unrolling pattern of her life, but he was here now, and the "now" must be all she could be concerned with. The "after" need not be thought of today. Tomorrow, perhaps. Or the next day. But not today.

She came up with him just before he started to limp into the trees, and touched his arm lightly. He spun to face her, and the brooding look in his eyes lightened to a tender glow.

She fought the need to throw her arms about his neck and managed to speak calmly. "Have you managed to hurt that ankle again, Captain Firebrand?"

"I've a notion old Rump accidentally trampled me," he said with a wry grin. "Nothing vital, I think. I must go and have a look at the rascal."

She took his sleeve in a firm grip. "He can wait a few minutes, sir. Pauley has attended to *that* particular rascal. Now I shall attend to the other."

"But—"

She shook one finger under his nose. "No buts. Wait here!" She left him and ran to Gregor.

Her proprietory manner was causing Mathieson's heart to pound with delight. More prosaically, he was suddenly rather tired, and sat gratefully enough on the chair the girl and Gregor hauled over.

The Scot grinned at him and went back to Cuthbert. Fiona knelt and began to pull off Mathieson's boot.

"Hey!" he gasped.

Her beaming look flashed at him. "Never fear. I do not mean to inspect your toenails this time."

He chuckled, then was gripping hard at the side of the chair and swearing under his breath as she had to tug harder. They both gave a sigh of relief when the boot came away. "Such a price you pay for your heroics," she murmured. "Though I fancy you will have an excuse, as usual."

He watched the top of her untidy head as she gently rolled down his stocking. "I don't know what you mean."

"Then allow me to assist with your scenario. Now, let me see . . . You will probably say that you really did not gallop to my—our rescue this afternoon. 'Twas purely accidental. A bee chanced to sting Rumpelstiltskin on his—er—self, and he went mad and hurled you at that great beast who was—" her voice shook a little "—attacking me, and— Oh, Roly! *What* an ugly bruise!"

He peered at his ankle. A lurid abrasion low on his shin was already much swollen and beginning to purple.

"You must own I am at the very least a—er, colourful fellow," he said whimsically.

She looked up and met a pair of eyes as soft as velvet, and a half-smile that seemed to enfold her heart. "Oh—at the very least," she murmured.

He reached out and touched her hair in a brief caress that intensified her need to be held close and tight in his embrace. But other eyes watched them; she must be sensible. She forced her attention back to his damaged leg.

Fighting his own battle, Mathieson said rather hoarsely, "Pray finish your tale—wicked chit that you are. Or are you done with your version of my—ah, heroics?"

Her fingers on his shin trembled. "I am as done with it as you are done with duelling, sir."

"*What* a ghastly fate! I must have forgot—with whom was I engaged to go out, madam?"

"With Sir Roger," she said, her face becoming very serious all at once. "You'll not be able to play the lead tomorrow, Roly. Not the way Captain Firebrand jumps about."

'Zounds,' thought Mathieson. 'Milady Dairymaid!'

191

Wondering how they could possibly restore everything in time for tomorrow's performance, and how many of them would be fit enough to play their parts, he glanced up. With bizarre incongruity the red carriage rolled magnificently into the clearing, Mrs. Dunnigan beside young Japhet on the box, and both staring in horror at the chaos.

Freemon Torrey threw open the door, jumped out and let down the steps. "What in God's name . . . ?" he gasped, his anxious gaze flashing to Fiona. "Not dragoons?"

My lady said, "We were visited by a pack of vicious yobboes masquerading as country gentlemen. They fancied us to be fair game. I thank heaven you were not here, Moira. Did you post the notices? Is there any word from—" She broke off, staring.

Torrey was backing down the coach steps, helping a man who swayed and stumbled uncertainly, Moira Torrey adding her young strength to support that wilting figure. A harsh, racking cough sounded.

Stunned, Mathieson thought, 'No! Dammitall—*no*! Not *now*!'

Robert MacTavish, his face drawn and haggard, his eyes sunken into black hollows, reeled forward, saying hoarsely, " 'Fraid I'm not—" He checked, blinking as he took in the wreckage. His grey eyes flickered from one to the other of the casualties, and then paused, widening in horror.

Very white, Mathieson sighed faintly, then stood and faced him, head proudly held and sneer marked. "*Bonjour*, dear my friend."

"*You!*" breathed MacTavish.

They were all staring, in every face surprise and uncertainty. Well, they'd soon know the whole. Faith, but he might have guessed there was no hope. But—mustn't whine; that was the way the cards had fallen. Mathieson smiled a mocking smile that did not reach his eyes, and found he could not look at Fiona—that to see revulsion come into her sweet face would be more than he could bear. "I fancy," he drawled, "you were expecting me, no?"

Lady Clorinda said, "So you know each other. I'm not very surprised. We've had trouble here, as you can see, and—Rob? Dear boy, you look—"

MacTavish pointed a shaking hand at Mathieson. "He—he's—" he gasped, but was once more overtaken by that horrendous coughing.

192

Mathieson wondered with dreary detachment if his luck had run out altogether; if he could get away from this collection of cripples with his shin throbbing like blazes; and why he had found his love only to lose her so cruelly soon.

MacTavish regained his breath, looked at him steadily, then suddenly crumpled. There were cries of alarm. Torrey leapt to catch him and ease him to the ground.

Near exhaustion herself, Lady Clorinda gathered her faculties and hastened to bend over this new victim. "Poor lad, poor lad!" She rested a hand on his brow. "Heavens, but you're on fire! No, do not try to talk. You must—" She stopped speaking as MacTavish's eyes closed and his head rolled limply. "Lud," she murmured, for the first time showing real alarm, "but he is extremely ill!"

Mathieson limped painfully to MacTavish's side and looked down at him with commendable distress. "Poor old fellow," he said. "He does look bad. What is it d'you suppose, ma'am?"

"To judge by his breathing, I'd say at the very least an inflammation of the lungs. And—at worst . . ." She straightened again, her eyes fearful. "At worst—the pneumonia! He must be put to bed at once, and someone must ride for an apothecary."

Torrey said, "I'll go. Pauley—give me a hand, here."

MacTavish was lifted gently and carried off. Mathieson watched his inert figure sombrely. He admired Rob MacTavish, but—if he died before imparting what he knew of one soldier of fortune with three identities, how much easier it would be . . .

Lady Ericson asked, "What was he trying to tell us, Mathieson?"

From the corner of his eye he could see Fiona holding his boot, her hopeful eyes on his face. "What I should have told you from the start, ma'am," he answered slowly. "Rob and I are old friends. I followed him up here because I feared he was going to run himself into a bog. He can't help you now, and—I'm not the man he is. But—in my own fashion, if you'll trust me, I swear I'll do everything in my power to help you complete your task in safety."

He fully expected them to reject him, even now, but my lady, her eyes dimmed with grateful tears, held out two unsteady little hands to him. Fiona's smile was blinding, and Japhet was grinning from ear to ear.

"Of course we trust you, Roland," said Lady Clorinda fervently. "After all you've done for us, how could we fail to do so? We can only thank heaven you were sent to us!"

Robert Victor MacTavish was a Scot of fine family, reared up to the standards of manners and morals expected of a gentleman, and of high personal courage and integrity. When the Uprising began he joined Charles Stuart at once. He fought well for his Prince until the tragic field of Culloden Moor left him wounded and running for his life. After some desperate doings, and with the help of Ligun Doone and The Committee, he reached France and safety. Within months however, he had turned his back on that haven and returned to perilous England to do all he might to assist his bedevilled countrymen.

So far as he was aware, he had nothing personally to gain from ensuring that the Jacobite treasure was safely stored so that it might eventually be restored to the original donors. His rather erratic sire was not kindly disposed towards the Stuarts and it was doubtful that he would have made a donation to their Cause. On the other hand, his own enlistment with the Jacobite forces might just possibly have influenced his father to contribute, in which case their name was on the list of donors. The list, therefore, still not safely delivered, was of greater interest to MacTavish than the treasure itself, for should it fall into military hands, all those named were doomed. Others, however, must ensure the delivery of that vital document. MacTavish had accepted the responsibility for retrieving the treasure from the three less than satisfactory locations where it was now stored, and arranging for its shipment to a permanent and safe hiding place. For the better part of eight backbreaking weeks he had bent all his energies towards accomplishing this task.

At the start of his efforts he had met the English lady destined to become his bride. When Rosamond Albritton had become endangered, he'd married her and taken her to his farm in Wales, where she now awaited his return. He rejoiced that she was safe, but the enforced separation from his love galled him and spurred him on to even greater efforts to complete his task as speedily as may be.

He had forged ahead untiringly, scouting the three present locations of the treasure; contriving to collect, often in the wee hours of the morning and at hideous personal risk, the clumsy and precious articles so vital to the welfare of so many—and so exceedingly difficult to transport. Many sleepless nights were spent planning these forays, followed by days so fraught with peril he dared not rest.

One cloudy morning he was dressed in the rags of a poor shepherd, herding a flock of Lincoln sheep (whose thick fleeces hid items that would have guaranteed the removal of his head) when he was stopped and questioned by a troop of dragoons. There were rumours that Jacobites were hereabouts. Had he seen anything of a suspicious nature? He managed to convince them he was comparatively witless and after they had enjoyed themselves by frightening such a bumpkin and scattering his sheep, he was released. It had taken some time for the inexperienced "shepherd" to gather his flock, and in the process he was soaked to the skin by a sudden shower. The sun was brilliant again before he reached his destination, but he'd had three hours of sleep out of the past seventy and was exhausted. Next day he suffered one of his rare colds. Except for the slight limp which the Battle of Culloden Moor had left him, he was a healthy young man and seldom had known illness, and with the cheerful arrogance of youth, had taken his good health for granted. Ignoring the worries and warnings of his friends and fellow-conspirators, he laughed at his indisposition and pushed on doggedly, not acknowledging until he found his skin afire, his head one gigantic throb, and his legs weak as water, that he was a sick man.

Following his collapse at the campsite, he lay as one dead in the cot Gregor and Japhet had set up in one of the property caravans. Nor did he awaken for the rest of that afternoon, a fact which brought increasing anxiety to the battered troupe and increasing hope to Roland Mathieson.

The necessary work of cleaning up and repairing went on meanwhile, the tasks performed painfully but uncomplainingly by the less severely injured among them. Lady Clorinda, worn out, was carried, protesting, to her bed, and fell asleep the instant she was laid down. Mathieson's ankle was aching with wearying persistence, but it was a relatively minor injury and he insisted on helping along with the other cripples. He had fashioned a makeshift cane from a sturdy branch, and during a particularly busy moment he slipped away and hid his saddle and saddlebags near the paddock, just in case he was obliged to make a dash for freedom. Returning to his labours, his gaze turned often to meet the pair of tired but happy green eyes that turned so often to beam at him, and he made many appeals, if in silence, to his overworked friend, St. Thomas.

Shortly after six o'clock Torrey returned with an apothecary he had found on the outskirts of Chester. The squat, dour Mr. Harte had come such a distance much against his better judgment, as he lost no time in telling them. His irritation was considerably dispersed when Fiona and Elizabeth exerted their charms on him. He was horrified to learn of the attack on the camp, and wasted several minutes in a loud harangue on the morals and behaviour of today's youth. Mending his own manners, he insisted on resetting Cuthbert's arm, much to the ire of that staunch individual who was left sweating, and swearing he'd felt better before he'd had the benefit of the apothecary's skill. Bradford was pronounced to be suffering a mild concussion which would take its own time to cease being a nuisance, the sufferer's ironic thanks for this inestimable verdict, following as it did a painful examination, passing completely over Harte's head. Heywood's nose was indeed broken, and he endured stoically while Harte set the damaged article, taped a piece of sticking plaster over it, and warned that Mr. Heywood would likely have two back eyes by morning. MacTavish was then inspected and the apothecary hemmed and hawed and observed gloomily that the man should be dead but appeared to have weathered the worst of the illness and with proper rest and care might survive. He delighted everyone by advising that it was not the pneumonia, but an inflammation of the lungs complicated by severe exhaustion. He left a bottle of medicine to alleviate the cough and help the patient sleep, and continued to the next case, this being Gregor.

Mathieson refused Harte's attention, exclaimed with the others over the good news about MacTavish, and knew he must act swiftly.

Supper was a simple meal of cold meats, cheeses, and fruit accompanied by hot muffins prepared by Mrs. Dunnigan. A sorry, silent, and exhausted group of Thespians partook sparingly of the food before dragging themselves to their respective bunks.

Despite her objections that he would hurt his ankle, Mathieson limped beside Fiona to her caravan. Now, at last, he was

196

able to snatch a few words with her, but after waiting so long for the chance, he found himself oddly tongue-tied.

"Are you feeling dreadfully, Roly?" she asked in a weary little voice, adding with a trace of her indomitable humour, "I think I may call you that . . . now. Mayn't I?"

He yearned to kiss her and hold her close, but had to content himself with placing one hand over the small hand that rested on his arm. "I am feeling perfectly well, I thank you. And you may call me . . ." His words died away. He stood at the foot of the steps, gazing down into her upturned face, wondering if he would ever again hear her call him anything at all. And what she would think of him, if he was unable to deal with MacTavish in time and had to make a run for it.

"Are you afraid for Robbie MacTavish?" Fiona asked, watching him anxiously.

"As a matter of fact, I was remembering something I read in school. By Jean de la Bruyère, I think. I can recall but one phrase—'Most men make use of the first part of their lives to render the last part miserable.' " His smile was tinged with bitterness. "I never knew till now—how true that is."

Fiona turned her hand to clasp his, and said stoutly, "If you used the first part of your life so as to become the man you are now, Roland Mathieson, then I think you contrived very well indeed."

He glanced around swiftly. Heywood and Elizabeth stood beside the fire still. Mrs. Dunnigan and Japhet were piling dirty dishes into a large pan, and Freemon Torrey, who was to stand the first two watches, had gone to his caravan to load his pistol. Mathieson lifted Fiona's hand to his lips and held it there for a long, intense moment. Then, he said, "You won't believe me when I tell you the truth of myself. But—if anything should happen— No—don't be afraid, I expect all will be well. But—just in case, will you remember something? I have never loved—till now. There is *nothing* I would not do to win my love. But if I lose her, I will never love any other."

Fiona's heart gave a great painful leap. She was being told the man of her dreams loved her! This dear, gallant, fearless, handsome gentleman loved *her*! More—he was pledging his lifelong devotion.

"Oh . . . *Roly!*" she squeaked and hurled herself into his arms.

Staggering on his weakened leg Mathieson almost fell. He might have known, he thought, startled and struggling to keep his balance, that this tempestuous little creature would not shyly yield him her hand to kiss. Or sway gently to his ardent embrace as any well-instructed lady of Quality would do. "You are supposed to at least *appear* shrinkingly timid and overcome by my exceeding improper declaration," he said with a breathless laugh.

"Stuff!" cried Fiona, muffled but ecstatic as she hugged him harder.

That unconventional response made him fairly ache with love for her. "My wild, wonderful little Mite," he murmured, and made an attempt to kiss her, but her face was pressed so close against his cravat that he could not find her lips. With a groan of frustration, he freed one hand and groping for her chin, tilted it upward. He kissed her then with a hunger that left her weak and shivering, but with a great effort he restrained himself from kissing her as he longed to do. She was too trusting, too innocent for those kisses. Whispering his love, he trailed his lips down her cheek, over her closed eyelids, around her ear.

Fiona lay limp and blissfully happy in his arms. Surely, no maid had ever been kissed like this? Surely, no maid had ever— She frowned, and whipped her head up so suddenly that Mathieson, who had been about to kiss her eyebrow, gave a yelp and jerked back, clutching his mouth.

"What do you mean—you expect all will be well?" she demanded. "You are telling me something. Warning me of something. What is it?"

He was exploring his lip gingerly. "You little fiend—you nigh knocked my tooth out!"

"You brought it on yourself with your ominous statements! Roland Mathieson—what did you mean? Tell me!"

He seized her by the shoulders and shook her fondly. "I told you several things. Can you not recall the others?"

"It is *because* I recall the others that I must know the threat to them. Roly—"

He touched her cheek. A lingering touch and a return of that smile of such gentleness, such complete devotion. "It was but a silly piece of drama to enhance my declaration to you, as becomes a Great Actor!" He dropped a quick kiss on her forehead. "Pay me no heed, little dairymaid, save to remember that—I love you, and always will. Now—good night, my very dear.''

He was gone before she could say another word. She gazed after him, torn between quivering bliss and a vague apprehension. But as she turned and wandered slowly back to her own caravan, she was remembering that last instant before she had thrown herself so wantonly into his arms. She could see his face as it had been at that precious moment. The smile, the mockery, the lazy boredom had been quite gone from the dark eyes, but gone also was the tenderness she had seen there when he had kissed her hand. That dear expression had been replaced by a grimness; a look of such icy and ruthless determination that the memory of it now frightened her.

'There is *nothing* I would not do to win my love . . .'

Had that been a piece of drama too . . . ?

Troubled, she slipped quietly up the caravan steps.

At three o'clock it was cold in the clearing. From the coach came the slow and regular grind of Cuthbert's snores; a log shifted on the dying fire, and distantly, an owl hooted.

Despite his ankle, Mathieson moved soundlessly, not the crack of a twig or the rattle of a pebble disturbing the comparative silence. Like a dark shadow he crept up the steps of the second property caravan. He eased the door open, froze into immobility when a faint creak sounded, and resumed again when there was no sign of anyone coming to investigate. A single candle burned steadily in a hurricane shade. Mathieson closed the door, and trod silently to the bed.

MacTavish lay on his back and his sleep was uneasy. The fair hair was tangled and disordered about the flushed face, his head tossed restlessly and he muttered something unintelligible. Mathieson stood utterly still. A fluid movement then, and the jambiya dagger slid easily from its sheath. Another soundless step. 'Poor old Rob,' he thought. 'I really am sorry, but . . .' And, dagger poised, he prepared to finish this desperate and unfortunate business.

𝒪 12 𝒪

The instincts of the hunted awoke Robert MacTavish to a throbbing head, burning heat, a gravelly chest, and a sense of strangeness and danger. Even in illness his was a quick mind. The bewilderment of finding himself lying in an unfamiliar place was banished by the sight of the blurred shape that leaned above him. His hands tightened on the blanket but his immediate and instinctive attempt to sit up brought a small sharp pain at his throat. At once he lay still, and as his vision cleared said hoarsely, "So good of you to call."

Mathieson gave him full marks for courage and when the coughing stopped, murmured, "Whisper. Don't talk. An your hacking wakes someone I shall have to finish this quicker than I would choose."

The tired grey eyes met the cold black ones without wavering, but the Scot had seen the dagger, and for a brief instant, despair brushed him with her icy fingers.

"You are thinking of Rosamond," Mathieson said, correctly interpreting that briefly shadowed expression. "Keep on thinking of her."

MacTavish whispered, " 'Twould have been kinder, Roly, to have struck while I slept."

"Yes. But so dashed unsporting, *mon cher*. You should have a chance, at least."

The pale but proud lips curled. "My sword is over there."

"Oh, come now. I'm not that generous. Besides, I doubt you could heft it at the moment." Mathieson sat on the side of the cot, his dagger no longer menacing the Scot's throat, but held ready. "You look awful, you know," he commented breezily.

"But the apothecary says you don't have the pneumonia after all, so perchance you won't die yet. Of that ailment, at least."

"More likely of ten inches of steel, eh? How many men *have* you murdered to get at our gold?"

"Scores." Mathieson's sardonic smile died. He said slowly, "I really don't want to have to do this, Rob. I've sometimes thought that—" He hesitated and added with heightened colour and rare diffidence, "that—under other circumstances, we might have—er, become friends."

MacTavish knew he was very close to death and so abandoned his own reserve. "Yes. I'd the same feeling. Beastly luck that you've such a bad case of greed."

"And that you're such a damned fanatical heroic idiot!"

His eyes widening in shock, MacTavish cried furiously, "What a filthy thing to—"

Mathieson sprang to clap a pillow over his face and force him back down. When the coughing stopped, he removed the pillow. MacTavish lay limp and still. Alarmed, he leaned forward, "Good God! Are you—"

The pathetic figure convulsed. One hand flailed the dagger from his grasp; the other swung a lethal blow at his chin. He reeled back, swore as his full weight came down on his hurt ankle, and sat down hard. Half out of bed, MacTavish lunged for the fallen dagger, but it was just out of reach, and he sprawled, making flailing and abortive snatches for the weapon.

"Serves you right," said Mathieson, indignant. "Of all the putrid tricks!"

MacTavish's efforts precipitated him into a most unheroical slide from the cot and he lay there swamped in one of Cuthbert's nightshirts and groaning curses.

Watching him, Mathieson laughed breathlessly. "If you knew how silly you look!"

"I—dinna doot that—a bit. Help me up, will you?"

Mathieson stood and limped over to haul the Scot back into bed again and throw the blanket over him. MacTavish was panting and his face shone with sweat. He looked longingly at the crate whereon was a water pitcher and a tin mug. Mathieson filled the mug and held it out, then withdrew it. "Promise not to heave it at me."

MacTavish grinned, promised, and drank gratefully.

Retrieving his dagger, Mathieson slipped it into the sheath, then relieved MacTavish of the mug and sat down again.

"Damn you, Fairleigh," murmured the sick man wearily. "I don't believe you came in here to kill me at all."

"My apologies. Dreadfully disappointing, I know."

"Then why the dagger? I wonder I didn't suffer a seizure."

Mathieson fingered the new red mark on his chin. "Yes, I can tell you're actually at death's door and weak as a cat! No—don't be obtuse, *par grâce*. Had I written for an appointment and said politely, 'Rob, can we have a little chat?' you'd have had me locked up." He added, aggrieved, "As you did once before! I've not been able to look at a toolshed since."

MacTavish chuckled. " 'Twas a woodshed, not a toolshed. And—" with sudden gravity "—I think I've not thanked you for my life, Roly."

"And Rosamond's," Mathieson pointed out demurely. "Are you thanking me now?"

"With deepest humility."

"So I should think. My cousin's troopers had been promised a bonus were you and your lady taken. When I saw you lying on that beach, knocked out of time, I could have called Jacob and won myself a very nice reward."

"Yes."

"As a patriotic Englishman, it was *en fait*—"

"*Englishman*, Roly. Forgive the interruption, but you cloud the illusion."

"So I do, by Jove. Thank you. Er—I've lost the thread . . . Oh yes, as a patriotic Englishman, it was in fact— Is that better?"

"Much."

"Good. It was in fact my *duty* to inform my cousin that you were *not* on the ship he saw rushing off to France, but were instead stretched out at the base of the cliff, right under his silly nose. I denied him his so longed-for promotion. He'd have my liver out if he knew that, you are aware?"

"I am aware."

"Furthermore, I could have lost my head for that piece of—of Christian charity."

"Rosamond said you told her you'd sworn an oath not to betray any of us."

Mathieson asked quickly, "Do you believe that?"

"I—er . . . I would never doubt my wife."

"No more you should. She's a lovely little creature. Quite a—" Mathieson's eyes reflected a sudden tenderness that had nothing to do with Rosamond Albritton MacTavish, "—a pearl beyond price." He smoothed his coat sleeve and went on idly, "Speaking of which—what value would you place on her life?"

In the small following stillness, each man knew that the small truce was done and the gauntlet thrown.

"There is no comparable sum," replied MacTavish, a touch of acid in his hoarse whisper. "Had you hoped for one-third of the treasure, perchance? Or is that too conservative a figure?"

Mathieson's hand, loosely clasping his knee, tightened. He stared at his knuckles, then looked into the Scot's grey eyes and did not lower his own in spite of the unutterable contempt he saw there. "Suppose I swore that I am not here for your damned gold?"

"Suppose—*what?* After you've tracked and hounded and hunted us since first you learned of the existence of Prince Charlie's treasure? After you've brutalized our couriers and manhandled their ladies in an effort to force the cyphers from them!"

Mathieson's head bowed at this, and it seemed to MacTavish that he shrank. "I didn't mean to hit Miss Montgomery so hard," he muttered. "But Chandler was coming at me with his blasted sword and—" He pulled back his shoulders and said irritably, "Hell, what's done is done. I'll not weasel out of the responsibility for what I've been. I bluffed my way in here for one purpose only—to get at the gold. I admit it. If anyone had told me I would find something that—that meant more to me than gold or jewels—or my own life . . ." He shook his head sombrely. "I'd have laughed at them."

MacTavish said rather brutally, "So should I."

Mathieson glared at him, then muttered, "I only ask . . . Rob—I *swear* I won't touch a groat—not a farthing of it!"

"Splendid. When do you leave?"

Mathieson gritted his teeth. "I don't. I *cannot!* I must stay. I *must* see you all safely done with—"

MacTavish laughed until the tears crept down his cheeks and he was overcome by more coughing. Wiping his eyes, he moaned, "They say—laughter is—is the best medicine . . . And I believe it! If you—" A hand was clapped over his mouth.

203

Mathieson's black eyes, narrowed and deadly, blazed down at him.

"Damn you! I should have killed you when first I came in! *Listen* to me!"

Impressed by the power of his personality, and baffled by his apparent sincerity, MacTavish lay mute, watching that grim face.

"I'll give you something to really laugh at." Mathieson smoothed the pillow and straightened up again, loathing what he meant to do, but sufficiently desperate to resort to it. "Have you heard of my family?"

"Which one? You've so many names, I—"

"Otton is assumed. It was necessary after a—ah, certain indiscretion concerning the wife of a London Alderman. My real name is Roland Fairleigh Mathieson. Does that mean anything to you?"

"No. Oh, I've heard of some Mathiesons, of course. The duke who helped Tony Farrar is—Good God! *Marbury?* You—you're not—?"

Mathieson bowed gracefully.

"Why—why then, you must be his—"

"His grandson. The infamous bastard. Then you've doubtless also heard of the splendid gentleman who was my sire?"

MacTavish nodded, and wrinkled his brow. "I think I saw Lord Fairleigh once when we all came to London to spend Christmas with relations. An exceedingly well-favoured man, and very popular. Yes—I remember that he was killed the following year and that my aunt was much grieved. A hunting accident, wasn't it?"

"Fortunately."

MacTavish's eyes widened predictably, and Mathieson smiled his cynical smile and went on. "When I was nine years old, I displeased that—'very popular' gentleman. Worse, I humiliated him. And he was an aristocrat who held himself very much up, and had done the noble thing by owning me to be his bastard and giving me his name—if nothing else. I disgraced that name, and him, in front of all his friends. The cream of the county aristocracy. And being the gentlemen they were, they sniggered behind their hands. He, poor fellow, was mortified. He never forgave me or ceased to punish me for it."

Frowning, and not a little incredulous, MacTavish asked, "He beat you?"

"That was of no consequence. My real punishment was to be kept from the one person in this world I loved—and whose happiness was, I knew, wrapped up in me. I was instructed very precisely as to what kind of a—thing—I was, and dear Papa saw to it that I was reminded of it with unfailing regularity. I grew up on a great estate, where I was treated with more contempt and far less kindness than the lowliest bootblack." He paused, his eyes looking back broodingly into the bitter past. "Just to be sure I knew what I was missing, I was sent back to Paris each summer, to be with her for a few days—we never knew for how long—so that we both might suffer the pain of parting again and the dread that the next year's meeting might be denied."

"Your mother?" asked MacTavish gravely.

"My beautiful, *Maman*. A lady who never had an unkind thought—never did a bad thing in her saintly life." Mathieson wandered over to stare down at the candle flame. "Much good it did her! Her health began to fail, and I went in terror that she might die, pining for me, before I could reach her. The summer she became really ill, I was not allowed to go. My valise was packed, the coach was at the door, and then—my father summoned me into his august presence and made me stand at attention while he read me her letters—letters that begged and pleaded . . . so piteously . . . that she was ill, and that I be allowed to visit her. Regrettably, he said, he had changed his mind. My Parisian journey could not be made this year. When I flew out at him, he knocked me down and—laughed, and told me what kind of vermin I was."

"Jupiter . . ." whispered MacTavish.

Mathieson turned, and shrugged, his eyes empty and his smile brittle. "But we can learn from everyone, *n'est-ce pas?* I began to study him. He was a handsome fellow, as you said, and could be very gracious if it pleased him. He was much admired. Especially by the aristocratic ladies—silly vapid women who are impressed never by character, but only by looks or money. They said he was charming, brave, gallant; a truly great gentleman. I learned how exceeding well *mon père* enjoyed all the good things of life. And I knew he was a great villain. And I saw *ma chère Maman*—broken-hearted, abandoned, slowly dying. And I knew she was a saint." He paused again, one of his slender white hands clenching spasmodically. He said low-voiced, "I laughed and danced for joy when he was killed in that stupid hunting accident! He could not keep me from *Maman*, anymore! I was free! I stole some money from his strong box, went to Paris, and stayed with her and managed to make her last year a comparatively happy one. When she died, my grandfather brought me back to finish my schooling. He hoped, I think, to turn me into—a gentleman.'' He gave a soft, mirthless laugh. ''I had already dedicated my life to villainy. I had learned, you see, that the good earn only sorrow and savagery, while to the evil go all the rewards.'' He straightened the ruffles at his wrist, and murmured, ''But—do you know, Rob, I am inclined to believe that, despite everything he accused me of being, everything he said I *would* become, as deplorable as I became in truth, I have never yet reached *his* level of villainy.''

MacTavish did not know what to say. And because he had for a while been blessed by the love of a gentle mother and had grown up under the guidance of a doting aunt and his wise and kindly father, he was appalled. In a very different voice from that of a few minutes ago, he asked at length, ''Why do you tell me all this?''

Mathieson looked up. He was very pale, and his hands were tight-gripped behind him. ''I never thought I would find true happiness in this life. I—don't say I have found it now. Or that I have any right to it if . . . I could win it. But I have caught a glimpse of it. I—who judged women by the creatures who adored my father; I—who believed *Maman* was the only angel who ever walked this earth—have found another angel.''

With the true Briton's horror of any display of emotion, MacTavish was nonetheless impressed. Whisht, but it was an intense creature! Only see how the sweat shone at his temples. No play-acting here! The man meant every word, by God! And which lady had won the heart of such a renowned rake—heaven help her? Surely not . . . ''Miss *Bradford*?'' he gasped.

''You may well be astonished,'' sneered Mathieson. ''Do you also believe one word I have said?''

''Aye. But—but . . .''

''But the leopard cannot change his spots—is that what you think?''

''Er—I'm sorry, but—yes.''

''Well, I mean to try, damn you! I mean to . . . to somehow . . . be worthy of her.''

206

MacTavish stared at him, baffled. "What is it you want of me?"

"You owe me, Rob!"

"Aye. As you've reminded me!"

Mathieson's intense pallor was tinged by a slight flush. "My apologies. I am—desperate, you see. We were attacked today, or were you too far gone to notice?" A little muscle began to twitch beside his mouth. He said harshly, "That peerless innocent—that trusting beautiful little creature would have been beaten and shamed and—and raped, had I not chanced to arrive! Oh, never curl your lip, devil take you! I don't claim to have saved them all, single-handed! I balanced the odds is all. Which has nothing to say to the matter." He limped closer to the bed again and bent lower in a sudden and unexpected pleading that shook MacTavish more than any brutality would have done. "Rob—don't you *understand*? She should not *be* here! You know what the military would do if they came up with us. You know what would become of her! *Mon Dieu!* The very thought—" His face twisted betrayingly; he gave an oddly wild gesture and wrenched away again. "Once more, I must apologize," he said, recovering himself after a hushed moment, and standing very straight and stiff. "You will recollect I am a half-breed, and sometimes I slip into the abyss and become *porté à l'émotion* and—very French. Horribly embarrassing for the British side of me. And for you. Much more comfortable when I appear as a—a base but rather amusing rogue, eh?"

"When I get up," said MacTavish wrathfully, "I'm going to poke you on the beak, Fairleigh—"

"Mathieson this time, don't forget."

"Mathieson, then. What the devil makes you think you're the first man ever to have loved a woman? How the hell d'you think *I* felt when your damnable cousin was hard on our heels with his troop, and that confounded ship sailed off and left Rosamond?"

"W-Well then," stammered Mathieson eagerly, "if you understand—"

"I'm to believe you mean to play the game like an honest man, for once in your life? I'm to keep my mouth closed to all my friends who have risked their lives countless times for our Cause? I'm not to tell them what you did to Quentin Chandler? That you were paid to ambush and kill Geoff Delavale and damn

207

near succeeded? That you drove poor Meredith Carruthers half out of his mind badgering at him to give up the cypher Lascelles carried? That you came slithering around Rosamond and her family, and—'' scowling at the bowed dark head, his voice softened ''—and wound up saving our lives, blast you?'' He was far from insensitive, and sensing what these revelations had cost the other man, he said earnestly, ''If 'twas my life only, as God be my judge, I'd leave it in your hands. After what you've done for me personally, even if you sold me to the block, I'd not count the debt paid. But—mon, d'ye no see? Wi' the past tae be considered— Y'r reputation . . . ! I *canna* keep quiet!'' He recovered his accent and said with stern dignity, ''No, Mathieson. I'm sorrier than I can say, but—there is far too much against you to justify taking such a risk. This is a desperate business, and these faithful people have sacrificed much. They *must* be told the whole. 'Twould be to betray them all, else! I've absolutely no choice in the matter.'' And anticipating the desperate appeal that would follow, he added hurriedly, ''Nor, I might add, would have Lady Ericson.''

Mathieson drew a deep breath. His eyes became glittering and hard, his mouth a thin, ruthless line. He stepped very close to the bed. ''I see,'' he said coldly. ''Well, I'm sorry. I tried to not have it come to this.''

The Scot tensed, and vowing to sell his life as dearly as possible, said, ''It's to be death for me then, is it?''

''Not at all.''

Mathieson smiled, and dealt his trump card.

By morning the weather had changed with a vengeance; a cold wind came out of the east bringing with it a steady drizzling rain that pattered at the caravan roofs, reduced the lane to a sea of mud, and made Lady Ericson's fingers ache with the rheumatism she would never admit to. She betrayed no sign of this however, as she sat beside the cot in the lurching, jolting caravan, and watched MacTavish's pale face incredulously. ''Lad—are you sure?''

''Quite sure,'' came his harsh whisper.

''But—the danger! And with you so ill . . .''

He smiled and patted the hand that clasped his own. ''I whisper only because it helps to keep me from coughing. I feel rather astonishingly improved compared to this time yesterday.''

"Thank God for that! But I fancy your improvement is largely due to the good sleep you've had. The first in weeks, I'll be bound, eh? Do you start rushing and tearing about, planning and organizing and using your own energy to bolster everyone else's—It still could turn to the pneumonia, Rob."

"I'll have plenty of help, and besides—"

"What help? My son's also a touch improved today and swears he'll play his part tonight, but much of that is vanity, for Bradford loves every minute he's on a stage. Cuthbert has more than his share of gumption and says he can manage his role, but he'll be considerably slowed is there trouble. And poor Heywood can almost see this morning. You know how much worse ailments become at night, and how we are to manage to do all the loading and—"

"My fellows from Chester will do it."

"But you said they were worn to a thread from the hard work you've done."

"True. We all are. Needs must when the devil—" He checked, frowning a little, then said, "Besides, I'll have Mathieson's help."

"Oh, splendid! He can barely hobble! He's going to disguise himself with pillows and a wig tonight, and play the villain as a fat man. The duel will have to go, which is a pity." She sighed. "It was such a delight for the ladies to watch him, he looked so splendid as Firebrand, and with that superb physique— But it cannot be helped. We'll be fortunate can he carry off the part of Sir Roger in his present condition."

"He does better than you may think, dear ma'am."

There was an odd expression in his eyes, and my lady said worriedly, "I don't mean to offend you, lad. I know you're good friends, but—Rob, how well *do* you know him?"

MacTavish stared at her small hand. "I know he can fight."

"La, but he can! You've no need to tell me *that*! But—are we right to trust him?"

He looked puzzled. "Have you doubts then? I thought you had accepted his offer to become one of us? That you all but fell on his neck as your saviour, in fact."

My lady flushed, irked, as she had been irked in the past, by this young Scot's sometimes caustic tongue. Her eyes met his smoulderingly, but she refrained from giving him a setdown. This was not the time. Still, her reply was rather stiff. "I was

209

somewhat overwrought yesterday afternoon. I—'' She bit her lip and a sudden vivid memory made her tremble.

Watching her, MacTavish realized with mild surprise that the remarkable woman he had always thought of as being fashioned from Toledo steel, was human after all; not quite as young as she used to be, and very tired. She had drawn her hand away, but he reached out to hold it again. "I wonder you were not fallen down in a fit," he said sympathetically.

"What a repulsive thought," she exclaimed glaring at him. "I never had a fit in my life!"

He chuckled. "Aye. I'm a clumsy clod, but—you know what I mean. Jove, but I never cease to marvel that you dainty ladies with your fans and laces and flutterings and megrims can yet turn to and suffer such privations—such terrors—with a courage and endurance many of us men could scarce equal."

"More accurately, my lad, that many men could *not* equal! I know my first husband could not have! Faith, but the creature would turn in his grave did he know what I was about! Such impropriety would have purely horrified the sanctimonious pomposity. Do you know why I've done it all, MacTavish? I lived so many years in England you likely consider me a Sassenach. Why do *you* think I've plotted and risked and contrived these past months?"

"For love of Scotland, ma'am. And human kindness. Nothing more."

Lady Clorinda smiled at him mistily. "Then you'd be wrong, lad. It was for something more. A large something more. Six feet, two inches of gallantry. The proudest, fiercest, most gentle creature I ever knew . . . All Scot, but a throwback to his Viking ancestors, if ever there was one!" Her pretty green eyes were full of memories and her voice had softened. "Ah, my dear, never underestimate the power of love. My first, and I suppose my greatest love, was denied me, and I was forced to marry a penny-pinching fool. But do not be thinking I've known little of happiness. When I was widowed, I went back to Scotland and married again, and 'tis worth getting old to have lived as the wife of Sir Dugall Ericson . . . To have been loved by such a one. *That* is why I did it. For my Dugall's dear memory. I came on this journey because I knew there *must* be women in these caravans. Only . . . I shouldn't have allowed my granddaughters to come, Robbie! God forgive me! I should never have exposed them to—to such fearful risks . . . !'' She put a hand that shook over her eyes and was silent.

MacTavish whispered, "They came because they considered it their duty. Their families were of the Jacobite persuasion. Who would you have selected in place of them, ma'am? Someone else's granddaughters?''

She sniffed and lowered her hand. "You've a hard heart, Robbie MacTavish.''

"Merely a logical one. But I do understand. And I appreciate why you were so grateful to Mathieson. I take it he saved the day.''

"Did he tell you that?''

He blinked. "No! Egad, ma'am, if you doubt the man—''

"You think me ungrateful. I am not, I assure you. But—I may be prejudiced, and I dare not take chances, not with us about to take up the treasure. Tell me honestly now, Rob. *Can* we trust this flamboyant soldier of fortune?''

He said slowly, "Perhaps I also am prejudiced, my lady. He saved Rosamond's life. And mine. I am deep in his debt. But even if I were not, and in spite of his lurid reputation, I'll confess I like Mathieson. And I think we are safe in trusting him. For—er, the time being.''

"Humph,'' she said. "So be it. For the time being.''

Mathieson had disgusted himself by sleeping late that morning. Because of the rain, their fires had been lit in the woods and Mrs. Dunnigan, Japhet, and Moira had bustled about, preparing a hasty meal. It was the smell of coffee, and bacon frying which had roused him, but by the time he hobbled to the cooking scene, the other men were already starting to rearrange the caravans. He had encountered Lady Clorinda on her way to check on MacTavish and had a brief chat with her, but there had been no sign of either Fiona or Elizabeth Clandon. Heywood, lingering over his breakfast, had informed him that the girls were still sleeping, and that my lady had given instructions they were not to be disturbed.

Insofar as was possible, my lady also sought to spare the cripples. Gregor was able to drive the lead caravan, but Miss Torrey, well instructed by her brother, took Bradford's place on the seat of the second vehicle, and Japhet replaced Heywood as driver of the fifth caravan.

With both eyes black and puffy and his nose tightly taped, Heywood could barely see, but he sat beside the youth, lending his moral support until they were well along their way and Japhet felt more at home with the horses. He ran ahead to Pauley's caravan then, and having rather precariously negotiated the steps and the back door, groped his way to his bunk and sank down with a faint sigh of relief.

Mathieson lay outstretched on the opposite lower bunk, an arm flung across his eyes. His ankle ached with wearying persistence and he knew that if he was to be in the play at all, he must rest, but it irked him to have to lie here when he longed so to see his love.

He was still dazzled by the delight of this tremendous change in his life; still awed by the power of it. He felt as if the rest of his existence had been but a prelude to this moment. His mouth twisted wryly. Not an altogether harmonious prelude . . . But that would change. He would become everything Fiona could wish him to be. He thought with a surge of tenderness, 'She loves me just as I am . . . bless her.' But it would not do. She did not *know* what he really was. The very thought brought a clammy sweat to his brow. Someday she might find out the truth, but by that time, with luck, she would be his wife, and he would have proved his love and his unalterable intention to change for the better.

He stirred uneasily. The Bradfords appeared to be in straitened circumstances, so his suit might not be refused on the grounds of Fiona being some sort of heiress. Still, he'd have precious little to offer. He could go back into the army, of course, but he didn't want that kind of life for her. She belonged in a place like Dance . . . He could envision her there—not as it was now, of course, but as he'd always dreamed of its becoming. It was the only one of the Fairleigh properties where *Maman* had been happy—the widespread Gloucestershire acres to which she'd been taken, believing herself a bride, little knowing that her "husband" had thought they never would be sought for at the decrepit old farmhouse. It was gone to rack and ruin now, of course, only because Papa had neither known nor cared that he had a lazy and inept steward. Likely Muffin had never bothered with the old place.

The thought of his grandfather caused Mathieson a qualm. It would be curst revolting to have to go whining around Muffin and beg for the allowance he'd turned up his nose at. But it was the most logical procedure; it would allow him to offer Fiona a comfortable life, a nice home, servants. So he must humble his pride.

"You awake, old lad?"

He ignored the cautious enquiry, his mind on the conversation he'd had with my lady this morning. She'd been kind; concerned because he limped and because she'd said he looked tired. He smiled cynically. If she knew *why* he'd looked tired, she'd have had good reason for concern. But after he'd convinced the Scot that he alone knew the whereabouts of the vital list, MacTavish had (however reluctantly) sworn to keep silent about him, and Rob MacTavish was not the man to go back on his word.

He lowered his arm. "Yes," he said. "Why?"

Heywood, who had been smiling foolishly at the ceiling, started. "Gad! Not the man for a quick reply, are you!"

"One has to prepare oneself to contemplate your glory," said Mathieson unkindly. "Can you see anything at all?"

"Not much. But—thpeaking of glory . . ." Between his numerous bruises, a flush appeared and he contrived to look shy and ecstatic at the same time.

Mathieson sat up, swung his legs over the side of the bunk with care, and reached out. "Women," he sighed, as they shook hands. "Who can ever understand the pretty creatures? Miss Clandon refused you when you gave the appearance of being halfway human. But now that you look like something a wolf spat out—"

"You're jealouth!" said Heywood, grinning rapturously.

"Jealous? I? Why a man would want to confine himself to one woman, when the world fairly swarms with 'em—"

Heywood laughed. "Jealouth ath hell! But you need not feel obliged to with me happy—for I am tho happy, I can hardly bear it!"

"So I see." Mathieson's smile was tinged with envy, but he said with real sincerity, "And—my dear fellow, I do indeed wish you happy! When did you pop the question?"

"Yethterday. While Beth wath binding my hand."

"What? In front of everyone? Gad what a clumsy block! I wonder she did not refuse you again. One chooses a moonlit night, Thad, or—"

"There wath a moon the latht time I athked her. Turned me

down cold. I vowed to wait for jutht the right moment before I rithked it again. I could tell Beth wath genuinely grieved by my pitiable condition, God love her tender heart, tho I—"

"Struck while the blood was in full flow, eh? Good tactics, I must admit. Have you spoken to Bradford?"

"Well, of courth! I hope I know how to go on!"

"I hope you do, too. So he gave you his blessing, eh? Now what's wrong? Never say the old boy refused to act for his—brother-in-law, is it?"

"Yeth. Ian Clandon. They live near Prethtonpanth. And Bradford wath willing to give hith approval—after I have made application to Lady Clorinda."

"Well, ask her, you clod. She likes you, and with your prospects she'll likely fall on your neck! What *is* your rank, by the way? Earl? Viscount?" His lips quirked. "Not a lowly baron, I hope?"

"Yeth, damn you!"

"What a pity! Never mind, she might overlook—No!" Laughing, he leaned back. "You would not strike a cripple?"

Heywood swore and sat down again saying dismally, "I'd hoped you might underthtand the bog I'm in. I am truly dethperate."

"Why? I fancy you'll have to go up to Prestonpans before you can publish the betrothal, but—"

"You blithering idiot, *will* you be quiet! I'll go up there, of courth, but . . ." Heywood's unfortunate eyes fell. He muttered, "The—the thought of approaching Lady Clorinda in—in a matter that meanth tho very much . . . I will make a mull of it, I know! I'll thtand before her like a—a perfect gudgeon, with my horrid lithp . . . Roly—the lady frightenth me to death!"

"Cannot say I blame you. She scares me, too!"

"That ith pig dribble and you know it! You wrap her 'round your little finger ath you do all the femaleth. And—I wath thinking . . . well, my lady thinkth the world of you, tho—could you—*would* you put in a good word for me, old lad? I'd—I'd be everlathtingly grateful."

"*Servilité! Infâme!*" exclaimed Mathieson. "Do your own dirty work, you spineless coward! I'll have no part in—"

Heywood looked crushed and held up one hand in acknowledgement of defeat.

Mathieson's indignation eased into a faint smile. He must try to remember not to be a villain. "Oh, very well," he grumbled. "But don't blame me if she hires me to put a period to you!"

Lady Clorinda had been quite sure when Mathieson limped to her caravan that he had come to find Fiona. They'd paused to rest the horses, and when she realized it was herself he had come to see, she sent Fiona hurrying back to the coach to discover how Rob went on. For a second, Mathieson's eyes had followed the girl betrayingly, but apart from that his manners had not slipped by an iota. His whole attention was on my lady, his considerable charm expended at length, and very persuasively in behalf of his friend.

Perched on the lower bunk, watching him thoughtfully, she said, "So you like Heywood, do you?"

"His kind are the backbone of this land. He is the type of man I wish—I had been."

"Well! There's a compliment, indeed." The warmth in her smile was unfeigned. "Yet we have reason to be thankful you are exactly the kind of man you are."

He said with bland immediacy, "For the moment, at least."

"Does that mean," she asked, accepting the challenge, "you think us thankful only for the moment? Or that you are what you are only for the moment?"

"I suppose—both. When this is over, I fancy I shall be *persona non grata* with you, no?"

Despite the sardonic drawl, the black eyes held a wistfulness that could not fail to touch her heart. 'Oh, you wicked creature!' she thought. "And—the second half of my remark?" she evaded.

Mathieson hesitated, then limped over to the door and stood looking into the rain. He'd had no intention of raising the business now, but perhaps it was as good a time as any. His pulse quickening and his voice low, he asked, "Do you believe a man can change, Lady Clorinda? Do you believe the love of a beautiful woman can make a worthless, unprincipled rascal into a—a worthwhile human being?"

"Oh, no," she answered softly.

He spun around, frowning, and she felt a delicious little pang of fear. "Pray do not throttle me," she said. "Perhaps I should qualify my verdict. For—it *is* a verdict, isn't it Roland?"

He paled, but gave a small bow.

"I do not believe the love of any woman can change a man. Particularly, if he is worthless and unprincipled and a rascal. I *do* believe that in rare—alas, very rare—instances, a man's love *for* a woman can inspire him to change. But—'twould be a long and hard road for such a man as you describe, and his love would have to be exceeding deep and faithful."

"But if he were to take that long and hard road, and if at the end he was—might be—considered worthy. Would he then have some small chance?"

"I—rather doubt it," she sighed. "Oh, *Lud!* Do not look at me so, dear boy! I vow you put me very much in mind of your grandfather, for in his youth he was just such another creature! All fire and ice and terrifyingly intense passions!"

He gripped his impromptu cane so hard that it bit into the palm of his hand. A betraying muscle flickered beside his mouth, but he had no intention of losing his poise as he had done so disgracefully last night, and responded coolly, "My sincere apologies, madam. Perhaps—you would be so good as to explain . . . ?"

"But, my dear, it surely must be obvious. If the lady were beautiful, and the gentleman in question must follow a long, hard road, the chances are that by the time his metamorphosis was complete, she would have—married someone else."

How white he was now, and how his eyes glittered with rage. He would like to pick her up and break her neck, beyond doubting. Poor lad—he was much more in love than she had guessed. Almost, she could be sorry for having been so cruel. But— sometimes, it was necessary. And, withal, kinder in the long run.

Mathieson said in a tight, controlled voice, "And—how if the beautiful lady is as deeply in love and as faithful?"

"Ah—that would be sad. For beautiful young ladies—of our class, at least—do not always have control over whom they will wed, do they?"

For an instant, again, she was almost afraid. Then the dark head was turned from her and she could breathe once more.

Mathieson stood very taut and still, looking blindly at the team behind them, but seeing instead a piquant, trusting face, the love in a pair of shining emerald eyes.

To spare him, and because of her own nervousness, Lady

216

Clorinda said brightly, "But since we speak of Thaddeus Bri—Heywood, we need have no such qualms."

"True," he murmured. And then, with a sudden wild gesture, he swung up his cane and snapped it between his hands as if it had been a thin twig rather than a sturdy branch. His control broke also. "No!" he cried, and limped forward until he towered over the tiny lady who leaned back on the bunk, looking up at him with wide, frightened eyes.

'I wonder,' thought Lady Clorinda, 'if his mind has given way? Is he going to strike me with those two pieces of his cane? Gregor has gone to talk to Pauley—if I scream, can he come back in time?' But she did not scream although she could not have told why.

Mathieson suddenly fell to his knees before her, and reaching out, took her by both arms. In a strained voice, he said, "You told me once that—that when you were young, you admired Muffin. Did you—love him?"

A dark flush stained her cheeks. Frightened, but still proud, she demanded, "Let me go at once! How dare—"

He shook her but very gently. "I dare! And you blush, madam. *Did* you?"

"Well—w-well . . . I do not see—"

"You *did*! Ah, my lady, do you remember how it felt? You did not marry him, so you must have been separated against your will. No, do not hide your eyes! Look at me! Ma'am, if you remember how it felt to be denied your heart, *Je vous en supplie*—do not inflict that on us! I worship her! I dare to think she loves me. I know . . . God help me, I *know* I am unworthy! But—" His voice broke, his head bowed, and suddenly the agonized face was concealed against her skirts.

She stared down at him for a moment. Such ungentlemanlike loss of reserve both shocked and touched her. But his words had taken her back to youth and its heartbreaking disappointments, so that her hand went out gently to touch the thick dark hair. She laughed rather shakily and murmured, "How much of your poor mama is in you! What Englishman would resort to such emotional behaviour?"

"I know," he said, his face still hidden and his voice muffled. "I am quite unused to—to loving, you see. I apologize for causing you such embarrassment."

"I find it refreshing, rather than embarrassing. Would that

more of our men had some of that hot Latin blood! Our ladies would be better loved, I think.''

Mathieson lifted his head and gazed up at her. His face was haggard, but hope had crept into his eyes.

She said gently, ''Yes. I do remember. At the time I thought . . . I surely would die of grief. And I *do* pity you, Roland. But—oh, poor boy, I cannot help. You see—I love my granddaughter very much.''

He seized her hand and pressed it to his lips. ''And, I am not what you want for her. Of course not. But my lady, you *can* help! How much you know—how much you have heard of me, I dare not guess. I only swear to you, here on my knees, that I *will* change! I shall not ask her to wait. For the time all I ask is to be allowed to be near her—to try and guard her from harm. And to—most humbly beg that—that you will not close your mind to all hope for us. That you will give me a chance to prove myself. Lady Clorinda . . . is there anything—*anything* I can do to win your favour?''

She shook her head in a troubled way, but said, ''Well, to start with, I would have you get up, for I fear you are hurting that ankle quite badly. No, do not utter polite platitudes. Now—be silent, and let me think if I may in the slightest degree give you any hope . . .''

Obediently, Mathieson dragged himself awkwardly to his feet and limped to the door again, his nerves quivering, horrified by this second lapse in conduct, and waiting in quivering apprehension for the verdict of this proud and invincible *grande dame*.

''I have your task,'' said Lady Clorinda after a few moments that seemed to him to stretch into an eternity.

He returned to stand very still before her, scarcely daring to breathe.

''You have told MacTavish you mean to help us get clear,'' she said gravely. ''You may think that, of itself, should be sufficient. Alas, it is not. Fiona must have a husband who is honourable as well as brave. Whose devotion is not a fly-by-night thing, but will endure. Who can offer her an adequate fortune and a gracious home. Who can command the respect not only of those who have cause to be grateful to him, but of—the finest man I know.'' She saw his right hand stretch out, then tighten into a fist, and she finished, ''Yes, Roland. When you can come to me and tell me Muffin has forgiven you—then I may consider your request to pay your addresses to my granddaughter!''

Mathieson did not move, but his heart thudded into his boots. He thought, *'La tâche hors de accomplissement!'*

My lady saw the despair in his eyes and prepared herself to resist his appeal.

He surprised her. With a commendably bland smile, he murmured lightly, *"Merci bien*, my lady. Now—what must I tell our poor Heywood?''

So the English side of him was in control again. There was the feeling that his outburst was unprecedented and had dismayed him as much as it had startled her. How calm and assured he appeared now. And who would dream that behind the lazy smile, the faintly bored and mocking air, dwelt such a volcano? Lud, but one could not fail to be titillated, nor to marvel that Fiona, dear as the minx was, had managed to attach so fiery and tempestuous a heart.

Stifling a sigh, my lady stood. "Tell him to come and speak to me himself," she said, standing and walking to the door with him. "He will not find me unsympathetic.''

He bowed and murmured his thanks. And leaving her, knew she was a formidable antagonist, indeed.

❧ 13 ❧

The village of Sandipool was not blessed with a town hall, so the Avon Travelling Players were to present their performance in the Vestry Hall of the church. St. Peter's was located atop a steep hill, and late in the afternoon of their arrival, the two property waggons toiled through the cold drizzle to the old church, escorted by every boy within a radius of five miles who had been able to escape his parents, and a motley crowd of dogs. The excitement rose to fever pitch when the hastily repaired set pieces, each swathed in oilcloth, were wheeled down the make-shift ramps. Many willing hands made short work of trundling the tantalizing objects into the Vestry Hall, but the joyous uproar stilled to a hushed silence when the red coach made its resplendent way across the cobblestones and the five female members of the Avon Travelling Players alighted. Three of these ladies were so dazzlingly beautiful that the curate, who had come out to quiet the children, completely forgot his errand and stood gawking in a manner that the vicar subsequently informed him was particularly unsuited to his calling.

There was a great deal of hammering and shouting inside the Vestry Hall. There had been no stage available, but when MacTavish had first spoken to the Squire as to the possibility of presenting the play in Sandipool, the local people had been so excited by such a prospect that they had undertaken to erect a stage themselves. This structure was now nearing completion, and my lady, Mrs. Dunnigan, and Moira went off to inspect the results, while Fiona and Elizabeth instructed Japhet, Pauley, and Freemon Torrey as to the disposition of their costumes and cosmetics.

A curtained-off area adjacent to the new stage was used by the choirboys to change into their robes. This had been hurriedly partitioned into two separate temporary dressing rooms, one for the men and the other for the ladies, with screens arranged so as to leave a short inner corridor by which it was possible to access the stage while out of view of the spectators. The large box of costumes having been carried in, Torrey and his two helpers departed, and the caravans soon went rumbling back down the hill.

Fiona and Elizabeth busied themselves with the proper disposition of the various garments, and in setting up the two travelling mirrors.

"Thank goodness the rain became no heavier," said Fiona, hanging up her "dairymaid's" apron. "I doubt this drizzle will keep many people at home, do you?"

"As if we cared," whispered Elizabeth, with a cautious glance at the curtain.

"Oh, I know." Lowering her voice also, Fiona said, "How worrying 'twould be was this really our livelihood. But—it *is* rather fun, do not you think? I vow that despite all the nuisances and discomforts, I never have enjoyed anything more!"

"That is *very* apparent," teased Elizabeth, then laughed at her cousin's blushes.

Fiona made a fast recover. "And what of you, pray?" Turning to seize Beth's hands, she said, "Poor Thaddeus! He is so battered, but fought for us so bravely." Her eyes became wide and haunted. "Do you know what I was thinking before I went to bed last night? I thought—how very close we came to—to—"

"I know!" Elizabeth hugged her, trembling. "I cannot get it out of my mind. I was—so terrified, Fiona—so very frightened!"

"Well, we were spared, praise God! We must not think of it anymore. Beth—Thaddeus is such a fine man. Now that the decision is made—you must be very happy."

Elizabeth smiled. "I thought I was—until I looked at you! Oh dearest, do you know how often you sing to yourself? How often you smile at some secret thought?" And trying not to betray her fears for her cousin's future happiness, she asked, "Is it not wonderful that love has come to us both at once? Has Captain Mathieson offered yet?"

221

"No." Fiona picked up the gown she wore aboard the pirate ship and hung it on one of the clothes trees that had been provided for the purpose. Carefully arranging the voluminous skirts, she said, "I've scarce had a word alone with him since yesterday afternoon. Is very difficult, you know, when—" Sensing a difference, she glanced up. Elizabeth had gone.

A gentleman stood beside the hall screens, watching her. A tall gentleman, rather portly, but dressed with great elegance. An elaborate periwig was upon his head, the long curls hanging down on each side of his face and flowing to his shoulders. His complexion was florid, his lean features marred by a sinister scar stretching from his left eye to his chin. A half-moon patch adorned his right cheekbone, and another, diamond-shaped, was beside his mouth. He made her a fine leg and when he straightened she saw that the diamond-shaped patch was quivering suspiciously and that the eyes he had kept modestly lowered now watched her and that they were exceedingly handsome eyes, black, and alight with laughter.

"Roly!" she squeaked, clapping her hands, and dancing over to him. "La, but I scarce recognized you!"

"I should hope not." He surveyed her through an ornate quizzing glass. "I am neither Roly, nor Captain Jack, but—" He leaned closer and hissed malevolently, "Sir—Roger! Beware pretty maid!"

"Splendid!" Ignoring this advice, she took his arm. "But—where is your cane?"

He reached to a long be-ribboned staff that was propped against the screen. "*Voila!* Madam—will you walk?"

"No, for you should not! And how you will essay the duel, I cannot guess. Even without your damaged ankle, that—er, protuberance would get in the way of your sword, I'd think."

"We are going to have to manage without a duel. Furthermore," he drew himself up, "can it be that you refer to my manly physique, ma'am?"

"No." Her eyes twinkled mischievously at him. "To your monstrous stomach, sir. Roly, I know you cannot play Firebrand tonight, but why must you make yourself so silly-looking, when—"

He drew her towards the side door that led to the churchyard. "Because I mean to make Sir Roger into a really despicable villain—as only I know how. I can scarce blame your reluctance

222

to trust yourself to stroll among the gravestones with such a menace.'' His lips curved into a leering smile, but his eyes were a caress.

Fiona's heart began to beat very fast. She glanced nervously to the stage, but they were already concealed from view by the curve of the curtains. ''We should not,'' she said, without a great deal of resolution. Then added with her beaming look, ''But I suppose that is no obstacle for a 'really despicable villain.' ''

''Oh, none.'' He opened the door and bowed. ''What they say about forbidden fruits is all too true.''

''Just for a minute then, Sir Roger. But I would not have you think 'tis my practice to be so naughty.''

''Whatever your practices, dear my Mite, I cannot but adore them.''

She drifted beside him, her hand confidently on his arm. How the cloak came about her shoulders, she did not know, but when they walked in silence to the side steps he contrived to lift the hood over her head. She turned to smile up at him, and his answering smile seemed to kiss her heart.

The rain pattered lightly onto the flagstones of the path they followed. The sullen wind had no power to chill them. Neither spoke, yet each was blissfully content. Limping along beside her, Mathieson scarcely felt the ache in his ankle, but when he drew her to a halt, Fiona scanned his face with an immediate anxiety. ''Are you all right? You must be very tired. Perhaps we should—''

''I am all right until you look at me like that.''

''Oh,'' she said, blushing and lowering her eyes.

''In fact,'' he went on, ''were you any other lady, I would certainly have kissed you by now.''

''Oh. Well—well, I grant 'tis bold in me to walk out alone with you, but this *is* a public place, and—''

''And this particular public is so—buried in its own concerns . . .'' Her enchanting little laugh sounded. He said, ''Only look at that obligingly large angel on the pink marble pedestal. Now—an you dare risk a few more steps beside me, my sweet—''

''Captain Mathieson!'' she exclaimed with a prim mouth and dancing eyes.

''Sir Roger, Miss Bradford.''

The tall angel offered an excellent screen. Mathieson tossed the staff down and took Fiona in his arms. "My most adorable sweeting," he said, low and huskily.

"Wicked creature," she chided, joying in the nearness of him. "Oh! This horrid cushion!"

He laughed and began to unbutton his waistcoat. "I will remove it at once."

"No! Roly—they will see us!"

"Much we care!" He cupped one hand about her blushing cheek. "Besides, we have a guardian angel."

"Of course we care. Foolish boy, do not pretend to scorn the proprieties, when you have so often lectured me upon my lack of them."

"I was a fool indeed," he breathed, running his lips down her temple. "You should have paid no heed to my nonsense."

How gentle, yet inexpressibly thrilling was the soft touch of his mouth . . . Fiona seemed to float; her senses reeled to an ecstasy she had never known before. He loved her. He was too honourable a man to say such things, to embrace her like this and not love her. And, dear Lord, but she loved him so very much! What a glory to surrender passionately, completely, to so adept a lover . . .

"My dearest darling girl," he whispered in her ear, "what am I to do? I must either run mad—or kiss you."

"Well," she gasped, "I certainly would not wish to be accused of causing you to run mad, sir . . ."

Even as she spoke his arm became steel bands that crushed her tight against him. Her pulses leapt. Without a trace of maidenly modesty she lifted her face, and his lips found hers.

Mathieson's boast that he had never forced an unwilling girl was largely true. Only once, inflamed by desire, had he kissed a lady against her will, and she had not only refused to kiss him back, but had soundly boxed his ear for his pains. Thus, with this girl alone had he known the kiss of innocence. The soft, yielding body, the tremblingly inexperienced lips, the shy sweet eagerness, wrought on him to such effect that when he lifted his head he was as dazed, as enraptured, as she. "Fiona," he gasped, and with an unparalleled lack of originality, "Oh—Fiona . . ." He bent to her again.

After a blissful interval, she found the strength to push at his chest. "Roly—my dear, I *must* go back."

"Another moment—I beg you. We so seldom have a chance to be alone together."

"I dare not. We will be missed and—and I know you'd no more hurt my dear papa or my grandmama than you would shame me."

He sighed and let her go, asking wistfully, "Do you feel shamed because I dared to kiss you, beloved?"

"No, ah no!" She stretched out a hand which he promptly seized. "Proud, rather," she said. "Though I dare not guess what your obliging angel must think of us."

He had been pressing more kisses into that warm pink palm, but at this his head lifted, and he stared rather blankly at her. For another instant her eyes, soft with love, gazed into his, then with a swirl of petticoats she had turned and was running quickly back up the path to the Vestry Hall.

Mathieson stood staring after her. Then he sat on the angel's marble pedestal and gazed numbly at a small golden leaf that floated on a nearby puddle. How wonderful, how incredible, that he had found her. That of all the many places in this great world where he *might* have been, he had instead been so blessed as to have ridden through that miserable storm and found the one, the only lady he would ever love . . . Stretched out at his feet and covered with mud.

He stood and began to wander slowly back to the church, smiling fondly to himself. He must have been blind not to have seen, mud and all, how exquisite she was. He *had* been blind. A blind fool. It was all ignorance—ignorance and arrogance combined! Not long ago he had laughed at the heartbreak of a friend whose lady had left him. "You're the type wants one woman for eternity," he had sneered. "From which may the good Lord deliver me!" Well, the good Lord had instead sent that imp Cupid after him, with a whole quiver-full of arrows marked with his name. A fine marksman was the imp, and he was caught for all time, even as Muffin had warned.

Lady Clorinda knew Muffin. She knew him well enough to know that the task she had set was impossible of achievement. Mathieson's jaw hardened. She was a brave and resourceful woman, and one he could not but admire, but she had underestimated her opponent. He had every intention of keeping his vow; of helping these people achieve their goal, of becoming a more honourable man, for the sake of his precious lady. But also

225

he would fight for his happiness and resort to whatsoever he must to ensure it. A sneer crept into his eyes and his lips curved to a smile that was not pleasant. He had beaten my lady at her own game. Nor had he been obliged to break his word to her. Not exactly. All he'd done was kiss Fiona. He chuckled. A girl of her upbringing and moral beliefs would consider that they had plighted their troth with that kiss. She would wait. Whatever Lady Clorinda Ericson or Mr. Mervyn Bradford, or anyone on the face of this earth said. She would deem herself betrothed, and she would wait.

A faint voice whispered, "Despicable!"

Alarmed, he jerked his head around. He was alone in the cemetery, save for a few grieving angels and a cluster of impudent sparrows who perched on the statuary and scolded him for having come calling without breadcrumbs.

He must, he thought, have imagined that horrid whisper. Still, he *was* on hallowed ground, and he'd not put it past St. Thomas to come frippering around just when he wasn't wanted. He hastened his steps and limped rather hurriedly from among the angels.

For as long as she lived Fiona was to remember St. Peter's Church in the village of Sandipool. The sanctuary was not large and on this rather chill and drizzly afternoon she was the only occupant. She had felt too overwhelmed with emotion to return at once to the Vestry Hall. She knew her cheeks were hot, and suspected that her eyes must reflect her happiness. She needed a quiet time to compose herself before she faced Elizabeth and Moira, either one of whom would be sure to notice her flustered state. There could be no formal announcement yet, and she was not ready to share her wonderful secret. She had crept into the sanctuary, therefore, and now sat quietly in the back pew, wrapped in the peace and tranquillity of the old church, her radiant gaze taking in the beautiful carvings of the pulpit and choir loft, the richness of the stained glass windows, the cross and the unlit candles on the altar. To her nostrils came the faint scents of flowers and furniture polish. Faintly, she could hear voices and laughter from the Vestry Hall. She wondered if Roland was among them now. She wondered if he felt as exhilarated as she; if he was as proud and awed by this new feeling of completeness, of commitment.

She had reached a turning point in her life. She was betrothed. Now and for all the years to come she belonged to the man of her heart, and that knowledge brought her a deep sense of gratitude. Sometimes, when Freemon had been particularly persuasive she had worried, wondering if she was throwing away the chance of a good life with a good man only because of her romantical longing to care for the man she would wed.

She smiled tenderly. Thank heaven she had waited. There were no doubts now. Fate had sent a gentleman to her who was everything she had hoped to find, and she could ask no greater joy from life than to place her future in his hands. It occurred to her then that she knew very little of his prospects. He had said he was a poor man. Much that mattered, she thought defiantly. She had her inheritance which may not be enormous, but would be ample for their needs.

What would Grandmama say? Some of the sparkle left her eyes and she frowned worriedly. Grandmama had warned that Roland was a rogue; a soldier of fortune; that he was not for her. Surely, she could not think so now, after all he had done for them? He was highly born, that was obvious, but if he was not received by the *ton* for some reason, why that was of little moment; she and Papa and Francis had never been much ones for going into Society, after all. Francis would like Roly, she was sure of it, despite his hopes that she would choose his friend for a husband. How proud she would be to introduce Captain Roland Mathieson as her affianced to all the members of her family . . . How very blessed she was.

She found that her eyes were misty and leaning down, pulled over a hassock, then sank to her knees to pray God's blessing on this betrothal and beseech His protection of the valiant gentleman she loved more than her own life.

Despite the varying degrees of misery with which the gentlemen coped as they played their parts, at the close of the first act a weary Mervyn Bradford acknowledged to his mother that it was the best performance they ever had given. "For Torrey is so pleased to be the hero again that his acting is inspired, and Mathieson has transformed Sir Roger into such a dastardly rogue that I wonder he's not been dragged out and lynched!"

"The customers certainly seem to be enjoying it," murmured

my lady, peeping through the curtains at the noisy and crowded benches.

Torrey had already changed into the rags he wore in the prison scene, and came to join them carrying the robe and tattered wig that transformed Bradford into the gaoler. "Is there any word from MacTavish?"

Handing his bag wig to his mother and shrugging into the long robe, Bradford answered grimly, "No change."

"It will be tonight, then?"

"Heaven knows how," said my lady. "If my poor battered actors can cope with the second act, 'twill of itself be a miracle. Cuthbert looks purely exhausted already, and though he hides it well I think Mathieson can scarce endure to walk. Bend your head before you put on that pitiful object, Bradford, the sticking plaster is coming loose." She remedied the matter, and watched her son worriedly as he cautiously settled the gaoler's wig over his bandage. " 'Tis a monstrous bruise. How do you go on?"

"Fair to middling, I thank you," replied the stalwart Bradford, whose head was now pounding so unkindly that at times he found it difficult to focus his eyes. "Never fret, ma'am, we shall do. Mathieson's pure steel, and I've never known Cuthbert to let us down yet."

In the gentlemen's dressing room, Cuthbert was arguing with Heywood, who was attempting to put the sling about his neck.

"Be damned if I'll wear the stupid thing," the big man grumbled. "Makes me feel a proper doddipoll."

Mathieson turned on him frowningly. "Your wrist is puffing up, you block. An that arm becomes infected, we'll have to leave you behind. And we need you, Cuthbert! The play may be 'the thing,' but we've a more important thing to worry with. The audience will understand, I've no doubt."

Another moment Cuthbert scowled defiance, but the younger man's will prevailed. With a wry grin, Cuthbert said, "Oh, very well, then!" and allowed the sling to be put over his head and his hurt arm eased into it.

Leaning heavily on his cane, Mathieson limped over to Gregor, who, flute in hand, was standing where the rear curtains came together, peering at the audience.

"Is everything ready on stage?" asked Mathieson. "No sign of trouble is there?"

"Alec has the set pieces in place for Scene Two. And they're getting waeful rrrresty oot yon. If 'tis trouble ye're sniffin'—why there's naun I glim, but . . . whisht, I've the scent o't. I'd a notion ye sensed it forbye." He shook his head gloomily, walked around the screens and into the little passage.

Mathieson had difficulty with the Scots accent at times, and he glanced uncertainly at Cuthbert, who chuckled and translated: "He said the audience is tired of waiting for the next act. And that he smells trouble."

Mathieson grunted and parted the end curtains just sufficiently that he in turn could scan the audience.

"I think that ith held to be bad luck," warned Heywood cheerily. "Never trouble trouble, till trouble—"

"I think Gregor's nostrils did not lie!" Mathieson stood back holding the curtain aside.

Fiona hurried in with Japhet beside her. Both the Dunnigans had been left at camp with MacTavish. It was clear that the youth was agitated and considerably out of breath. Heywood sprang to his feet and they all gathered closer.

"The soldiers came again," said Fiona. "Japhet ran all the way here to warn us."

Gregor's flute commenced the introduction to the prison scene which was played before the closed curtains, and without scenery. Cuthbert glanced in the direction of the stage. His part required that he appear very shortly and he swore in exasperation. "Lake again?"

"No, sir. A different officer, but I think it was the same troop."

With a flutter of draperies, a much shocked Lady Clorinda came through the hall curtains. "Fiona! This is the gentleman's—Japhet! Oh, Lud! What's happened?"

The boy told her rapidly and she looked dismayed, but asked at once, "Is your mama all right? What about MacTavish?"

"I don't know, ma'am. I was with the horses when the dragoons rode in and they didn't see me. My mother was arguing with them, but she spotted me and gave me a nod, so I ran all the way here. But I surely didn't like leaving her and Mr. MacTavish."

"Never fear," said Mathieson, reassuringly. "An English officer would not allow his men to harm a woman alone with a sick man."

"They were not touching Mama, but—they were bedevilling Mr. Rob," said the boy with a grim look.

My lady asked anxiously, "In what way? He was in bed—an invalid to all appearances, no?"

"No, ma'am. He'd insisted on getting up and dressed, and the officer wouldn't listen when my mother said he was ill, and kept questioning him. He left off when Mr. MacTavish coughed so much, but told his men to keep at him. It looked ugly, I thought. When I left they were getting rough."

"Be damned," muttered Mathieson.

Cuthbert swore under his breath.

Heywood snatched up his cloak, and started for the rear curtains.

Mathieson thought 'A typical hero!' and watched him with faint amusement.

My lady said sharply, "Thaddeus, don't be a fool! You cannot go down there!"

"Besides which, you cannot see well enough to *get* down there," Mathieson drawled.

"I'll go," growled Cuthbert.

"You're due on stage in about thirty seconds," argued Lady Clorinda.

Mathieson pointed out, "Besides, if any of you go charging down there, they'll know we've been warned and that we responded most urgently. Such desperation might well awaken their suspicions that we had guards posted—that we've something to hide."

"You told me just now you couldn't afford to lose me," said the big man. " 'Tis sure as hell that we cannot afford to risk *Rob's* life!"

"We need a diversion all right," agreed Mathieson. "Preferably from someone they've not seen." They might, he thought, prevail on some sturdy yokels to provide a distraction. He glanced up. Japhet watched him, his bright eyes alight with admiration. Fiona's loved face was turned to him adoringly; she fairly glowed with pride. Uneasy, he said, "I was—er, thinking—"

She said in that husky little voice that reduced his common sense to idiocy, "Yes. How brave you are! I *knew* you would know what to do, Captain Mathieson!"

Stunned, he realized they all were smiling at him . . .

* * *

Heywood's rawboned grey horse made short work of the hill and Mathieson was galloping towards the camp while he was still wondering why he had been so stupid as to agree to this ridiculous and decidedly risky endeavour. But, heigh-ho, what was done was done. He certainly could not have driven that glowing look from the Tiny Mite's dear face, or shaken the pedestal on which Japhet had so obviously set him. Besides, with luck the soldiers had already gone, and he would merely have to turn around and gallop back up the hill again so as to make his appearance in the third act.

He heard male laughter as he approached the camp, and knew his hope had been ill-founded. Still, the new officer would likely be some Johnny raw, and he'd be able to use the calling card my lady had given him and intimidate the young fellow into taking the troop away. He came around the end caravan then, and drew the grey to a halt, staring motionless at the scene before him.

Once again, their belongings were strewn carelessly about. Once again, troopers were searching through the caravans. Mrs. Dunnigan, looking angry and frightened, stood to one side, ignoring the sergeant who was talking quietly to her. Nearer at hand, three troopers were grouped about Rob MacTavish, shouting questions at him, but interrupting his faltering attempts to reply by shoving him violently from one to another and raucously mimicking his gasping coughs. An immaculate and amused young officer lounged on the steps of Lady Clorinda's caravan, his snowy breeches protected by the blue gown he had used as a cushion.

It was very apparent there was no real suspicion here. Just a jolly spirit of sportiveness. And a sick man their helpless foil. Rage seared through Mathieson. "Hey! You, there!" he roared.

So intent had the troopers been on their fun that his arrival had gone unnoticed. His shout had unexpected results. One of those baiting MacTavish spun about. MacTavish, barely conscious and reeling from a hard shove, lurched weakly through the opening and fell heavily.

The officer sprang to his feet with a cry of anger. "Damme if the beastly fellow ain't splashed mud on me!"

There was no moon yet, and the clearing was lit only by the flickering flames from the campfire, but the officer's tall figure was lithe and perfectly formed, and the deep voice struck Mathieson like a blow. He thought a shocked, 'Lambert!' and for an instant time stood still.

Lieutenant Brooks Lambert, he well knew blamed him for the loss of his inheritance, the loss of his lady, and the loss of his captaincy. To an extent, he was justified. With this in mind, staring at the man who had every reason to wish him dead, Mathieson knew he was batting on a very sticky wicket indeed.

At this moment, Lambert's anguished attention was on his violated breeches. "Who the hell is this person, Patchett?" he snapped, trying to repair the damage with his handkerchief and not looking up.

The sergeant left Mrs. Dunnigan and strode rapidly to Mathieson's stirrup. He was a thin man of average height, somewhere in the mid-thirties, with a deeply lined face and dark eyes devoid of expression. He said in a London voice, "Lieutenant Lambert would like your name and papers, if you please, sir."

Mathieson had been questioned by this man when Lake had commanded the troop, but Patchett clearly did not recognize him. Sir Roger must be believable then, and between the dimness and the pillow under his belt, he began to hope he might manage to bluff his way through without having to fight his way out. Lambert's was a stubborn and contrary nature however, necessitating that his own intended tactics be discarded. His mind racing, he decided on a new approach. He had a bad moment when Mrs. Dunnigan, running to MacTavish, glanced up at him, and her eyes widened suddenly. But she went on, giving no other sign of recognition, and knelt beside the exhausted Scot.

"Papers?" roared Mathieson. "Don't be a blithering idiot! I do not carry papers about with me—especially when I come to kick a parcel of worthless gypsies off my lands! Here—" From his waistcoat pocket he extracted the card my lady had given him. "My card, sir. Innings. Sir Roger Innings." A gleam of unholy joy came into his eyes, and unable to resist the temptation, he added, "They don't call me that, though. Call me 'Second.' If I don't getcha in the first innings, begad, I'll getcha in the second!" He gave a bray of a laugh that brought a grin to the sergeant's lean features. "Jolly good—what? Haw!"

"Gad!" muttered Lambert, disdainfully waving the card away. "State your business, whatever your name is."

"Innings," trumpeted Mathieson. "Just toldya. And my

business, sir, is what jolly well should've been *your* business long before this! This is *my* land, sir! And I asked that this trash be cleared from it yesterday! Gave you the job, did they? Took you blasted well long enough, sir! Does no good to mollycoddle this kind of scum, y'know.''

Lambert glanced at MacTavish who was trying feebly to sit up. "I'd not say we've been er, mollycoddling exactly."

"I'd say you've been wasting time, sir! Wasting time! I want these people rousted off my land, and now, sir! NOW!"

"Your wants do not concern me. Nor do I see any need to shout," said Lambert, coldly. "My men will do precisely as they are told—*when* I see fit to tell 'em!"

"*When*, sir? *When*, is it? Now, stretch me bleeding, but you're an insolent fellow! I'll remind you, sir, that 'tis humble folk like me who pay your wages, sir!"

Lambert, who would have liked very much to stretch Innings bleeding, said drily, "Which would, no doubt, explain why we are so underpaid."

"For doing—what, sir? Disporting yourself at ease and allowing yon harridan to pamper that confounded clod? Move away from there, woman, afore I move you with me boot! Now—get about your business, Lambert, else I'll see to it you're promoted to corporal! Set your men to cleaning up this mess and sending these gypsies packing! At once, sir! I demand it! Never mind fussing with your drawers, sir! NOW, I say, d'ye hear?"

Drawn by the uproar, most of the troopers had gathered around to watch this scene delightedly. Lambert, upon whose noble brow a dark frown had gathered, was not amused. His new breeches would almost certainly be stained, which was infuriating, and his demotion was still an exceedingly sore point. His dislike for this hectoring, bucolic clod became acute. "In the first place, sir," he began icily, pulling on his gauntlets, "the acting troupe is up at the church, and—"

"Putting on their drivel at St. Peter's are they? I expressly forbade it! Go up and roust 'em all out and make 'em come down and do something useful for once by tidying—"

"In the second place," interpolated Lambert, his voice rising above Mathieson's sustained howl, "until you become my commanding officer, I can think of no reason why I should do—one—damned—thing—you ask!"

"No—no *reason*? Confound you, sir! Your *duty*, sir!" Mathieson, who was becoming hoarse, bellowed, "I want these people off my lands! Tonight, I tellya! TONIGHT!"

Lambert waved to his orderly, who came up leading a fine bay mare with four white stockings. "Then, I would suggest you set about it with no more loss of time, sir," sneered Lambert. "Patchett!"

"Mount up!" shouted the sergeant.

Sir Roger Innings shook his fist and raved. The troopers grinned. The fine bay mare danced and spun and cavorted her way out of the clearing, and the troop came to a trot and disappeared into the night.

"Disrespectful young jackanapes!" roared Mathieson, even as he dismounted and limped to bend over MacTavish. "I'll report you, sir! Be-damned if I don't! Stand warned, sir!"

MacTavish leaned his head back against Mrs. Dunnigan's shoulder and grinned up at him. "You lunatic . . ." he whispered. "What a chance to take!"

"Not my idea," murmured Mathieson, oddly gratified by the thankful glow in this man's drawn face. "Start picking up this rubbish, woman!" he roared after the troopers. "I'm going after your accomplices!" He turned back to MacTavish and went on softly, "I was forced into it against all my better judgment. A nice game they had with you. Can you get up?"

Japhet, who had followed Mathieson but stayed out of sight, now came running to join them, tears streaking his cheeks. Between them, they got MacTavish onto his feet again, and Mathieson pulled the sick man's arm across his shoulders.

Mrs. Dunnigan asked anxiously, "Why are you crying, son?"

"I laughed so hard I ache," sighed the boy. "Captain, when you said that about your nickname being Second, I wonder I didn't bust a blood vessel!"

MacTavish chuckled feebly. "Yes—that struck a chord with me. Something Charles Albritton told me, but I cannot think— Jupiter! Wasn't Lambert the officer involved in that business with Merry Carruthers?"

"He was a captain then," grinned Mathieson. "Poor block was clumsy as be-damned. Nigh got himself drummed out of the service."

"And he likely blames you! You everlasting lamebrain, you had to taunt him with your 'Second Innings!' If he'd recognized you . . . !"

234

"Hasn't got the brains. Still—you'd best keep your sharp eyes on 'em, Japhet. If they turn towards St. Peter's, Heywood will have to take over as Sir Roger. I've pushed La Belle Luck about as far as I dare tonight!"

In response to the lieutenant's wave, Patchett rode up to join him.

"You said you had searched their caravans before, sergeant?"

"Yessir. Only there was more to look through then, because—"

"Because they've taken all their paraphernalia to the church for their play. Obviously. Who inspected the pirate's treasure chest? You?"

There was contempt in the drawling voice and the sergeant, who had already conceived a deep dislike of this handsome young officer, said stiffly, "Captain Lake, sir. And right thorough he was, if—"

"Were there other big men among 'em?"

"Mr. Ford—er, I think his name was Ford."

"Your thought is erroneous. His name is Bradford, so the woman told me. A poor memory is not an aid to advancement, sergeant. Go on."

"Mr. Bradford—sir," said the sergeant, drawing a steadying breath, "is a very large gentleman, and—"

"I count myself a gentleman, Patchett, and dislike being grouped with the member of a troupe of common actors. Correct, if you please."

'Cap'n Lake,' thought the sergeant, 'why'd you go and leave us with this pretty sod?' "Sorry, sir. A very large *man*, sir."

"Hmmnn. Has he any resemblance to the regrettable Sir Roger? Don't gape like a trout, man! Ah, but perhaps I used big words. I must not overestimate you, must I? Let me put it to you again. Does Bradford in any way look like Innings?"

Thinking balefully of what he'd like to do with a couple of big words, the sergeant answered, "Not at all sir. Mr. Bradford is an older gen—er, man. About fifty, I'd think."

"I see. And a man might make himself appear older, but I doubt could make himself younger . . ." He drew rein, and the sergeant threw up his arm, halting the troop.

Lambert turned in the saddle and looked back to where, dimly

235

against the brightening sky, the tower of St. Peter's soared heavenwards. "No other large men among 'em?"

"One big cove, sir. Name of—ah, Cuthbert, as I recall. But—a much bigger frame than Sir Roger." Patchett hesitated, watching the perfect profile cautiously. "P'raps we should go and see that play, if he looked like someone you know, sir?"

" 'Twas not his looks, exactly . . ." Half of Lambert's mind was on the dinner he'd bespoken at a picturesque old inn they'd passed that morning, the proprietor of which had a daughter with a pair of saucy dark eyes and a dimple. It would be an hour's ride at least, and he had no desire to delay any longer. But . . . "There was something about the gentle Sir Roger," he murmured. "Some mannerism or feature . . . I cannot quite place . . ."

"They could tell us in the village where Sir Roger lives, sir. Likely it's not too far, and you might enjoy the play they put on. It's a nice play and—"

"Shakespeare, at the very least, eh?" sneered Lambert, aware that Patchett would be only too glad to go back.

"Well, no. Nothing clever, sir, but the ladies is pretty. It's about this milkmaid who—"

Lambert shuddered. "Spare me. At all events, it was likely just a similarity to someone I've met at sometime, and of no real importance." And dismissing Sir Roger Innings from his mind, he rode on.

The sergeant waved to the troop and followed, his lips silently mouthing a pithy and profane assessment of his superior officer.

ॐ 14 ॐ

Mathieson was so deeply asleep that his awakening was very gradual. Something was strange, but he could neither think what it was nor be greatly concerned, for he was warm and drowsily comfortable. There came by stages memories of yesterday; the delicious episode with Fiona in the cemetery; his bluffing of Lambert; and his wild dash back to St. Peter's where he had arrived in time to rescue a pale and panicked Heywood from taking over his role in the second act. Fiona's relief when he'd limped in had touched his heart, but there had been no time then to say anything more than that the soldiers had gone and Mrs. Dunnigan and MacTavish were unharmed. Later, when the red coach and the two largest caravans rolled up the hill to collect them, their scenery and properties, there had been need for caution because the vicar and the more influential local landowners had gathered around with what Mathieson had come to term "the three c's"—criticism, condescension, and congratulations—and it had been some time before they'd been able to escape.

On reaching the campsite Mathieson had been astonished by the complete restoration of order. There was no sign of the military upheaval; everything was neatly put away; MacTavish was asleep in Gregor's bunk; and Mrs. Dunnigan had hot cider waiting for the weary troupe. In response to his incredulous, "How a'plague did you manage to get it tidied up so fast?" the lady had merely replied with a coy smile that she did not propose to share her secrets. Oilcloth had been stretched between the roofs of Lady Clorinda's and Bradford's caravans to create a small shelter from the damp night air, and in front of it a fire

237

had been built. They'd gathered there in the warm good fellow-ship that comes from shared danger and hardship, enjoying the cider, slices of cold pork and cheese, and hunks of fragrant, buttered bread.

Japhet had come back from tending the horses and proceeded to regale them all with a highly dramatized account of the incident with the dragoons. Their fury over the rough treatment accorded MacTavish cooled a little when Mathieson's arrival was described, and by the time the tale was told the campsite rang with laughter. It was a rare experience for Mathieson to win praise and admiring looks from other men, and Japhet's obvious hero-worship, the awareness that he had done something that would have pleased *Maman*, and above all else, the loving pride in a pair of sparkling green eyes had not been hard to bear. He smiled faintly, hearing again the laughter and teas-ing, recalling the smell of the fragrant woodsmoke, seeing the firelight dance on one vivacious and lovely face.

It was very noisy in the caravan. Disturbed, Mathieson turned over and gave a startled shout as he was flung to a floor which jolted and shook and bounced under him. Fully awake at last, he realized that the back window was alternately a pale grey square or criss-crossed by the dark shadows of tree branches. It was, it would appear, the beginning of dawn, but they were moving—and moving very fast.

Pauley's head came over the edge of the upper bunk and peered down at him. "What're ye doin' awie doon there, laddie?"

"We're moving," said Mathieson redundantly.

"Aye. We are, that."

Heywood's bunk was empty. Mathieson clambered to his feet, moved erratically to the back door and saw the dark shapes of horses and a following vehicle. He made his way to the front, pulled the curtain aside and peered through the window which someone had taken the time to clean. Heywood, muffled to the ears, was driving the team. Mathieson opened the narrow door, drawing an indignant complaint from Pauley. The air was cold and damp. Mathieson snatched up his blanket and wrapped it about him. "Thad," he shouted. "What's to do? Did the troop-ers come back?"

"Not that I'm aware."

"Then why are we travelling at night?"

"Got a long way to go, dear old boy."

"But—"

"SHUT THE BLUIDY DOOR!" yowled Pauley.

Mathieson closed the door. "Apologies, Alec. What's happening? Am I allowed to know?"

The snore that answered him was as loud as it was unlikely. He gave a resentful grunt but made no attempt to pursue the matter, for if Pauley had been told to say nothing, he could say nothing. Mathieson reached for his clothes and managed with some difficulty to get dressed. Shivering, he groped under his bunk for his boots, was flung to one side as the caravan swayed wildly, and grabbed instinctively at the supporting post quite forgetting the protruding nail. The nail wasn't there. Puzzled, he ran his fingers up and down the post, but it was perfectly smooth. It had been there yesterday. Now it was gone. With all that had transpired in these busy hours it seemed unlikely that anyone would have found the time to attend to an incorrectly driven nail. But—beyond doubting, it was not there.

He pulled his boots on, noted absently that his ankle was much less painful, and, having wrapped his cloak about him, clambered through the narrow door and sat beside Heywood. The single caravan in front of them was the largest of their train, the property waggon in which four of the set pieces were stored. If he knew MacTavish, the Scot would have insisted on driving.

The sky was grey, the great dark clouds which skulked below the overcast warning of rain to come, and a chill wind sent occasional gusts to agitate the treetops.

"Lovely morning," he said ironically, peering about at the dark loom of hills, broad meadows, and endless meres and streams that reflected the dull skies.

"Charming," responded Heywood.

There were few signs of human habitation and none of other vehicles. They thundered over a long bridge. The water below was rapid and full of whitecaps. If it was the Severn, they had turned east. He asked, "Where are we? This doesn't look like Chester."

"Avoided it."

Avoided it . . . Mathieson frowned. "Good God! Was that the Dee? Are we in Wales, then?"

Heywood pointed the whip ahead, and again to the left, and, dimly, Mathieson glimpsed the proud loom of mountains.

"Stop," he demanded. "I must go and see about Rump."

"Can't, dear boy." Heywood pulled back his shoulders in an involuntary gesture of weariness. "But never fear, Japhet will take care of him, and we'll have to pull up again thoon at all eventh, to retht the cattle."

"You look properly out of curl. How long have you been driving?"

Heywood turned to reveal a drawn face but a bright grin. "Half the night. We left just before one o'clock, which you'd know had you not been ath one dead."

"Then why did you not waken me, you clod? Here—let me take the ribbons for a while."

"Never be tho eager! You'll have your turn. Ah! Rob ith pulling off. Alleluia!"

The caravans slowed and turned aside into a meadow that sloped gradually downward from the lane. A line of elms loomed up and they drove along behind the trees until there was small chance of being seen by any passing travellers.

Mathieson clambered down at once and limped back along the line. The caravan directly behind them was Bradford's. By some illusion of the half-light, it appeared to have grown taller. Torrey, stretching wearily in the driver's seat, gave him a cold stare and sneered, "Have a good sleep, did you?"

"Yes, I'm ashamed to admit. You did not, I take it."

"No. Nor did I snore while the women did the work."

"You are of the true nobility," smiled Mathieson, and walked on, wondering what that gibe had meant.

The next caravan was the one now occupied by Fiona, Elizabeth, and Moira, my lady having moved in with Mrs. Dunnigan. Dismayed to see his love on the driver's seat, Mathieson hastened to lift her down and only in the nick of time avoided the teeth that the near horse snapped at his shoulder. "Hey!" he cried, bringing his hand down smartly on the black's nose. He had never been attacked by any of the animals in the past, and he'd thought Rump the tallest, if not the largest of their horses, but this big brute was as tall, certainly. He dismissed a momentary confusion as Fiona reached out to him, and he caught her in his arms.

He was a man of fastidious habits, and knowing his beard grew rapidly, was not surprised when she giggled and told him he looked like a hedgehog. "Never mind about that," he said,

she has done, she insisted upon volunteering to become a member of our troupe.'' He took up Lady Clorinda's hand and touched it to his lips. "Ma'am, I think you cannot know how deeply we all love and honour you.''

There was an emotional chorus of "Aye's" and expressions of affection and gratitude. Poor Lady Ericson was overwhelmed, and, having commandeered her son's handkerchief, in a muffled voice from the depths of it, told MacTavish that he was a wretch and to stop making her into a watering pot and "get on with it!''

"Aye,'' said Gregor. "Tell us the noo what happens next, Robbie.''

MacTavish nodded. "As my lady said, we've reached the final step. Last night when the dragoons came, I was awaiting the arrival of the men who have helped me in my own assigned task—the gathering of the treasure.''

"That must have been a prodigious chancy business,'' put in Bradford. "You've told us very little, Rob, but we all know it was no easy task for you to accomplish so much so soon.''

"You were working fairly under the noses of the dragoons,'' said Cuthbert. "How did you manage to escape capture?''

"Largely because I'd ten of the most gallant fellows alive, to help me. We had to retrieve the treasure from areas that were thickly patrolled. To do it, we were variously coal heavers, shepherds, rag-and-bone men, pedlars, and bakers. I cannot speak highly enough of my men. They were superb throughout. They used disguises, worked day and night, knew little of sleep and much of peril. The toll was high. Of the ten who were so brave as to work with me, only six were able to finish.''

"Not killed, I pray God,'' interjected my lady anxiously.

"I hope not, ma'am. One was shot and had to run for his life when a dragoon challenged him. Two were hurt when we were hauling a load on a stormy night, and a waggon overturned. Another was injured by a footpad who guessed rightly that the articles in his rag-and-bone cart were worth stealing. The survivors are all exhausted and at the very limit of their endurance.''

"Let's gie a wee yell fer our Robbie and his lads,'' cried Pauley.

A soft but enthused cheer went up.

Torrey asked, "When do we help your poor fellas by taking the treasure off their hands, Rob?"

MacTavish rested a measuring glance on Mathieson. "We already have done so."

They all stared at him, baffled.

"I ken we've fine fresh horses," said Gregor, slowly.

'And bigger brutes, at that,' thought Mathieson.

"Oho!" exclaimed Heywood, the first to comprehend. "Jolly clever! I *thought* my caravan had a different air about it!"

The missing nail on the bunk support flashed into Mathieson's mind.

"Do I hear ye say ye *changed caravans*?" asked Pauley in patent amazement. "And we all sae daft as not tae notice? When?"

MacTavish grinned like a mischievous schoolboy. "Last evening. My fellows came in just after you left, Roly. All the time those dragoons were having such a jolly time wrecking our camp and knocking me about, the treasure they sought was less than a quarter mile away! My lads transferred all our goods to the new caravans and drove off the old ones. Mrs. Dunnigan and Japhet knew, of course, but I thought some of you would notice the difference when you loaded the set pieces and properties after the performance. I'm sure you would have done so, had you not all been so weary."

"I'd my suspicions," said Bradford grandly.

"I feel a proper cawker," Heywood admitted more honestly. "How could I have been tho blind?"

Confused, Moira Torrey said, "But—there's no treasure in our caravan. Where is it?"

"I think I can guess," said her brother. "These caravans are taller, now that I come to notice 'em. Likely a lot heavier, too. False bottoms, eh Rob?"

"And a few other tricks I'll . . . er, not go into."

'The treasure chest holds no imitations now,' thought Mathieson. 'And I'll wager the spaces in our set pieces are well filled!'

"So this part of our task is done," said Bradford, redundantly. "But our fine new horses mean we've still far to drive, eh Rob?"

"Not so very far, sir. From here, our cargo will travel by boat."

"Back up tae Bonnie Scotland?" asked Pauley, his face aglow with excitement.

MacTavish shook his head. "To the south of England." He held up one hand to quiet the flurry of dismay. "'Is an isolated spot where we believe the military will never think to seek, and the treasure can lie in complete safety until we dare begin to distribute it."

"Are you quite sure of the captain of this boat?" asked Torrey.

"Quite sure. Unhappily, he believes he has fallen under suspicion and a frigate of the Royal Navy hovers about. Within the past week he has twice been boarded and searched. Our plan was to rendezvous with him in two days, if he could slip away, but last night he sent word that the frigate is off to Belfast, and he must sail at once. I'll own I wasn't sure we could get to him in time. 'Twill be a scramble, but this is our best chance. Perhaps, our only chance."

Lady Clorinda put in, "To lend wings to our efforts, we learned that dragoons are prowling the Mersey Estuary and that another troop is en route from Manchester."

"Lord alive," exclaimed Cuthbert. "Do they suspect our plans, then?"

Bradford boomed dramatically, "Heaven forfend we have been betrayed!"

"They suspect something, certainly," admitted MacTavish. "The more reason for us to make our dash as soon as the horses are rested."

"But—not to the Merthey, I think," murmured Heywood.

They all looked at him, unease written large on several of the strong faces. MacTavish said coolly, "Exactly so, Thad. Our captain will come in on the falling tide and weigh anchor. The estuary is relatively shallow, and when the tide goes out, the boat will be in river water—a narrow channel only—so we'll be able to cross the sands of Dee, load her up, and—"

Mathieson tensed, his gaze darting to Fiona who at once turned to him, her face paling.

Lady Clorinda's fine eyes widened with shock.

Bradford gave a start. "Dee! Good God!"

"*Cross the sands of Dee?*" gasped Pauley, the colour draining from his pleasant face. "Och awie, mon! Ye're sick in y'r brrrainbox!"

Gregor shook his head. "The Dee Estuary? Whisht! Not a chance, laddie! We'd be visible fer miles. 'Tis all marsh and mud when the tide's oot y'ken, and the flood tide comes in like a typhoon! I wish I'd a grrroat fer all the poor souls ha' gone oot there thinking they'd time enough tae get back safe, and drowned fer their folly!"

"Besides which," muttered Cuthbert, "there's a storm blowing up."

Mathieson, who was a poor sailor and dreaded sea voyages, had only recently suffered through a rough Channel crossing, and his heart thudded. He was in full agreement when Pauley asked, "Rob, could not we keep on overland and meet the ship at some sheltered cove on the Welsh coast?"

"No, for two reasons. Firstly, the country is very wild and with few passable lanes. The caravans now carry heavy loads and 'twould be well-nigh impossible to manoeuvre them over such rough terrain. Secondly, we are running out of time. Each day we're on the road increases our risk—especially now that we carry such a priceless cargo." MacTavish looked around the circle of faces and saw dismay. He said gently, "I do not say this will be easy, my friends, but we'd have small chance of conveying the treasure overland without being discovered."

Bradford declared, "I'm willing enough to dare the fangs of fate, Rob. But how do you propose to drive our caravans, or our horses for that matter, across what Gregor has described as 'marsh and mud'?"

"Aye," said Gregor, nodding bodingly. " 'Tis a muckle mess, laddie!"

"I'll show you." MacTavish got up and found a fallen branch. The rest of them gathered around as he used it to draw a crude map in the damp ground. "Now—here we are," he dug a hole and drew a line above it, "and here's the river. Over here to the northwest of us is the estuary. Another three miles and there's Flint, with Holywell about four miles farther along. Now, all the way to that point are mud banks and marshes, just as Gregor told you, lying between us and the deep channel of the river. Even when the tide is all the way out we wouldn't be able to get the caravans across. Up here to the northwest, however, the mud gives way to sand and shale and will offer a better surface."

"And are there no more marshes?" asked Torrey, frowning.

MacTavish gave a wry grin. "Er—well, there are, but there's a way through them."

My lady said, "And you know that way, Rob?"

"Alas, ma'am, I must own I've never so much as seen the estuary, but the captain of our vessel has taken on a local fisherman who knows every inch of the shore and has arranged for markers to be put up—likely they're up now, waiting for us. We'll be able to follow them through the marsh onto the sands and then drive straight out to the boat."

Mathieson drawled, "One assumes the ladies stay clear of all these desperate doings?"

"The ladies remain on shore in the red coach," confirmed MacTavish.

"Do I mithtake it," asked Heywood in his mild fashion, "or ith our little jaunt going to be a clothe run thing?"

MacTavish nodded grimly. "A very close run thing. We've to make an exact rendezvous. I think the military do not suspect we'd attempt to sail from the Dee, but even so, we dare not hang about in full view very obviously waiting for a boat to come. No more can the boat wait long for us."

"Surely 'twill be a tricky course for the captain," said my lady. "Has he negotiated the estuary before this?"

"No, ma'am. But if you picture a schooner sailing to our rescue, pray disabuse your mind of such a scene. Our captain is a Jacobite gentleman, and his craft a big sailing barge. He'll have other rebs aboard to help us, and he's a skilled man who knows the tricky coast betwixt here and the south of England. The local man will pilot him into the estuary, and they'll wait as long as they dare. But our friend has said he will try it once, and once only."

Torrey muttered, "In effect, we've to wait till the last minute, make a mad dash across the sands on the falling tide, unload the caravans in broad daylight, and be safely back on land again before the flood tide drowns us all!"

"Not—quite," said MacTavish. "Firstly, we'll only have about a half-mile dash. Also, we've had a special ramp built which is on the barge, ready to be lowered from the deck. With luck, we'll be able to drive the caravans right on board, and then unharness the teams and ride them back to land. When the barge reaches its destination in the south, there will be others of our people ready to take charge of the caravans, so *our* task ends here.''

Gregor pursed up his lips and exchanged a dubious look with Pauley.

''Wager you a pony we do it,'' said Heywood with his bright grin.

Torrey looked eager to take the wager, but said nothing.

''Whisht!'' snorted Gregor.

Fiona's heart was beating very fast. She turned to Mathieson, but his gaze was on the lowering heavens. Her own thoughts at this moment were less with the threatening weather than with Robbie MacTavish's final remark: ''. . . our task ends here.'' It was almost done then, this strange, terrible, wonderful interlude that had so changed her life. God willing, Roland would be able to ask Grandmama for permission to pay her his addresses. Mrs. Roland Mathieson . . . The thought was so delicious it caused goosebumps to break out on her skin, and she wondered that Roly did not feel her gaze on him. He looked so remote, so stern. As it should be of course, for all his concentration must be on the task before him. She forced her eyes from his beloved face and looked upward also. Lud, but the sky looked threatening. But it would go well. It *must* go well. Surely, Fate could not be so unkind . . . She shut off that line of thought hastily. Everything would be all right. By this time tomorrow their task would be done, and they would all be safely en route home.

The horses, Mathieson was thinking, would need at least another half hour of rest, and already the wind was rising. To attempt the daring procedure MacTavish had outlined would be difficult in calm weather, but with a storm blowing up, heaven knows what could happen. On the other hand, lowered visibility might protect them from being seen, and at least the threatened sea voyage had not materialized. It would be dangerous, beyond doubting. Still, if they could pull it off, by this time tomorrow he would no longer have to go in dread of Fiona being arrested at any moment. He could see her safely home—wherever that might be—then begin the business of arranging for their future. A new life—a life full of hope and happiness to share with the precious lady he had found, the lady he worshipped.

'By Jupiter, Thomas,' he thought. 'I do believe I may have done it right this time! I think I've at last found safe harbour!'

He saw Fiona watching him, and, with a sly wink at her went hurrying off to shave and have a word with Rump.

By the time they left the meadow the light rain had become heavier, and the wind more blustery. MacTavish, in the lead caravan, set as fast a pace as could be managed with their heavy vehicles, and they bumped and rumbled and rattled along the lanes, mud and puddles beneath them, and the skies above becoming ever more dark. Mathieson had taken over the reins of the second caravan, allowing Heywood to snatch some sleep. They passed scattered dwellings at first, each one proud with white plaster and artistic black half-timbering, but there were few people about on this gloomy morning, and the habitations dwindled until only an occasional fisherman's cottage loomed up through the rain.

The weather continued to deteriorate, and after about an hour, a brilliant flash signalled the beginning of a storm which swept down upon them with increasing fury until it seemed the thunder crashed directly over their heads. There was a short lull, but just as Mathieson was thinking gratefully that the worst was over, he was momentarily deafened by an explosive crack, the acrid smell of brimstone was in his nostrils, and a sullen yellow glare dazzled him. He had his hands full then, as the horses screamed and reared in panic. Of no help at all was a strange and piercing creak, followed by an earth-shaking crash. From the corner of his eye he saw that a lightning bolt had split a big tree on the hill beside them. Half the tree had fallen and flames were licking up the part that still stood. He could hear the neighs and whinnying of terrified horses and even as he battled the reins and called reassurances to his own team, his anxieties were with Fiona.

Ahead, Robbie MacTavish's caravan plunged forward, then rolled away much too fast and rocking wildly.

"Can't I rely on you to keep thingth quiet for jutht a little while?" enquired a plaintive but cool voice in Mathieson's ear.

"Ungrateful wretch," he responded, with a faint grin. "I very cleverly avoided the lightning bolt. *Whoa!* Down, you confounded *aliéné!*"

MacTavish's caravan had stopped again, but his team sounded thoroughly panicked and the rocking vehicle made it clear there was trouble. Subduing his own animals, Mathieson tossed the

249

ribbons to Heywood and clambered down. He peered back worriedly along the line of colourful vehicles, now spread untidily across the lane. The red coach in which the ladies were riding appeared to have sustained no damage, and even as he watched, Fiona leaned from the window and waved.

Much relieved, he returned the wave, and answered Heywood's shouted enquiry by relaying that all seemed well with the ladies. It was very clear that all was not well with MacTavish, however, and he ran unevenly to determine the cause, Alec Pauley sprinting along after him.

MacTavish was already at the heads of his team. The big black stallion Mathieson had earlier decided was a bad actor, having been restrained from bolting, had evidently determined to travel sideways. Both front legs were over the pole and the terrified animal was squealing and lunging about frenziedly. MacTavish, looking grim, was attempting to quiet the stallion who in turn tried to bite him.

Mathieson drawled, "Wrong approach, Highland laddie," and dealt the black a firm rap on the nose. The animal subsided and perched there looking foolish and uncomfortable and trembling violently. "That's right, you great looby," murmured Mathieson, stroking the foamy nose. "*De mieux en mieux . . .* easy now. A fine time to teach him to dance, Rob!"

MacTavish's smile was strained. "The devil's in it that we *have* no time," he muttered, struggling with harness straps. "Alec, we'll use one of the spare animals. Tell Japhet to bring up that big roan mare. Anyone else in trouble back there?"

Pauley said, "Nought tae speak of," and ran off.

Mathieson helped MacTavish untangle the stallion. The black had succeeded in scraping both his forelegs and every succeeding clap of thunder inspired him with the need to bolt. His terror unnerved the well-behaved bay gelding, and the resultant debacle took up more of their precious time, so that twenty minutes were lost before they were ready to resume their journey.

MacTavish took out his watch and frowned down at it.

Emptying rainwater from his tricorne, Mathieson asked, "Will he wait?"

"For the tide, only." The Scot replaced his timepiece and began to climb up to the seat again. "It's almost ten o'clock. We've to be there at eleven. We will have an hour at most before the floor tide begins.'' He took up the reins, his grey eyes troubled.

''And how far have we to go?''

''About six miles.''

''No difficulty there, friend. Not with these horses. *Bon voyage!*'' With a jaunty wave of his hand, Mathieson limped rapidly back to his own vehicle.

MacTavish glanced after him unsmilingly. ''Mud permitting,'' he said under his breath, and slapped the reins on the horses' backs.

The next two hours were a nightmare. Mercifully, there was no sign of the scarlet coats of dragoons, but the weather had become as relentless an enemy. The rain which shielded them from prying eyes had also turned the lanes to mud and the wheels of the heavily laden caravans several times became so mired that Fiona marvelled they were able to continue. Somehow, the horses managed to pull them free, but then a wheel of Torrey's caravan slipped over the edge of the comparatively level surface and sunk deep. For long frustrating minutes the men stood in the rain pushing and straining, the horses pulling bravely, and at last, with the help of branches and boards thrust under the wheel, and a great deal of physical effort, the caravan lurched out of the mud. MacTavish, tight-lipped and worried, urged that they proceed as swiftly as possible, but the pace he had at first set could not be maintained, and it seemed to Fiona that they were crawling along.

They were in Flintshire now and the few houses they saw were, true to their location, fashioned of grey stone which, combined with the leaden skies and the cold grey sheets of the rain, presented a rather depressing picture. They had been able to see the river from time to time, but for the most part they kept away from the estuary, their way winding around low hills and pools, with an occasional glimpse of mountains to the south, their massive shoulders vanishing into the sullen clouds. The river had not at first looked formidable, but as they followed it to the northwest it seemed that each time Fiona saw that broad surface, it had doubled in width. As the fateful moments slipped away, anxieties mounted and there was little talk in the coach. Lady Clorinda called often to Cuthbert, who sat on the box, for a report on the time, and then muttered nervously that they were very late.

MacTavish was also worrying about the time. They had left the concealing slopes now and were heading straight for the estuary. The hills and mountains lay behind them; to the south-west rose the soaring peaks of Snowdonia, but the land ahead sloped gradually downward through diminishing and ever more stunted trees and shrubs. The track they followed petered out. MacTavish pulled up and waved the signal that alerted Cuthbert to wait here. The red coach halted. The caravans went on, bumping over rough sandy turf, toward a wide band of sullen, black water and tall reeds interspersed by soggy patches of land that looked uniformly untrustworthy. Already, MacTavish was full of dread that at any minute a wheel would get stuck, but although he strained his eyes he could find no sign to guide him, and began to fear their fisherman had failed them.

At last, more by luck than good judgment, he detected a sodden strip of white cloth hanging limply from a bush. Lord! Did the fisherman think they had the eyes of hawks? Still, knowing what to look for he was now able to pick out other strips, and began to guide the horses carefully down into the reeds and bushes between the markers, the land holding firm but their path descending ever lower, until there was nothing to be seen but the encompassing reeds.

Without warning, the foliage fell away and the estuary lay before them.

Following, Mathieson halted his team and stared, his heart sinking.

Thaddeus muttered a dismayed, "Oh, Jupiter!"

The tide was out, and the sands stretched away broad and flat and bleak under the pattering rain until they were parted by the curvingly erratic sweep of the river. The opposite bank, a good three miles away, looked desolate and deserted, deeply fringed by mud and marshes. The barge was already waiting, but instead of lying only a half mile dead ahead, she was at least a mile farther up estuary. Her sails were close reefed, and she rocked gently to the pull of the current, secured by lines that stretched to stakes driven into the sands.

Beyond her, dimly visible through the rain, far up towards the Irish Sea, was a wider gleam that stretched from bank to bank.

'Mon cher Thomas,' thought Mathieson grimly. 'You are off fishing again! The tide is coming in!'

Standing at the top of the bank beside the coach, her eyes glued to the line of swaying caravans that wound towards the distant barge, Fiona felt weak and trembly; her hands were icy cold and her heart seemed to thunder against her ribs.

They would have time surely? The incoming tide was so far away yet. They *must* have ample time. If anything should happen—God forbid!—the lives of those brave men, her dear papa and the one to whom she had so completely surrendered her heart, would be at terrible risk.

She dashed rain from her eyes. The caravans were moving more rapidly now. At least they did not seem to have encountered mud, and her fears that the heavy vehicles would sink into the wet sands eased a little. Again, her apprehensive eyes darted to the west. That terrible gleam of water seemed not to move, yet was it her imagination, or was it closer? She felt sick. If Roland was drowned, her heart would drown with him! She could not go on living now, without him. She closed her eyes, praying fervently.

A cold hand slid into her own. Elizabeth, very pale, murmured, "Fiona, I'm waeful scared. If the tide cuts them off from us here, will they be able to get oot by another path?"

This terrible possibility had not occurred to Fiona, and her desperate search along the bank did not help her state of mind. Chilled, she said falteringly, "I expect, if it goes badly, they—they will sail with the ship."

"Oh yes, of course," sighed Elizabeth. "What a silly goose I am not to have thought of that."

But, clinging to one another, they were both trembling.

♫ 15 ♫

The wind was rising, sending rain flailing like a grey sheet against the caravans, and closing them into a diminishing landscape. Ducking his head against another cold blast, Mathieson shouted, "Can you see it still? I cannot."

Heywood narrowed his tawny eyes and peered ahead. "Nor I. But it ith coming in, Roly. Beyond doubting! 'Time and tide' you know, my tulip . . ."

"Which being the case—can you swim, old boy?"

Heywood gave him a scared look. "I'll be a gimlet and cling to you!" He brightened. "If it ith too clothe, we will have to make the voyage."

Mathieson shuddered. The caravan lurched, and the fear that they were stuck in the sand chilled him. There came another jolt, and they were again moving toward the river channel, and the boat which loomed from it. The lines were holding her steady and the sturdy ramp MacTavish had described was already in position, sloping down from the deck of the vessel to the sands. "D'you see our staircase?" he said cheerfully. "That should speed things up, eh?"

Heywood grinned, but his reply was drowned in a growl of thunder.

The sailing barge was long and low, and much larger than she had appeared from the bank. When they came near her, MacTavish halted his team. A seaman who had run down the ramp to call up to him now sprinted to the second caravan. Pausing beside Mathieson, his oilskins wet and glistening, he shouted, "The tide's at the flood and coming very fast! Robbie MacTavish will try the ramp, but we're higher i' the water than we'd hoped. If aught goes amiss, he says the rest o' ye are to turn around and run like hell for the shore!''

It sounded ominous. Mathieson nodded, and the seaman ran on, to relay the message to the following caravans.

Heywood said, ''I'm glad we're not to lead the way! That ramp lookth heavy enough, but . . .'' He gave a wry grimace.

Mathieson eyed the ramp uneasily. It certainly appeared to have been sturdily constructed, and timber supports had been wedged between it and the sands, but the pitch was fairly steep and it would be no mean task to drive the horses up such a structure.

MacTavish was wasting no time, however. His whip cracked. The team started up, then backed again, snorting nervously, afraid of the unfamiliar ramp. Two men ran down from the deck to take the bits but there was insufficient room for them to walk beside the horses, and they were obliged to go back. A heavy gust swooped at the caravan causing it to sway. The horses sidled skittishly and squealed with fright.

Saying nothing, Heywood gripped Mathieson's arm. Mathieson glanced at him. He was pale, his eyes fixed on the west. Turning his head in the same direction, Mathieson's blood ran cold. The rain had eased a little and he could see farther now across long flat stretches of sand ending in a white line that reached from bank to bank. Foam. He thought, 'By God, but it's coming fast!'

The seaman, running past again, shouted, ''We'll be lucky to have ten minutes! Say y'r prayers, lads!''

'Thomas,' thought Mathieson. 'Attend to business, if you please!'

With a thunder of hooves and rumble of heavy wheels, MacTavish's caravan moved onto the ramp. The straining horses, their eyes rolling with fear, fought the slope. The caravan inched and bumped forward. It was obvious that the intrepid Scot had taken the lead position because if the ramp could support his caravan, it would take the rest. It seemed to Mathieson that the ramp bowed very slightly to the weight, but although the timber supports beneath it dug into the sand there was no sign of catastrophe.

The skies had darkened once more; the rain came pelting down with renewed vigour, and another gust of wind rocked the caravan. The horses swerved to the pull of it, and Heywood's breath hissed through his teeth as those big wheels strayed to the very edge of the ramp. Someone howled, *"Pull 'em in, Mac! This way!"* The right wheels were halfway over the edge. Mathieson whispered, *"Sacré colimaçons!"* and held his breath. MacTavish's whip cracked, and at the last instant the caravan pulled in and straightened out. Seconds later, it jolted onto the connecting down-sloping ramp and bounced onto the deck.

A wild cheer went up on the barge, echoed from the waiting caravans. Those on board raced to unharness the team, and MacTavish took the reins and led the pair to the ramp again. The downward slope evidently frightened the big roan mare, and she shied and reared up. MacTavish talked to her, his hand firm on the ribbons. Another man ran to slap the mare's rump. Ears flattened and eyes rolling, she kicked out, sending him jumping back. Then she tore free from MacTavish's grip, bolted down the ramp and splashed past Mathieson's caravan. The Scot followed, leading the bay gelding.

His pulse quickening, Mathieson saw that water was all about them now, shallow as yet, but creeping with silent menace over the sands.

MacTavish ran straight to him and called urgently, "Japhet's caravan must go next! Let him pass."

Japhet drove the second property caravan in which was the pirate's treasure chest. 'Logical,' thought Mathieson, and reined his team aside and watched the youth drive toward the ramp.

Heywood said. "Jupiter!"

He was staring westward again. That terrifying white line of foam was much closer. Mathieson thought, 'It looks as if we'll sail with them, after all,' and frowned, worried for Fiona.

An ear-splitting screech returned his attention to the barge. The ramp shifted slightly. With a noise like a gigantic violin string snapping, one of the stakes shot from the sand, the line snaking through the air, the men on deck flinging themselves flat as it whistled over their heads. Japhet's horses screamed with fright, reared, and plunged, the youth looking terrified but striving bravely. Shouting to Mathieson to get aboard, MacTavish raced to climb up beside Japhet, but even as he gained the seat the horses bolted madly back down the estuary.

The barge dipped uneasily. Watching it, Mathieson would have sworn it was tilting slightly to one side. He set his jaw, and glanced at Heywood. Apart from his bruises, the man was deathly pale, but winked at him irrepressibly. Mathieson whipped up the team. "Thomas . . . ?" he muttered prayerfully, and then the horses' hooves were reverberating on the ramp. This time, the heave of the barge was unmistakable. Mathieson gave a gasp as that keening screech resounded above the growl of thunder. The ramp tilted and shuddered convulsively beneath them. The horses screamed and staggered. Mathieson thought, 'Like hell!' and hauled on the reins, backing the team.

Heywood howled, "No! Go back, Roly!"

"What d'you think I'm trying to do?" said Mathieson between his teeth, and roared, "Back! *Back*, you fools!" Dimly, he heard shouting. The men on the ship were waving them off frantically. The big horses danced and fought in terror. Mathieson heaved on the reins and Heywood yelled encouragement to the team.

The ramp scraped deafeningly, slid, then tore free from the side. The timbers beneath collapsed, and the heavy ramp plunged downward, landed with a thunderous crash, then bounced up again. Mathieson's caravan was battered by flying sand and spray, but the team's hooves had cleared the ramp a scant instant before it collapsed, and the surging timbers missed them by a hair.

Pale and sweating, Heywood clung to the seat, his shoulders slumping. Mathieson met his eyes and gasped, "Whew!"

MacTavish had evidently mastered Japhet's team and was swinging them around again, but there was not a moment to lose. Mathieson clambered from the seat and with Heywood ran to wrench open the back door, trying to ignore his shaky knees and the water that swirled over his boots to the ankles. A standard-sized gangplank had now been swung over the side of the barge, and three men sprinted down it to assist them. Bradford came running, moving with surprising speed for such a big man, and with Heywood's help removed a section of the caravan's floorboards. A long, flat crate was hauled from the aperture. Heywood and Mathieson took it, and carried it to the sailors, the wind battering them. Torrey and Gregor ran to help. With desperate haste, boxes and bales were hauled out. Mathieson staggered to the barge with a barrel that seemed to weigh a ton. Relieved of it, he turned back and began to splash through ever-deepening water towards the caravan.

"The tide!" Driving up at frantic speed, MacTavish's shout was high-pitched with urgency. *"The flood! 'Ware the flood!"*

Mathieson whirled around. A wave was rushing at them. The wind tore foam from the crest, and seemed to drive it ever faster. All across the estuary it stretched, and behind it came a dark enormity capped with white. The air was suddenly shaking to a low, petrifying growl of sound.

"Mon Dieu!" he breathed.

Above the uproar, MacTavish howled, "Everyone back to shore! Spring 'em!"

Racing for his caravan, Mathieson was vaguely aware that the horses were hock-deep in water; that the lines holding the ship had been cut and she was moving inland; that Heywood was already leaping onto the seat. He made a dive for the side as the frightened team fought Heywood's restraining hands on the reins and started off. Mathieson's fingers closed around the edge of the seat; with his right hand he gripped the roof. His boot thudded against the flying wheel, and he fell onto the seat, clinging for dear life as the team raced madly for the distant path and safety.

Torrey's caravan, which had fallen to the last position, was in the lead now. Mathieson's heart jumped into his throat as the right rear wheel of that racing vehicle hit some hidden obstruction. The caravan bounced up and keeled over. Perhaps the very speed of their going saved them, for they righted, and kept on.

The horses were straining against their collars, but they were running into the teeth of the east wind and were further impeded by the pull of the undertow. The violent moments dragged past, and the bank still seemed far away. Mathieson threw a quick look back. The sea was rushing in like a maelstrom, boiling up turbulently where it encountered the deeper river water. Appalled, he heard Heywood roar, "Cut off, by Jupiter!" He jerked his head around. A fast-moving flood was between them and the bank. The horses were plunging, sending up gouts of water. Shivering and soaked to the skin, he strained his eyes through the spray and the rain, vainly seeking the red coach that would be their guide to the safe path.

A minute later, Heywood shouted, "Torrey'th out!"

A caravan ploughed like some demented great fish from the greedy sea and tore, rocking wildly, into the tall reeds. Mathieson thought, 'I hope he found the markers!'

The water was deepening, tugging at the wheels, slowing the horses, as if the tide was determined they should not escape. Caught by the current, the caravan slewed and shook. Mathieson knew a moment of paralyzing terror. How many had experienced such despair before they were claimed by the coldly relentless sea? A grey curtain of lashing rain and spray reduced visibility to about thirty yards. They seemed to be scarcely moving. He wondered numbly if Thad could see to guide the horses, and then realized with a stunning shock that Heywood had lost the reins and was clinging to the seat, as helpless as himself. In that horrifying instant, in that turmoil of sound and cold, pounding wind and icy water, and the awful imminence of death, the eyes of the two young men met. Mathieson thought with strange clarity, 'If I have to go, I could not have a better man beside me!' He tore one hand from the edge of the seat, and reached out. Heywood's icy fingers closed hard around his own.

A staggering shock; a violent impact as his head slammed against something. Hurled from the seat, he thought, 'Fiona!' and waited to be engulfed.

He landed hard and rolling. A dark shape shot past with a thundering roar. Bewildered, he realized suddenly that he was sprawled on the bank, mud and reeds beneath his cheek. The rush of relief brought tears to his eyes. With a choked laugh, he kissed a soggy clump of grass. Then, frantic little hands were pulling at him, a dear voice was sobbing his name. He looked into Fiona's white, tear-stained face and gasped, *"Mon cherie! Mon cherie!"* And sitting up, screened by the reeds, held her tight for a blissful moment.

She clung to him, whispering, "Thank God! Oh, Roly! Thank God!"

They had to run clear then, as another caravan thundered past. Shaken but exultant, Mathieson led the girl up through the reeds, and at the top peered around, counting. "Two . . . three . . . four." Japhet's caravan, minus a wheel, was leaning against a stunted and tilting tree. "Five! By the Lord Harry—*five*! We all got back!"

"More or leth," said Heywood breathlessly, hobbling up leaning on Elizabeth's arm and clutching his leg. "Are you all right, dear boy? Rob dethided to go tree climbing, and Torrey hath a broken head, but I rather think we're all alive."

Holding Mathieson's hand very tightly, Fiona said, "Well, I

259

wonder *we* are! We were terrified lest you all be drowned!'' She turned and looked down at the raging waters that surged below them. ''Another minute, only . . . ,'' she muttered.

Mathieson patted her hand. ''Well, it didn't come to that, child.'' He strained his eyes into the rain and could dimly make out the barge, apparently attempting to come about, the sail going up jerkily, and billowing out in the wind.

Anxious, Fiona asked, ''Will the sail split, do you think?''

Mathieson glanced at Heywood and said whimsically, ''They've an easterly breeze, at the least. I fancy they know their business. Likely, she'll be safe away before we are.''

And he thought, 'But what the deuce shall we do now?'

They made camp that evening in a quiet and secluded little vale south of Chester. A copse of ash trees provided some shelter from the rain which had dwindled to a steady drizzle, and from nearby came the endless chatter of a swift-flowing brook.

They were a rather subdued group; drier now, but downcast because of the failure at the estuary, and apprehensive as to their chances of bringing the remaining treasure safely to its destination. They all knew they had brushed very close to tragedy, but they had not escaped unscathed: Heywood had twisted his knee when he'd been flung from the bouncing caravan and limped painfully; Torrey's head had made violent contact with the side of his caravan, resulting in a large lump and a severe headache; Japhet had suffered a badly cut hand; and MacTavish, who had been thrown into the tree, had some badly bruised ribs, was white-faced, and looked to be at the brink of exhaustion. Perhaps, of them all Mathieson came closest to guessing the depth of the Scot's inner distress, knowing that he would blame himself because only one caravan had been successfully loaded, and that the bulk of the treasure, including the chest of jewels, still faced a long overland journey to the south coast.

While the men tended to the horses, built the fire, inspected damage done to the caravans, and hauled water, the ladies prepared stewed chicken, carrots, and onions. Soon, the little camp was redolent with the smells of woodsmoke, stew, and fresh bread procured en route from an isolated farmhouse. There was a keg of home-brewed ale also, and by the time the meal was over, the spirits of the Avon Travelling Players had lifted somewhat.

Gathered around the fire, they discussed their plans. To travel by day would be extremely dangerous now, for they carried a fortune in gold, jewels, and *objets d'art*. Were they to be searched by dragoons who had previously inspected the caravans, they might have a chance of escaping detection, but a patrol stopping them for the first time might soon discover that the jewels were not imitations, and that the spaces in the set pieces were no longer empty. Mathieson was astounded to learn that in addition to gold and plate, several paintings of great value now resided inside the set pieces, including part of a tempera triptych by Giovanni Bellini, a small portrait by Van Dyck, and an *en grisaille* drawing by Rubens. The owners of these works of art, MacTavish explained with a rueful smile, had been too fearful to attempt to sell the pieces themselves, and had instead donated the works intact to the Cause. "The Prince had requested gold," said my lady, "but—" she shrugged and spread her hands, "he was too gracious to express anything other than his grateful thanks."

They discussed the possibility of travelling only by night, which would also be dangerous—partly from the risk of accident to horses or caravans when traversing unknown roads in darkness, and partly because nocturnal travellers invariably aroused curiosity which might bring the military down upon them more surely than if they ventured by daylight. Also, as MacTavish pointed out, it would mean a long, slow journey, undesirable with winter coming on.

Bradford frowned thoughtfully and turned to his mother. "Can you tell us now ma'am, exactly how far south is the chosen spot?"

Lady Clorinda hesitated, glanced at MacTavish's grave countenance, then replied carefully, "I will say only that 'tis within a few miles of the south coast."

A dismayed chorus arose. Heywood spoke for them all when he said, irked, "I wonder they didn't make it a wee bit difficult for uth. Like Manchuria—or Africa!"

"It was chosen," said my lady with some asperity, "because initially 'twas hoped to send the treasure all the way down from Scotland by sea, and the selected location lies near some ideally secluded coves. It is a great house with cellars containing secret rooms where the treasure could be kept concealed for as long as is required. The most zealous of English officers would never think to search the south coast for a Scots treasure trove. It seemed ideal—until the first ship was nigh wrecked in a storm in the Irish Sea and was forced to put in to Liverpool. It was little short of miraculous that the Jacobites guarding the treasure were able to off-load it without being caught. But it was because they found themselves in a veritable sea of dragoons that they had to make hasty choices for temporary storage places.'' She sighed and gave a little gesture of helplessness. ''None of this, alas, was foreseen.''

''Fate's best-laid traps are never foreseen,'' muttered Freemon Torrey, watching Fiona sad-eyed.

''True,'' agreed Bradford. ''And we are, I suspect, hoist by our own petard. We've some of our scenery and most of our costumes, but we dare not stop to give performances now, else 'twould take forever and a day to get to the south coast.''

''Our first plan was to become a gypsy group,'' said Cuthbert. ''Perhaps we should revert to it.''

''And explain to any stray troopers how a gypsy group chances to be carrying set pieces and a pirate's treasure chest,'' drawled Mathieson sardonically.

For once in agreement with his rival, Torrey said, ''We'd be clapped up before you could wink an eye!''

The discussion continued, but everyone was tired, no more satisfactory solution to their difficulties was propounded, and in the end they decided to continue as they were going. They would stay away from all main roads and highways; travel as fast and as long as was possible each day; and send out advance scouts to survey their route and provide warning of any sign of the military.

The ladies prepared to retire, and Mathieson abandoned his hope for a private moment with Fiona and slipped away to check on Rumpelstiltskin. The big stallion kicked up his heels when he heard the familiar whistle and came at a run, eager for the caress of his master's hand, his head tossing, his nose searching for the carrot he knew lurked somewhere about. Laughing, Mathieson produced the treat from his pocket. ''Cupboard love, is it?'' he scolded, holding the carrot just out of reach. ''Let me see you ask properly.'' He whistled a short three-note melody, and at once the chestnut began to dance in circles, scattering the horses in his path. A low warbling note and Rumpelstiltskin came at the trot, to halt at Mathieson's spoken command.

"Now—make your bow, Rump." Obediently, the horse leaned back on his haunches, and rendered his equine bow.

Fiona, who had crept up unobserved, asked, "May I give him his reward, Roly?"

His heart leaping, Mathieson swung around. The girl stood a few paces away, the distant light of the flames showing her little face aglow with the radiance that was not exactly a smile but that had come to mean more to him than any smile in the world.

Without a word, he handed her the carrot and she trod nearer to the rope paddock.

"Gently, Rump," he admonished.

She proffered the carrot; the big horse accepted it, his lips scarcely brushing her hand, and stood chomping contentedly.

"How splendid he is," she murmured.

Mathieson glanced about, and drew her into the shadows. "But, of course. He belongs to me. I will own nothing less than the best."

Her head came up and she turned to him. The hood of her cloak fell back and he heard her low chuckle. *"Ma belle,"* he reached for her hand. "How very brave of you to come. I was afraid I'd have no chance for a word with you."

"Well, Grandmama has gone to bed, and Papa and Mac-Tavish are still talking. Moira and Elizabeth will not betray me, so I very naughtily followed you. And now that I am here, what words have you, sir?" Her voice very soft, she swayed to him. "A scold for my—lack of propriety?"

His arm slipped around her. He said, "There are advantages to being a scoundrel, and—"

Her warm fingers shut off the rest. "I did not come to hear nonsense."

There was no need to ask the obvious. He knew why she had come, and he wasted no more time, but bent to her lips. She gave them up willingly and matched his ardour with her own shy but eager caresses. He knew he could take more than a kiss and for the first time in his life knew also that the only important thing was her—that she must not be frightened, or hurried, or persuaded to what would be even a small violation of her trust and her purity. He was not pursuing a brief flurry into passion, or even a more lasting *affaire de coeur*. This was for all his days. This was his madonna, and she must be handled with reverence and kept safe—even from him. With an inward sigh, he thought, 'Especially from me!' And smiling wryly, put her from him.

"Roly," she whispered yearningly. "If you knew how afraid I was. How very grateful that you came back safely. I-I was praying so hard . . ."

He pressed a kiss into one soft little palm. "Which would explain why I did come back safely. Tiny Mite, I don't like this plan of MacTavish's. I want you out of danger and back at your home. There is no longer the need for you to journey with us."

Touching his cheek lovingly she murmured, "How do you know I would be safe at home, sir? You know not where I live—or how."

"True. But it must be a beautiful place, for you grew up there. Where *do* you live, Tiny Mite?"

She chuckled again. "Guess. Tell me what you suppose."

What did he suppose? He frowned a little. It was doubtful that Bradford was completely poverty stricken. Besides, Fiona was Lady Clorinda's granddaughter. "A country manor house, or a gentleman's farm perhaps," he said thoughtfully.

Faintly annoyed, she said, "Where I helped feed the chickens and churn the butter." And with a teasing smile, "Or am I London bred, and accustomed to the balls and routs and endless seeking after pleasure which—"

"Never that," he murmured laughingly. "You're no London belle, Tiny Mite."

Definitely annoyed, Fiona stiffened. "Indeed?"

"Indeed, miss. You are too honest; too free from sophisticated artifice and—"

"Too simple-minded? Gauche?" There was an unexpected hauteur in her voice, reminiscent of her grandmama. "A rustic do you mean, perchance? I'll have you know, Mr. Mathieson, that I've not dwelt all my lie in a caravan!"

"Of course you haven't," he agreed, much amused. "You spend at least half your time wallowing about in the mud, and baking plaster crumpets, to say nothing—"

"La, what a fine picture you have of me, sir! Only think how people will mock you for having chose a muddy rustic for a bride!"

"To say truth," he teased, "I court you only because I covet Picayune, and because my grandpapa will get his just desserts when he samples some of your crumpets!"

"A somewhat less than compelling reason for matrimony, Mr. Mathieson!"

The chill in her voice startled him. He scanned her face and saw the proud tilt to the chin, the angry glint in the green eyes and cursed himself for a fool. "*Vraiment* but you are tired," he said remorsefully, "and I have made you cross with my foolish nonsense. Forgive me as quickly as you can beloved, for we have so little time."

"Oh, I am a great stupid," she said, at once repentant. "Very well, my dear. I live in an old house called Blackberry Manor. It is situated in Wiltshire, and we are so fortunate as to have the River Avon flowing through part of the estate. You would, I think, find it as beautiful as do I."

Unease touched him. He said in oblique probing, "And you, who are so humble, are in fact a great heiress, I understand."

She laughed. "Now you have been listening to Torrey. My brother Francis will inherit the estates of course, but I'll own I have a comfortable inheritance which comes to me from my mama's family." Her fingers touched his chin. "Why look so glum? Only think, now you can claim to be a dastardly fortune hunter and—"

"Not I! I shall say instead that my own fortune is vast. Since you never believe the truths I tell, you will then know that I am *in fact* a dastardly fortune hunter and will be able to warn Heywood that Miss Clandon's fortune lures me in her direction!"

"Ah, have you heard about that, then? Good gracious! I wonder if Thad knows."

Mathieson gave no sign of his surprise, and said blandly, "I think he would not care had she sixpence to her name."

"She was never that badly off, but just five months ago a cousin of her father's went to his reward. The old gentleman had removed to Italy years since, and we all fancied him a pauper, but it seems he won a mare at the tables, and her foal became a great racehorse. The old gentleman built up his stables and died vastly rich—and childless."

"Jupiter! Did he leave some of his wealth to Miss Clandon"

"All of it! He had loved her dearly as a babe and never forgot her, so now—"

"Fiona . . . ?" Moira's soft call interrupted her.

Mathieson said urgently, "Listen to me! You must go back to Wilshire *at once*! I don't want—"

"Foolish boy. As if I would leave you—or my people. Good-night, now." And she was gone, running quickly to her friend.

For a long moment Mathieson gazed after her, frowning. He was roused when Rumpelstiltskin shoved him and uttered a friendly whicker.

"It would seem, you old rascal, that we have two rich ladies among us. One with a comfortable inheritance, and the other a great heiress . . ." Mathieson scratched the stallion under his chin in the way Rumpelstiltskin particularly liked. "That puts a rather different complexion upon things—*n'est-ce pas*?"

Eyes half-closed with pleasure, the horse made no response, and after a while Mathieson left him and walked slowly to the caravan, his thoughts very busy indeed.

The rain stopped on Thursday night, and Friday morning dawned bright and sparkling with a return to warm autumn weather again. Old Shrewsbury town, proud on its perch above the River Severn, showed well on such a brilliant day. To walk its streets was to walk through history, and as Trooper Willhays told Sergeant Patchett, he expected that at any minute the door to one of the ancient timber-framed houses would open, and a lady in wimple and farthingale be handed down the steps and into her sedan chair.

Marching briskly beside him en route to the livery stable, the sergeant returned only a grunt. He liked Willhays; the boy's clean-cut face and earnest grey eyes had impressed him the instant they first met. 'A decent, God-fearing youngster,' he'd thought then, and he was still of that opinion a year later. Further, Willhays possessed a mind that was full of interest in the world about him. He could, thought Patchett, work his way up through the ranks—might even earn a battlefield commission some day. He had it in him to make a fine officer—if Lambert didn't crush him first. Taken a dislike to Willhays had the charming lieutenant, because the boy had made an intelligent observation about the Jacobite Cause in his hearing. Lambert had enjoyed a jolly few minutes, cutting the trooper to ribbons with his caustic tongue. The lieutenant, thought Patchett bitterly, was acid to his fingernails—and would probably rise to be a general, ruining God knows how many promising subordinates along his way. He cursed the army mentally and shocked the trooper by spitting into the kennel.

The subject of his thoughts pushed back his chair in the coffee room of the small hostelry where the troop had headquartered for two days, and walked out into the sunlit street, pausing on the steps to draw on his gauntlets. Unlike Trooper Willhays, Lambert paid no attention to the gracious old buildings. The sunshine glinting on their deep latticed or mullioned windows and brightening the flower boxes escaped him utterly. His deep blue eyes rested with indifference on the glittering river that girdled the high peninsula whereon was the town. Shropshire, beautiful in the eyes of so many, he judged a bore, and everything in it a damnable nuisance. Each moment he was here was a moment he might have been in Town with an eye to winning back his captaincy. Small chance there was of tracking those blasted rebs up here. Since Lake had gone flaunting back to the south country he'd caught not so much as a whiff of—

His bitter musings were interrupted by loud voices from inside the building. The host was saying angrily, ". . . hired to mend my roof, which you said as you could do. Well, it *ain't* been done. Not right, that is. I told you as I wouldn't pay full money for a half-done job of work, and I meant it! Now take yourself off, or I'll call the constable!"

Lambert's lip curled as he started down the steps. Disgusting that a guest should be obliged to hear such a vulgar dispute! You'd not find such behaviour at a decent inn, but—

He checked, standing shocked and motionless as another voice rose. A whining, rasping, crudity of a voice that whipped him back to a small dim chamber under Castle Carruthers, and the traitorous hireling whom he had shot down to protect himself from a charge of kidnapping and attempted murder. He whispered, "Hessell!" and walked on, knowing this threat must be properly silenced or he would face a greater loss than his commission.

Moving swiftly, he went down the steps and along the street to the baker's shop, continuing to the far side of the deep bow window. Affecting to inspect the cakes displayed there, he had a fine view of the front of the inn, and in less than a minute saw Ben Hessell's ungainly figure come shambling down the steps and slouch off. At once, he followed. Hessell was going towards the livery stable, which was bad, because that insolent clod Patchett would likely be bringing the horses at any minute.

Lambert hastened his steps until he was very close to his

quarry. Hessell started across a narrow alley. Coming up behind him, Lambert said softly, "My pistol is at your back, Hessell. Turn in here. No—not a word! *Move*—or I'll do the world a favour and shoot here and now!"

The big shoulders jerked and then cowered, as Hessell identified the voice. His cunning mind told him that if he once walked into that alley, he'd never come out alive. Pulling his shattered nerves together, he halted and said, "I told me mate as I'd seen yer, Lieutenant, sir. And I told him what we'd done . . . you and me. If I don't come back . . ."

"You filthy lying bastard," ground out Lambert, shoving him hard. "You've got precisely ten seconds, and then—"

"But I bin follering you, sir. Honest I have! May me liver rot if I'm telling a whisker! I don't hold no grudge, Lieutenant. I know what you and yer friend Captin Otton is up here fer, and—"

Lambert's eyes widened in shock. Rage made him very fast. Hessell's arm was seized in a bruising grip and he was spun into the mouth of the alley and slammed against the wall behind a tall rain barrel. Two narrowed eyes blazed into his own. The muzzle of a pistol was rammed under his chin, so that he gave a yelp and in terror and desperation, gabbled shrilly, "Don't yer never scrag me, Lambert! Don't you never! On top o' all the rest, you'd be—"

The pistol smashed against his throat cutting off his words and bringing tears of pain into his small dark eyes.

Lambert snarled, "Have you seen that dirty swine? When? Where?"

Hessell's devious mind raced. So this horrid wicked cove didn't know where his accomplice in crime was. And he was desperate anxious to find him. He wanted Otton. Bad, he wanted him. And that could be worth a penny or three, maybe. He whined and moaned, and clutched his throat.

Lambert eased the thrust of the pistol. "Answer, carrion!"

"I dunno the name of the place," Hessell said hoarsely. "I could show you though, only I'm so weak, sir. Fair clemmed I be in me poor innards. Ain't et fer days'n days, and—"

The pistol struck hard again. "I'd as soon put an end to you now, traitorous dog that you are. You took my money and then betrayed me—"

"No, sir! Oh, no sir! I thought as you was working together, straight I did! I nigh got rid of yer uncle fer you, didn't I, sir? Own up.''

"You *missed*—filth!"

"I *tried*, guv'nor, you gotta admit, I tried. And I stole the lady, just like you told me. Then when Captin Otton made me take her and hide her again, I thought it was what *you* wanted, too. *Honest*, Lieutenant, sir. Benjamin F. Hessell don't cheat them as what pays him! Only tell me what yer wants, and it's did, sir. I swear it, see this wet, see this—''

"I'll see your brains all over that wall behind you in about two seconds! *Where—is—Roland—Otton?*"

Hessell read death in those splendid blue eyes, and his knees shook. "I dunno, sir! Honest! Oh, Gawd! I'd tell yer if I knowed. Cheated me, he did! I owes him one! He said he was goin' back ter London, only yer can't trust a word he—''

"Where did you see him? Where was he when he told you that? *Where?* Damn your eyes! *Where?*"

Hessell gulped. "You're chokin' me, sir. I can't—ah, that's better. Thank you kindly, sir. Thank you. Why, why it were up near some awful village. This side o' Chester, and—''

"Chester!" Lambert's lips writhed back from his teeth in a snarl that appalled Hessell. "*Chester!* Was he alone?''

"He was when I see him, sir. Only—I seen him agin. With a buncha actors, he was. And actresses, sir . . . tasty bits they was, just the kind you—'' He struck in mid-sentence, beating the pistol from Lambert's hand. With the strength of desperation, he grabbed the tall rain barrel and brought it tumbling. It was only half full, but the flood of dirty water sent the fastidious Lambert leaping clear. Hessell took to his heels and ran for his life.

Cursing bitterly, Lambert searched for his pistol. The water had poured over it, thoroughly wetting the powder. He picked it up, but scarcely noticed the green slime that covered the fine weapon.

So Otton was with the acting troupe after all . . . 'If *only* I'd gone to see that accursed play . . . ! Damn! Damn! Damn!' Belatedly, he realized that there was slime on his hand. He drew his handkerchief and wiped his fingers, revolted. And then he stood very still, for the littered clearing was before his mind's eye. He could see again the abominable Sir Roger Innings offering his mocking bow. A fat man—yet the hand he extended was white and *slender*, with unusually long fingers. Had the two middle ones been of uniform length? Lord, how could he have failed to notice? Roland Otton bowed with that same graceful ease, that same Frenchified flourish! Stunned by his own obtuseness, he was struck by a new awareness that caused him to catch his breath.

"*Second . . . Innings . . . !*" The words hissed through his white teeth and his eyes widened into a glare that would have purely terrified one Benjamin F. Hessell.

For four days the weather had continued unseasonably warm, only the nights and mornings holding the chill tang of approaching winter. There had been no more rain, and they'd been able to travel at a good speed from first light until dark. Long days, full of effort, and all of them were tired, yet delighted by their rapid progress. Indeed, Fate seemed to smile on them. The horses had done well, for now they were able to change teams when the animals became tired; not once had they so much as glimpsed a scarlet coat; and the only threat had been presented by an irate farmer who brought his workers to drive "the dirty thieving vagrants" from his lands. His son had taken a fancy to Elizabeth, and his generous decision to favour her with his attentions had transformed the mild Thaddeus Heywood into a raging savage. Mathieson at once seconded him and a pitched battle might have ensued had not the farmer suddenly noticed that he and his men were outnumbered by a surprisingly militant group. The farmer beat a strategic withdrawal, the "vagrants" moved on, and the danger was averted.

By sending scouts ahead at dawn each morning they were able to avoid other hazards such as festivals and autumn fairs; too busy roads that were likely being scanned by military; lanes so rutted and flooded as to be impossible for the caravans to negotiate; villages or hamlets where they would be eyed with suspicion. As far as possible they had kept to wooded lanes and secluded by-ways, and on this late afternoon had stopped to make camp beside a pleasant little corpse of silver birch trees in the Clee Hills, a few miles north of Ludlow.

As soon as the fires were crackling, my lady settled herself in a chair beside one and began to make a dreadful botch of darning one of Bradford's stockings. Fiona brought her own pile of mending and sat with her, but Picayune put her good intentions to flight by snatching at the thread until, laughing, Fiona began to play with the little animal. Within minutes Freemon Torrey was sitting cross-legged at her feet. He said little, but watched the girl with such yearning worship that my lady became vexed with him and sent him off to fetch her a shirt that he said needed a button.

"I vow he stares at you like a perfect moonling," she muttered as the tall young man went hurrying off. "Heaven knows why, for you are positively tanned by the sun and wind, which is unfeminine in the extreme."

Fiona sent her a glance of sparkling mischief and said meekly that she knew she could never hope to compare with Elizabeth who had been so fortunate as to take after her grandmama.

"Well, you are quite right," said Lady Clorinda, her own eyes bright. "Although Beth is one of your fair beauties, whereas I had the benefit of dark hair. Which will teach you, my love, not to twit your elders!" She laughed, swooped to kiss her granddaughter's smooth cheek, and drew back saying fondly, "I'm proud of you both, I'll admit, though I shouldn't for 'twill make you vain, and there's nothing less attractive than a vain woman. But, I will own, my love, that the tan makes your eyes like emeralds. Small wonder Roland and poor Torrey are so bewitched."

Fiona blushed. "Captain Mathieson has been very good, Grandmama. You will own he has posed no threat to us."

"Far from it! He has been splendid and of great assistance. But," my lady's eyes grew stern "years of folly cannot be wiped away, however one might wish they could. I'll not see your name besmirched by an alliance that could only bring shame to you, however 'good' the boy has been for a few weeks. Or however sincere he may be—at the moment." She saw the sparkle fade from the green eyes, and as Fiona started to protest, added hurriedly, "Speaking of Mathieson, where is he?"

"He is one of our scouts today, ma'am. He left before dawn."

"And is not back yet? Lud!"

"Never fret, Grandmama. Ro—Captain Mathieson always stays out longer than the other scouts, have you not noticed? I think 'tis partly because his horse has such wondrous endurance, and partly because . . ." she hesitated, her lashes drooping "—because he is so extreme—dedicated."

"Hum," said Lady Clorinda. "Let us hope his dedication finds nought to disturb it, though I fancy there is small cause for alarm on that count. One is persuaded the hunt must be wandering at last, for we have not so much as glimpsed a dragoon."

Despite his customary optimism, on this particular occasion Mathieson did not share Lady Clorinda's sanguine views. At first elated by the absence of military coats, that very absence began to disturb him, and as day succeeded day with never a sign of soldiers, his unease deepened into apprehension. All the way from Sussex there had been troopers everywhere. Lord knows they'd been thickly dispersed throughout Cheshire. Yet now it would seem they all had been recalled. So sudden and complete a withdrawal was illogical, to say the least of the matter, and Mathieson had learned to mistrust illogical developments.

As a result, he took to ranging ever farther afield, and today had crossed the River Teme, and ridden on as far as the Lugg, still with no sign of danger—at least not military danger. And still he was plagued by a deepening sense of peril. The lovely Herefordshire woods and valleys, the rich farmland and fields dotted with sheep and fat cattle, basked under the warm sun. Mathieson had crossed the Teme with a wistful sigh for the trout and grayling that abandoned there. Now the Lugg, home of similar temptations rippled and sparkled and sang to him. He dismounted, allowing Rumpelstiltskin to drink. The very thought of fresh trout sizzling in a pan made his mouth water. Surely, the Avon Travelling Players would welcome such an addition to their dinner table. He had no fishing pole, but there was, of course, a length of twine in his saddle bags . . . Ever the optimist, he unsaddled the stallion, told him he was allowed to graze, and wandered about, twine in hand, searching for a likely branch. He came to an inward curve of the riverbank where a weeping willow cast its lacy shade out over the water. Starting forward, he halted as low-pitched voices drifted from within that large green sunshade.

" 'Course we could've! You think we're scared of a buncha dirty traitors? Thing is, the Lieutenant says there's some of 'em sailed off on a boat with some of the treasure. He's got it in his mind they're all going to meet again in a special place, which is where this lot's going, and where we're tippy-toeing after 'em.''

"If you was to ask me, Sergeant," said a younger voice, "he'd do better to take what he's got now, 'stead of playing a waiting game and risking them slipping through his fingers. Wouldn't be the first time, by what I—"

"*Ssshh!* You perishing fool! If he heard you—cor! I'd think you'd had enough of his tongue! 'Sides, I won't deny as he's a sight too eager to get his rank back, but this little game of his is working right nice, I must admit. Here they comes, tripping so tidy as you please—right into his snare, and then—" There was the sound of a sharp clap. "Gotcha!"

Mathieson started to move back very slowly, but paused again as the younger voice said, "And how if they stop tripping into his snare, and go hopping off where he don't expect, and get clean away?"

"Don't be such a silly blockhead! They got damned great caravans to haul about. Where they going to 'hop off' to when we got a troop between them and the west coast, and another just to the north of 'em, watching every move they make? The south road is so clear as a bell, Lambert's seen to that, and if they should smell a rat and try to run anywhere else, why our fellas is ready and can move a sight faster than them caravans.''

"Um. Then he's got them, fair.''

A pause, then the sergeant muttered, "He's got 'em all right. Those poor silly bastards is running like scared rabbits just where he wants. And Gawd help the trooper what lets one inch o' his uniform get seen. Our lovely Lambert'll peel him alive! A slice at a time!''

Very grim and silent, Mathieson crept away. As he retreated, the younger voice drifted after him. "Y'know, I can't help but feel sorry in a way. Did you see the girls they've got with 'em? Poor little things . . .''

"You look absolutely worn out, dear," said Elizabeth, eyeing Fiona anxiously. She glanced around the camp, a bright spot against night's dark curtain, and added softly, "I know how you feel about Captain Mathieson, but *must* you rise so very early? These past three days you've been up long before the rest of us. What time was it this morning?"

Fiona stifled a yawn. "I am not sure. Before dawn."

"And here it is, almost ten o'clock! Small wonder you can scarce keep your eyes open. No really, we'll have you ill do you not get some rest. Surely he does not expect you to see him leave each day?"

"No, of course he doesn't. But . . ." Fiona hesitated. There had been not the slightest change in Roland's attitude towards her, nor in fact had his manner changed in any respect. Yet these past few days she'd sensed that he was troubled. During one of their all too few moments of privacy she had taxed him with it. They'd been at the paddock, and he had laughed at her, called her a silly little goose, and risked a quick kiss on the tip of her nose. Before she could say any more he had called Rumpelstiltskin and by means of a hand signal sent the stallion into a frenzy of bucking that had made her laugh and brought Thaddeus and Elizabeth hurrying to see the performance. But she had not been deceived. Roly was worrying and therefore she worried too. "I just feel . . . I must see him before he leaves," she finished rather lamely.

"Are you afraid he will be taken during his scouting expeditions? He seems a man who knows what he is about, and Rumpelstiltskin is so very fast, I'd think that unlikely, dear."

"I know." Fiona sighed, and thought, 'but a musket ball can bring down the fastest rider.' Cold fingers shivered down her spine. She said slowly, "I do not think that is what I fear—exactly. I cannot say what it is, Beth. Just . . . a feeling. I'll not rest easy until I know he is safe home."

Her resolution was overborne an hour later when she dozed off by the campfire and my lady demanded she go at once to her bed. She obeyed, but somehow managed to stay awake until Moira retired also and much to her relief told her that Mathieson had just ridden in.

"He is all right?" asked Fiona, starting up onto one elbow and blinking at her friend anxiously.

"Quite all right, and looking no more tired than if he'd been napping all afternoon. I'd no chance for a word with him, for the saucy rascal was chattering to Elizabeth and had her in whoops about something. Poor Thaddeus looked quite glum, which is so silly, when we all know where Captain Mathieson's interests lie."

Fiona smiled and fell peacefully asleep.

Wednesday dawned brisk and bright; perfect weather for travelling. But Mathieson had brought word of a troop of dragoons scouring the countryside to the south, and my lady and Mac-Tavish decreed that they would do well to stay in their quiet haven for a day or two, until the troop had moved on. The decision was a welcome one for the weary travellers. There was harness to be mended, a caravan wheel that was tending to run hot and would be the better for filing down the axle, and three of the horses needed to be reshod. Accordingly, Pauley and Gregor set forth early in the morning, taking the horses to a blacksmith they had passed a few miles back. Mathieson was judged to have earned a rest, and he declared his intention to give Rumpelstiltskin an overdue currying but otherwise to spend the day "idling."

This plan delighted Fiona, who at once began to rack her brains for a way to arrange a *tête-à-tête* with the man she loved. Her delight was premature. Despite her efforts, not once during that long frustrating day was she able to have a private moment with Mathieson. Every time she manoeuvred events so as to be able to slip away with him, someone would delay her, or he himself would wander off with Heywood, or Robbie MacTavish in the most provoking way. Twice, he managed to conduct long and apparently amusing conversations with Elizabeth, and Fiona could not but recollect Moira's words of the previous evening. It was foolish, as Moira had said, but she had not exaggerated. Heywood watched Mathieson narrowly, a small frown between his brows and a set to his lips that should have warned both his friend and his lady, but Mathieson seemed either blind or indifferent to these danger signals, and Elizabeth fairly glowed and came perilously close to outright flirting.

By supper time, Fiona was feeling quite capable of scratching the cousin she always had loved so dearly, and when they went to bed she at once pointed out to Beth that Thaddeus Heywood had waited long and faithfully and this was no time to be teasing the poor gentleman. Elizabeth listened gravely, laughed merrily, and hugged her. She was, she said, extremely flattered, but Roland Mathieson had no more interest in her than the man in the moon, and had merely been gratifying her interest in France in general, and Paris in particular. He knew that great city as well as he knew London, and had been so kind as to relate many droll incidents of *le beau monde*. Truly, oh but *truly* there was no cause for dearest Fiona to be jealous.

This somewhat arch remark caused Fiona to sputter with wrath, and give her cousin a sharp set-down. She was horrified to see tears spilling down Elizabeth's lovely face, whereupon, repenting her hasty temper, she was obliged to kiss and comfort her. This proved to be rather more of a task than she had envisioned. Elizabeth tried to compose herself, but Fiona woke in the night to the sound of muffled weeping, and, remorseful, made a mental vow to handle her cousin much more gently in the future.

The next day it was MacTavish who rode in while they were at breakfast to report the military was thick to the south and they dare not move. The conspirators eyed one another uneasily. Fiona, who had helped prepare the meal of gammon rashers, fresh farm eggs, and newly baked muffins, was plagued by foreboding as she carried a well-laden plate to Mathieson.

He sprang up at once and took the plate with a flourish. "Never look so troubled, Tiny Mite," he murmured under cover of a surge of anxious comment. "Perchance you can contrive to come to the paddock this afternoon." His eyes twinkled at her. " 'Tis past time my saddle was polished."

Her heart gave a little leap, and she nodded, happiness banishing her anxiety over the message the Scot had brought.

When the meal was finished and the dishes washed and put away, Mrs. Dunnigan and Japhet began to prepare runner beans for luncheon. Today, this could be a proper meal rather than the hasty fare they were obliged to serve when they were travelling at speed. Faces were concerned rather than pleased, however. They all longed to finish their task as quickly as possible. That one day had been lost had been a vexation, but also a welcome rest. That another day must pass with no progress being made was worrying. The weather held unseasonably fine, but autumn's rich brush had painted the trees with gold and rust and scarlet, and already the leaves were beginning to drift down. Winter could break upon them at any time now, and there was still over a hundred miles to be covered before they would approach their destination. A hundred miles of well-patrolled country and the constant risk of seizure and arrest.

Fiona was summoned by her grandmother to help repair the hem of a skirt which had been accidentally stepped on. My lady was in a strange mood, variously bright and sombre, her usually unflagging energy showing signs of dissipating; and Fiona went out of her way to seem confident of a happy resolution to their problems. "We'll be safe home within a week or two, dear Grandmama," she said gaily. "And then we will set to work to redecorate your suite, for you will stay with us—no? At least until after the holidays?"

My lady loved her Scottish home, but she acquiesced in this, and the two spent a pleasant hour sewing together and planning the new curtains and colours for the suite Lady Clorinda occupied whenever she was in Wiltshire. Cuthbert, who was actually my lady's steward and major domo, must also be thought of in connection with these plans, but it was not until his name was mentioned that Fiona realized she'd not see the big man for two days.

"One might suspect you to have had your mind on other matters, child," said my lady drily.

"Yes, but—" A pang of fear struck. Fiona asked, "Wherever has he gone? Dear ma'am, is something more wrong than we have been told? I've a sense of—"

A shrill cry that was almost a scream interrupted her. Even as she and Lady Clorinda started up exchanging alarmed glances, angry shouts rang out followed by the unmistakable sounds of a scuffle.

With a heightening sense of disaster, Fiona ran outside and down the steps.

Everyone seemed to have congregated at the edge of the trees. Her father and Rob MacTavish were hurrying to join the little crowd, and Fiona, her heart in her mouth, followed. Elizabeth, her long golden curls hanging in loose disarray about her shoulders, stood weeping in Moira's arms. Heywood was attacking Mathieson like a wild man, but Mathieson seemed more amused than irked as he ducked and dodged, calling to Heywood to "let be," and not be "such a silly makebait."

"You thlippery damned libertine," roared Heywood, livid with rage. "There'th no woman thafe . . . within a mile of you!"

Her heart as if pierced by a lance of ice, Fiona was suddenly incapable of speech or movement, and stood as one turned to stone, watching in mute shock.

Her father came up behind Heywood, grasped his arms and held him strongly, disregarding his impassioned demands to be released.

MacTavish said a curt, "Quiet, Thad! What is all this? Have

we not sufficient to worry about that we must now quarrel among ourselves?"

" 'Tis Mathieson's doing, I'll be bound," said my lady tartly. She held out her arms and Elizabeth flew into them, sobbing incoherently. "Tell us what happened my sweet child."

Mathieson drawled, " 'A storm in a teapot,' ma'am, I assure you."

With a growl of rage, Heywood wrenched free, bounded forward, and lashed out. Mathieson avoided the blow, and struck back at once. Heywood was sent reeling and went down hard.

Gregor ran to kneel beside and prop the dazed man, glaring up at Mathieson, who gave a sardonic shrug.

"Will somebody be so good as to tell us what happened here?" MacTavish's fine face was grim, and when Mathieson began to answer, he flung up a silencing hand and nodded instead to Japhet.

The boy looked miserable and said reluctantly, "Miss Elizabeth had gone with Captain Mathieson to watch Rump dance. I saw them go over to the paddock. Then—Miss Elizabeth came running back, crying and—er, well, sort of—" his young face became scarlet "—er, tidying her frock."

"The devil," muttered Bradford, fixing Mathieson with a disgusted frown.

"I thought Heywood was your friend," said my lady accusingly.

"You are right to—to uthe the patht tenth, ma'am," Heywood gasped. "You'll meet me for thith, Mathie—"

"Certainly not," snapped Lady Clorinda.

Gregor said incredulously, "But ma'am—Mathieson *strrruck* him! I dinna see how they can fail tae—"

"There will be no duelling," put in MacTavish.

Mathieson smiled. "I know you'd see reason, Rob. There's no call for all these heroics. 'Twas a simple matter of—"

"Of your forcing your unwelcome attentions on a lady," said MacTavish, stern and relentless. "I might have known 'twould come to this. You force my hand, you fool."

"What a needless conflummeration," sighed Mathieson, bored. "I am quite willing to overlook poor Thad's hysteria. I had no intention to offend. Miss Clandon did not seem averse to me, but—"

"Damned lying rake!" cried Heywood, struggling to his feet.

My lady said angrily, "I'll not have my granddaughter insulted, Rob!"

"Of course not, ma'am," said MacTavish, looking weary. "The fault is mine. I knew what he was, but—"

Mathieson's dark eyes became narrow and deadly. "Have a care, Rob," he murmured.

Winking away stinging tears, Fiona looked in anguished bewilderment to MacTavish's grim face.

"What does he mean?" demanded my lady sharply. "And why should you blame yourself?"

"I lied to all of you," said MacTavish. "I knew this rogue by another name, and I knew *of* him as—"

"Don't be a fool!" cried Mathieson ringingly. "Merely because I stole a kiss, you would risk—"

"Be silent," thundered Bradford, supporting Heywood's unsteady figure.

Mathieson scowled, threw up his hands in a gesture of irked resignation, and sauntered a few paces from them.

His face stern and pale MacTavish said, "I told you all that Mathieson helped me—that he saved my dear wife and me from sure disaster. That much, at least, is truth. What I did not tell you was that he came to me on the night of my somewhat dramatic arrival, and told me he had served in the Low Countries with one William Bond . . ."

Lady Clorinda gave a gasp of shock. "Not—not *our* Will?" she stammered.

MacTavish nodded. "Our Will, ma'am. The same Will Bond who was our fifth courier. And who carried the list of donors!"

Bradford, pale and horrified, asked, "Why do you use always the past tense, Rob? Never say the poor lad is . . . is . . ."

"He's dead, sir."

There were concerted exclamations of dismay. In their alarm they pressed in closer around MacTavish. Only two of those present watched Mathieson. After one swift glance he avoided the anguished eyes of the white-faced girl, and, ignoring the youth who stared with such bitter but silent disillusionment, he stalked away.

"How? When?" asked Gregor. "Are ye main sure, Robbie?"

"I'm afraid so. 'Twould seem the poor lad was shot, and too far spent to recover. He died in the hills . . ."

William Bond had been a long-time friend of Alec Pauley, and the young man turned away, his head bowed with grief. My lady gave a little sob and her handkerchief fluttered to her eyes.

"Alone?" asked Torrey sharply. "How d'you know, then?"

"Because he was not alone. Just before he died, Will was found by an old friend and—"

"Mathieson?" asked Bradford.

MacTavish nodded. "Will believed him to be an honourable gentleman, and entrusted him with the list."

"My God in heaven," gasped Pauley, turning a drawn face. "Then we must—"

MacTavish held up a hand for quiet. "Let me finish, please. That is why I lied to you. Mathieson came to me with a bargain. I could have the list provided I allowed him to stay with us until we collected the treasure and that I say nothing of his past. That's why I kept it so secret that my fellows were going to switch caravans. Mathieson demands one-third of the gold and safe-conduct, else we never will see the list and he'll—"

Came a sudden thunder of hooves. A mocking voice shouted, "Catch me if you can, *espèce d'imbéciles!*"

"Mathieson's away!" howled Gregor.

"After him!"

"He's turned the horses loose!"

"There he goes! Shoot him down!"

"No! We'll have the dragoons upon us! *No shooting!*"

The little encampment became a confusion of running, cursing men, who raced for saddles and their milling horses.

Swinging astride a piebald mare, Torrey did not wait for a saddle, but sent his mount galloping in hot pursuit of Rumpelstiltskin, already a rapidly diminishing blur across the meadows. A minute later, Heywood was also mounted and tearing after the other two. Gregor threw his saddle onto a rangy black horse and began to wrestle with leathers and buckles.

MacTavish shouted, "No more! Gregor—help get the horses into the paddock! Let Torrey and Heywood catch the swine!"

"Small chance of that," said my lady, her worried gaze on Fiona's drawn, white face.

"Rob," said Bradford, his own face reflecting shocked dismay, "you are absolutely sure? He seemed such a—well, such a likeable young fellow."

"His charm has fooled many," said MacTavish, also slanting

281

a compassionate glance at the silent Fiona. "But he sometimes uses another name, sir; one you may have heard. It is—Otton."

"What?" Still clutching his saddle, Gregor jerked around. *"Otton* you say? Isnae that the murrrrdering scoundrel tried tae torment information oot o' poor Quentin Chandler? And Chandler already sore wounded? He's *Mathieson*? Och! It fair boggles ma mind ye coulda stomached him, Robbie!"

"I'd little choice. He had the list. Without it . . ." MacTavish shrugged helplessly.

"Without it!" exclaimed Bradford. "The question is what'll the conscienceless scoundrel do *with* it? All our heads will roll if he sells it to the military."

Dazedly, Fiona whispered, "No! He'd not do so base a thing! However—however b-bad he may be . . . he'd not do *that.*"

Elizabeth left her grandmother and crossed to Fiona. "Dearest, *please* do not look so heartsick. He's—he's nae worth a single tear! He only courted me because he'd somehow learned of my inheritance."

Racked by grief, Fiona closed her eyes. *She* had told Roland of that windfall. He'd wasted no time, acting on it. Elizabeth was so very beautiful . . . Perhaps he'd decided she was the— the better bargain . . . She turned to MacTavish, a bewildered pleading in her pale face that made him wince. In a cracked, thin little voice she asked, "Do you say that—that Captain Mathieson tortured one of—of the couriers, Robbie?"

MacTavish could not bear to look at her. His accent becoming pure Scots, as it tended to do when he was upset, he said gruffly, "I'm waeful sorry tae tell ye, lassie. But—aye, he did that. And sent murrrdering assassins after Ligun Doone hissel'. His crimes 'gainst our people are many, and he's fair withoot honour or merrrcy."

Fiona swayed a little, and a faint whimper escaped her.

Bradford hurried to her side and Elizabeth moved back allowing him to slip a consoling arm about her daughter. "Come, child," he said very gently. "You have had a bad shock, but 'twill pass. You mistook your heart, is all. I know it hurts now, but—as well you found out in time, m'dear. Come . . ."

He led her away and she went with him like one in a trance, scarcely aware of what she was doing.

My lady looked after them, her own bright eyes dimmed by tears. "Poor little soul," she murmured. "So much for his vows and declarations, the ingrate!'' She blew her nose daintily and dried her eyes. "Well, Rob? Do you really think Mathieson will use that list 'gainst us? He holds many lives in his bloodstained hands.''

MacTavish stared at the campfire. "I think Miss Fiona was right, ma'am. There is a limit even to his baseness. And—I believe he once gave his word never to betray us.''

Gregor sneered low-voiced, "Ye canna think such as *that* verrrmin would hesitate fer one instant tae betray us was there money it for his ainself? Hah!''

"He'll not betray us," said MacTavish, still frowning fixedly at the flames. "He'll more likely try to blackmail those on the list, but we'll get it back, never fear. Meanwhile, that shall have to wait, for I think we must now abandon our hopes to get through to the chosen place. 'Tis too far—the odds 'gainst us too great.''

"Yes, I agree, alas." Disheartened, my lady sighed wearily. "Would to God we'd a closer hiding place. We've come so far . . . tried so hard. To be defeated now is cruelly hard!''

MacTavish lifted his eyes and smiled at her. "I know of a closer place, ma'am. A place where the treasure can lie hid for as long as need be. And—I've a plan. 'Twill be chancy but— with luck, it just may work!''

The next day was a greyness through which Fiona moved and spoke and even managed to eat a little, although she was so hurt and sick with grief that she could scarcely have felt more pain had Mathieson struck her. In some strange fashion she seemed quite cut off from her family and friends. She knew that they were all around her, that they spoke gently and lovingly, that in their way they strove to comfort her. But it was as if she existed in a glass cage with the windows faintly blurred so that nothing looked clear and voices came only dimly to her ears.

She had waited all her life for the one, the true love. And love had come. But it had been a false love offered by a charming, handsome, deceitful gentleman whose eyes had held adoration, and whose heart was full of guile and greed. A savage who could stoop so low as to visit more suffering upon a helpless wounded fugitive, only for the sake of gold. A man who had been willing to hire murderers to track down the peerless and heroic Ligun

Doone—thank God he had been circumvented in that wickedness!

She sat in the caravan, staring blindly at the windows, seeing not the splashes of rain, for the weather had turned again, but a pair of dark, long-lashed eyes that could hold such a brilliant dance of laughter, or be soft as velvet with tenderness. She pressed shaking hands to her lips to hold back the sobs. It could not be true! It *could* not be! Yet every time she recalled some instance of valour or even heroism, his own words came back to haunt her.

When they first had met and he'd saved Picayune, he had denied his bravery almost with indignation and said that his " 'cue was villainous melancholy.' " She smiled sadly and the tears slipped silently down her cheeks as she remembered him sitting there wrapped in the blanket, looking so far from heroic—yet so very dear, with his wet black hair curling about those superb features . . . How put out he had been when she'd told him it was funny to be wooed by "a real rake"; little had she known the depth of his depravity then. When he had saved the poor lady from the ducking stool he'd said that had he been alone, he'd have ridden away and left her to her fate . . . True, no doubt. Fiona sighed heavily. Always, he had spoken truth. And always, nobody had believed him . . .

Someone was talking to her. A hand was taking her own, leading her from the caravan. Beth's hand. How anguished dear Beth looked. How kind, to be so understanding. She managed a smile somehow and could not know how that pathetic travesty of her former bright beam wrung her cousin's tender heart.

She was mildly astonished to find it was dusk, and they had not yet left the little meadow. Her mind pondered it vaguely while she ate a few bites of something—heaven knows what. Gregor played his flute, and Heywood began to sing softly in his fine baritone. Fiona started and stared at him. "Oh," she gasped, interrupting the song. "You are come back!"

The others looked at each other, their troubled glances telling her she had been told of this and had not comprehended.

Lady Clorinda took her hand. "They did not come up with Mathieson, my dear. He is likely miles away by now. I fancy we'll not hear from him again until he lets us know what we must do to get the list back."

Soon, Fiona was sitting alone in the caravan again, thinking in that oddly detached way that he was safe. Beyond doubting, she should have wished he'd been caught. But she could not. Roland Mathieson had come into her life and brought an ecstatic happiness; a depth of love she had never dreamed would be hers. He was gone now. Out of her life forever, for he had never loved her as she loved him, and to leave her must have meant no more to him than to change from riding clothes to evening dress. But whatever he was, however evil, in going, he had taken her heart with him, leaving her alone in a cold empty world, and she knew she would never love again.

Despair engulfed her, and she wept until she fell asleep. Her next clear memory was of waking during the night and hearing the rain pounding down. They were moving once more. They must be crossing a bridge, for the wheels rumbled in an odd echoing way. They were slowing to a stop. She could no longer hear the rain, but the hollow rumbling continued. She heard her father's voice call softly, "Shall we clear?" and Torrey's answer, "By an inch, sir!" And after a minute, again, her father, "God-speed! And go in His keeping!"

Curious, she clambered from her bunk and hurried to peer from the back window. At first she thought they were in a tunnel. Then she saw a faint beam of light from a hooded lantern and was astonished to realize they had halted on a covered bridge, and barely scraping past them was a line of five caravans—five familiar caravans. She blinked, scarcely believing her eyes. They were the same caravans they had brought up from Gloucester! She gasped an astounded, "What on earth?"

Lady Clorinda's voice spoke in her ear. "We are trapped, dear. There are dragoons all around, and no possible way for us to escape."

Fiona gave a stricken little gasp as she turned to look into the small face that could seem proud and pretty, even framed by the beribboned nightcap. "Then—then Roland *did* betray us?"

For an instant my lady hesitated. Then she said, "We cannot know that is certain. But—but this is our one hope."

Fiona blinked out of the window again and saw the last caravan rumble past. "I don't understand. I cannot see the gentleman who is driving. Where did they come from? Where are they going?"

"Cuthbert went to find them and bring them down here. The 'gentleman' you saw was a dummy, tied to the seat. They will travel only at night, and there will be just one driver, in the first caravan. The following horses are all tied on to the vehicle ahead. Hopefully, in the dark it will look as if we are very quietly trying to slip away.''

"But—but if the soldiers are all around us, they will be stopped before they have gone a mile.''

"No, child. It seems the military discovered that some of our treasure has been sent on aboard ship. They very cleverly decided to let us get through—to follow and watch and wait until we reached our destination, and there to seize not only us, but the Jacobite gentlemen who await our arrival in Dorsetshire.''

"And—the entire treasure,'' whispered Fiona, horrified. "Oh! How frightful! Then those caravans are decoys, to lead the soldiers away?''

"Yes, my love. They were brought onto the bridge at dusk this evening, long before we came near, and they have hid here, waiting. The dragoons were all watching *us*.''

"Did you see them?''

"No, but we know they are there. They have kept well out of sight. I suppose they think that if we saw them and suspected their trap we might turn aside from our proper destination so as to protect our friends.''

"And you think they are watching now? In the middle of the night?''

"Rob says they are. They saw us drive in, and they'll see the five empty caravans drive out of the other end of the bridge. They will follow, thinking they still follow us.''

"But—if they follow, they will come in here, and find us, no?''

"No, child. There is a new bridge a half-mile north of here. We believe they will choose that one. The instant they're well away, we will turn about and drive into Wales, where, God willing, we will reach MacTavish's farm and safe haven before—'' She paused and shrugged wordlessly.

"Before—what? Oh, my Lord! Before the other caravans are found to be decoys, you mean! Then—then the gentleman who drives, goes to certain death!''

My lady's face was inestimably sad. "Yes, child. Is a very gallant gentleman indeed. For all our sakes he was willing to take the risk. I'll own,'' her voice cracked a little, "I did not expect it of the boy.''

Her heart commencing to pound hammer blows at her ribs, Fiona whispered, "Who is he, Grandmama? Tell me, I beg you! Who is sacrificing his life for our sakes?"

For a moment Lady Clorinda was too moved to reply. Then she said in a voice that quavered, "It is the man who has loved you so faithfully and so well, Fiona, that he has given up his life to protect yours. It is . . . Freemon Torrey."

ॐ 17 ॐ

Freemon Torrey huddled over the small fire, trying not very successfully to warm his hands. He was cold and hungry and wet, and the oilskin he'd draped over his head and shoulders hadn't afforded much protection from the rain which had continued with dreary persistence all night. Above the surrounding trees the skies were beginning to lighten to a gloomy dawn. Lord, but he was tired!

He glanced up as a plate and a tankard of ale were handed to him, and took them with a murmur of thanks. "Where are we?" he asked rather thickly, as he bit into bread and cheese topped by a slice of ham.

Stifling a sigh of weariness, Mathieson sat on the steps of the caravan. "A few miles above Tewkesburg, I think." He balanced his tankard beside him and stretched out his long legs. "We've done surprisingly well." He bit into his own breakfast. "Made very good progress last night, considering the weather."

Torrey grunted and after a minute asked, "Have you seen any sign?"

"No. They're keeping well out of sight." He smiled faintly. "Brooks Lambert is a damned good officer in some ways. Knows his business."

"And knows you," muttered Torrey. "I sometimes think 'tis because of his knowing you that all this trouble came down on us."

Mathieson was silent. It might very well be truth. If he'd been able to restrain the impulse to taunt old Brooks with his impersonation of Sir "Second" Innings, they might not be in this fix. He stared down at his tankard. A terrible guilt, that because of

288

his rashness his dearest love was now in peril. 'I wonder if they've reached MacTavish's farm yet,' he thought achingly. 'I wonder if she's safe; if she is grieving . . .' Torrey had said something. "Your pardon?"

"I asked about the horses."

"My apologies. They're right as—Egad, I almost said as rain!"

Torrey met the laughing eyes with inner resentment. Mathieson looked as debonair, as lazily untroubled as though they enjoyed a picnic at Vauxhall Gardens, or strolled along St. James's. One might suppose the man to be made of iron. Did he never tire? Was he never fearful of the terrors the future likely held for them both? These past three days and nights had been one long nightmare; trying to keep all five caravans in line; urging on the horses who balked at the unusual arrangement; knowing that through every minute death hovered about them, that the slightest error would bring the dragoons down upon them. His visions of horrible punishment haunted him waking and sleeping, and the tension was making his nerves tight as a bowstring. An Lambert detected their imposture and they were arrested, they would both be put to the question, no doubt of that. He shuddered, wondering if he would be able to hold firm—if he might fail that ultimate test.

Watching the haggard face, Mathieson knew the man had come near to the end of his endurance. He said quietly, "MacTavish said he must have three days, Torrey. We've given him that. There's no cause for you to go any further. Faith, but there was no cause for you to come at all."

Torrey's heart gave a great hopeful leap, but he growled, "Much chance you'd have had, leading them off alone."

"I'll own your help has been invaluable, but—I can manage now."

Finishing the food, Torrey took up his tankard again. "Damned if I don't think you *want* me to go. Why? To hog all the glory and then present yourself to her as the valiant hero who saved us all?"

Mathieson chuckled. "Is a pleasant picture you paint. I'd not be averse to it."

"I know that, damn you! 'Tis why I came also! You've not won her yet, Mathieson, and I'll fight you to the finish! She's

289

been promised to me since we were children and— Where are you going?''

''To check on Rump. Get some sleep, you would appear to be in sad need of it.''

Bristling, Torrey sprang up and caught his arm, wrenching him around. ''If you think I'm afraid—''

Removing his hand, Mathieson said, ''I don't. But you have done your part—more than that. Man, there's no call for both of us to lose our heads! 'Tis your turn to scout the lie of the land. Slip away while you're out this afternoon, and get as far and as fast as you can. So long as you head anywhere but back to her. We can take no chance of your being followed.''

Yearning to seize this chance at life, despising himself because the temptation was so powerful and his nerves so shredded, Torrey snarled, ''Why such solicitude for my welfare? You've no love for me. I know that well enough.''

Mathieson shrugged. ''Belligerence bores me.'' He saw wrath in the fair face and relented. Whatever else, the man had cared enough about Fiona to take this risk for her sake. And it *had* been a great help not to try to carry it off alone. Quite apart from doing his share of the backbreaking load of work, Torrey's presence might very well have helped preserve their desperate illusion for as long as it had lasted. He added in a kinder tone, ''But—I'd not see her left without one or other of us.''

For a moment Torrey's eyes searched the handsome countenance he both detested and admired. The guards were gone from the dark eyes now, and what he read there caused his own to fall. He muttered sullenly, ''If you really care for her, why did you let her think—I mean—were any of the things Rob said about you really, er . . .''

''True? But of course. Some were. Even so, if I come through this with a whole skin, you may believe I'll run you a race to win her. But in case—If things go wrong, that is . . .'' He reddened and said awkwardly, ''If you should get back Torrey, and I do not—you must never tell her the part I played in this. Never. I'll have your word on that.''

Torrey frowned at his boots. He bitterly resented the need for such a promise, and evaded, ''I suppose you think that if she knew the truth of it she'd hoist you up on some sort of pedestal in her heart, and deny any other suitor for as long as she lives. Or enter a convent or something equally ridiculous.''

Mathieson had seen the worshipful light in Fiona's dear eyes. Torrey had not. He countered, "Have I your word?"

"There's not the need. Fiona has far too much sense to indulge such dramatics only because you and Miss Clandon staged that silly attempted assault." His lip curled. He added sneeringly, "You must have enjoyed mauling the girl and tearing her gown. What did you tell her? That it was necessary so as to convince everyone, even the old lady?"

It had not been necessary for Mathieson to lay one hand on Elizabeth Clandon. That brave young lady had ripped her own gown even as she wept with pity for him. And before she started screaming, she'd kissed him on the cheek and said she prayed this horrid scene would prove to have been for nought—that he would come back safely and claim the girl he was going to such lengths to protect.

There was no point in trying to convince Torrey of that. Nor did he give a damn what the man thought of him. He repeated wearily, "Your word?"

"Oh, very well, if you must have your high flights! I fancy you know I'd be the last to tell her of your latest piece of acting, when—" He jumped visibly as a twig snapped nearby, and springing up exclaimed in a voice that shook, "God! Are they that close, do you—"

Standing also, Mathieson hissed, "Keep your voice down, you dolt! I'm going to look around. Make it appear you are speaking to someone inside this caravan as you pass!" He went striding off to where they'd fashioned their clumsy paddock.

Nerves quivering, Torrey glared after him resentfully, but followed instructions, pausing at the rear door of the caravan and engaging in a low-voiced "chat" with the invisible occupants before he slouched on towards the vehicle where was his bed.

Mathieson reached the paddock to find Rumpelstiltskin in a skittish mood. The big stallion, ears erect, had been gazing off into the trees, but came dancing over when his master whistled. The gloom was lightening; while he gave the chestnut his carrot, Mathieson's eyes darted about, his ears straining for the slightest whisper of sound. He saw nothing, heard nothing, and went slowly back to the caravans. It had likely been only a hare or some nocturnal creature going home. If Lambert was quite sure he had his victims neatly trapped, he'd not risk the game by coming too close, which was precisely what he had counted on when he'd proposed this scheme. He settled down on the steps again, gazing into the fire, but listening intently.

No untoward sound disturbed the early morning stillness, and after a while his thoughts wandered, for he was very tired. Torrey couldn't last much longer. The strain had quite obviously pared him down to the bone. Small wonder. Three days and nights of backbreaking effort, of striving to give the impression there were twelve of them with the caravans instead of only two, was enough to wring out any man. He'd kept his promise to Rob MacTavish and could end it now, but he wanted to give Rob a small extra time—just in case of an accident, or a breakdown, or something of the sort. Tonight should suffice. But more than that he dared not do. Lambert was nobody's fool; already, he might be suspicious.

His head started to nod. He stood and stretched, then strolled to the second caravan and put his head in at the door. This was the vehicle Fiona had occupied on the northward journey. He could still catch a whiff of her fragrance. He closed his eyes and breathed it in, smiling. "Goodnight, *ma belle*," he called, and wondered what she was thinking now. Hopefully, she was sleeping peacefully, thinking nothing at all. Her bright little face came into his mind's eye as he last had seen it, anguished and pale, believing him to have attempted to violate her cousin. That ghastly scene had been one that would haunt him for as long as he lived. It had been all he could do to keep his eyes from her distraught face, to maintain a defiant demeanour while knowing how her dear heart must be breaking. But it was for her sake he had done it. If he didn't come through this, she must not spend a lifetime mourning him. She must be free to make her life with someone else. Torrey loved her—he'd proved that. He would be good to her, and in time she would forget the man to whom she had given her heart, and who had turned out to be—his mouth twisted wryly—such a dedicated villain.

But, God willing, it wouldn't come to that. He and Torrey would get clear in time, and he would find her again. Perhaps, then, my lady might look more kindly upon his hopes. Muffin, God love his crustiness, might find it in him to forgive his erring and unwanted grandson—even as Lady Clorinda had stipulated.

And when all was said and done, it was worthwhile, however it turned out. The only thing that mattered was that his adored Tiny Mite should be spared the horror of arrest, questioning, and execution. The very thought turned his bones to *blancmange* and awoke such nightmarish visions that he terminated his "conversation" hurriedly and made his way to his own bunk.

Torrey shifted in the saddle and looked about him hollow-eyed. As tired as he was, for a long time he'd found sleep denied him. The slightest sound had sent him jumping up, ears straining desperately, his heart hammering with dread. When he'd finally fallen into a troubled slumber he'd dreamed Lambert had caught him and that he'd been tied to a stake while dragoons with bayonetted muskets danced around thrusting the razor-sharp bayonets at him until he screamed aloud with the pain of it. He'd awoken, weak and sweating, to find Mathieson's hand clamped over his mouth. He had felt sick and shamed, but there had been no contempt in the dark eyes, and all the man had said was that he had some soup heated and it was time to ride out.

It had stopped raining, but the day was cloudy and cold. Still, he'd been almost glad to escape. As usual, he'd seen no trace of redcoats on his journey, and the knowledge that this was their last day—that after dark tonight they would both slip away, heartened him immeasurably. Their plan was to leave the camp-fire burning, and the caravans in their usual places so that the dragoons would be lulled into thinking they were going to buy ale, or dinner, and that the rest of their little band expected their return. If worst came to worst, they would be armed, and mounted on fast horses so they'd have a good hope of winning free. At least, this damnable pretence would be done with!

He turned back towards the camp at four o'clock, a package of cold roast beef, a crusty loaf, and some pickles, in his saddlebags, and an escape route charted in his mind.

He was whistling cheerfully as he rode from the trees and started down the hill towards their camp. The whistle died in a gasp. He wrenched his bay to a halt.

Mathieson stood by the fire, talking with three men. Three big men. Torrey's eyes dilated. He didn't like the look of this.

Mathieson didn't like the look of it, either. He'd been harnessing up two of the horses when a voice had given him a friendly hail and he'd turned to find the three behind him. They were roughly dressed and said they were farm labourers, but he doubted that. Their eyes were everywhere, and their accents were too variable. One man, he spotted at once as London bred;

another was Sussex born, or he'd eat him; and the third he guessed to hale from Lancashire or thereabouts. Further, to a chance traveller this would appear to be a gypsy camp and he was quite dark enough to be taken for a gypsy. Those long-suffering people had for centuries been wanderers, denied the right to stay in one place for very long, and usually half starved. Their reputation for thievery caused them to be driven from town and village, and they were more often met with blows than with kindness. Yet these three rough men were all smiles and camarderie. 'Dear Brooks has put out a few spies,' he thought, and turned their questions smoothly. His little band, he said, had been so abused of late that they now dared journey only at night, with the result that the rest of his mates were sleeping.

"I heard as ye'd some saucy little fillies what danced right nimble loike," said the Sussex man slyly. "They be sleeping too, be they?"

"Ar, master," murmured Mathieson, keeping his eyes humbly lowered. "Tired out, poor girls."

"You got some nice cattle in that there pen," said the Londoner. "Where you come by 'em, Mr. Gypsy?"

"Worked for 'em, sir. Worked years, we did. Never got no pay, 'cepting the grys."

"Soomthin' harsh it be," put in the Lancastrian, his shrewd eyes on Mathieson's long, well-manicured hands, "the way you poor folks be treated. Happen ye don't get noothin' easy in life, eh, gypsy?"

Mathieson slipped one hand into his pocket and moved back to block the steps as the Londoner made toward the caravan. "We have to fight, sir. All through life," he said, with a wry smile.

The Londoner checked and eyed him speculatively. "Ain't no cause ter fight *me*, Mr. Gypsy. I jest wanta littel peep. Ain't never seen inside one o' them carryvans."

"Sir, ye can look all ye wants, after me mort's awake. She'd have me ears did I let a strange man pass his glims over her sleeping."

He smiled easily, but the Londoner noted that his hand remained in the pocket of his coat. 'He's got a pop in there,' he thought, and paused, irresolute.

The Lancastrian took a pace to the side. "Mighty quiet, like," he said, glancing at the other caravans. "Is *everyone* snoozing, mate? Bean't ye got no brats, or dogs? I never see a gypsy camp yet what wasn't—''

"Who's he?" The Londoner was staring up the hill at Torrey. "Hey!" he shouted. "You! Come on dahn here 'fore I—"

Panicking, Freemon Torrey rammed home his spurs and fled.

And the game was up. Without a second's hesitation, Mathieson's fist jabbed at the Lancastrian's jaw. With a faint "Ooof!" the man went down. The Sussex individual made a grab for his coat pocket and his hand emerged clutching a horse pistol. Before he could aim it, Mathieson's flying boot caught him in the ribs and he hurtled backward. The Londoner whirled about, swinging a lethal right. Mathieson ducked under it, but the Lancastrian was already clambering to his feet, pistol lifting.

Mathieson flailed the side of his right hand across the Londoner's middle, and leapt to grab the Lancastrian's pistol wrenching it upward. The weapon discharged deafeningly. "Hell!" groaned Mathieson, then was sent reeling as the Lancastrian's left smashed home against the side of his jaw. Gasping for breath, he went to one knee and managed to whistle a brief but shrill summons. Rumpelstiltskin cleared the paddock rope with a beautiful leap and charged to him, teeth bared. The Lancastrian, who had fancied this man hopelessly outnumbered, took to his heels and ran, leaving the Londoner doubled up on the ground, and the Sussex man clutching his ribs and gasping out faint but lurid predictions of Mathieson's fate.

From not too far away came shouts and the sounds of horses travelling at speed through the woods. Torrey had ridden eastward. A quick glance in that direction revealed no sign of him. Panting, Mathieson bounded up the steps, and grabbed his saddle. He beat all speed records throwing it across Rump's back and buckling the girths. Another mad dash for his sword-belt and cloak, then he was down the steps and had vaulted into the saddle.

The big stallion was at a full gallop before he was halfway across the meadow. Wind whistling through his hair, Mathieson guided the horse over the low fence and into the lane. A shout was followed by the roar of a pistol. Mathieson ducked as two dragoons rode straight at him along the lane. Another shot, from behind this time. He felt the breath of the ball as it whizzed past his ear. The east was clear, but to ride that way would be to lead them after Torrey, who had done his best to help, poor fellow.

He touched the spurs lightly to Rump's sides and the stallion gathered his mighty muscles and was back over the hedge again, galloping due south. At the foot of the slope was a culvert; a tricky jump, but it would likely stop his pursuers until they could find a way around. Mathieson set the chestnut at it, steadying him with hand and voice. They soared into the air and cleared it with a foot to spare, but the far bank was slippery and the horse staggered. Mathieson's firm grip on the reins held him together, and they were away again, up a rise and over the top. A shout of alarm. An oncoming troop was thrown into hopeless confusion as Rumpelstiltskin charged through them like a bowl through ninepins, scattering them, then galloped on at incredible speed, Mathieson crouching low in the saddle and laughing exultantly. "Bravo, *mon ami*! Well done!"

An infuriated bellow followed him. "You two men—see what's happened at those caravans over there! The rest of you—after him! No shooting! I want the bastard alive!"

Lambert.

Mathieson's smile became grim. Rob MacTavish had been given his three days. Now he must make his own bid for life. But—whatever the outcome, the lieutenant's wants must not be gratified.

Rosamond Albritton MacTavish hesitated in the doorway of the book room, her big blue eyes tender as they rested on her husband. MacTavish stood with one hand on the wall, looking out into the rainy gardens. For perhaps the hundredth time since his return she sent up a silent prayer of gratitude. He had come back safe and unhurt. His task was done, for the treasure was safely stored away in the old earthwork under the barn which was all that remained of some long ago version of Blue Vale Farm. She moved to his side and laid her cheek against his sleeve.

At once, MacTavish turned to smile down at her and take her in his arms. "Well, my madcap bride," he said. "Are you happy now that I've brought you all this company?"

"*I* am happy because you are back safely." She caressed his lean cheek. "But *you* are not. What is it, Rob? You should be very proud, but—"

He tugged one fair and glossy ringlet. "What an imagination," he said with a chuckle. "I was merely thinking that we must plant some Twining Splendour in the garden, and—"

She gave a little gurgle of laughter, but put her hand over his lips. "Fustian, my bonnie braw laddie! If—Robbie *MacTavish*! Give heed to your behaviour! We've guests in the house!"

He grinned and kissed the top of her golden head. "Then do not be speaking with that pseudo-Scots accent, you little varmint! You know it drives me wild! As for our guests—what d'you think of 'em?"

"I think they're splendid. I adore Mr. Bradford and that marvellously theatrical manner. My lady frightens me a little, though she must have been a great beauty at one time, do not you think?"

"She was. And still is a lovely wee creature, no?"

"Yes. And I am very glad to meet Lord Thaddeus again and to see him so happy with that beautiful girl. Will she wed him, do you think?"

"Aye, I do. Another hapless bachelor shackled into—"

His wife shut off that wicked remark by the simple expedient of standing on tiptoe and covering his lips with her own.

"Shameless hussy," he murmured, after a few delightful minutes. "And what have you done with our guests?"

"That nice Scots boy has taken Miss Torrey for a ride about the farm. My lady is having a nap, and I believe Lord Briley and his lady are exploring the buttery. Gregor and young Japhet, are down at the stables."

"And—Miss Bradford?"

It was idly said, but her eyes flew to his face. "Perhaps resting, too. I know her papa and Cuthbert both are snoring in the blue sitting room. They all are so tired, poor creatures. But— dearest, I never saw such sorrow as I find in that child's eyes if I catch her unawares."

"Child," he scoffed. "She's much of an age with you, matronly one."

"Pish! She is an innocent. A veritable babe. And do not change the subject, sirrah! I would swear Lady Clorinda is also deeply distressed, but—poor Miss Bradford! I vow at times it hurts me to meet her glance. Rob, tell me. Why does she grieve so? Has someone she cares for—died, perchance?"

Startled, he exclaimed, "God! I pray not! Whatever makes you say such a thing? Not your woman's intuition again?"

He had actually paled. Shocked by his vehemence, she stared at him, then took him by the hand and led him to the deep cushioned seat in the bay window. "Sit down, Lieutenant Robert Victor MacTavish," she commanded sternly. "And—tell me."

Her husband looked at her, frowning. "I cannot, love. At least—not without you give me your word of honour to keep the secret."

"Oh, delicious!" She clapped her hands. "Yes, I promise. Is it an *affaire de coeur*?" Seeing his sombre expression, her own changed to anxiety. They sat side by side and she asked, "Not a tragedy, Robbie? She is too young to know—" An idea struck her. "Rob—how *were* you able to get away? You told me you were fairly trapped, but then eluded the dragoons. Is—Miss Bradford's grief in some way connected with your escape?"

MacTavish sighed. "You'll remember that rascal, Roland Fairleigh . . . ?"

She nodded, searching his troubled face anxiously. "We owe him our lives. How could I ever forget—Rob! Did he follow us? Was he—"

"If ye'll close your pretty lips for a bare instant, madam wife—I'll tell you."

Rosamond closed her lips.

Five minutes later she sat pale and silent, her head turned from him, staring at the rain splattered window.

MacTavish took her hand. It was very cold, and he held it tightly.

In a shaken voice, his bride said, "So—again, I have him to thank for your precious life . . ." She blinked at him through a film of tears. "If Lambert takes him—"

He put his hand over her trembling lips. "Dinna think aboot it, lassie."

"I—cannot help it. *You* are thinking about it! I doubt you think of anything else! Oh, Rob, is there any chance for him? Any chance at all?"

"Perhaps. He has Torrey to back him. That might help."

"Why did Torrey go with him? Were they good friends?"

"Torrey hates him, I think. He's fair crazed for Miss Bradford, you see. Has been for years, I gather. I fancy he volunteered to help so as to convince the lass—or himself perhaps—that he's as good a man as his rival. Still, it took courage, love. I—rather think, if things get verra bad, Roly will see he gets clear. Somehow.''

"And—that poor child sits up there, her heart breaking, never dreaming the truth." She turned on him, flushed with anger. "Oh! 'Tis infamous!''

He blinked at her. "But—do ye no ken, sweetheart? Roly did but think tae ensure she'll no waste her life grieving for him. 'Twas for her own protection he—''

Rosamond jumped up and stamped her foot at him. "Men!" she said and turning to the door, stopped with a gasp.

Fiona walked in. She was a different girl to the pale silent creature Rosamond had first met. The little head was held high now; a militant gleam lit the green eyes, and her small hands were clenched at her sides.

Apparently completely unaware of Rosamond's presence, she walked straight to MacTavish who had sprung up at her coming. "I have thought and thought, Robbie," she said. "And I know that I have been a great gaby, because 'tis all wrong. Whatever he has done, whatever he may have been, Roland vowed to mend his ways, and he is not the man to break a vow. He loves me. No—" one hand lifted imperiously. "There is no use to deny it and tell me he is a libertine. He may *once* have been a rake. He will not be so again. I am perfectly sure I have his heart. I was very weary, and so shocked and hurt that my silly head was not working, perhaps. But it is working now. I want the truth, Robbie MacTavish. Where is Roland?''

His face commendably blank, MacTavish said coolly, "Ma'am, I've not the remotest notion.''

"I see. You have been sworn to secrecy." From the corner of her eye, Fiona caught a glimpse of Rosamond, who had crept closer and watched the scene, entranced.

"Your pardon, ma'am." Fiona held out her hand. "I collect I did not talk to you. My—my behaviour at times leaves much to be desired, so you will forgive an I come straight to the point. Are you also sworn to secrecy?''

Rosamond ignored her husband's warning frown. "Yes," she said, with a very kind smile.

MacTavish groaned and looked helplessly at the ceiling.

"I see," said Fiona. "Then—if you cannot tell me, I shall have to guess and—" she bit her lip, trembling, then went on bravely. "If I guess correctly, you need say nothing at all, so

299

you will not be breaking your promise, will you?'' She blinked and dashed tears away with an impatient hand. "I'm not going to cry, for I have not the time. But—you see, I remembered that Roly once told me about an officer who had a fear of covered bridges. I only wish I'd—recollected sooner. It was Lieutenant Lambert, of course. And Roland told you of it. And—and if he planned that business, then . . . Oh, I *beg* of you—tell me. Is—is Roland driving one of those caravans?''

MacTavish said, "Miss Bradford, truly I am sorry, but—'' He spread his hands in a gesture of helplessness.

Blinking rapidly, Fiona knew he would not cooperate—not even to this extent. Anguished, she turned to his lovely young wife and in a voice that broke pathetically, repeated her question.

Mrs. Robert MacTavish folded her pretty hands, looked at the ceiling, and said not a word.

A pale sun broke through the clouds in late afternoon, but the wind was cold. It had drizzled all day and Mathieson was soaked to the skin. Poor Rump was wheezing again. As he stroked the foam splattered neck, he could feel the stallion trembling. He glanced back into the valley. No sign of Lambert now, but each time he'd thought to have lost the troop, they appeared again. They, of course, had access to fresh horses, whereas his only choice was to ride Rumpelstiltskin to death. For two days and nights they'd been hard on his heels. The military was out down here, all right. He'd had to detour many times when he'd all but run into stray patrols. The detours had cost him dear, and he'd been shocked earlier in the afternoon to hear gunfire and find dragoons streaking after him from a narrow valley. Rump had been tired then, and he'd had to push him unmercifully, poor brave fellow.

As often as he dared, he'd stopped and dismounted, allowing the great horse to rest while he watched the slopes around him, pistol ready. As soon as Rump's painful, sobbing breaths eased a little, and the powerful legs ceased to tremble, he'd walked the stallion, explaining the situation, apologizing for this cruel treatment. And the worst of it was that Rump had never failed him. Even in the most racking of moments the glazed eyes rested on him with love, the muzzle would heave up and the velvety lips would caress his neck as if in forgiveness.

Shivering, he slid from the saddle again and staggered. He was so tired he could sleep standing here, leaning against the stirrup. Mustn't do that. *Mon Dieu*, no! But he'd had only a few hours sleep since they'd left the others on the covered bridge. Poor Rump was near exhaustion again, his head hanging low. Dear old fellow—what other horse could have stood such a gruelling pace for so long? This last hill had been steep, but he'd taken it gallantly, God bless his hooves and hocks. Mathieson stroked the bowed neck and told the stallion how splendid he was, and once again, when some measure of normalcy was regained, he walked beside the horse, his red-rimmed eyes ever watchful. He had avoided Cheltenham, had been obliged to swing east at Gloucester, and now he'd not the faintest notion of where they were. And, Lord, but he was so hungry he ached with it.

He thought he heard hoofbeats and spun around, snatching for his pistol, but saw no sign of life on the hillside. If capture seemed imminent he must have the courage to put a period to his life. He daren't fall into Lambert's hands. He knew too much—too many names, too many details, and he knew where the list was. That Bradford's name was on that list, he had no doubt. Likely Mac-Tavish's was; and Boudreaux, and de Villars—so many other good men. And, although he was trying hard to be worthy of his love, he knew his limitations; he was a novice at the hero business and a poor risk for stoical resistance. If he weakened under torture and told Lambert what he would surely ask, he would betray Fiona also—his perfect little lady, who—

There was no doubt this time! Hoofbeats—coming fast! He spun around. Three troopers were less than half a mile away, and they'd seen him! Cursing, he clambered into the saddle again, and the chase went on.

An hour later, at dusk, disaster struck. He'd eluded the soldiers and had begun to think himself safe, but it was very obvious now that all through these hills the search was up. A party of civilian hunters burst through some trees almost level with him, and roared their triumph. Desperate, he spurred hard. Rumpelstiltskin obeyed, but he was dazed with exhaustion. Neither he nor Mathieson saw the stream beyond the hedge they jumped, and not until they were in mid-air did Mathieson realize it was too wide, and the far bank too sheer. The stallion strove gallantly, scrabbled at the edge, and fell back. Mathieson kicked his heels from the stirrups. He was hurled into icy water and

301

dragged under. His breath snatched away, he battled to reach the surface, bursting out at last, gulping air. The water was fast and up to his shoulders and it took all his strength to get to where Rump plunged and fought to regain his balance. Mathieson tugged at the reins and somehow managed to guide the horse to a shallow spot. He heard shouting and wild excitement and held Rump's nostrils, pressing desperately against the overhanging bank. The hunters raced above him to a narrow board bridge, thundered over it, and rushed on, all shouting at the top of their lungs and not one of them thinking to look under the bank.

In a few minutes Mathieson ventured to peep over the top. They were already lost to view. The light was failing rapidly, and the air ever more chill. Shivering convulsively, he led Rump along, fighting the current, until they came to a low spot in the bank where they could climb out. And then he saw that the stallion was shaking all over and barely able to stand. He was done. Another mile, and he would drop and never get up again. Mathieson's heart twisted with anguish. He must abandon the gallant animal. No choice. Rump must not go any farther without proper food and a good long rest.

He led the stallion slowly in amongst some trees, burrowed under the fallen leaves until he found some that were comparatively dry, and rubbed the horse down for the last time. His teeth chattering, he talked to Rump fondly.

It was a wrenching parting, culminating when he threw his arms around the neck of this beloved friend and hugged him tight, before giving him a stern command to stay. Far off, he could see the flares of torches. Men—many men—coming this way. That party of hunters returning, and with reinforcements, by the look of things. One of them was sure to stop and take care of old Rump. Few men would pass an ailing horse— especially such a horse as this. He delayed long enough to remove the saddle and found it a taxing and wearisome task. Then, repeating his command that the stallion remain, he started off. He heard Rump whinny anxiously. Tears blinded him and a lump was in his throat. "Thomas," he managed, "Look after the old fool for me." Hoofbeats again, coming from the west. His heart missed a beat as he saw blurry but unmistakable red uniforms. He took to his heels and ran into the woods.

At midnight, he was crawling, his lungs on fire, a spear turning remorselessly in his side, but he refused to stop, concentrating on Fiona's sweet face and what life would offer if only he could win through. Sometime in the night he slept, but started up again to the sound of a ragged drum beat and staggered on.

Dawn came. He was dizzied and his head felt strange. It must be, he thought dully, because he'd not eaten for so long. He frowned around at the trees that loomed up through the gloom. They looked familiar, especially that oak which had been struck by lightning. Had he been here before? *Maledictions!* Was he going in circles? He peered at the sky, but the sun was not yet risen, the clouds so thick he could not tell which way was east. Only he could hear the drum—ever louder, and eager excited howls. Lord, was there no end to it? Did they never sleep? They must have found some sign of him. He'd fallen so many times, he'd likely left broken branches to mark his route. Must keep on. Must keep trying.

The hours crawled past and he struggled on doggedly until the voices were louder and seemed to come from every direction at once. Panic took him then. He ran with the strength of desperation until he fell, sobbing and gulping for breath like a hunted animal. It came to him that this must be how poor Quentin Chandler had felt when he and that hound Joseph Montgomery had tracked the wounded Jacobite down. He gave a faint, ironic laugh. The way of the hero . . . as he'd always known. A fine pickle he'd got himself into!

It must have been noon when he dragged himself up a slope and at the top the ground suddenly fell away. He rolled helplessly and lay sprawled in the mud at the foot, too tired to lift a finger. The stubborn flame of hope was quenched at last. He was finished, he knew, and he was so exhausted and spent he was almost glad. Heavy feet were running to him; a harsh, exultant voice rang and echoed in his ears. It would be Lambert, of course, so he must find the strength to reach the pistol. He fought to drag the weapon from his pocket, cursing when it resisted his efforts. At last it was in his hand. It was very heavy. He saw the running boots now, and swung it upward. The boots halted.

Mathieson whispered, *"Maman . . . Je vous demande . . . pardon . . . "* And he closed his eyes, pressed the muzzle to his temple and pulled the trigger.

There was a click, nothing more. The powder, of course, was wet. What a sorry fool not to have realized it!

The boots were beside him. He blinked up into a rage-contorted face, saw the glitter of a high-swung bayonet, then was gasping to the sharp agony of goring steel.

The last thing he heard was Lambert . . . raving . . .

❦ 18 ❧

Life, reflected Benjamin Hessell, was a bitter pill. What's more, it was fulla meanness and trickery. Here he'd wheedled and stole and trudged his way clear up to Liverpool and back again, thinking as that there Otton was on to something good at last. And what had it got him? An empty belly, a perishing cold, and he'd damn near been scragged by that wicked and evil Brooks Lambert—may he rot! Bitta luck he'd cadged a ride with that carter, even if it had only got him this far. At least he was not much more than thirty-five mile from home. Give or take a mile.

He interrupted his gloomy introspection to look around the tap. Perishing farmers. All wot they could talk abaht was cows and corn, cows and corn! Cor! Enough ter make yer sick! The ale wasn't too bad though, considering as this was such a small tavern, on the north fringe of Cricklade which wasn't exactly no roaring city. Lor', but he hated the country! Give him the Big Smoke any day!

He fumbled in his pocket, wondering if he had enough coins to pay for another tankard. He'd gotta think of dinner. Might be able ter prig something, but you couldn't always count on it. He wouldn't've been able ter buy himself the sausage and pickles or the first tankard, if he hadn't of earned a shilling loading a river barge fer two days. A fine thing when a man had to *work* fer his vittles! He found himself the possessor of a groat, a ha'penny, three farthings and the silver button Otton had given him. At least, it *looked* to be silver. He eyed the host thoughtfully. Wonder if the fat old clown would buy it—or take it in exchange fer—

A commotion from outside cut into his musings. A steady

305

drumbeat, many horses, and a confusion of catcalls and whistles. That'd be soldiers. Likely they'd caught some slippery Jakeybite. Together with the other occupants of The Swan, he stood and hurried to the door.

Outside, it was drizzling and cold. A troop of horse was coming along the tree-lined lane, well accompanied by urchins. The officer in the lead drew an awed, "Oooh! Ain't he *handsome*!" from the barmaid, but sent Hessell dodging back into the shadows with a whispered, "Lambert!"

"Oh! Poor man!" said the barmaid a minute later, her tone so sympathetic now that Hessell's curiosity awoke. Lambert had passed, so he was safe. He shoved his way to the fore, jostling the barmaid, who turned a shocked face.

"What's got yer shivering, me pretty?" he leered.

"I think that's cruel," she said indignantly. "He's hurt—see, his sleeve's all bloody. And to drag him along like that! It ain't right!"

Hessell shrugged, and turned an indifferent eye on the prisoner who staggered and reeled behind the sergeant's horse, his bound hands secured to the rope that pulled him along. Hessell's eyes sharpened. The black hair of the prisoner straggled wetly about haggard, beard-stubbled features; the drenched clothes were a far cry from anything he would ever have expected to see upon that usually elegant individual. But he'd know Roland Otton anywhere. His astonished gasp was drowned by several other exclamations as the prisoner fell to his knees and then toppled, to be dragged unmercifully.

The catcalls had ceased by this time and now several angry shouts went up. The officer glanced over his shoulder, then raised a gauntletted hand and the troop halted. A command was called. A sergeant dismounted, tossing his reins to a corporal. He went back and dropped to one knee beside the sprawled figure, then rolled the prisoner onto his back.

"Get him on his feet!" shouted the lieutenant.

Expressionless, the sergeant hauled the limp figure up, and let go. There was some laughter but more indignation from the small crowd as the prisoner crumbled and fell headlong again.

The lieutenant reined around, leaned down and spoke a few pithy words to the sergeant, who flushed and motioned to a trooper. Between them, they lifted the prisoner and slung him face down across the trooper's saddle. Another brief conference, then the sergeant mounted up again and troop and prisoner went on at a slower pace.

The trooper however, remained, and pushed his way through the knot of people at the door. He glanced around the tap. He was a clean-cut, good-looking youth, and when he spoke his voice was educated. "Is there a doctor hereabouts, host?"

The barmaid sidled over to him. "There's the apothecary," she cooed. "Last cottage at the end of the lane 'fore you turns into Cricklade, m'dearie."

The trooper's young face reddened. He touched his tricorne, gave her a shy smile and hurried out.

"Mind you come back again, Colonel," she called after him. And when he was gone and the laughter had died down, she murmured, "I wonder they bother. That poor fella they caught looked proper done for."

" 'That poor fella' is likely one o' them murdering rebs, my girl," said the host sternly. "And they're not about to let him die till they're done with questioning him."

She looked frightened and retreated into the back of the tap.

Hessell sat down again and stared at the button he still held. So Lambert had caught up with Captin Otton, or Mathieson, or whatever his real name was. And if they was looking fer a sawbones it might mean they'd be told they must let their prisoner rest here for a day or so afore hauling him orf to London and the questioning. Poor perisher. He had no love for Captin Slippery Otton, but—cor! he wouldn't wish that lot on no one! He wouldn't give much fer his own chances neither, if horrid Lambert saw him here. He'd best be getting—

"Want to sell that?" The host had wandered up and was looking at the button.

"Might," said Hessell, craftily nonchalant.

The host picked up the button and inspected it closely. With a grin he asked, "Acquainted wi' his Grace, is you?"

"Wot grace?"

"The duke. Marbury. Them's his arms. I know, 'cause I used to work on his estate."

Hessell, playing his cards cautiously, laughed. "You're wrong there, mate. This was give ter me by a young fella name of Otton—or Mathieson, and—"

"Right you are, then."

Hessell gaped at him.

"Mathieson's the family name," explained the host, willing to air his knowledge of the Quality. "Clifford Augustus Fairleigh Mathieson, Earl of Nettering, Earl of Mathie, and dozens of more titles—Duke of Marbury. That's the old man." He frowned thoughtfully. "I didn't know there was another one of 'em. Come to think on it, there *was* a son, I heard. Long time ago, though. I'll give you a tanner."

His eyes very bright, Hessell scooped up the button and restored it with great care to his greasy pocket. "No thanks, mate. Fancy you working on a great estate, though. Cor! In London, was it?"

"I never did see the London house. Very grand, I heard, No, I worked at Dominer. Now *that's* a palace if you ever wanta see one!"

"A palace, eh?" Hessell's hopes rose with every second. "I wouldn't mind having a look. You think this duke cove would be there?"

"Hmmnn. October . . . He might. He's got a lot of houses. I dunno for sure. I heard he was in Sussex a week or so ago, but—he might. Why? You thinking to take a dish of Bohea with him?"

Hessell laughed dutifully at this witticism, but his mind was busy. Otton might be a nephew or some sorta relation, and the old man might pay fer a mouth kept shut about the disgraceful arrest. The Quality didn't like real scandal in the family. It was, he decided, worth a try. "And where might this here Domino o'yours be, me clever covey? Not bloomin' France, I hopes?"

The host grinned. "No, not that far off, mate. And it's Dominer—not Domino. About ten miles this side of Bath. Matter of fact—" He checked, eyeing Hessell thoughtfully. "If you're really thinking of going down there, I got a waggon-load of bricks to get to Bath. My sons make 'em, but my eldest boy's hurt his back, so my fourteen-year-old's loading now and he'll be off in a hour or so. I'd as soon he didn't drive, but we're already late delivering. If you'd be willing, I can offer a good meal 'fore you start, a free ride, and sixpence if you help him load now, and unload at t'other end. He could put you down near Dominer on the way back, if you'd like. What d'you say?"

Hessell hemmed and hawed, and with inner jubilation accepted the offer.

* * *

Trooper Willhays propped his musket against the barn door, took off his tricorne and mopped his brown. The afternoon was warm and the rains of yesterday had left the air damp, the resulting sultriness not pleasing when one wore a red uniform coat with a high-buttoned collar. He flinched slightly as a faint cry from within the barn reached his ears, and he knew that he did not sweat entirely because of the heat. He snatched up the musket hurriedly and began to pace up and down, keeping his gaze on the farmhouse and trying not to hear those occasional sounds of pain, or the lieutenant's harshly repeated questions. He whipped about as Lambert's enraged voice broke into a flood of cursing. The door to the barn fairly burst open and Sergeant Patchett exploded through it, his face mottled with wrath. He charged past the trooper, halted beyond a nearby beech tree and swore at it with fire and fluency until he ran out of breath.

Trooper Willhays ventured closer and watched the sergeant unhappily. "I—haven't heard the whip this time," he muttered.

The sergeant glared at him and tore open the buttons at his throat. "Lovely Lambert don't need it now. He's already cut that poor fella to ribbons. He's got a new trick."

"Oh," said the trooper, wishing he'd joined the navy.

"He's got him strung up to the beams by his wrists," snarled the sergeant, twirling ferociously at a button. "With his feet just off the floor."

Willhays blanched. "But—but what about that—hole in his arm?"

"You know what. All the lovely Lambert has to do is hit him now and then—not very hard—just so as he—swings." He spat savagely.

"Oh, Lor' . . ." The trooper glanced at the barn in horror. "Sarge—I didn't know we had to—to do this er, sort of thing. I mean—I don't mind fighting a cove when I've got a sabre in my hand and he's got a sabre in his. But—this! It—fair turns my stomach! Sarge—oughtn't we to be taking the poor rebel gentleman to the Tower? Or to the barracks?"

"Yes, we should. But we ain't. And we won't. You know why? Because that pretty sod in there's got a score to settle. I heard him telling the poor cove. Proper gloating he was. I'll swear to God he loves every minute of this!" He ground his teeth, then added sharply, "And don't you let the dear lieutenant hear you call the prisoner a gentleman. He's got a funny little

309

turn of mind that says *he's* one. Hah! That poor cove he's killing a inch at a time is more a gentleman than—'' He swore again as a roar emanated from the barn. ''Your *super*ior officer wants a bucket of water, me lad. Hurry up. He don't like to be kept waiting while he's playing his nasty little games.''

Willhays asked hesitantly, ''Did the reb faint again, then?''

''Not—exactly.'' The sergeant's grin was mirthless. ''The lieutenant said his knuckles was getting skinned, and it was too hot to put his glove on. Poor chap. So he invited me to have a swipe at the reb. Nice of him, eh?''

The trooper stared, much shocked. ''You never did?''

''What, and upset our gentle little Lamb? I done what I was told, like a good soldier.'' He slammed his fist into his palm. ''Straight to the jaw, hard as I could. Put the poor cove to sleep for a while, at least. Our lamb was raving! Likely you heard him. And you better hurry up with that water. I'd not put it past him to string you and me up, just like poor Otton!''

''Otton? I thought his name was Mathieson?''

''I dunno, son. Lambert's got it in his head he was using a false name. Probably was. I fancy he'll be buried as Roland Otton. Now get along with you!''

The water was cold, drawing Mathieson back towards a consciousness he fought desperately, for to awake was to return to agony, and the everlasting fear of his own weak longing to give up; to tell Lambert what he wanted and be done with it. But the next bucket brought him sobbingly awake again. He had prayed that this time he would be dead. Surely he *should* be dead after what they had done to him. But he was still tied to the beam . . . And dear God, but he was one mass of pain. His arm was anguish, and he was so thirsty his mouth felt swollen shut, but his back was the worst. Why didn't he die? He *must* die, else there was no doubt he would answer Lambert, for he couldn't stand any more.

He could hear Lambert shouting something, but he wasn't being tormented . . . Was it possible he'd told them? Had he already betrayed his love . . . his friends . . . ? If Lambert didn't hurt him anymore, he must have—

He fought a groan as his head was wrenched back. Lambert's voice hammered at him, asking the same unanswerable questions, just as he'd done since the apothecary had kindly said the prisoner was "doing well enough now." When had that been? A week ago . . . ? An hour ago . . . ?

"Where are they? . . . Who is Ligun Doone? . . . Where is the list?"

And between each question, another blow, another swing that racked his torn and brutalized body and made him dig his teeth into his lacerated mouth to keep from screaming. So he had held out—this far. Lord knows how. But he was not a brave man . . . 'Thomas—let me die soon, before I—'

Lambert struck hard and Mathieson could not keep back the cry. It felt as if a rib had gone that time . . . 'Oh, Thomas . . . where are you? Help me! For the love of God—help me!' Writhing, he tried to speak, but only a cracked whisper sounded, and his head sagged.

Lambert wrenched it up again. "What? Say it louder!"

"Wa . . . ter . . . *Please* . . . Wa—ter."

"But of course. Trooper—bring Captain—er, Otton a drink of water."

Mathieson closed his eyes, trying not to sob as each breath scourged him; waiting, praying, for the water.

"When you've told me what I want to know," purred Lambert and rammed his fist home again.

As the savage moments passed, Trooper Willhays tried to close his ears and blot the scene from his mind. It was dark and stuffy in the old barn; he began to feel sick, and wondered how long it would be before the reb broke. Lord knows, he was a brave man, but—

Lambert said dulcetly, "Trooper. Bring me that lantern."

His hand trembling, Willhays carried over the lamp. "Careful, sir. That side is nigh red hot."

"So I see," smiled Lambert, and turned back to his prisoner. Willhays looked away quickly, and prayed.

A moment only. Mathieson groaned one choking word and mercifully sank back into unconsciousness.

Lambert shouted, "What was that? What did he say? Dammitall, I didn't hear!"

The trooper thought ragefully, 'You were too busy laughing, you dirty bastard!' But he answered in a faint but controlled voice, "It was only one word, sir. I don't know what it meant."

"Well what *was* it, damn your eyes?"

"I think he said—'Retribution.' "

Lambert swore a flood of gutter oaths. "I thought the scum would break before this. Oh—cut him down, blast him! We'll have to try something else."

"Sir," said the trooper, standing on the upended bucket and trying not to see Mathieson's back, "he's getting very weak. If he doesn't have some water, he'll go mad and die, and the colonel—"

Lambert tensed. "What colonel?"

"Fotheringay, sir."

"*Fotheringay?* He's not up here, you fool. He's hot after a traitor—in Sussex, I think."

The apothecary had said Colonel Fotheringay had ridden through only yesterday, but Willhays was silent as he eased down Mathieson's limp form, not caring now if his uniform was stained. 'Dear Lord,' he thought. 'The poor fellow! Let him die soon. Please let him die soon!'

It was a prayer Mathieson echoed as he drifted back to consciousness, but he did not seem able to die. He had been cut down and was lying outside on grass that was wet and blessedly cool. He could see very little, but it seemed to be late afternoon. A tankard was at his lips and he gulped icy water, well laced with brandy. It stung his cut mouth but eased the hellish thirst. Unfortunately, it also restored him to a full awareness of his misery. Someone was supporting him, and the hands were kind so that his shrinking preparations to withstand more pain seemed unjustified, at least for the moment.

Lambert's smiling face came into his blurred view. That deep and hated voice enquired solicitously, "Can you see, dear Roly? Sergeant—do something about his eyes, there."

A damp rag was applied, and he could see a little better. What were they going to do to him now? He mustn't cry out again. Lambert loved that. But—merciful heaven how terrible was this pain . . . 'The Lord is my shepherd . . .' He clung to what he could remember of that kindly old Psalm.

Lambert purred—"Only look who we've found to keep you company . . ."

Roland blinked. Oh God! Had they caught Torrey? It was hard to see, but . . . beyond Lambert's handsome face someone loomed . . . Only—it wasn't a someone! With a gasp of terror he saw a faintly discernible white blaze, heard the enquiring whinny. 'Rump!'

Lambert laughed softly. "I shall ask you again, my poor fellow. Where is the list . . . ? Where is the treasure . . . ? Who is Ligun Doone? Spare yourself, Roly . . . and—your faithful friend, here . . ."

Mathieson was shuddering with fear. 'If he didn't answer, they'd hurt Rump . . . They mustn't hurt dear old Rump! He couldn't bear that! No! He'd have to tell them . . . he'd have to give in . . . But . . . Fiona . . . *Mon Dieu! Mon Dieu!!*'

Lambert reached out and shook his arm very gently, but it was not the waves of agony that brought sobs welling up in Mathieson's throat. 'Rump . . . oh, Rump . . . *Je suis . . . vraiment . . . désolé!* . . . So *very* . . . sorry . . . !'

Lambert shook his head regretfully. "What a stubborn fool you are, to be sure. You do but make it hard for everyone. Sergeant," he added with his pleasant smile. "Put a bullet in the horse's right knee, will you?"

"No!" groaned Mathieson, his battered face reflecting a deeper torment than he had yet known, his one visible eye pleading desperately, and his moveable hand clutching feebly at Lambert's boot. "Please, Brooks . . . Have . . . mercy! I implore . . . I *beg* you! Not—not *him!*"

"But—my dear boy," explained Lambert reasonably. *"I'm* not responsible for this. *You* are! You've brought it all on yourself, Roly. There now, never look so grieved. You can put an end to this distasteful business. 'Tis so very simple. Just tell me what I want to—" He jerked back, his face convulsing as Mathieson choked out three pithy words which (as Patchett was later to happily relate) described the lieutenant down to the ground. Lambert's powerful fist clenched and flew up, his narrowed eyes glittered with fury, but he took a breath, and with a supreme effort, mastered himself. "Sergeant . . ." he snarled, "you heard me. *Now!*"

Patchett reached down and drew the long pistol from its holster. He could feel the reb shaking, poor cove. Lor', but it was a fine animal! And only look how it watched Otton—like it fair loved the chap. How the hell was he to cripple that great horse? It would break the reb—little doubt of that . . . This was the first time he'd groaned in that sobbing way—the first time he'd begged for mercy, 'cept to ask for water. His own hand trembled as he lifted the weapon. He couldn't do it! But—if he didn't, Lambert would ruin him. He'd be discharged with dishonour.

And that meant he wouldn't be able to get work anywhere. Kitty and the babe—they'd starve, belike . . . Gawd! He thought, 'Sorry, mate! It's a hard cruel world!' And he let Mathieson down and stood, taking careful aim.

With every ounce of his strength, Mathieson dragged himself to one elbow. To breathe now was torment, but he fought the pain and whistled a shrill, steady note.

Rumpelstilskin whinnied, and reared, hooves flailing the air, sending the trooper who'd held him jumping for his life. Lambert flung himself sideways, tearing at his holster, shouting, "Shoot him, you dolt! Shoot him!"

The stallion went into a bucking spin, his back legs kicked out, and Patchett also was obliged to jump aside, chancing to collide with Lambert and thus spoiling his aim, so that his shot went wide.

With a thunder of hooves, Rumpelstilskin was away, a chestnut streak across the yard and into the woods.

"After him!" howled Lambert. "You two men as well! If you can't catch him, shoot him down! Let him get away, Sergeant, and by God, I'll break you!"

Paling, the sergeant raced for the nearest horse, mounted with a flying leap, and was off, the corporal and a trooper following.

Lambert rounded on Mathieson, who lay there, a shattered and bloody wreck, but with a quiveringly defiant grin on his torn lips.

Maddened, Lambert's temper snapped and he swung back his boot.

Clifford Augustus Fairleigh Mathieson, Duke of Marbury, elegant in dark blue velvet and silver lace, stood at the window of his study in this, his favourite house, and contemplated the pleasure gardens with their gracefully winding paved walks, benches, and statuary; the tastefully placed trees and shrubs; the glistening sweep of the ornamental water, and the bejewelled sprays of the fountains. He loved Dominer. To a degree, many people shared his affection for the crescent-shaped three-story mansion, for it was one of England's most admired houses. The setting was equally as delightful, Dominer being situated upon a low hill in the beautiful Cotswold country, compassed by lush green valleys and richly wooded higher slopes. It was a joy to the eye at any season of the year, retaining its beauty no matter

314

what the weather. Sometimes, he became lonely in the great house, for he was not one to surround himself with people unless they were friends whose company he really valued. He had been away a great deal this year, however, and as always Dominer seemed to welcome him. He smiled faintly. It was good to be home.

He was glad he had deeded the mansion to the Aynsworths. Kit and his Leone were the type of young people who held out the best hope for England's future. And heaven knows, poor Kit had known his share of sorrow. He frowned a little. It had not been easy to intercede with His Majesty and win an amnesty for the boy. He rather thought, in point of fact, that he was the one man in Britain could have pulled it off. Only the fact that Kit Aynsworth had such a splendid military record, and had not been personally involved with those confounded Jacobites had convinced King George in his favour.

Marbury pursed well-cut lips and clasped long-fingered hands behind him. It had been a close run thing all right, despite his friendship with the monarch. And, of all things, no sooner had he become deeply involved with Lord Christopher Aynsworth's desperate dilemma, than he'd been obliged to sally to the rescue of young Anthony Farrar. A vicious plot, that, and had almost cost poor Tony his life. He'd suspected there must be some connection to the Jacobite business when he'd seen his scapegrace grandson hanging about Sir Anthony's estate, but he'd not dreamed how deeply, and how dangerously, he'd got himself involved once more. He would have to be careful henceforth— very careful. George was a friend, and had been kind, but kings went knee deep in treachery, and tended to believe the worst, and if a king could have his head cropped at the shoulders certainly a duke was not exempt from such tender mercies. No, there must be no more dealings having the slightest taint of Stuart about them!

His thoughts turned to his errant grandson. How pleasant it would have been to deed this house to Roland. Not that he begrudged the Aynsworths, God bless them! But—to have had a Mathieson here to care for the great house after he was gone . . . He sighed. Useless dreams. Roland was just as worthless as his sire had said. And Dudley had been a fine judge of worthlessness. Why was it, his Grace wondered rather wearily, that a man strove so hard to protect his son—to guard him against the trap that had blighted his own life—and the son went from folly to folly until he got himself a bastard born of a cheap, money-grubbing French slut, and then as good as killed himself?

The duke sighed again. Would it have made any difference, he wondered, if he himself had married the girl he'd loved long ago? If they had been blessed with children, would it all have turned out the same, anyway? Had it been preordained that he be forced into marriage with a woman he despised and walk through life unutterably lonely—unutterably despairing? That his only son must break his heart, and his grandson disgrace and befoul the proud name he should have been grateful to bear? For all the blessings of wealth and power, was not the lowliest peasant with a happy family life more blessed than a duke who had no one to—

The door opened softly behind him, and he started to turn, but Beast's head was on his foot and Beast was fast asleep. Wherefore, my lord duke waited until his butler's hauteur hove into view.

"Your Grace," intoned that rotund magnificence. "Your pardon—'tis most irregular, but—"

The mighty Kildwick was flustered. Astonished, Marbury prompted, "But—?"

"'Tis—Sorenson, your Grace. Captain Roland's man. Begs a—a private *word*, sir!" The pale eyes lowered from the ceiling to rest upon the duke in anguished apology and appeal.

Marbury had long since come to grips with the fact that he was a too sensitive man of small stature in a large, insensitive and remorseless world. The barriers he had built to protect himself were, or so he had fancied, invincible. Now, for no appreciable reason, an invisible hand came over the top of that invisible wall and touched the back of his neck with a finger of ice. He removed his foot from under the somnolent dog with such rapidity that Beast's head thudded to the floor.

"Show him in at once," said Marbury crisply.

Kildwick looked shocked, but departed.

Both reproachful and bewildered, Beast sat up. His Grace rested a white, beringed hand on the dog's head and apologized, then crossed to the great armchair, limping a little since his foot had gone to sleep. He sat down, drumming his unusually long thin fingers on the rich red velvet of the chair arm, and wondering why he felt so apprehensive. Beast heaved himself to a standing position, staggered over, and sat beside him. He did not at once collapse, and Marbury's sense of something very much amiss, deepened.

The door opened for a second time and the man known simply as Sorenson entered, bowed, and waited just inside. The duke gave a graceful and encouraging gesture. Mr. Sorenson, sleek, urbane, discreet, drifted nearer.

"How may I be of service," enquired his Grace gently.

Behind his calm mask, Sorenson thought, 'By allowing me to cut out what poses as your heart, sir.' He said, "I apologize for this breach of etiquette, your Grace. I am—disturbed about your—Captain Roland."

"My grandson. Yes. Well," said the duke drily, "I have been disturbed about him for years, but—"

Briefly, an expression of such ferocity lit the veiled brown eyes that Marbury was rendered speechless. Then the lashes were discreetly lowered over those betraying eyes. His Grace blinked. "In what way are you disturbed, may I ask?"

"He went off without me, sir. Some seven weeks since. I—I have reason to believe he has met with an—er, accident."

Briefly, Marbury's hand tightened on the arm of his chair. Then, he drawled, "Your concern is to be commended. Would it reassure you to know that I encountered him last month? And that he was, regrettably, his usual—self?"

"Thank you, your Grace. But—no." The duke's brows lifted very slightly. Sorenson felt rebuked, but persisted doggedly. "Captain Roland knows I—I worry, if he is away very long. He always sends a note—just a line perhaps. I have had not a word, sir."

The duke stood, looking bored. "He is a grown man. Really, I fail to—"

Desperate, Sorenson committed the cardinal sin and interrupted. "It was my birthday last Monday, sir. Master—I mean, Captain Roland has *never* forgotten! Not these fourteen years! Not *once*, your Grace!"

This man had served Roland since he was barely out of the schoolroom; had even gone to Flanders as his batman. The rather sallow face was beaded with perspiration, and the anxiety in the dark eyes was intense. Marbury said curiously, "You are fond of my grandson, Sorenson."

"I would follow him to the ends of the earth. I—I implore you, sir, to make enquiries. I would do so myself, but—I have small means, and—and I don't even know where he went."

"He went north," said Marbury, baffled because he sensed loathing and was astonished that so careless a young rake as Roland could inspire such devotion. "Hunting that damnable Stuart gold."

Sorenson uttered a faint sound of despair. "I know you think me quite mad, sir. But—"

The door opened for the third time.

Irked, the duke snapped, "Kildwick, I do not wish to be disturbed!"

"Do you not, indeed, Marbury!" The imperious feminine voice presaged the appearance of a small personage who swept past the despairing butler with a whisper of silks and the flutter of a large fan. "Then you are like to be prodigious disappointed, for I mean to disturb you enormously!"

His Grace stared in astonishment at a lady he had not seen for more than half a lifetime, but whom he knew at once. A tiny lady with suspiciously bright cheeks, but a skin as smooth as a woman half her age, and a pair of rogueish green eyes that frowned on him briefly, softened in the light of his lax jaw and stunned shock, then frowned again. She extended a tiny gloved hand. The duke recovered himself sufficiently to bow over it. She still wore the same scent, he realized numbly. And she had not run to fat . . . *"Cl-Clorinda,"* he stammered.

"I am here," she said, "seeking my beloved Roland, and—"

"Your . . . beloved . . ." gasped his Grace.

"Roland," she nodded. "Has he reached here? Have you had word of him?"

Recovering sufficiently to guide her to a chair, the duke struggled for composure and managed to say with some semblance of coherence, "I was not— Did not know I was to receive a . . . er, visit from my grandson. Surely, you are mistaken, but—"

Again, incredibly, the door opened. Really angered this time, Marbury said in a voice of ice, "Kildwick! I must not have made myself clear. I *do not wish to be disturbed*!"

The butler was almost in tears. "Your Grace—forgive . . . Truly, he is a . . . a dreadful *person*! But—he insists 'tis a matter of life and—and death, sir! And he sent—this . . ."

He held out one hand. On the palm was a silver button.

With a muffled imprecation, Sorenson fairly sprang to snatch it up. "Show him in," he said in an odd, strained voice.

Kildwick curled his lip and glanced at the duke.

Marbury was beginning to be uneasy. He frowned, but nodded, and the butler went off again. "Might I perhaps be allowed to see that?" the duke enquired with faint sarcasm.

Sorenson hurried to hand him the button. " 'Tis Master Roland's token, your Grace. He sometimes sends it to me with anyone having a message for my personal ear."

The duke gazed at the button. "I was not aware that the Captain uses the Mathieson crest."

"He doesn't, your Grace. Only in the signet ring, and a few private and—most treasured objects."

Marbury glanced up. Again, Sorenson was regarding him coldly. Unaccustomed to such a glare, he quite forgot the little lady who sat so silently, watching. "Perhaps you might care to explain—" he began, but the opening door interrupted him.

A fawningly obsequious individual came in, bowing at every step, his smile an offense, his clothing a disaster—especially a lurid belcher neckerchief—and about him the air of the unwashed. "Very kind, I'm sure, sir," he whined, edging nearer. "Arternoon sir, and ma'am. Benjamin F. Hessell, at y'r service, Duke. I see ye got th—"

"What do you know of Captain Otton?" interposed Sorenson, disregarding protocol.

Hessell's crafty eyes brightened. He'd struck gold here, all right. "Why—I *might* be able ter tell yer something. But—I'm a poor man. A honest, but poor man, and—" He was shocked then by the look in the tall cove's eyes and the remorseless approach of that same tall cove. He drew back, flinging up a shielding arm. "Don't yer dare hit me!" he gabbled. "The dragoons got him!"

Lady Clorinda dropped her fan.

His face white as chalk, Sorenson gasped, *"Sacré bleu!"*

The duke, a little nerve beginning to beat at his temple, stepped forward. "Mr. Hessell, I fail to understand what dragoons would want with my grandson, but if you indeed bring word of him, you will be well paid. Do I take it Captain Mathieson has been arrested?"

'His *grandson*!' Hessell brightened and stood straighter. "Yussir. But, er—*how* well, if yer don't mind of me asking?"

Marbury crossed swiftly to his desk, sat down and scrawled a draft on his bank. He held it out. "Can you read?"

Hessell nodded and hurried to take it. "Me wife taught me. I—" He gave a gasp. "Oh! Oh—lumme!" He'd kill for that much! It would mean a new start somewhere, and all the booze he could ever want! Blimey, he might even take the old woman a buncha flowers! A damn great cart-full! "Sir," he said, for once in earnest. "Wotever I can do . . . *Wotever!*"

My lady stood, and her voice quavered a little. "Is—is Captain Mathieson hurt?"

Hessell nodded.

Whitening, Marbury asked, "But—why has he been arrested? I—"

"I'll explain in private, Muffin," interpolated my lady, bafflingly. Her eyes were suddenly full of tears. She gripped her hands tightly. "They—are taking him to—to the Tower, I suppose?"

"What?" gasped the duke.

"No, ma'am," said Hessell. "They stopped at a farm outside o' Cricklade and took it over like." He had a very small measure of compassion, but the stricken look on the face of the little old mort awoke that tiny emotion, and he added, "The cove wot's in charge is a nasty customer. I 'spect he means ter make the captin tell what he knows. And I'll tell yer plain, I don't think he'd stop at much a'doing of it!"

My lady's hand flew to her mouth. "Not—Lambert?"

So she knew the perisher. "Ar," said Hessell. "The very same, ma'am. Got it in fer the captin, too."

Marbury felt very cold. "Hessell—be frank. How much time have we?"

Hessell looked at him thoughtfully. "Sorry I am ter tell yer, sir, but—I'd say very littel, melor'. Very littel indeed."

For a moment, Marbury could scarcely breathe.

He wasn't really surprised when the door opened once more.

His face pallid and distracted, Kildwick ushered a young damsel inside. She was tiny and fascinatingly pretty, rather than beautiful. Dismissing the shattered butler with an airy wave of her hand, she entered, followed by two men, one of whom was well known to the duke. The girl's rather narrow green eyes flashed around the assembled company. She advanced on Marbury, hand outstretched.

"Good afternoon, your Grace. I am gauche so you must forgive that I cannot wait to be formal. My name is Fiona Bradford and I am your grandson's betrothed. I believe you know Lord Briley, and this is Mr. Cuthbert Potterby."

Dazed, the duke bowed over her hand.

Even as he touched her fingertips to his lips, she went on swiftly, "Hello, Grandmama. Have they heard aught of Roland? Oh, my God! They have!"

Marbury straightened and slipped an arm about this frail yet dynamic little miss. Snatches of thought slipped through his mind. He might have known Roland would choose so unconventional a lady; he was glad of it . . . So she was Clorinda's granddaughter; that was good . . . But if she was deeply in love, would she be able to withstand the shock of what he must tell her . . . ?

A few minutes later, he had his answer.

Her face white as death, her voice shaking, Fiona looked up at those who watched her so compassionately. "I—have a plan," she said. " 'Tis very simple, so it just may work. Have you any onions, your Grace?"

They had killed poor old Rump . . . If it had been just the sergeant who'd come in with that news, there might still have been some hope, for the sergeant, hard as was his fist, had seemed a decent sort somehow. But all three of them had come and in obvious trepidation confessed that the big stallion had outdistanced them; that in obedience to orders, they'd all shot at him, and that he'd stumbled, and . . . and almost gone down . . . but had run on until he'd apparently been unable to see the quarry . . .

Lying very still in the corner of the cold barn where they had thrown him, his every breath a shallow tortuous rasp, Mathieson felt the slow burn of tears again. Poor old Rump . . . He hadn't rated that kind of death. He'd done nothing bad . . .

The news had seemed to drive Lambert berserk. He had given up more subtle methods, and used his boots again . . . After that, very little was clear . . . Intervals of horrible agony interspersed with Lambert's voice, roaring his stupid questions. And the boots . . . But the moments of consciousness were shorter, thank God, and they must fear he was dying, because now they gave him time between their savageries . . . This was just such a respite, and already, heaven help him, it was done . . . They were coming back . . . He could hear the boots—so shiny, so incredibly vicious coming straight at him. He shrank as far as he was able, knowing it was not far enough, trying to drag his hands up to protect whatever was left of his face.

Waiting in trembling terror, he thought that when Brooks kicked him again he would go out at last . . . bound from this hell to another. Only the other hell would not be so frightful, even if it was physically worse, because it would not be men who subjected him to unending torment, it would be something evil and cruel, but not human, and thus more endurable. The steps had ceased. Through the pause, his shrinking mind prepared him. Any second now . . . be ready. Don't scream—for God's sake, don't give him that satisfaction. He wondered he had a mind at all, and knew his sanity hung by a thread, sustained only by the memory of a pert little laughing face, and the love in a pair of entrancing green eyes . . . A face he would never see again, even if by some misguided miracle he survived this nightmare, because by now, Lambert's boot had blinded him . . .

Something touched his shoulder and he jerked back, sobbing out an involuntary plea that they not hurt him any more, and despising his weakness, even as the faint, halting words were torn from him.

"My poor old pippin—what a meth you're in! Here—have a pull at thith . . ."

He was delirious. His mind really had gone at last! That low-pitched voice *could* not be . . . But he breathed a feeble, "Thad . . . ?"

"Righto! But we can't chat now, old lad. Here—take it. Roly? Can't you thee what—" A gasp, and then with compassion. "No—of courth—you cannot. Here, then . . ."

A cold touch at his swollen lips. It was very hard to drink; he managed, then coughed to the bite of the brandy, and was muffling groans while strong but very gentle arms cradled him, and Thad's voice murmured encouragement.

"Are you—mad?" he whispered, as soon as he was able. "Go! You'll . . . you'll be . . . taken! Dragoons . . . everywhere."

"Then we mutht pop along, my tulip. No, don't argue." His lordship's voice rose very slightly. "Over here, Cuthbert . . . ! I'm afraid we're going to lift you, Roly. We'll try to be careful, but we have to move quickly, you know."

He heard a rustling, then a muffled, "Christ! Is that—" and Thad's voice, soft and oddly uneven, "Yeth. I'm afraid he—he can't thee . . . Only till we get him cleaned up, you know. But— we'll have to carry the—the old cawker . . ."

Another hand touched him. He shrank, gasping.

Cuthbert muttered, "Holy—! *Thad*—his back! Those filthy bastards! How can we—"

"No choice, dear boy. Careful, now. Up, Roly . . ."

He was too weak to point out that they should save themselves because he had no wish to live, and it was a waste of effort. It was such a superb effort. He was overcome to think that they would *do* this—*risk* this—for his sake! He tried to thank them, but then they were lifting him and it was pure hell. He couldn't help . . . he couldn't walk . . . he couldn't see . . . And he simply couldn't bear any more. Sighing faintly, he gave up and let himself slide deep and ever deeper into a stifling and complete emptiness . . .

ᘒ 19 ᕬ

Dominer was under siege. All through the night lights blazed in many windows of the central block and in the principal guest suite on the first floor. By the light of day carriages raced at intervals along the wide drivepath, and the most skilled of the west country physicians trod quickly up the steps and passed under the graceful portico to the doors that already stood wide to receive them; for the bell had been taken down lest its clamour disturb the sufferer who lay in the great tester bed of the sumptuous guest suite. Across the circular sweep of the Great Hall each physician trod with gravity and confidence, ushered along by soft-voiced servants. Up the famous spiral stairs, and into the quiet bedchamber they went. And after a while, down they came again, faces pale and eyes grim, and made their shaken way back to their carriages, never to return.

Other carriages came, and coaches, and riders, for rumour had spread its wings, and it was known far and wide that milord duke's bastard grandson lay dying in the lovely old house, and that his Grace (who had never thought well of the young man) now, after the strange fashion of humanity, was crushed by grief. Some of those who brought their cards, or flowers, or fruit, were close friends who could not be denied, and verified their fondness by staying but a few moments. Most, however, were informed that his Grace was at the bedside, and could not receive them, though their expressions of sympathy were deeply valued. The great double doors were closed without a sound; the footmen crept away again, and the lackeys who remained on watch at the side windows, whispered together, glancing around from time to time at the nurses who came softly down the beautiful staircase looking tired and despondent, and the nurses who tip-toed up, exchanging a few anxious words with those they relieved, and shaking their heads as they continued to their tasks.

On the fourth day there came another carriage through the rain, splattered with mud from its long journey, the solitary occupant a tall thin gentleman of middle age with an air of faint exasperation and a militant eye. The footman who handed him down received his leather bag, and the two lackeys who opened the doors exchanged knowing glances. Another doctor. His Grace refused to accept the verdicts he already had been given, but clung stubbornly to the hope that so obviously was vain. Marbury was well loved by those who served him, and watching this latest physician's rapid ascent of the stairs, the lackeys sighed.

Forty minutes later, Marbury ushered the doctor into his study, waited with unfailing courtesy until he was seated with a glass of Madeira in his hand, then asked the inevitable question.

James Knight started to reply, glanced curiously at the composed features of the aristocrat, and hesitated. It was difficult to believe that this suave and polished gentleman with the tired eyes and the cool but anxious voice was the same Marbury reputed to be such a tiger when aroused, his acid tongue feared by all. He appeared to have himself well in hand at the moment, but he was no longer young, and a few times, when it had been necessary to move that poor devil upstairs, the faint moans uttered by the semi-conscious man had caused my lord duke's fine hands to tremble.

Reading his thoughts, Marbury said quietly, "I brought you down here, Knight, because I was impressed by the splendid job you did with young Kit Aynsworth. I want the truth however—not a polite gibberish that says nothing."

Knight frowned. He was not cowed by rank, and he said in his harsh deliberate voice, "I'll own I was flattered when you summoned me. But the reason I left my other patients to come here, Duke, was because your man told me something of the nature of your grandson's injuries, and I hoped I might be able to help."

The duke's chin lifted imperceptibly. The chilly blue eyes and the narrow hazel ones met in mutual challenge.

Knight sighed then and a faint smile dawned. "I'm sorry if I'm prickly. Damned tired. What did your local men tell you?"

"That—he is . . . dying."

The cool voice shook on the last word. Knight felt angry and helpless. He said in a very different voice, "Sir—I can only marvel he is still alive. He must have been in perfect condition, but youth and a fine body can only prevail to a point. The flogging alone might well have proved fatal. The wound in his arm is relatively trivial of itself, but he has lost much blood. Three fingers of his right hand, his nose, and four ribs are broken; I suspect a concussion; his entire body is covered with bruises and contusions; there are several bad burns on his left arm, and . . ." he paused, his lips tightening.

"And—he is blinded." Marbury gulped at his glass, then asked huskily, "If—if he *does* live, is there the slightest hope he will ever see again?"

Knight stared at his knees. "Your Grace—I wish I could give you a kinder answer, but—alas, I am no deity. The young man cannot live. I doubt he will last the night out. You must—"

"Give up?" The duke slammed a clenched fist on the top of his desk and his pale eyes blazed defiance. "By God, but I'll not! I'll have you know, sir, that the Mathiesons are fighters! And—"

"And—*is* he fighting, sir?"

Marbury stared. The light faded from his eyes to be replaced by misery. His shoulders slumped. He whispered, "No. He—wants death . . . poor lad."

"So I thought. Sir—who could blame him? You've seen how he suffers. And when he is moved, however carefully—Lord! In his place, I'd want to die too. As soon as may be!"

"There's always . . . hope," muttered the duke stubbornly.

Knight sighed, finished his wine, and stood. "I must get back to Town, sir, I've many patients waiting."

"Nonsense!" Marbury's lifetime of schooling in the behaviour demanded of an aristocrat enabled him to put aside grief. With quiet courtesy he argued, "It's raining, and you cannot hope to reach Town tonight. You shall stay for dinner and a warm bed, and in the morning you can start back."

"Thank you. I'll not say no to a good meal, but then I really must go. With luck I may reach Devizes before the light fails."

Together, they walked to the door. The doctor paused to turn back and look at the portrait that hung above the mantel. He shook his head wonderingly. "Is that really—what he looked like?"

"Yes."

"Good God! Sir—whoever did this should be—"

Marbury smiled a slow and rather terrible smile. "I do assure you, doctor, that the matter will be dealt with."

Knight nodded and almost could feel sorry for whoever had perpetrated such atrocities. He put out his hand. "You are anxious to get back upstairs, your Grace. Do not think you must stay with me. I shall do."

They shook hands. Gratefully, Marbury gave the doctor into the care of the butler who waited in the wide, lovely hall, then turned his own steps to the stairs.

A few paces, and the doctor looked back. "Sir," he counselled gently. "Let him go easily. 'Twould be kinder."

Marbury turned to face him. He made a slight bow and continued on his way without a word.

Dr. Knight sighed, and went frowning to the small dining room where, unexpectedly, he found several anxious people waiting for him.

With his foot on the bottom stair and his fingers resting on the banister rail, my lord duke halted. *Was* he being harsh by urging Roland to keep on fighting? *Would* it be kinder not to prolong his sufferings through what might well be a doomed effort? His head bowed and he so far forgot himself as to put a hand across his eyes.

Small, warm fingers closed over his own on the rail. He jerked his head up and beheld a weary but very sweet face, the shadowed eyes full of compassion.

"Do not give up, Muffin dear," murmured Lady Clorinda. "Fiona won't."

He managed a smile. "Thank God for Fiona," he replied, offering his arm, and together they went up the stairs.

The battle was joined again. On the one hand prayers, the devoted nurses, every possible care and potion, softly whispered words of love and encouragement. On the other, weakness, shock, pain, and despair. Surely, the forces marshalled against defeat must prevail, thought Marbury. Surely, the doctors were wrong. But as the weary hours passed it began to seem to him that there was yet another force in that quiet room. A dark and shadowy, yet not unkind presence, that hovered in the

327

far corner; waiting. He began to fear that corner, and to dread looking in that direction. But with each day it seemed to him that the dark figure drew a little nearer to the bed, and his fear intensified.

Gradually, it dawned on Roland that he was waking again. So he was alive still, which was as disappointing as it was savage. The pain was merciless; there was scarcely a part of him that didn't hurt—his left eye the worst, for it sent spasmodic shafts of agony through his head so that it was all he could do not to cry out. But his back was almost as bad, and even to draw breath was torture. This time he was lying on his back, whereas before he had always been face down. Wretchedly uncomfortable, he tried to ease his position, but was unable to move, save to lift his right hand half an inch, which not only required an enormous effort, but at once reminded him that Lambert had stamped on it.

All this misery brought a confused thought that perhaps he really was dead after all. But however hell might be furnished, he could not think that he would be provided a soft bed to lie on. And this must be a bed; he could feel smooth sheets, and smell lavender. How long had he been here? Days, surely, for he could remember blurred earlier awakenings that were too intolerable to have endured for long. Awakenings in which agony of body was joined by agony of mind. Somehow, in spite of everything, he'd at first clung to the hope that his inability to see had been a temporary thing; that perhaps the blood from his cuts had sealed his eyelids, but his return to consciousness had been accompanied by a complete blackness for which there could be only one explanation. He was blind. And very probably hideously disfigured. The initial acceptance of those terrible facts had all but driven him into madness. His tottering mind had found a degree of comfort in the realization that he was dying, and he was grateful, for life now could mean only misery and despair. But there were people trying to keep him alive. People with kind voices that echoed weirdly and unintelligibly, and hands that carefully but cruelly heaved him about from time to time, which he took rather a dim view of, when all he asked was to be allowed to die in peace.

It was strange that one of those voices had seemed to be the dearest voice in the world . . . That so often he had thought

Fiona was close beside him. He had dreamed to hear her murmuring of her love, imploring him to cling to life, for her sake; he'd even thought to feel the touch of her hands on his cheek, the brush of her lips on his own, and a salt taste to that sweet caress, as though tears had touched him also. And—oh Lord, if only it *was* real! If only he could see her! But even if she came, he wouldn't be able to see her. And that precious girl, with so much of life to experience and enjoy, must not be tied to a helpless blind man. That buoyant vivacity must not be crushed under the weight of staying beside him; reading to him, caring for him, helping him stumble and grope his way about—as she would surely do. That giving heart must not be given out of loyalty . . . and pity.

His left hand stirred in agitation on the coverlet. Something very sharp scratched his fingers and he caught his breath. If he didn't know better . . . He set his jaw and struggled desperately, and managed to move his fingers again. They touched a warm softness, a small form. He heard a faint trill and horror seized him. He tried to call out, gasping with the pain that effort cost him.

A muttered exclamation; quick, soft steps, and a woman's voice said kindly, "It's all right, Captain Mathieson." A blessedly cold cloth touched his cheek. "Just try to lie—Sir! Thank goodness you've come! He's awake and in an awful state!"

"Where . . . ?" Mathieson whispered, fear lending him strength. "Where . . . ?"

"You're at Dominer, dear lad. Perfectly safe. And . . ."

The rest of it was lost in astonishment, because his mind could only handle one thing at a time. *Muffin?* Was that Muffin's voice—so kindly, so concerned? Was this Muffin's hand, gently smoothing back his hair? But—if he was at Dominer . . . !

"Sir," he panted in febrile agitation. "Treason . . . dragoons . . . Mustn't keep me . . . here!" And he drifted again into the emptiness before he could ask the all important question.

The next time he awoke, his bed was on fire and he was struggling feebly to escape Lambert, who kept pushing him down into the flames, hurting him as only Lambert knew how to hurt. He gasped a plea for water, and almost at once a glass was at his lips. A gentle hand was bathing his face. He awoke fully. It was so hot, so terribly hot, but there was something— some question . . . He remembered, and whispered, "Fiona . . ."

329

"Yes, beloved. I'm here."

Horrified, he groaned aloud. "No! *Ah, mon Dieu! No!*"

A muffled sob. "Darling," said the voice he loved above all others, "I know all about it. How wickedly . . . wonderfully, you lied to—to protect me. How—gallantly you went away and left me."

"Didn't . . . want you—to know . . . to see me . . . like this . . ." he moaned, his head tossing distressfully on the burning pillows. "Go! Don't—don't want . . . you . . ."

Her cool hand was caressing his cheek. She said lovingly, "Stop being so silly and thrashing about, Roly, or you'll hurt your dear self. I found you, and I have no least intention to leave you. Ah, beloved, never grieve so. Do you think I could have lived without you?"

But distraught and half delirious, he raved and tossed and would not be comforted. Her tender voice faded. The shadows closed in around him and he was lost and alone in an unending dark nightmare of heat and suffering, wanting only to give up this cruel fight, but always held back by two little hands that clung to his own, or bathed his face, or held water to his dry lips. By the voice he so loved, yet dreaded to hear. By the tender kisses pressed on his cheek, on his hands. By her love that was so deep, so faithful.

After a long time, he woke again. His hand moved in a faint groping; his head tossed fretfully. She wasn't there. Perhaps she never had been here. Perhaps he'd dreamed it all. He was weaker now and the pain was very bad, and cravenly, he whispered her name. At once, his hot hands were clasped by her small, cool ones. He gave a faint sigh of relief. "You—didn't go, then . . ."

"Foolish boy. I shall never leave you. Don't think to be easily rid of me."

"Should—make you go . . . Selfish. Wrong to—to . . ."

"To let me stay? Because you are—just for a little while—unable to see?"

"Not—just for—little while, sweet . . . child. Should—send you 'way. But—I'm only . . ." His voice faded.

Wiping away her tears, Fiona leaned closer to the bed. "Only—what, beloved?"

"Only," he sighed wearily, "very amateur . . . hero." And then, as the pain worsened and the deep pit loomed, he cried, "Fiona! Don't—don't leave me . . . ! Please . . ."

Her hands tightened on his. "Never, beloved," she said huskily. "I swear it."

Comforted, he let the pit claim him.

Marbury sat with his elbows on the desk and stared blindly at Beast, stretched out in a sunny spot on the carpet. The end was very near. There was so much he had wanted to know—so much he would like to have said. But there was no time now . . . Fever had come, as though Roland had not enough to bear, and was destroying what was left of the boy. Before their eyes, despite the frantic efforts of the doctors and the eight nurses and Clorinda and that splendid girl, it raged ever more destructively, the delirium racking him, the tossing and the pain exhausting the last vestiges of his strength. And that ghastly shape in the corner was halfway across the room now. The girl, so magnificent, so untiring, fought to hold it at bay, but from the corner of his eye, at dawn this morning, he had thought to see it . . . creeping, creeping . . .

"Clifford . . . ?"

The duke wrenched his head up and forced a smile. My lady was peeping shyly around the door. Hopefully, she'd not seen him drooping like a spineless fool. He rose and went to greet her.

Lady Clorinda had never entered this comfortable room, and once inside she stood still, staring through the pale beams of winter sunlight to the mantel. "Oh—Muffin . . . ! Did—did *you* do that?"

He glanced at the portrait. "Yes. I—used to keep it in my bedchamber, but I—rather like to have it by me . . . now. I think—later, you know—I shall hang it in . . ." His voice faltered; he went on bravely, "in the Great Hall."

Her little hand tightened on his. Her eyes were very soft. "Yes. I agree. That is where it belongs. In the place of honour." She took the chair he drew up and watched him walk around the great desk. How very tired he looked. They all were, of course. Fiona, in particular. Dear little Fiona, who seldom left that quiet room for fear that she might come back and find the battle lost. And thinking all this, my lady said none of it, murmuring instead, "I knew you had great talent. But—you surprise me, Clifford. That was painted with—with love, I think? Yet . . ."

Marbury sighed. "I know. I've never been able to understand

331

it myself. Loving him—in spite of what he was. And now . . .'tis even more puzzling, for from what you've all told me, it would seem he is a very gallant young man. Whereas—''

''You had been told otherwise?''

He shrugged. ''I did not have to be told,'' he said wryly. ''He made no secret of it. His misdeeds were common knowledge. The gambling, the women, the wildness. He was expelled from school, you know. Not surprising. In a word, m'dear— notorious. Later . . . there was his reputation for—shady dealings, and that driving fixation for the gold . . . And now—this! So out of character. I just . . . cannot understand.''

''Poor soul,'' she said kindly. ''You never have.''

He shot a startled glance at her. ''Have you?''

''I knew Dudley.''

''Well, so did I. He was my son! And he—''

''Lied to and deceived you from start to finish! No Clifford! Never freeze me with your icy stare, for I'll not be frozen, and so I warn you! He hated Roland—did he tell you that?''

Marbury was shocked. ''*Hated* . . . his own son? Madam, I—''

''Oh sit down do, and don't be confoundedly ducal. Yes, I said confounded, sir! I am tired and irritable, and I swear at times—lots more wicked words than that, I assure you!''

A faint smile coming into his eyes, my lord duke sat down again. Of course she was tired. And she had been so good with the boy. Day and night she had helped through this last terrible week. He said gently, ''You mistake the matter, ma'am. Dudley was *disappointed* in Roland naturally, but—''

''*Un*naturally, more like! But pray tell me now about the so-called slut your son seduced. Did you ever see her?''

''Fortunately—no. And *she* seduced *him*, Clorinda—just as I was seduced!'' He looked at her, wistful-eyed. ''Cast your mind back, my dear. Do you not recall?''

She smiled sadly. ''We were so young, Clifford . . . So terribly in love. And that wicked Mary Frobisher said you had assaulted her and got her with child. Such nonsense, when you were but seventeen years old—and so gently shy. And she was what—twenty-five?—and bold as any tart!''

He blinked and corrected, ''Twenty-two, Clorinda. And one should not speak ill of the dead, my dear.''

''Why not? She was pure alley cat when she was alive. I doubt she has changed a whisker! Oh, how I hated the vixen! Did you really rape her?''

''*Clorinda!*''

''Of course you didn't. 'Twas more likely t'other way round! But they made you wed the little b—Oh, I'll not shock you further. And then Dudley was born . . . and grew up to be so very handsome.''

''He was—but with all his mother's failings, and far too many of my own, alas. I had such hopes for him, Clorinda. I tried so hard . . . but . . . And then—to run off with—that creature! It was years, you know, before I found out about their child.''

''You made Dudley acknowledge Roland as his son. He didn't like that, Muffin.''

''Had I known what the boy would do—''

''*Did* you know, then? You surprise me. I always fancied Dudley had lied to you—as he lied about poor Juliette de Fleury.''

Marbury stood again and came to draw a chair nearer and sit beside her. ''What do you mean? Dudley had no reason to lie to me—I had made him quite financially independent, and he knew he would inherit my fortune and titles. Why should he poison me against his mistress? Against his illegitimate son?''

''Partly, as I said, because you found out about the child, and shamed him by forcing him to admit it. But—did you know he married her?''

''*WHAT?*'' Marbury leapt to his feet, and the chair went over with a crash. For a moment he gazed at her; flushed, shocked beyond words, while she met his wide, horrified eyes coolly. Then, he recovered his aplomb, righted the chair, and occupied it again. ''You—quite startled me, my lady. But you are mistaken, I do assure you. Had they been wed there would have been records; marriage lines, banns. Dudley would have brought his wife to be presented, however much he knew I would have despised her—he would have made the attempt. Or she, knowing that now she had a right, would have applied to me for funds. Neither of those things happened. I once ordered a search, Clorinda, for I had a small suspicion— But there was nothing. Neither in England, nor in France.''

''No. Quite so. The tragic thing is that poor Juliette thought there was. He arranged a 'ceremony,' do you see? A quiet one, but with a 'priest' and a proper 'service.' He couldn't have her, else. And he wanted her. She was so very beautiful. He hid her away in a secluded little love nest, but he feared you might hear of it, so he took her back to France. And— for three years she thought herself Lady Fairleigh. Poor, innocent child. When she discovered the truth—it was much too late. She was ruined.''

Very pale now, Marbury stared at her small grim face in horrified disbelief.

"Oh, yes,'' she went on, relentless. " 'Tis quite true. He deserted her when he realized she no longer loved her betrayer. He had to be loved, you see. He would probably never have looked at Roland again had you not discovered his misdeeds. Then, he had to make some pretense at meeting his obligations, so he brought the boy over here for his education. It was an education, all right!''

Marbury said feebly, "Clorinda, you—you have been misinformed. What you say is—is not—*cannot* be so! Dudley was weak, and—and an immoral wastrel, but—''

"He took Roland on his first hunt when he was nine years old,'' she overrode inexorably. "From the time he had been obliged to acknowledge him, Dudley kept him away from his mother save for a brief yearly visit. But the damage was done. For five years Juliette had schooled Roland in her own gentleness. She taught him to love all living things—especially animals. This, then, was the child Dudley took hunting!''

"And—?'' asked the duke, despite himself.

"I don't know. Dudley claimed Roland disgraced him. Afterward, he used every possible means to break the boy—to make him into what he himself was. As Roland grew older and became more and more handsome, his resemblance to Juliette ever more marked, I really believe Dudley was almost insanely jealous of him. He delighted to tell Roland that he was worthless—that he would always be bad.'' She sighed. "The boy began to believe it, I suppose.''

Aghast, Marbury murmured, "But—but, if what you say is truth—what was it that he did? How did he so enrage Dudley, as to cause such terrible rage and bitterness?''

"I do not know. Nor did I know all of this. But I brought the man who told me, and who can answer you.'' She raised her voice. "Sorenson—you may come in now.''

The door opened, and Sorenson slipped in, as neat and elegant as ever, but with despair written large on his haggard face.

"Pray tell his Grace," said my lady, "what happened that day at the hunt when Roland was nine."

Sorenson frowned. His feelings for the old gentleman had mellowed considerably this past week. The duke looked worn and rather pathetically bewildered. "My lady," he said hesitantly, "perhaps another time would—"

"Now, if you please."

He sighed, and capitulated. "Master Roland was a very gentle lad in those days, your Grace. He didn't want to go on the hunt, but Lord Fairleigh insisted. The end of it was—the dogs caught the fox. And—well, it was the boy's first hunt, you see."

Muffin stared, appalled. "But—he was just a *child*!"

"His father was a proud man, sir. He wanted to be proud of his son. The tail was torn off—the blood smeared over the boy's face. My lord said it was—the initiation."

"Good . . . God!"

"Master Roland was horrified and fought to get away, sir. His father was—displeased. When the—er, ceremony was done, the boy—well, he fainted. My lord's friends laughed." Sorenson shrugged.

"And—that's *all*?" stammered the duke. "Do you say that for so—so trite a thing Lord Fairleigh took his son in dislike?"

"My lord felt he had been, shall we say—let down, sir. He was embarrassed. Publicly embarrassed. From that day, he made Master Roland's life most miserable. He never forgave him; never ceased to sneer at and revile him."

Marbury sat in stunned silence. After a long pause, he looked up. Sorenson had gone. Lady Clorinda was holding out a glass of wine. He accepted it gratefully. She stepped closer, scanning his face anxiously. "Clifford—forgive. 'Tis just—I thought you should know why Roland was—or believed he was—such a very wicked fellow."

His Grace could not speak. With a hand that shook, he lifted the glass, then paused as running footsteps sounded in the corridor. He thought, 'Oh, Lord—not yet! Not yet!'

Sorenson rushed back inside. "Sir!" he gasped. "They think . . . the crisis!"

My lady gazed with great frightened eyes at the panting valet.

Marbury slammed down the glass, and not even noticing that

335

it toppled, ran most undignifiedly for the door. For the first time in memory, Beast ran also.

A lackey came sprinting towards them from the Great Hall, his expression terrified. Marbury slowed, and halted, preparing himself for the worst.

"Your—your Grace," the man panted. "A—a colonel, sir! And a troop!"

Marbury stood very still. "Hell!" he whispered.

Lieutenant Colonel Mariner Fotheringay settled his long, lean self in a comfortable chair of this charming morning room, took a sip of excellent Madeira, and allowed a pair of hard dark eyes to meet the duke's veiled ones. Marbury was neither a large man, nor of formidable aspect, but Fotheringay, a shrewd judge of character, knew that all he had heard of this aristocrat was very likely true. Not giving away a *soupçon* of information was my lord duke. He looked taut and pale however, and the light eyes were tired, ringed by dark smudges. Understandable.

Mariner Forthingay was a hard and demanding officer who kept very much to himself and had few friends, but he had a reputation for fair play, and his men liked him if only because they always knew where they stood with him. A career soldier, his rank had of late been as stable as England's weather. Until earlier in the year his military record had been superb. And with this Jacobite Uprising he had fancied himself well on the way to becoming a full colonel, but he'd been demoted for a stupid bungle which had allowed a valuable Jacobite fugitive to slip right through his fingers. Almost immediately he'd won back his rank with the capture of another fugitive under most adverse circumstances, and now he meant to let nothing stand in the way of his determination to become a general before he was sixty.

His face unreadable, he said, "I believe your Grace has a grandson named Roland. Who sometimes goes by the name of—Otton?"

Marbury became even more pale, but he answered steadily. "I—hope I have, Colonel."

Fotheringay's hand jolted slightly. "He *is* here, then?"

There was small point in lying, thought the duke wearily. He wished Clorinda was not here, but perhaps she and the others could be shielded in some way. Did he dare to hope that the king would stand by him this time? Odd, that he could consider his own death in so dispassionate a fashion . . . He replied, "I think you are well aware that he is here, Colonel. I take it you also are aware—"

Fotheringay interpolated hurriedly, "Sir—there are no words! That any one of my officers should—should so abuse his authority!"

Marbury's ears perked up, and he became very still. With not the slightest change of expression he said a cool, "Then, you were not directly responsible for my grandson's—interrogation?"

"Responsible! Good God, duke! I am known as a hard man, but—from what the sergeant told me—By Jove, 'twas damn near unbelievable! I can only hope . . ." he levelled a rather hunted gaze at the cold blue eyes so unnervingly fixed on him, " 'tis not as bad as I was told."

Considerably bewildered by now, Marbury gave no sign of it. "Your hopes are ill-founded, Colonel. Captain Mathieson is at this very moment waging a—a losing battle for his life."

Fotheringay heard that slight check, the break to the voice, that was so sure a betrayal of grief. Genuinely aghast, he set down his glass, and said earnestly, "Sir—I cannot convey the depth of my shame. That such—such bestiality could have been perpetrated by an officer of my own regiment is—is an affront— a blotch on the pride of every one of us!"

"I agree," said Marbury arctically. "My grandson has been unable to tell us of the reason for his savage treatment. Perhaps you would be so good as to enlighten me."

The colonel tightened his thin lips, but refused to back away from this. "I do not normally discuss military procedures, duke. But—in this case—I will keep nothing from you. I presume you know that your grandson was held at a farm outside Cricklade? I learned of it by chance, and the instant I arrived there, and learned what had gone forward, I launched an investigation. Lieutenant Lambert had the unmitigated gall to try and pull the wool over my eyes! He informed me that Captain Mathieson was shielding Jacobites; that he had information about them that we have long sought; that he had, in fact, cooperated with fugitives to get the

Stuart treasure aboard ship to France, and then tried to shield them by leading the troopers a wild goose chase.''

He gave a contemptuous snort. ''I have no wish to offend, your Grace, but I have for some time been aware that your grandson has been, shall we say—relentless in his pursuit of the Jacobite gold. I know that he had a hand in the capture of one of the rebel couriers, who subsequently bested him in a sword fight and escaped. Of all men, Captain Mathieson would be the last to hold a brief for the Jacobites who damn near killed him! And to expect me to believe he would have helped fugitives ship off the very treasure he has assiduously pursued these many months—! Zounds, but I hope I am not such a fool!''

''A ridiculous tale, indeed! 'Tis my understanding that Roland was questioned at great length and without mercy. Surely, he must have offered some defense?''

''From what I can gather— From what I suspect, your Grace— Captain Mathieson—er, appropriated five caravans from the Jacobites, believing them to contain the Jacobite treasure. When Lambert's troop came up with him, he apparently feared to be caught with the treasure, so he ran.''

Marbury said cautiously, ''From what I know of Roland your surmise is—very likely the true one. And that being the case, he was certainly liable to arrest, though I'd think he could have claimed to have intended to restore the treasure to the Crown and—''

''There was no treasure, sir. Your grandson was tricked by the rebs. At least, so I believe.''

''But . . .'' The duke frowned as though trying to make sense of all this. ''If there was no treasure, what had Roland done that could warrant such inhuman savageries? One trusts you have been able to obtain an accounting from this Lambert?''

Both tone and words stung. The colonel gritted his teeth, but humbled his pride. ''I have occasionally suspected that there were aspects to Captain Lambert's character which— But that is by the way. One of the men in his troop chances to be a sergeant who served with me in Flanders, and of whose integrity I am very sure. 'Tis a practice I detest, but in this instance I felt well justified to question Sergeant Patchett in private, under my personal guarantee of his protection against possible—reprisals. What he told me—!'' The colonel shook his head grimly. ''I could scarce believe it. The other men confirmed his story, however.'' He stared broodingly at his glass and was silent.

"I remain at a loss, sir. Surely, Lambert must have had *some reason*?''

The colonel said reluctantly, "Apparently there had been bad feelings between the two men for some time. Patchett heard Lambert taunting Captain Mathieson and saying he intended to 'even the score,' and that no man made a fool of him without he paid the price.''

"My God!'' thundered the duke, leaping to his feet. "Do you say this monster used his military rank to capture and destroy my grandson out of—personal animosity?''

The colonel flinched. "It—would appear so, your Grace. I— I cannot fully convey my horror, my regrets, but—''

Marbury drew himself up. He seemed to the miserable Fotheringay to be ten feet tall. In a voice of ice he said, "I apprehend your horror and your regrets. Pray respect mine. Roland has been stricken with a raging fever, and I have just been told that he has reached the crisis; otherwise colonel, I think I would demand that you come upstairs and see what your officer has wrought with his—his legalized savagery! I take it you know Captain Mathieson is—blind?''

Fotheringay had also stood. At this, his proud head bowed. He said in a near whisper, "Oh—Lord!''

"Any man,'' gritted the duke, "who would stoop to such barbarism—who would use his boots to blind a helpless and badly hurt man, is not fit to dwell among decent human beings! Whether Roland lives or dies, I intend to make it my business to see Captain Lambert punished to the fullest extent of the law. I only wish it were still possible to enforce the 'eye for an eye' decree! As 'tis, I would prefer to have the swine hanged, but—''

"Impossible, your Grace.''

"We'll see that! At the very least, I'll have him imprisoned and transported.''

"You will not be supported in either attempt, sir.''

Marbury stared. "Am I to understand the army means to do nothing? I find that hard to believe!''

"My apologies, your Grace. But no action will be taken against Brooks Lambert.''

"The *devil* you say! Why don't you give him a medal for—''

But something in the colonel's expression stopped him. He said shrewdly, "Explain yourself, if you please."

Before complying, Fotheringay drained his glass. Setting it aside, he said in a low, grave voice, "When I had what I believed to be all the facts in the case, I called Lieutenant Lambert into a private room, and I proceeded to tell him exactly what I thought of him, and what he could expect in the way of discipline. I think I never saw such rage in a pair of eyes. I knew that Lambert would like to have throttled the life out of me, but he said not one word in his own defense. When I invited him to do so, he just stood staring at me in what I can only describe as a—most peculiar fashion. Then—he started to giggle." The colonel took a deep breath. "He ignored my commands, and began to—to take off his clothes. All the while, he leered at me and giggled, and whispered the most horrible obscenities." Dragging out his handkerchief, Fotheringay mopped his pale, sweating face and said unsteadily, "I do assure you duke, I had a lot rather face— a massed charge of Scots Highlanders, than ever endure another such interview! Brooks Lambert is stark raving mad. He has been put in Bedlam."

Five minutes later the Duke of Marbury raced up the stairs, watched by many sympathetic eyes. He paused at the door of the sickroom. From within came the sounds of weeping. His heart suffered a great pang. He tried to tell himself that God, in His wisdom, knew best, and gathering his courage he opened the door. Fiona was kneeling beside the bed, lost in smothered but heartrending sobs as she clung to one of Mathieson's limp, emaciated hands. Lady Clorinda turned and ran to the motionless duke. Her face was flushed, her nose red, her green eyes brimming over with tears—and radiant. "The—fever has . . . br-broken," she gulped, and sniffed unashamedly. "Muffin—dear Muffin! There has been no more of that dreadful delirium that so exhausted him. He is—he is sleeping so peacefully. And—only see . . . he sweats! Thank God! He sweats!"

For an instant the scene dimmed before the duke's eyes, but he peered with new hope at that certain far corner of the room. There was no need to draw the curtains against the pale winter sunshine, and the corner was bright and quite unoccupied, with not so much as a suspicion of a shadowy presence.

Somehow, Marbury groped his way to the bed, sank to his knees also, and brokenly, gave thanks.

Beast, who had followed, padded up and sat not beside, but behind his god, peeping rather warily around the duke's elbow. He had learned to his sorrow how sharp were the pins of the Guardian of the Bed.

∽ 20 ∾

The corner had been turned and Mathieson began to mend. It was a slow and wearisome mending, and there were still setbacks to be endured from time to time, but whenever he reached out, there was a hand to clasp his own; if he felt crushed and lost in his dark world there would come kind words of understanding and encouragement and, however bad things became, he was humbly grateful to find he was never left alone.

Fiona spent so many hours with him that he protested guiltily that she should have some respite from the sickroom, to which she responded that she wanted no more "respites" and could only be happy when she was near him. Each day she would describe the weather and the scene outside the windows; often she played with the little cat, telling him of its antics and making him smile; sometimes, she brought him flowers from the greenhouses, and would hold them so that he could smell the fragrance. Truly, a *rara avis* was his love, and knowing he was wrong to keep her here, that the life he had to offer her would be one of servitude, he clung desperately to her love and knew that without it he would surely have died.

Not one day passed but that his grandfather spent part of it with him, and was so kind, so attentive that Roland marvelled at the old gentleman's devotion. Sometimes, the duke would talk gently to him, attempting to allay his terrors with assurances that his blindness was but a temporary thing; that his eyes would heal and he would see again. Mathieson knew it was not true, that it was said only to bolster his spirits; but just to hear the soft voice, to know that at last he had won his grandfather's love was a cause for rejoicing.

His nurses were incredibly kind and patient. There were four shifts of two each, and they were in the room at all times, day and night. He came to identify them by their voices and to learn which ones were cheery and which all starch and no-nonsense; that one loved dogs but hated cats, and would shoo Picayune away if she was on the bed; that another sang softly and rather off-key when she thought he was asleep; that one had very stiff petticoats that rustled like sheets of paper; that one was very fat and bustled about pantingly, and that another always smelled of lavender.

Lady Clorinda spent part of each morning with him, reading to him from the *Gazette* unless he was too tired or uncomfortable, chatting to him of the *ton* and their doings, laughing with Fiona over the Society columns.

The days slid slowly past. Very gradually the pain began to ease until it hurt only when he was moved, and he realized with something of a shock one morning that his head no longer throbbed so viciously. That same day, he was carefully raised and allowed to sit up in bed for half an hour. The next morning, he had a boiled egg for breakfast, and he knew he was getting well.

The time came for a great occasion—he was to have a visitor. The nurses went off for a cup of tea, and Thaddeus Briley crept in. He stayed only a few minutes but imparted the glad news that the barge had arrived on the Dorsetshire coast, and its cargo had been safely unloaded and "tucked away." A further enquiry elicited the information that MacTavish had retrieved the vital list, and that The Avon Travelling Players had been disbanded and gone their separate ways. Thaddeus hesitated, then said in a very gentle voice, "They all know, Roly, that but for you there would have been a very different ending to our journey."

There was so much more Mathieson wanted to know, but his lordship was banished then, because Fiona declared he had succeeded in upsetting her patient. Mathieson, still so infuriatingly weak that he could not deal with emotion, was left to picture his Tiny Mite when she had learned why he'd left them, and to wonder how they had come here, and how they'd rescued him from that awful barn, all of which were matters he was forbidden to speak of for the time being.

He had not expected anyone else to call, and as he grew stronger, he was amazed to find his lordship's visit was but the start of a steady stream. Meredith Carruthers came, with his lovely lady, bringing great bouquets of flowers and fruit from the succession houses. Piers and Peregrine Cranford drove up; Peregrine thumping along on his pegleg, the volatile young twin brothers interrupting each other constantly in their efforts to describe the wedding of their sister to Sir Anthony Farrar.

Tony Farrar himself came strolling in one afternoon and said breezily, "Well Roly, now what devilment have you been about? I vow your Grace, this grandson of yours is driving me berserk! My wife and my aunt do nothing but chatter of him, and have positively bedevilled me to come and check on the rogue!" And before Mathieson was able to recover from his surprise, Farrar's hand rested very lightly on his shoulder, and he said with quiet earnestness, "Well done, old lad! I'm damned proud you're a friend of mine!" Which was blasted unsettling and caused him to make a fool of himself, yet again.

His cousin Jacob arrived, sounding grim and uncomfortable, yet with an underlying note of concern to his voice that was touching. But despite the pleasure of his visit, it proved to be a trying one, for as he left he said gruffly, "Don't worry, old fellow, we'll have you riding again in no time. I'll guarantee to find you a good horse." And another memory Mathieson had shrunk from, had to be forced away again until he should have the courage to bear it.

In mid-November he was permitted short visits to the sofa, and on a cold, rainy afternoon Fiona sent the nurses away and admitted Thaddeus once more, warning his lordship to behave properly or be ousted.

Undeterred, Briley said cheerfully, "How glad I am to find you up and about, my tulip," and hastened to bend over the sofa and take the skeletal left hand that was so eagerly outstretched.

"Thad, you rascal," said Mathieson, overjoyed. "I owe you my life, for which I've never properly thanked you, I think and—"

"Good-bye!" said his lordship, retreating hurriedly. He relented in the face of some hasty and humble pleas, and drew up a chair. "You did thank me, you cawker! I have been fairly buried in, deluged by, and inundated with gratitude! It ith, in point of fact, about to drive me to dithtraction—although I detherve every word of it—tho let uth have no more, or I'm off!"

"*Ça va! Ça va!*" said Mathieson with a laugh that warmed Fiona's faithful heart. "But I'm a sick man, and must be humoured, even by noble lordships. No one will tell me anything, Thad! And I'm so devilish curious. How the deuce were you able to find out where I was? How did you manage to haul me out of there?"

Briley sent a questioning glance to Fiona, received a nod, and sat down. "Ah me," he sighed. "I rather thuthpected I wath in for an interrogation."

Mathieson had suspected that Freemon Torrey had raced up to Wales and summoned help, but this proved erroneous. None of them, it appeared, had seen Torrey, and Lord Thaddeus prefaced his own story by enquiring as to the way in which the two desperate fugitives had parted.

Mathieson hesitated. "We split up," he said. "Thought we'd stand a better chance separately, once we'd been rumbled, you know. I'm sure Torrey must have got clear, else my grandfather would have heard of his arrest. He was going *ventre à terre* towards Oxford the last I saw of him."

The smile, thought my lord, was a little forced. He watched the invalid's scarred and gaunt face, wondering what really had happened, until Mathieson became impatient and demanded the details.

It had been Fiona who'd precipitated matters, said his lordship. She had told MacTavish's bride of her suspicions and having persuaded that lady to a confirmation of them had at once declared her intention to follow Mathieson, and had proved so unshakable in this resolve that Lady Clorinda had been won over. They had left that very day; Cuthbert driving a fast coach and four, and Briley and Mr. Bradford riding escort. They had travelled at breakneck speed in an effort to catch up with the decoy caravans. Failing, they'd found themselves not too far from Dominer, and on the chance that Mathieson might have taken refuge with his grandfather, they had come here, arriving just after Hessell brought in the now famous button.

"We dethided you might be a trifle bored with a dull old barn, dear boy," said Thaddeus blandly. "Tho we thought it betht to—ah, bring you home. And—there you are!"

"What d'you mean—there I am?" demanded Mathieson, tiring but indignant. "*How* did you do it? There were dragoons from here to next week! How—"

"All right," said his lordship with a great resigned sigh. "I am loath to confeth, but if you mutht know, I had very little to do with it. We racked our collective brainth, for we didn't want to hurt any of the military—with one notable ektheption!—but we knew we had to act quickly. You've your lady to thank for your—ah removal, old lad."

"And some onion skins," put in Fiona with a smile.

"Onion . . . skins . . . ?" echoed Mathieson.

"We boiled them," she explained. "The outer skin makes a lovely dye, and my skin was too fair for a gypsy—which I had to become, for an hour or so."

Mathieson frowned. "You should not have allowed that, Thad. Fiona, you little scamp—what did you do, go in there and find out where I was?"

"No," she said meekly. "I was so kind as to sell the poor thirsty soldiers some nice cold ale. Which put them very nicely to sleep."

"*Drugged?* Ah—*mais . . . non!*" gasped Mathieson, chilled.

"*Mais oui,*" said his lordship. "Could've knocked me down with a feather, I don't mind telling you!"

"So I should think!" Shaken, Mathieson reached out and Fiona took his hand. "What a chance for you to take, dear heart! I wonder Colonel Fotheringay didn't bring charges against you!"

"Nobody recognithed Mith Fiona," said Briley. "And I think the colonel wath very eager to keep it all quiet."

"As was my grandfather," muttered Roland.

"You are beginning to look tired," Fiona said sternly. "Now lean back and rest while Thaddeus tells you what happened, or I shall send him away again! And do not dare lecture me about taking chances, after what *you* did, sirrah! No! Not a word, just be still! At all events, my plan was very silly, and Thaddeus was dreadfully worried and said it would never work."

"So I should think," said Mathieson. "He had no business allowing you to—"

Fiona put her hand across his lips, shutting off the words.

"I'd jolly well like to have theen anyone thtop her!" said Briley. "Her Papa wath all for the idea. And her plan *did* work!"

"Yes," put in Fiona. "Luckily, it was such a warm day, and the farm a long way from the tavern."

"We had to wait till the almighty lieutenant wath in the houthe at hith luncheon," Briley resumed. "The dragoonth practically jumped into the ale barrell—all but one, that ith, and I tidily felled him with a magnifithent right to the breadbathket! We hopped into the barn, popped you out dear boy, and—*voilà!*— here we all are, thafe and thound. In truth, Roly, I have to admit it wath rather fun to dreth up ath a gypthy, and I—'' He halted, the light words dying on his lips as he saw that his friend was fast asleep.

For a little while, he stayed, holding a whispered colloquy with Fiona. Then, very quietly, he tiptoed down the stairs again.

December slipped away, and January came in on icy feet, dropping snow onto the great house and sending inquisitive gusts of wind to rattle the windows and whine in the chimneys. On a cold, but brighter afternoon, fully dressed for the first time in over two months, Mathieson sat in the windowseat, stroking Picayune who had curled up in his lap. He had been allowed to walk about the room this past week, and was to go downstairs today. Another milestone! Sorri, who had taken command again after most of the nurses left, would be here at any moment, to help him negotiate the staircase. He was a trifle nervous about those stairs, but be damned if he'd let them carry him down! Lord knows, he must look sufficient of a scarecrow as it was, what with all his scars and the narrow bandage that was bound across both eyes.

He had come to grips with his blindness to an extent, but there were times still when he fumbled clumsily, trying to feed himself; or when fear of the future dragged him very low. He dared not let his thoughts linger in that direction, and turned them quickly to the many things for which he should be grateful.

Most of all, of course, there was his beloved, who had proved so brave and so devoted. Next, was Muffin. The dear old curmudgeon had been magnificent throughout. How many invaluable talks they'd had, learning to know each other. The old fellow loved him—really loved him! *Incroyable!* Certainly, he had been forgiven, just as Lady Clorinda had demanded, and if only things had been different, he might be able to— But now . . . had he the right to ask Fiona to become his wife? If he *was* so selfish, if they should be blessed with children, he would never see their little faces . . .

He lapsed, thinking with a raging bitterness, 'Damn, damn, damn! Wasn't the rest of it enough? Did it have to be my eyes, too?' And then he despised himself for giving in to self-pity. True, he could no longer see, but—he *had* seen. He'd seen the glory of countless sunrises and sunsets over England's varied and beautiful countryside; he'd seen his beloved Paris, so lovely at all seasons of the year. He'd seen roses, and the Spring flowers peeping up through the grass; he had seen his vision of perfection and so many of her swiftly changing expressions that could be hoarded in his mind's eye, and—

His musing was interrupted, the duke ushering in a most unexpected visitor, and saying with an odd note to his voice, "Mrs. Shadwell has come to see you, Roland."

Putting down Picayune and reaching for the cane beside him, Mathieson stood, thinking a mystified, 'Mrs. Shadwell . . . ?'

He received an impression of shy hesitancy and his outstretched hand was taken by one that was bony and workroughened. Then, a small, sweet-smelling bag of dried blossoms was thrust into his palm. A humble voice said, "Please to sit ye down, sir. Like Oi am doing. Ye saved me life, Captain. Oi'll never ferget ye. Oi wish as Oi could bring ye more than this."

He remembered then, and in a flood of nostalgia, said, "Ah, yes. You are a long way from home, ma'am. How very good of you to come and bring me such a nice gift."

The duke intervened with an offer of tea, which the woman declined in no little embarrassment. "Oi do know as Oi've no right to be here, yer Grace," she murmured. "But—Oi heard as yer young gentleman was very ill . . . Glad Oi do be t'see ye so . . . sprightly again, Captain."

The slight hesitation, the rather forced final words told their own story, but Mathieson thanked her again, and asked if the villagers had bothered her any more.

"Never went back there, sir. The Folk was coming south, and Oi come with 'em. Oi thought so many times o' what you did fer me. You and yer sweet lady."

"The lady is anxious to see you," Muffin said. "And I would be most pleased to learn of what my grandson did for you, ma'am."

Before she could reply, Mathieson said quickly, "Mrs. Shadwell, when last we met you warned Miss Fiona 'gainst me, and said I would—er—"

"Break her heart," she supplied. "Oi did that, sir. Oi read

348

yer palm, ye'll mind? And Oi saw you would soon come to a fork in the road o' life and—and it looked as if . . ."

"As if I would make a hasty exit?"

A brief pause, then she admitted this. "Oi bean't allus right in me readings, thank goodness. So it looks as if the second fork will be the one you'll be taking."

"The—second fork?" asked Marbury, intrigued.

"Aye, yer Grace." A small hesitation, then she said, "Oi'd best not say more, and Oi must not stay and tire the gentleman. Oi wanted only to see him and wish him well."

It sounded, thought Mathieson, as though she was keeping something from him, and he wondered if Muffin was warning her against more predictions. "I wish you will stay a little longer," he urged. "Sir—perhaps we could ask Miss Bradford to come and . . . ?"

"Nay, Oi must go now, Captain," said Mrs. Shadwell, standing again. "Me people be waiting. Now, don't ye get up, sir, and never despair because ye cannot see. From what Oi heard, they doctors thought as ye'd die weeks an' weeks ago, and ye're still here. Prayer can work miracles, sir, and you're in mine and allus shall be. Every day Oi do live!"

Muffin went out with her. He did not at once return, probably discovering for himself the details of that involuntary rescue. For once quite alone save for Picayune who had promptly reclaimed his lap, Mathieson allowed memory to drift. During that rescue which now seemed so long ago, he'd been aided not only by the valour of the Tiny Mite, but by his incomparable and so missed Rumpelstiltskin. Even after all these weeks, that wound was still raw, the death of the stallion so keenly felt that it ranked second only to the loss of his sight in the depth of grief it caused him. Dear old Rump . . . He sighed, lost in recollection until the cat jumped down as the door opened, and went pattering off across the room.

Mathieson took up his cane and stood eagerly. "Is that you, Sorri?"

"No, dear boy. 'Tis your grandfather."

Stepping forward and reaching out in the uncertain groping that never failed to wring the duke's heart, Mathieson asked, "Are we to go down, sir? Could you spare a moment before we do?"

"Of course." Marbury came quickly to sit beside him. "Well

349

now, what troubles you? I saw it in your face when that kind lady was here just now. Speaking of which, by what she tells me—''

''Oh, *par grâce*, no sir. Do not speak of it, for I am very sure she told you a lot of fustian. But—she did say something that—that makes me wonder . . . *Grandpère*—er, am I—well, what I mean is . . . Do I—*Mon Dieu!* how does one say this?'' And in a desperate and rather jerky rush, he finished, ''Is it—unpleasant for—for people to—look at me?''

The duke winced and looked down for an instant. Then he scanned his grandson's anxious face, and tried to be objective. Sorenson had carefully brushed the black hair into an attractive tumbling over the left side of Roland's forehead. It partially hid the wound that had irreparably damaged his eye, and the bandages concealed the rest. The scar across his right cheekbone would fade and be no worse than a sabre cut. The welts and bruises were already gone. His nose would never again be as perfectly straight, but by some miracle the fine mouth that had been so terribly swollen and lacerated when first they'd brought him home, had healed, leaving only a white half-moon scar on his chin. Inevitably, however, his ordeal had left its mark on him; there were lines deeply graven between his brows, that had not been there before; a sprinkling of silver at his temples. He was still very thin and looked haggard, but that hopefully would change with time. Cautiously, his Grace began to describe these visible signs of his ordeal, thinking that it was as well that few people would ever see the boy's back. ''You are something changed, there can be no doubt, Roland. But—I'm not at all sure 'tis a disaster. In point of fact—I think you look—rather more manly. Now—if we're done with your fascinations—''

With a grin that made the duke's heart leap with gladness, Mathieson said theatrically, ''Ah, but how can you be so *sans remords*?''

''I know, I know,'' chuckled Marbury. ''I am merciless. But—'tis very cold outside and I think we may have more snow, so I want you to come whilst there's still time. Fiona and her grandmama are already in the Great Hall. Unless, of course,'' he added whimsically, ''you'd as soon not bother with—''

''Bother! Sir, do not tease me so. I scarce can wait!''

''Very well, but we must go slowly, and I want you to promise you'll tell me an you tire.''

Mathieson promised, his spirits lifting as they left the room to which he had been confined for so long. In the corridor, he sniffed the air and smelled not medicine and salves, but flowers, and beeswax and woodsmoke. "I love this house," he said impulsively.

Marbury experienced a pang of guilt. "Then I shall settle another of my estates on the Aynsworths. I'm very sure Kit will under—"

"What, and give Dominer to me? Sir, I didn't mean that!"

"I know you did not intend to hint. Now, you *must* hold to the rail, dear boy! Dominer is not entailed and if you want it, 'twould make me proud to—"

"But I don't want it, your Grace. Ah! How crude! Your pardon! I *do* love it, and I shall be happy to be here with you. But had I ever— I mean, the place I always hoped you might give to me someday, is—is Dance."

The duke looked at him sharply and saw the brief look of defeat. What he'd started to say was 'had I ever married . . .' Poor lad. So that was what was fretting him, which was quite understandable. "Hold to the rail at once, sir!" he said gruffly. "Else you shall be returned to your bed!"

Mathieson laughed, but bowing to that terrible threat, he gripped the rail once more.

"Dance . . . ?" said Marbury curiously, as they edged their way down again, watched by at least five and twenty pairs of anxious eyes. "Why on earth would you want that run-down awful old place? Your father let it go to rack and ruin, and 'tis so marred by that ugly quarry. Why not the farm in Surrey? Or—the house at Richmond is not entailed either! Now, there's an idea! You shall certainly have the Richmond house. 'Tis right on the Thames, and the view—" He bit his lip, cursing himself. "But—*Dance* . . . !"

"You are too good, sir. And you're right about Dance, of course—now. But it was where my father took *Maman* when first they were—or she *thought* they were wed. She often spoke of it, for she was so happy there. She used to say it might have been made very beautiful. I began to think of how rewarding 'twould be to work on restoring it myself. I even—drew up plans. The quarry, you know, could be made into a lake, and gardens built around it. And—" In his eagerness he stumbled.

There were several muffled cries and a faint scream. The duke gave a gasp, steadied him, and said, "Thank heaven! Here comes Sorenson with your cloak. He'll keep you in your place my lad!"

When they reached the foot of the stairs Fiona came to take his hand and walk to the front doors with him. On the terrace the air was bitingly cold and stung his cheeks, but Mathieson felt invigorated and alive again. "What does it look like?" he asked.

The voice was slightly breathless, and Sorenson, supporting him, glanced uneasily at the duke.

"Heavy grey clouds," said Fiona, watching her love's eager face. "But there's a break here and there and the sun occasionally peeps through."

"The trees are bare, of course," Marbury added, "and we've turned off the fountains for the winter, but it's all very pretty, just the same."

He would have given his entire fortune for Roland to be able to see this, but he must not rail against fate, when it was so great a blessing that the dear lad had survived at all. "Are you able to manage the terrace steps, do you think?" he asked.

Mathieson was mildly surprised. He'd not suspected he was to be allowed to go so far, and he was already rather shaky in the knees, but he didn't want to go inside yet, so said he could race the duke to the old stone bridge and back, and heard his grandfather chuckle as he was guided carefully down the terrace steps.

He halted then, suddenly afraid. He'd always had a keen sense of smell, and since he had lost his sight, that sense seemed even keener. A horse was very close to him. Had Muffin bought him a new hack? He didn't want it! He didn't want even to touch a horse! *Mon Dieu!* How could they think he would want this? In a sweat of panic, he wrenched free and stepped back.

Marbury nodded to the groom. "Take off the blindfold now."

His voice shaking, Mathieson said, "Sir—I don't want to—"

He was interrupted by a ringing whinny.

He stood as one turned to stone. Stunned. Disbelieving. Not daring to believe. His lips formed the name, but no sound came.

A gusty breathing. A friendly whicker. A soft mouth whuffling at his neck, shoving at him gently, making eager loving little grunts.

"R-Rump . . . ?" he whispered numbly. "*Rump?* Is—is it . . . ?"

Marbury said in a choked voice, "Yes, dear boy . . . 'Tis—Rump . . .' "

Mathieson gave a strangled sob, flung his arms around the stallion's neck and buried his face against the sleek warm firmness of it.

Fiona was overcome and the duke took her in his arms. Sorenson blew his nose vigorously, and many of the servants who had crowded onto the terrace were in tears.

Stroking and stroking the silken side, the tossing nose, the smooth neck; so moved he could scarcely speak, Mathieson managed at length, "I—I don't understand . . . How . . . ?"

Marbury said gruffly, "I'll let this gentleman explain. Sergeant?"

Another shock, compounded by a voice that brought memory flooding back devastatingly. "It's me, Captain. Patchett. I'm the one what give you such a wallop in that damned barn."

Mathieson clung to the stallion dazedly. "Yes. I remember." He drew an impatient hand across his face and fought to be sensible. "I—you must excuse my—my behaviour. 'Tis just . . . well, you see—I thought you'd . . . shot the poor old fellow."

"So did our lieutenant, sir. I'd like you to know I wasn't—we all wasn't willing parties to—that lot."

Still holding Fiona, the duke shook his head warningly, and the sergeant went on at once, "Me and the two chaps as went with me cornered this big fella when he made a mistake and run into a churchyard. It wasn't easy, sir, but—cor, we couldn't scrag something as fine as what he is! We kept him hid for a while. I'm very sorry we had to let you think— But—there wasn't any other way. We all got families to think of, y'see, sir. Soon's it was safe, and we found out you was here, I come and told the duke."

Still caressing the stallion as if he dare not let him go, Mathieson spoke to where he thought his grandfather stood. "Sir—why . . . why did you not tell me?"

Watching that white twitching face, Marbury was inclined to think that even now it had been too great an emotional shock. "Well, you see—" he began.

He had moved, and Mathieson turned to where the voice now came from. In that same instant the stallion tossed his head happily. Mathieson had no inkling. Sorenson shouted, "Look out!'' even as a violent impact smashed him sideways and he staggered and tripped on the step behind him.

Fiona screamed.

With cries of horror the duke and Sorenson both leapt in abortive attempts to reach him.

Confused and alarmed, Mathieson had thrown out his hands to break his fall, but he had no way of knowing where he was falling and his head struck the low wall hard.

"Roland,'' gasped the duke, falling to his knees beside his grandson's sprawled figure. "Oh, dear lad, what have I done? Are you—''

He stopped, appalled. Through these interminable weeks he had never seen Roland betray abject fear, not even when he was delirious and reliving those ghastly hours in the barn. Now, the thin face was twisted with terror, the teeth chattered; the mouth twitched uncontrollably; in most unheroical fashion, Roland shook from head to toe.

Also on her knees, Fiona cried frantically, "Are you all right? Have you hurt your back again?'' Her little hands went out to him, and he clutched one, starting onto an elbow, then cowered against Sorenson as the man knelt to support him.

" 'Tis a seizure,'' groaned the duke. "Send for the doctor— quickly! God forgive me! I should not have—''

"W-w-wait . . .'' gasped Mathieson, still racked by that violent shuddering. "Sir . . . is—is the sun . . . out now?''

Scourged by guilt, the duke glanced up. The sun was setting, and from a break in the clouds sent pink rays beaming out.

"Yes, lad, but—'' He met Sorenson's stunned eyes and threw a hand to his mouth.

Fiona, staring in awe at Mathieson's face, whispered, "Muffin . . . Oh, Muffin!''

"Grandpère . . .'' stammered Mathieson, "Take off the bandages. P-please. I—I think . . . I think . . .''

Marbury fumbled with the bandage, but his hands were shaking too much to be of use.

Sorenson drew his pocket knife and between them, he and Fiona cut through the narrow strip of linen, then unwound the bandages.

Sick with the fear that he might be imagining things, Mathieson blinked. His left eye did not respond in the slightest. His right eye twitched open. He saw a rosy dimness that gradually brightened. Blurred at first, he began to distinguish low-hanging leaden clouds pierced by pink rays that fanned out in an awesome glory . . . Dazed with rapture, he saw a face come into focus. Muffin's white face, as contorted as his own must be, and so full of love. He reached out blindly, but not blindly, and his hand was gripped crushingly and pressed against a wet cheek. Sorenson bent above Mathieson, and clutched his shoulder speechlessly, his dark features working. A vaguely anxious whinny, and Mathieson perceived a white blaze, then the great dark eyes and the magnificent head of the stallion. Turning slowly, drinking it all in, he knew that he was weeping, and he didn't care.

Someone else knelt close beside him. A beloved face materialized; an exquisite face, ineffably dear, the green eyes filled with tears, the features paler than he remembered, and reflecting some of the worry and strain she had lived through these past months. Overcome, he clung to her hand. "Fiona . . . Ah *ma chèrie*! My bravest Tiny Mite! You are even lovelier than I remembered."

"My darling . . ." sobbed Fiona, pressing damp kisses on his forehead. "My darling . . . !"

"Oh, Thomas," Mathieson whispered brokenly. "Thank you! Thank you!"

At the duke's insistence they were married early in April at the new Church of St. George in Hanover Square which had, in a little over twenty-two years, already become exceeding fashionable. All London was there, agog to see if it was truth that Marbury really had forgiven his wayward grandson. Rumour had it that poor young Roland Fairleigh Mathieson had been captured and terribly disfigured by a jealous and demented army officer, and when the prospective bridegroom and Lord Thaddeus Briley appeared at the altar, necks were craned and an excited murmur rippled through the graceful sanctuary. The eyes of the ladies brightened, and fans fluttered a little faster. The eyes of the gentlemen narrowed speculatively.

Captain Mathieson was impeccably clad in white velvet lightly embroidered with black. His thick black hair tumbled attractively over the left side of his brow. The lean planes of his face were marked by a scar across his right cheekbone, and his nose was not as classically straight as it once had been. His left eye was covered by a patch: a black patch, with a small cluster of diamonds jauntily placed at the corner.

"Lud!" whispered the much admired Comtesse di Benedetto in the ear of her friend. "That rogue may have lost his eye, but I vow he's almost as handsome as ever!"

"And no whit less dashing!" Lady Deborah Martin, who had once enjoyed a dalliance with that same rogue and was London's present arbiter of fashion, hissed, "Only look at the men! Roly has set a new style! I'll wager half our gallants will be wearing jewelled eye patches 'fore the week is out!"

Another ripple disturbed the congregation and every head turned to view the bride.

Mervyn Bradford clad in mulberry satin paced with regal step and high-held head up the aisle, looking every inch a grand seigneur. On his arm, his daughter drifted in a cloud of white net and lace, a tiny cap embroidered with seed pearls atop her clustered and powdered curls, the fine veil unable to hide the radiant beam on her face.

Watching her come to him, Mathieson saw no other, and his breath caught in his throat because he thought her so exquisitely lovely.

Much later, after four hundred of the guests had enjoyed the wedding supper in Mathieson House, and the dancing had continued for an hour, Mathieson guided his bride from the crowded floor of the grand ballroom and swept her behind a potted palm. She was very thoroughly kissed breathless (to which she raised no least objection), and then led into the corridor.

Watching them go, the Duke of Marbury smiled fondly. How beautiful they were, he thought. Young and indomitable, mercifully uncrushed by the dark time they had endured so bravely, standing together on the threshold of their new life. He had been glad to note of late the return of the proud carriage of Roland's dark head; the slightly arrogant cavalryman's swagger to the walk. A flogging could do terrible things to a man's pride, but there was little doubt that his grandson was impudent as ever. He chuckled, and turning, found a young captain of dragoon guards at his elbow, resplendent in full dress regimentals.

"Hello, Jacob," said the duke. "You look surprised."

"I am astounded, your Grace," said Jacob Holt. "I think I must be dreaming. Roly so often told me he would never be leg shackled."

"Ah, but that was only because he had never truly loved. He does now."

"She is a very pretty lady." Knowing his cousin well, Holt pursed his lips. "Not quite the type I'd fancied he would choose. I hope he may never disappoint her."

"Oh, he never will," murmured the duke confidently. "He thinks of her as his madonna, and because each time she looks at him she sees a knight in shining armour—he will make very sure that she never sees him in any other light. Besides, there is a legend of our House, you know, that says Mathieson men love once . . . and once only."

Holt looked at him curiously, and because they were distantly related, he dared to ask, "Was that the way with you, duke?"

Marbury smiled again. A rather secret smile. "Oh yes," he said, and glancing across the ballroom saw the roguish eyes of Lady Clorinda Ericson peeping at him over her fan. She wore pale pink satin tonight. She had worn that same colour the last time he had escorted her to a ball—long and long ago.

Murmuring an apology, he went to her, his own eyes bright and his step remarkably light for a gentleman of his years.

In the corridor Fiona clung to her husband, considerably more breathless. "We must—go back inside," she said dazedly.

With his lips against her hair, he murmured, "I was about to suggest that we leave now."

"Faith, but—I wonder you wish to! The way all the ladies flocked round you, and you—"

"Hated every minute," he declared piously.

Fiona looked up at him, and saw the twitch beside his mouth. "Liar! You loved every second!"

He chuckled and spread his hands in the charming Gallic shrug that made her loving heart beat even faster. "It appeared, Mrs. Mathieson, that *you* did not lack for admirers! As for me— *par grâce*, but have I not said many times that all the ladies are adorable, but none is worth more than a week of my time?"

"Pish!" said Fiona irreverently. "The trouble with you, Captain Roland Fairleigh Mathieson, is that you never say what you mean! But—I *know* what you really think!"

The laughter fled from his face and a very different expression replaced it. "I wonder . . ." He lifted her hands and looked down at them. "Am I thinking that my life rested in these two dear little hands?'' He pressed a kiss on each one. ''Am I thinking that they belong to me now, even as I belong to the bright angel of my life?'' He raised his head to look at her steadily. ''Do you *know* that you will have all my adoration through this life and into eternity? Do you know *that* my Tiny Mite?''

Fiona found a lump in her throat. She blinked mistily, and wondering if any other lady had ever loved this deeply, asked with a rather quivering smile, ''Even if the bright angel of your life is lacking the proprieties, and says gauche things at times?''

''She requires educating,'' he admitted with a twinkle. ''Especially in . . . certain matters.'' His long, skilled fingers drifted tantalizingly down beside her ear and awoke a delicious shiver. He murmured softly, ''And—there is no time like the present, to commence . . . my most precious bride . . .''

. Blushing and ecstatically happy, she swayed to him, and with his arm fast about her, they drifted slowly along the hall and up the wide staircase, quite oblivious of the amused glances of lackeys and footmen; conscious only of each other.

It had been a long and stormy journey, with the future often in doubt, but the storm was over at last, and Roland Fairleigh Mathieson had found his safe harbour.

✍ *About the Author* ✍

PATRICIA VERYAN was born in London and moved to the United States after the Second World War; she now lives in Bellevue, Washington. The author of sixteen previous novels, she has been acclaimed "a worthy successor to Georgette Heyer at her very best" by the *Chattanooga Times*.

ROMANCING ADVENTURE...
by Patricia Veryan